THE WOMAN
THE DESERT DREAM

The Woman Who Was the Desert Dream

THAMES RIVER PRESS
An imprint of Wimbledon Publishing Company Limited (WPC)
Another imprint of WPC is Anthem Press (www.anthempress.com)
First published in the United Kingdom in 2013 by
THAMES RIVER PRESS
75–76 Blackfriars Road
London SE1 8HA

www.thamesriverpress.com

A CIP record for this book is available from the British Library.

ISBN 978-0-85728-131-9

This title is also available as an eBook.

THE WOMAN WHO WAS THE DESERT DREAM

William Coles

THAMES RIVER PRESS

Further Praise for William Coles

The Well-Tempered Clavier

"What a read! Every schoolboy's dream comes true in this deftly-written treatment of illicit romance. A triumph."
—*Alexander McCall Smith*

"This is a charming and uplifting read."
—*Piers Morgan*

"An outstanding debut novel. A wonderful story of first love. Few male authors can write about romance in a way which appeals to women – but Coles has managed it quite brilliantly."
—*Louise Robinson, Sunday Express*

"Charming, moving, uplifting. Why can't all love stories be like this?"
—*Tunku Varadarajan, The Wall Street Journal*

"A beautiful book, managing to use a simple narrative voice without consequently bland style – honesty, beauty, and passion pervade the novel but so do humour, youthfulness and energy."
—*Stuck in a Book*

"My own piano teacher was called Mr Bagston and frankly I don't think any power on earth could have persuaded us to create a scene of the kind Coles so movingly describes!"
—*Boris Johnson, London Mayor*

"Passionate and excruciatingly compelling."
—*Curledup.com*

Dave Cameron's Schooldays

"A superbly crafted memoir."
—*Daily Express*

"Try *Dave Cameron's Schooldays* for jolly fictional japes. It helps to explain the real Dave's determination to whip us into shape."
—*Edwina Currie, The Times*

"A piece of glorious effrontery… takes an honourable place amid the ranks of lampoons."
—*The Herald*

"A fast moving and playful spoof. The details are so slick and telling that they could almost have you fooled."
—*Henry Sutton, Mirror*

"A cracking read… Perfectly paced and brilliantly written, Coles draws you in, leaving a childish smile on your face."
—*News of the World*

Mr Two-Bomb

"Compellingly vivid, the most sustained description of apocalypse since Robert Harris's Pompeii."
—*Financial Times*

To Doug Lawson
Lookin' Good! Feelin' Good!

ACKNOWLEDGEMENTS

The Marathon des Sables is this strange, glorious mid-life rite of passage which mad middle-aged men tend to put themselves through. Women also run the race, but they are not nearly as downright odd as the men.

In 2012, I was lucky enough to take part; almost all of the events in this book actually happened.

I would like to thank my friends from Tent 71 who gave me their stories and their delicious gossip: Doug Lawson, Bryan Wilson, Al Getgood, Paddy Gillespie, Steve Smith and Eddie Brown.

My thanks to Margot, my wife, who had to put up with my endless training.

Lastly I'd like to thank Kate Muddiman, from Canada, who recounted to me one of the most inspirational stories that I have ever been told.

CHAPTER 1

This is a story of love and desire and mid-life crises. And blisters and warm bottled water and dehydrated pap. Sandstorms, thunderstorms and hailstorms so vicious they leave your skin bloody and bruised. It's the story of what it's like to run in the desert, as you trudge up mountains of stone and slip-slide down the dunes.

It is the story of heat.

You'll know all about thirty-degree heat. It is Centre Court at Wimbledon when the sun is blazing. It is the hottest day of the year in Cornwall when the ice creams are melting even before the first lick. It is a scorcher on the motorway, stuck on the hard shoulder as the radiator bubbles over.

Fifty-two degrees is different. When you're running at noon with the sun high overhead and the shadows small upon the ground. When you're running in the afternoon, as the sand and the rocks have started to fry. When there's a sixteen-kilo rucksack strapped to your back.

I will tell you the meaning of fifty-two-degree heat.

It's drinking eleven litres of water – and never once needing to stop for a pee. It's taking twenty salt tablets a day so that you don't start to cramp up. It's losing water as fast as you can pour it in.

On your face, the sweat dries instantly, leaving tidelines of white salt scum; on your back, your shirt is constantly saturated, and the sweat soaks through to the inside of your rucksack; and on your feet… yes, that is the big problem that faces all of the runners in the Marathon of the Sands. Until you've started the race, you have no idea how hard it's going to hit you.

Runners take all the precautions they can to prevent sand from getting into their shoes and their socks. They have their silk gaiters sewn into the soles of their running shoes and they tie the tops of their gaiters tight around their calves. But whatever you do, how ever snug the gaiters, you can never totally stop the fine sand from working its way into the shoes and into the socks and then next to the skin. And what happens next – not always, but sometimes – is that the sand mixes with the sweat in the socks and then it quickly turns into sand paper. If you are not taking care, and if your feet are already numb from all those Ibuprofen tablets you've been chugging, the first you will know of it is when you get back to your tent. You tug off your shoes and your gaiters and from the burn of the sharp hot spots on your feet you know it's going to be bad. Like all the other runners, you are wearing the very latest Injinji socks, special toe gloves. They look faintly reptilian. You tug off the first starchy sock and all the plasters come off with it in a fine mist of sand and blood. It's only then that you realise that you are in for a whole world of pain. The sand has combined with the sweat in your sock, and the skin on the bottom of your foot has been sanded clean off. Your foot has been 'delaminated.' I was almost sick the first time I saw it.

On the second day, the heat was the least of my problems.

Like a lot of the other runners, I had contracted the most severe diarrhoea. It was a combination of the heat and the exercise and the disgusting dehydrated food and the salt and all the powdered electrolytes that I'd been cramming into myself to stay alive. Your body can't take it, and goes into immediate spasming revolt, as if to say 'get this muck out of me.'

And normally, if you were at home, you would take some Imodium and perhaps take the day off work. You would sip coffee, read the papers and lounge around near a lavatory as your stomach slowly sorts itself out.

That isn't an option in the Marathon des Sables. It doesn't matter how bad your injuries, how severe your stomach cramps. For come 8.30 in the morning, you have to be on the start line, ready for another twenty-four miles through the desert.

I felt like absolute hell. The daily starts to the Marathon des Sables overwhelm the senses. There is pounding rock music and the manic jabbering of the organiser Patrick Bauer. The sun is already blazing and you're crammed into this tight space with all the other runners – almost every one of whom is, like yourself, just that little bit stark-raving mad.

I was wondering how long I'd last before I needed to relieve myself behind some friendly bush.

The worst of it was that I was parched. There are a lot of things that can put you out of the race, but one of the most certain is dehydration. Over a dozen people had been knocked out on the very first day after messing up with their water.

Your water is severely rationed on the Marathon des Sables. Extra water is, of course, available. The first time you take an extra 1.5 litre bottle, it's thirty minutes added onto your race time; second time it's an extra hour; and when you take a third bottle... well, you don't take a third bottle, because if you take a third bottle, then you're out, and bang goes all your training, bang goes your £3,500 entry fee and bang goes your desert dream.

The previous night I had watched, horrified, as the water had drained out of me, litre after litre of it; even with the pills, there was no stopping it. Sometimes I'd been so desperate that I couldn't even make it to the camp's makeshift latrines, and would squat in the middle of the desert, staring miserably at the moon. I took more pills and more pills, but nothing seemed to work.

And the next morning, I knew I was bone dry. I had already had my first extra bottle of water. But at that early stage in the race, I didn't dare take another.

We were assembled exactly where we'd finished the previous afternoon. Each day's finish line is the next day's start, and then you all charge straight through the bivouac, where the tents have all now been stacked onto the lorries and the site returned to what it once was.

Lawson was stretching, touching his toes, palms almost to the sand; his walking poles were forever falling to the ground. He would pick them up, balance them against his legs, stretch, and then the poles would drop back to the ground. He never tired of this routine.

He saw me watching him and grinned. 'May I offer you a wheelchair?'

'I didn't know you cared,' I said.

'Lookin' good!' Lawson inspected his stubbled reflection in my sunglasses. 'Feelin' good!'

The two Irish medics earnestly talked to each other, as if you could ever have any sort of game plan for running twenty-four miles in the desert. 'I'm going hard,' Martin said.

'I'm going out slow, so I am,' said Carlo.

Simon, on his second Marathon des Sables, was edging his way towards the front of the pack, hoping to shave a few seconds off his time so that he could finally find redemption with that elusive top-100 finish.

Kurtz, an ex-Para, was the only one of us who really knew how to handle pain – and he was going to need it, too.

I looked round for Kate, but I couldn't see her. I'd have liked to have seen her that morning, if only to wish her luck, for I wasn't at all sure I was going to make it through the day. I had not seen her for half an hour. She was probably being interviewed by some TV station, or swooned over by a troupe of tanned athletes. I knew that and I was fine with it. Kate was a beauty and beauty is much in demand in the Marathon des Sables. The men are naturally drawn to it. Of the 853 runners on the first day's start line, I guess there were about 100 women. And of these 100 women, I can both subjectively and objectively tell you that Kate was a stand-out.

But enough of that. I'd looked around and I still couldn't see her. It's difficult to spot a woman in white and red when you're in the thick of hundreds of bigger, burlier runners, all of whom are wearing near identical shirts and caps. Of all the other runners, I would have liked to have started the day with her; the sight of her damn cheery smile alone was a pick-me-up. But she wasn't there, so I'd just have to tough it out by myself. And I could do that. I wasn't looking forward to it. But I could do it.

At least, I was going to give it my best shot.

A huge, craggy face, hewn from scowling stone, peered into my face. He was a few inches away from me, eyes hidden by wrap-around mirrored sunglasses.

'You look like shit,' he said.

'At least I'm ill. What's your excuse?'

Del's face continued to linger in front of mine. He was about the same height as me, and of much the same age, though with his wizened skin and receding grey crew-cut, he looked much older.

'It's not too late to pull out.'

'Don't you worry about me, Del,' I said. 'I'm not going for speed.'

'Like the sunglasses.'

'Thank you,' I said. 'They're my wife's.' They did indeed belong to Elise. I'd brought them out as a standby, though after a mix-up in the race shop I'd ended up having to wear them. They were Christian Dior, large, white, very expensive – and very inappropriate for a race like the Marathon des Sables.

'You haven't done the training. You haven't got the kit. And you've been up all night with the runs.' Del smiled at me with yellowing gnarled teeth. 'You are so totally screwed.'

'I wish I could be like you, Del – you're a running machine.'

He took a swig from his water bottle. There was still a lot left in the bottle. He let the water cascade over his cheeks before pouring it down the back of his neck.

Nearby, Patrick Bauer was standing on top of a white Land Rover next to his pretty translator. A few years earlier, she had had a spat with Patrick and quit midway through the race, though he had charmed her back.

Patrick first started the race in 1986 as a way of introducing the world to the spiritual, cleansing heat of the desert. And even twenty-seven years later, and with some forty-eight nationalities now in the race, he hardly knew a single word of English.

He was a bluff bull of a man, tufty white hair on his tanned head, and he loved the sound of his own voice. At the start of each day, as we all itched to get going, he would chunter on for a good quarter of an hour. But he also had passion and joy. He was living the dream: he had brought the desert to the world. I liked him.

We spared a few thoughts for the fifteen runners who'd given up the previous day. Some of them had been shipped back to their hotels in Ouarzazate, but a hardy few had decided to continue the week with their tentmates. I don't know if I'd have been able to do that – still part of the Marathon des Sables, but no longer in it.

It was getting hotter and hotter. It wasn't even nine o'clock, and already we were way past a summer's day in England. I licked my sun-blocked lips and sipped some water from one of my water bottles. Almost all of the runners had two 750 ml water bottles attached to the shoulder straps of their rucksacks. Turn your head slightly and you could take a sip. In eight miles' time, at the first checkpoint, we'd be given the next 1.5 litre bottle of warm water which would keep us going until the next checkpoint... and so it would continue for mile after mile and checkpoint after checkpoint until after 150 miles of it we were finally done.

My tentmates looked the part. I did not feel a part of it. Maybe it was just my bowels making me feel so cheerless.

Ahead of us was a thin range of mountains, though in the shimmering heat it was impossible to tell how far away they were. Could have been five miles, could have been thirty. You can't tell distances in the desert. But you don't want to know distances in the desert. You don't want to know how far it is to the next checkpoint, or how many more hours you've got left. You're not thinking about that palm tree in the distance, or that hill that you might eventually reach by the end of the day. No, when your stomach is gyppy and you're parched and you don't even know whether you'll make one mile let alone twenty-four, then the only thing is to be in the moment and to focus on that next step. And after that, you think about the next step, and you string all those thousands of steps together, and with luck you've made a checkpoint before you've been timed out; and with even more luck you've beaten the camels to the finish line, and congratulations, son, you are now allowed to do it all over again tomorrow, and the next day, and the next day, and the day after that too.

But it didn't do to think about the future, because all these preliminary stages were a just a mere taster before the main course. Though it wasn't so much a main course as an absolute monster: a double marathon, right through the day and into the night.

You always knew the monster was on the horizon. It was out there, waiting for you. But it was way, way off in the future. What was the point in fretting over a double marathon, when I might not even make the start line in two days' time?

Patrick was winding down and the music had started again. It was the birthday of two of the runners; a fully orchestrated version of 'Happy Birthday,' very cheesy, was being pumped out through the speakers. The birthday boys waved to the French cameramen. The first time we'd heard it, we had crooned along. Not now though.

After all the preamble and all the hype, we were ready for the off, when the mad cacophony ended and we would be left only with the silent sound of the desert. Patrick gave a wave and we were surrounded by the blare of the Marathon des Sables signature tune: ACDC, 'Highway to Hell.' I've never particularly liked the song, but it has become such a part of the fabric of my life that, for better or for worse, it will have to number among my eight Desert Island discs.

Screaming, shouting, helicopters thundering overhead, blasting us with the downdraft. Runners waving for the cameras, Patrick bellowing out his countdown and ACDC drilling right through to the core of my brain.

And we're away and the mad ones tear off into the desert at a flat-out sprint, and the joggers amble out at a more sedate trot, and after them are the brisk walkers, striding along with their poles, and then, right at the back, are the walking wounded, the people like myself, who are wondering just what on earth possessed us to sign up for this insane race.

There are a lot of reasons why people enter the Marathon des Sables. We do it for the challenge and we do it to avert our impending mid-life crisis and we do it because it's called the toughest footrace on earth. It's a rite of passage and a test of manhood, so that, in small part, we can have a taste of what our grandfathers went through in the wars.

As I ambled over the start line, with my poles glinting in the sun, it seemed like just about the most stupid thing I'd ever done in my life.

Trek 150 miles through the desert, with all my food and kit strapped to my back? What was the point? And it was such an arbitrary distance too. Why not 300 miles in a fortnight? Why not make us carry all our own water?

Any way I looked at it, the Marathon des Sables was just painfully ridiculous. And in the unlikely event that I ever did finish this nightmare, then I'd pick up the medal and get my kiss from Patrick and – so what? Would it make me more of a man? Would I wear the medal in Hyde Park and watch as all the tourists fell at my feet? Would it give me bragging rights at the smart London dinner parties, or...

It was ludicrous. I was plainly insane.

And the endless monologue of thoughts would continue to spin through my head, this cycle of daydreams, as one abstruse thought moved seamlessly and inconsequentially onto the next.

And I would take the next step and then the next step. That is the way of the Marathon des Sables. Even when you're delirious and on the very cusp of giving up, you still always have to take the next step.

The Sahara is not really the endless sand of most people's imaginings. There are rolling dunes, but much of it is dusty and hard and littered with stones that can tweak at your feet and burst your blisters.

The front-runners were already so far ahead that they were nothing but a sand cloud. They'd probably finish the second stage in less than three hours.

I wondered if I'd make the eleven-hour cutoff. I might not. Whatever happened, I'd keep on walking.

At least my feet weren't hurting. After the first day, I'd only had three blisters. Compared to the others, that wasn't too bad at all. On the Marathon des Sables, it doesn't matter how awful your injuries are: there will always be somebody faring much, much worse than you. As in life.

I hadn't been paying much heed to the desert. I was heading northeast through stones and scrub and camel grass, the sun searing down and the drab sand crunching underfoot.

As you start out each day, you send out probes through your body, checking out how everything is holding up. My feet and legs were OK, but my guts were tremoring. It all just felt like incredibly hard work. My energy levels had fallen through the floor. If I'd been walking in London, I'd have stopped in a café, rested my weary feet and bought an ice-cold bottle of water.

Absorbed in the minutiae of my own little world, I had not been aware of the other competitors. But I gradually realised that somebody was walking right on my heels. They were about two yards behind me and walking at exactly the same dawdling pace as myself.

First time that day I actually smiled.

She divined my very thoughts.

'Pick it up at the back there,' she said.

I didn't bother to look round. 'What are you doing back here with the waifs and strays?'

With two smart steps, she was alongside me. 'Making sure you don't get caught by the camels.' She was giving me her very cheekiest smile, with just a coy glimpse of her tongue tucked into the side of her lower lip. That was the thing about Kate – she didn't just look lovely; she *was* lovely. She threw her head back, gesturing behind her. 'They're only a hundred yards away!'

I thought she was joking. I looked back – only to find that, if anything, the camels were barely three cricket pitches behind me. The two camels were called, believe it or not, Charles and Camilla. They were led by a couple of Berbers and would trudge the Sahara at just above a leisurely two miles per hour. It was their job to pick up the stragglers. Once you had been overtaken by Charles and Camilla, then off came your tags and you were out of the game.

'They are a little close,' I said. 'So what have you been doing?'

'Looking for somewhere to pee,' she said. 'They'd taken down all the latrines. I had to find a dune. It was miles away. You know how I need my privacy.'

'Just so long as you weren't waiting around for me,' I said. 'You should be running now. I'm fine.'

'I like walking with you.'

'Thanks.'

'Who said this was a race, anyway?'

'Yeah – it's an ordeal. It's a rite of passage. It's a…'

'Despicable form of torture?'

'Yes, most definitely a form of torture, as well as being a challenge, and a bit of a schlepp. But a mere race? Well maybe for some people, but for the rank and file such as myself, absolutely not.'

And I looked at Kate, and even though she was wearing mirrored sunglasses I could see that she was looking at me. She didn't have poles and was striding along, arms pumping, the very picture of blooming good health. Kate hadn't followed the dire MdS fashion of having her hair tied in tight, greasy cornrows. Instead, from the bottom of her white casquette – like the French Foreign Legion kepis – peeked the end of her ponytail. Taut, toned legs, with delicious tanned knees and thighs; skimpy shorts in the most brilliant crimson and a white shirt that, compared to my stained smock, was absolutely pristine. Even her gaiters looked good. My orange silk gaiters made me look like some bumpkin yokel who was out for a bit of rat catching; but somehow, on Kate, they looked cool and sophisticated. From top to toe she looked the part; she was a woman who was ready to run the sands.

Now this might seem wrong for a middle-aged married man.

There were any number of reasons why I'd entered the Marathon des Sables. But I must also admit that one of the reasons was, pure and simple: I found this twenty-six-year-old woman quite intoxicatingly beautiful.

CHAPTER 2

I work on the *Sun* newspaper. I never mention that to people; it can provoke the most severe reaction.

The *Sun* has come to represent the grossest excesses of tabloid journalism and when people discover that you work there, they can get very excited.

These days, the paper is not quite the Wild West that it was when Kelvin MacKenzie was in his pomp. Nor does it have the same clout that it did twenty years ago when it was 'The Sun Wot Won' the 1992 general election.

But it is still a heavyweight and we do still have a few big guns at our disposal, though they aren't wheeled out quite as often as they used to be.

If you asked most people to describe a *Sun* reporter, they would almost certainly paint a picture of some greasy reptile in a trenchcoat – though they would be quite wrong. It is a classic error to assume that the *Sun*'s staff is entirely made up of *Sun* readers.

Not that I'm a news reporter any more – nor am I a feature writer. I am midway up the tree now, and have the word 'editor' attached to my title. I currently write the leaders, though I am also capable of coruscating polemic, as well as those little testers that require finesse and nuance. I even have my own goldfish bowl now, with windows that look into the newsroom. So that's what I do, and although to my friends outside the *Sun* it all sounds intensely exotic, I can assure you that it is about as humdrum as being a lawyer or accountant. Though considerably worse paid and with a lot more shouting. I used to love my job, but not any more. Now, I am just going through the motions. These articles I write, I could tap them out standing on my head… in fact, it might be interesting to give that a try. Imagine the editor's face as he, yet again, barges into my office, only to find his esteemed leader writer doing a head stand in the corner, with the keyboard on the floor not three inches in front of my nose.

I digress. For six years, the *Sun* had fired me up like nothing on earth. I had been ravenous for stories, trampling over rivals and colleagues alike in my constant quest for the next exclusive.

But after a while, it begins to pall. You realise that every single story is just a slight variation on those that you have already written. Sportsmen sleeping with temptresses; stars bleating 'woe is me'; and, I don't know, tired TV has-beens trying to have one last shot at fame. You get bored, and after a few more years you realise that the entire tabloid news agenda is so unutterably banal. One editor used to describe the *Sun* as being '*Hello!* magazine with teeth.' When I first heard about this remarkable new editorial strategy, I felt like Hermann Goering as he remarked, 'When I hear the word culture, I reach for my revolver.'

So: a middle-aged man, bored witless with his job, yet does not have the gumption to try something new. Strike One for the Marathon des Sables. If you're stuck in a dead-end job, then somehow the prospect of a 150-mile trek through the heat of the Sahara can have the most awful allure.

I noticed Kate on her first day in the newsroom. You would not know that our office is the hub of the *Sun*'s empire. With those long lines of desks and the phones and the computer terminals, it could be a bank or a call centre – apart, of course, from the blown-up *Sun* front pages dotted around the walls.

The staff are difficult to place. The women are well turned out and the men, always and without exception, wear suits, which are usually either blue or grey. The news reporters, in particular, are not like the other drones in the City. They have a swagger, a certain panache, as if they have taken to heart that rousing little slogan that still stands above the front doors of the newsroom: 'Walk tall – you're entering *Sun* country.'

Once upon a time, I used to be like those reporters.

Not any more though; faded glories. The *Sun* has become my gilded cage, and if I were to leave it, I would not know where next to head for honey.

I was at the back bench blathering to Rudi, who at long last had become one of the mad masters. We had known each other since we had been trainees together, 20 years ago, on the *Wilts and Gloucestershire Standard*, when we had dreamed of one day making it to the top of the tabloid tree.

Be careful what you wish for.

Rudi had been talking about the showbiz tattle of the day when Kate walked past us. She was wearing a grey coat and had a tan leather briefcase, and was accompanied by one of the senior feature writers. She looked trim. She looked like she worked out, and that is not common on Fleet Street. We watched as she walked through the newsroom.

'Wow,' said Rudi.

And that just about summed her up.

It was her first shift at the *Sun*. She was made for *Sun* features. She was breezy and fun and, unlike most young journalists, was not stuffed up with grandiose journalistic ideals – which are all well and good, but which do not tend to make for a great career on a Red Top. Above all, she had no problem whatsoever in posing for stupid pictures and writing a jokey story at her own expense.

Being a *Sun* executive, I had very little to do with her. We would nod and smile when we walked past each other, just as you would do with any colleague in a big office.

And if she walked past my office, I would discreetly look up. It was like chancing upon a masterpiece. It wasn't just her beauty though. Pretty women, Page Three girls, models and PR lovelies would saunter through our office every day of the week, but I am not necessarily drawn to them. There has to be something more there: some spark. It's difficult to put your finger on it, but there has to be this intuitive connection – and if it's not there, then even a supermodel will leave me cold.

The first time I spoke to her was when I was queuing up in the News International canteen with Grubby, one of the staff photographers. Grubby was a little overweight, greying, raddled and ravaged, and though he wore a blue suit, there lingered about him this general air of, well, grubbiness. But he still had a twinkle in his eye; he was absolute catnip to women. When I'd been a news reporter, we had done many stories together, often spending a full week in each other's company, 15 hours a day. That's a lot of time to talk. We probably knew more about each other than our own wives. And if it ever came to dalliances, we would turn a blind eye. What happens on the road stays on the road.

Our canteen is airy and light, and well-stocked with cheap, healthy food. It's so good that some reporters even eat there on their days off. The chairman sometimes eats there too, just to show that he is occasionally prepared to slum it. And as for all those lavish expense-account lunches at El Vino's, when we'd roll back into work at 4pm for a couple of hours of light typing – those days are long gone.

We had ladled out our dull, healthy salads. I do not much like eating salad. But if you want to lead the sedentary life in front of a computer screen, then you have to compromise. It's either salad for lunch or a belly that's popping out at the shirt buttons.

I was in the queue waiting to pay. There was a woman in front of me. She was in her sixties. I'd seen her about the building, though I did not know her. From her office pass, I could see that her name was Sara and that she was one of the copy-takers. She was in a bit of a flap. She had a jolly face, but she was going red with embarrassment. The tills didn't take cash and there wasn't enough money on her charge-key.

'You'll have to charge up your key,' said the checkout guy.

'Can I eat it now and pay afterwards?'

'You've got to pay now.'

'I've only got ten minutes. Please.'

'No—'

I stepped in. 'It's all right,' I said. 'I'll pay.'

Sara couldn't quite understand what was happening. She looked worried. I leant forward and put my key into the slot. She gaped as the receipt spooled out.

'Thank you!' she said. 'I'll... I'll pay you back.'

'No, no. There's really no need.'

'I'd like to pay you back.'

'Honestly – it's a pleasure.'

I watched as Sara walked to her table. She looked back and waved at me. A random act of kindness; I'm a big fan. I paid for my lunch and for the food on Grubby's tray.

'You're being very nice today,' Grubby said. 'What about this girl behind us? You going to pay for her too?'

I looked over. Grubby was in the way, so all I could see was a young woman's hand, free of rings, scooping up a huge spoonful of macaroni cheese. Already on her tray was some bacon and three crispy sausages, as well as a two-litre bottle of fizzy water. She plucked up a bowl of trifle, and an orange and a banana and an apple. And then a Kit Kat.

Grubby looked on in admiration. 'You're really going for it!'

And that's when I realised just who had been loading up this gargantuan meal.

Kate's blonde hair was loose about her shoulders. Her skin was flawless, so fine that she did not need makeup and she had just the merest trace of lipstick. She was wearing thin white cords and a red shirt; compared to the rest of the raddled hacks who inhabited the *Sun* newsroom, she just looked so unbelievably wholesome. She glanced down at her tray and laughed. 'It does look a lot.'

'Do you know Kate?' Grubby asked me. 'We were working together on a feature last week. Kate – this is Kim, leader writer of 'The Sun Says' and other dreary articles never read by the readers.'

I smiled at him – for what he said may have been in jest but it was also the truth. *Sun* readers, I am well aware, have no interest in my hard-hitting columns or my pithy nuggets that appear on the Page 2 graveyard.

I shook hands with Kate. She had a solid, cool handshake and she looked me right in the eye. And she had that something in her eyes which you can sometimes actually see: it's a twinkle, a wry spark.

'I read your column every day,' she said. 'I like it.'

I was both staggered and quite immensely pleased. Leader writers rarely hear anything about their purple prose. We are neither praised nor criticised, and most of the time it feels as if we are filing our pristine copy into a black hole.

'Well...' I said. 'That's particularly sweet of you to say so, Kate – you must be one of the only people on the paper who actually reads the leaders.'

'One of the subs probably has to read it,' offered Grubby.

'Yes – and maybe the editor reads it,' I said. 'That'll be about it.'

'Rupert Murdoch reads it though,' said Kate. She slotted in her key and paid for her lunch. 'Doesn't he discuss the leaders with you?'

'Oh yes,' I laughed. 'Rupert and I are chatting all the time – nothing he likes more than calling up for a good chinwag.'

Kate laughed as she picked up her tray. She beamed at me. 'Nice meeting you,' she said.

'And you too, Kate.'

I was quite charmed.

And that was that for a few months. When I walked past her in the newsroom, I would say 'Hello Kate,' and she would smile and she would say, 'Hi Kim,' back to me. We did not say any more than that.

If she walked past, I might glance at her for a second or two, but certainly no more: I was not that starved dog staring in through the butcher's window.

Now in those days, I used to jog a bit. It was my small attempt to avoid the fate of all the worker bees who spend their dull days sitting on their bottoms.

Two or three times a week, I would run back home in the evenings from work. It was only six or seven miles from Wapping to Hammersmith , though very often the trip was quicker on foot than it was by car. At 6 p.m., I would change into my running gear and leave my blue suit in my office. I had a small knapsack and would carry my phone and a notepad and bits of office paperwork; it never weighed more than two or three kilos.

I had just left the building. It was a delicious evening in early summer. I had spent the last nine hours cooped up in the Sun's new offices in Wapping and I sucked the air deep into my lungs and started shaking my arms down. God it was good to be outside. How on earth could I have got into such a position that for my entire working day I never left the building? It was another of those things that I had long wanted to rectify yet never did.

I never start running immediately. I prefer the slow immersion, walking for a while before trotting down The Highway at a very slow jog. It takes me an age to warm up.

I saw Kate squatting on the pavement. She was fiddling with the contents of a very slick looking Inov8 rucksack. I did not know it at the time, but it was a runner's rucksack. She was wearing skimpy black running shorts and I could not help but notice her legs. I'd never seen her legs before. They looked fantastic.

She appeared to be putting several thick hardback books into her rucksack. I watched in silence.

'Unusual sort of stuff to be carrying in a rucksack,' I finally said.

'Yes.' She looked up at me and laughed. 'There won't be many runners with Proust, Shakespeare and Dickens.'

'Are you joking?'

'Surprisingly – no,' she said.

'I'm with you on the Shakespeare and the Dickens,' I said. 'I don't know about Proust.'

'They were the heaviest books on my shelves. Even Proust seemed more appealing than a couple of dumbbells.'

'Imagine bringing out a copy of Proust when you're at Tesco's.'

'And in the original French, too.' She clipped up the top of her rucksack and swung it up onto her shoulders. Then, very proficiently, she fastened the rucksack tight around her waist and her chest. She jumped up and down on her toes to check the rucksack was snug. 'Ten kilos,' she said. 'Not bad. Where are you heading?'

'Hammersmith.'

'You're on my route.' She put on some ice-cool sunglasses. 'Shall we run together?'

'I'm very slow, you know. I don't want to hold you up.'

'Slow is fine by me – I had a long run in Richmond yesterday.'

We started out towards Tower Hill as lorries and buses hurtled past us; it's not a great part of the city. But all I was aware of was that – unbelievably – I was running on the pavement with Kate. I looked at her briefly; she was a thoroughbred, easy, loose-limbed, lifting her feet high off the ground. And her arms were just gliding, so smooth, with her fingers lightly together.

'You must be training for something,' I said. Another lorry rumbled by, drowning us with its exhaust.

'The Marathon des Sables. I'm running it in April with a friend. At least I'm supposed to be running it with a friend.'

'The MdS?' I said, using the ultra runner's jargon. 'I'm impressed.' And I was. The MdS is usually the domain of nutty middle-aged men who, for whatever mad reason, feel the need to shell out a fortune to be beasted in the desert. Beautiful young women tend not to be quite so drawn to the charms of the Sahara.

'I don't know about that.'

We stopped at a set of traffic lights. She hadn't even broken a sweat. Her phone went and she took the call. 'Hi Edward,' she said. She looked at me, raising her eyebrows. 'I'm just running now. I'll sort it out when I'm home.'

She let out this huge sigh as she tucked the phone back into her pocket.

I was keen to know more about her race. 'I did a feature on the MdS a few years back after one of the runners died,' I said. 'I've always rather fancied giving it a go.'

'What are you waiting for, then?' she said.

'I don't know,' I said. 'What *am* I waiting for?

'Why don't you wait until you've contracted some awful illness and then it won't be a problem any more.'

I laughed. We were down by the river and had stopped to stretch. When I first started out running, I didn't like stretching. It seemed like a waste of time, when I wanted to be out there on the streets. But now I enjoy it. I am in the moment, focusing on keeping my body supple and my legs loose. Kate was leaning against a wall, one leg straight and one bent, stretching off her hamstrings.

'Or on your deathbed,' she continued. 'That'd focus the mind.'

'I don't know what will happen when I'm on my deathbed, but I suppose there's a chance – if I haven't got Alzheimer's – that I'll be looking back at all those missed opportunities.'

'And this race might be one of those misses?' Kate had brought up one leg to hip height and was resting it on a wall as she massaged her thigh.

'So why are *you* running it?'

'That'd be a long story,' she said. 'Shall we go?'

We ran for a mile or so in silence, the sun speckling the Thames and the cars queuing in the evening traffic. We were running quite close to each other, shoulder to shoulder.

We queued with the tourists to cross the road at Westminster. Kate turned to me and smiled. She took off her sunglasses so that she could look at me.

'If you're even half tempted by the MdS, I think you should go for it,' she said.

'You're right.'

'You might even enjoy it.'

'I've…' I paused, wondering what to say. 'I don't know.'

And that was more or less that.

For perhaps a day I was all fired up about the Marathon des Sables, but it's not at all easy to get a place in the race. Each year, for one day in April, there's a window of precisely one minute when the Brits can sign up for the race in three years hence. When that one minute is up, every single one of the 250-odd slots will have been taken. There are a few charity places and a waitlist, but the point, anyway, is that getting a place on the Marathon des Sables is tricky. Unless you've got a real hunger for the race, then it's very easy to get bogged down by the hassle and bureaucracy, and the next thing you know, you're another year older and still no closer to getting your entry. And why, exactly, do you want to go in for the race anyway? It's expensive, thoroughly time-consuming and will almost certainly involve more pain than you have ever experienced.

For an hour or two, Kate had once again kickstarted my dream of running the desert. That night, as I tried to read in my armchair, I finally gave up my book and thought about the Sahara. The desert can be cathartic, extraordinarily cleansing. It clarifies and puts things into perspective. It has a raw, spiritual power like no other place on earth; all of the world's great monotheisms – Christianity, Judaism, Islam – have originated from the desert.

In my mind's eye I could see myself in the Sahara, the wind flapping at the tent as I gazed up at the clear star-bright sky.

I took another sip of red wine and sighed and got on with my book. Because it couldn't happen. Like so many of my pipedreams, it would remain an absurd little fantasy; I might touch on it occasionally, brush it down, admire it from all angles.

But let me be quite clear: it was never going to happen.

At least it would never have happened if it had just been down to me. Sometimes, though, there is that catalyst and we find that – much against our will – we have been cajoled, butted and downright railroaded into doing something that, deep down, we know is going to be thoroughly unpleasant. Character-building, perhaps. But I cannot think of many things in life that are 'character-building' that do not also happen to be aggravating and vexatious and deeply painful.

Two months passed. I still continued with my jogging commutes. Occasionally I'd run with Kate.

And if you go running often enough with a person, you get to know them well. I heard about Kate's mum, a nurse, and her father, a bristling academic; and her older brothers, who she was forever chasing, but had never been able to catch; and the granny who lived in a granny annexe, and who only put in her false teeth at meal-times. I learned about her English degree, and her parents' astonishment when she aspired to join the *Sun*; and, now that she was working on the *Sun*, how her parents' astonishment had turned into no small amount of pride.

And I learned why she'd joined the *Sun* in the first place: she liked the paper's clout, and she liked its money and its humour, not to mention its mischief-making. She was a maverick, and, while all her friends aspired to work on the worthy broadsheets, she aspired to work on a roaring Red Top like the *Sun*. So I got to know Kate's passions and her foibles; what turned her on and what ticked her off. Above all, I learned what made Kate laugh.

By autumn, we had developed quite a rapport. We were mates. I liked that. I didn't have many friends who were twenty years my junior.

Then: It is a Monday, 4 p.m., and I am finally earning my crust for the day. My mad master the editor had emailed through his requests for tomorrow's topics in 'The Sun Says,' though I had some latitude. We often like to end with a funny, nothing more than two sentences, and usually based on a joke I'd heard in the office. It may not take me long to write the *Sun*'s leaders but I am the guy who delivers. Doesn't matter how tight the deadline, there will be my 500-words of polished pun-free prose, with each sentence preferably no longer than 17 words.

Kate knocked at the door, hovered for a moment on the threshold. My door is always open, but some of my politer colleagues still like to knock before they come in.

I looked up, my fingers still lightly poised over the keyboard.

'Hello Kate,' I said. 'What brings you to my little oasis? Like a coffee?'

She was wearing a white dress and a necklace of daisies. You would not have thought that she worked on the *Sun*.

'I would like a coffee, please,' she said. 'An espresso?'

'I'll join you,' I said.

My wife Elise had given me a Nespresso coffeemaker the previous Christmas and I kept it in my office. I also had four coffee cups, Royal Doulton, very fine bone china, that had belonged to my great-grandparents. I don't know why, but coffee tastes better when sipped from an elegant cup.

I rummaged around with the coffeemaker and, as the water dripped, she came to the matter in hand.

'You know how you wanted to run the Marathon des Sables?' she said.

'I do.' I gave her a cup and saucer. The coffee steamed and had an enticing thin froth. I gestured for her to sit down.

She sat across the desk from me, legs together. She was nervous. I didn't know why. In my mind's eye, I see myself as just this companionable sprig, barely out of short trousers. But I suppose it is possible that, to others, I come across as this grizzled, snappish bear. We don't really know how others see us. But all we do know is what they see will be so very different from our own self-image. 'Do you still want to run it?'

I looked at her. She had the saucer in one hand and held the tiny coffee cup between thumb and forefinger. She took a sip and she looked down at the coffee cup. Have I mentioned that Kate was lovely?

Strike Two for the Marathon des Sables.

I did not pause. It's how I am these days. Jump first, think about the consequences later. 'Yes,' I said. 'I'd love to.'

'It's in six months,' she said. 'You know that?'

'Your friend must have dropped out,' I said.

'Injuries and other commitments,' she said. 'There's a waitlist. But seeing as you're such an influential journalist – or so they believe – you're being given first refusal.'

I rubbed my hands together, palm to palm, in a slow circular motion. I do this when I'm thinking. Not that I really needed to think.

'I'm in,' I said.

'Well that's...' She looked up at me and gave this huge smile. 'That's fantastic.'

I shrugged. 'Got to be better than coming into the office. Besides – a week's fun-run in the desert? Carrying all your own food for 150 miles? How bad can it be?'

'A walk in the park.'

★

I told my wife Elise the news after dinner that night. Actually, that's not strictly accurate. It may have been a done deal with Kate, but it still required some delicate footwork. As do all dealings with a spouse.

We were upstairs in the bedroom and the girls were asleep. Elise was lying in bed reading *Grazia*, while *Question Time* droned in the background. I went round to her side of the bed and placed a bar of Lindt chocolate and a cup of green tea on her bedside table.

'Thank you,' she said.

I sat on my side of the bed and undid my black lace-ups. I put them neatly under the bookcase. Once, when I was callow and wilfully defiant, I used to enjoy the very act of hurling my shoes across the room. Now, at least to all outward appearances, I am terribly respectable.

'I've been thinking of doing the Marathon des Sables,' I said.

Her eyes flicked from the magazine to me. She is still very beautiful. And she is still very good at knowing when not to speak.

I started on the knot of my tie. 'There's a place come up for next April,' I said. 'I'm quite tempted.'

Elise stretched for the TV remote and turned off the television. The magazine was put to the side.

I had her undivided attention. I always find that slightly unnerving.

'You're quite tempted?' she said. 'Or have you already signed up?'

'I've been thinking about signing up.'

And then Elise did something very unexpected. If I'd had to make a prediction, I would have said that Elise's reaction would have been generally hostile. I would have guessed that she'd be dead-set against the amount of time I'd need to train. That she would have been concerned, perhaps, that I might end up dead or horribly injured.

I didn't even like to think what she'd make of my beautiful running mate. Elise has intuition like no other person I have ever met.

'Why not?' she said. 'You could do with a challenge.'

'Really?' I said.

'Better than what most men tend to do when they're having a mid-life crisis.' She cocked an eye-brow. 'As I think you already know.'

Ahh yes. Well, I have already written about that, for Elise is *The Woman Who Made Men Cry*. But we move on, do we not? I like it that marital infidelity is no longer – necessarily – a deal-breaker. That it can be a matter for jokes is even better.

'*Touché*,' I said.

'So what's she like?' said Elise. She was wearing a white t-shirt, one hand alluringly behind her head. She's still got it.

'What's who like?'

'Your running mate. Is she pretty?'

'Quite pretty. Though not in your league.'

And in my mind's eye…

I move towards Elise on the bed, and I stroke her magnificent auburn hair. It is still as thick and as lustrous as when I first knew her all those years ago in New York City. Then I slip my hand beneath her shirt, stroke her stomach and realise, delightedly, that she is wearing just her t-shirt and nothing else. She kisses me, artfully, wickedly, and writhes against me with great expertise as her hands frisk at the tops of my trousers.

In my mind's eye.

And in reality…

I move to stroke Elise's hair. She ignores my hand. 'I'm tired,' she says. 'Good night.' She switches her light off and turns away from me to face the wall. The white duvet is drawn up tight about her shoulders.

*

It was my editor, maddest of all of my mad masters, who put the seal on my Marathon des Sables dream.

He lumbered into my office. He is fat and sleek, in the way of a sea lion. His expensive Hermès tie rested jauntily on his smooth potbelly.

'Doing the Marathon des Sables?' he said.

'Yes.'

'You haven't got a bloody prayer.'

I felt like an old warhorse who hears a long-forgotten clarion call. For there is nothing in my life that is quite so guaranteed to get me going as people telling me that I am not… fit for purpose.

Strike Three for the Marathon des Sables; and a strike for the fusty, crusty forty-somethings; and a strike for wilfully, thrillingly doing that which I was so not supposed to do. Strike Three for the bored man who was suddenly throwing himself in at the deep end.

It would be tough.

It would be eye-wateringly painful.

But it would also be invigorating; and life-enhancing; and gloriously rebellious.

I'd regret it. Of course I would.

But having that fat clown parading himself in my office… and having him say I didn't have a hope in hell… Well it was that – much, much more than anything else – that put a seal on it.

I looked at him from over the top of my computer terminal. And I smiled, a smile of genuine delight – because when a gauntlet has been thrown in front of me, I am quite incapable of not picking it up.

'Don't stand a prayer?' I said. 'Well, you just watch me!'

CHAPTER 3

I am a late Charlie.

My wife Elise is also a late Charlie. My daughters are late Charlies. My colleagues are, by definition, late Charlies. We are addicted to the thrill of the deadline.

But of all the late Charlies, I am without doubt the Bonnie Prince.

I don't know how it's come about. But for me there always has to be that squeaky-bottom moment as you realise that, perhaps, this time, you might have cut things a little fine. If there's no tension, then where's the fun?

So: one very early morning in February and, as my family sleeps, I am clattering around the house looking for a blow-up mattress; and nipple-guards and gels; and a towel and lycra shorts and two lycra shirts; and gloves (I mustn't forget the gloves, because it's absolutely freezing out there); and maybe a pillow; and by Christ, I almost forgot my sleeping bag; rucksack and water platypus; and Dettol and needles and a scalpel and bandages; and at least two pairs of Injinji toe socks and a bobble hat; and a book and a head torch; and soap and shampoo and toothpaste and toothbrush; and seeing as I'd be with Kate for the next 36 hours, I'd need to be looking my best so therefore shaving gel, razor and aftershave balm and mosturizer.

And money. Money is essential if you're a late Charlie. When you're neck deep in the mire, you can always buy your way out of trouble.

Elise feigned sleep as I banged around in the bedroom. I was searching for a spare pair of running shoes. I found them eventually, tucked under the stairs, and the lot was all tossed willy-nilly into a huge yellow North Face holdall.

After four months' training for the MdS, I was entering my first ultra. Ultras sound more impressive than they actually are. All it means is that you're running a distance that's longer than 26 miles.

I put on the porridge that would power me through 33-odd miles along the Pilgrim's Way from Farnham to a school near the M25 in South Merstham. On the second day of the Pilgrim, we would be running the identical route back to Farnham.

I wasn't necessarily ready, but I was about as ready as I was ever going to be. After Christmas, I had started doing my daily commute to Wapping on foot. That was 12 miles a day, 60 miles a week, without even breaking a sweat.

My route varied, but I had come to know Hyde Park, Green Park and St James's Park very well. I got to know the other joggers, too, and I especially got to know that strip of sand on Rotten Row. I would run two miles of sand a day, side-skirting the horse droppings and smiling at the other madmen who had that slightly crazed look that comes over people who are training for the MdS.

Every morning at 8 a.m., you could see us scurrying out of our holes with our knapsacks and our suits on our backs as we trotted to our computer terminals. Lunch times were spent in the gym working on core strength and other such essential things that the MdS requires of you. Though it's difficult to tell what actually *is* essential for the MdS.

Lots of experienced competitors will name numerous essentials – though they usually only pipe up after you've arrived in Morocco: Keeping the weight of your rucksack down; training in the heat; training in the sand; having all the kit – including state-of-the-art footware. But this is by no means sufficient. Even if you're kitted out top to toe and even if you have trained harder and longer than any other athlete in the world, there are still so many things that can put you out of the race. Oh yes. Just ask the top seed in 2012, Rachid el Morabity.

He had won the race the previous year, and was absolutely made for the Marathon des Sables. I saw him on the fourth day of the MdS, running at full pace, and he looked just unstoppable – flowing, strong as a horse.

And yet…

But we'll come to Rachid's story later.

At the weekends, I went for much longer runs. I now know Richmond just as well as the London parks and Rotten Row.

It's difficult to say whether all this road-running is any sort of preparation for the MdS. I think it sets you up mentally. It toughens you. If you've done 33 miles back-to-back in sub-zero Hampshire, then, mentally, you might be ready for the punishment of the Sahara.

But, of course, it's a different form of punishment. Even if you get used to the blistered feet, you're never quite ready for the extraordinary heat. Some people can take it – and some can't. Some plough on even though their feet look like meat on the butcher's slab, while others throw in the towel. They had forgotten that you still always have to take that next step, and then the one after it.

I remember the second day of the MdS, trudging along after my night of the runs, Kate a hundred yards ahead of me. I was almost lightheaded and whenever I stopped I felt woozy as a wave of delirium washed over me. And then I would start walking again and it would gradually fade.

I had a conversation with a man from Ireland. He was very thin and very pale. He wore green – green shirt and green trousers. He said he was in a lot of pain; well, my friend, have you perhaps thought about joining the club?

It was hot and it just kept on getting hotter. I had never known heat like it. Well, actually, I had once known heat like it – in Death Valley in Nevada. But in Death Valley, I'd been zipping through the desert in my rented Lexus with the air-con at full blast. Not quite the same.

It had started getting hot by nine in the morning, and by noon, it was like being slow-stewed in an oven. It was a very still day, not a breath of wind nor a cloud in the sky; hot and relentless and a journey that seemed to be without end. My feet were boiling in my shoes and my back was wet with sweat. I had my casquette very low over my brow, and with my head slightly bent forward, I could see no more than six feet ahead of me. That was good. There are times when seeing the whole panorama of the desert can be intensely uplifting: to know that you are there in the middle of it all and that you are a part of it. And there are other times when all you want is to withdraw into your own little cocoon, for your wretched world to shrink to a few miserable feet of sand and nothing but the next step.

The Irishman was complaining and he was driving me crazy. What is the point in paying £3,500 to be in the MdS and then complaining that it's hot? What else did he expect?

It was all he could talk about: 'God this is hot,' he'd say in his thick Irish accent. 'I am *so* hot. It is so unbelievably hot.'

When the whining got too much, I quickened my pace and left him. The last words I remember him saying were, 'Sod this.'

A couple of minutes later I heard the firework fizz of a red flare going up. It reached a good height and then the parachute deployed and it gently glided back to earth.

I strained to see who had set it off, and caught a glimpse of green as the Irishman sat down on his rucksack. And that was his race over on day two. He had snapped at the first bite of pressure.

But that's why many of us do it: We want to be tested. For once in our pampered little lives, we want to experience pressure, to find out if we've got the guts to tough it out. We want to be stretched to breaking point – and then just that little bit more.

★

I ate my porridge and I sipped my black coffee. Kate would be ringing on the bell in three minutes. She was never late.

Elise came into the kitchen. I kissed her on the cheek. 'Good morning,' I said.

She kissed me with dry lips, rather functional. 'How did you sleep?'

'Very well – you?'

'You were tossing and turning a lot.'

The doorbell rang and I went to get it. Kate was standing there, her blonde hair peeking out from a beanie. She was head to toe in black, tight leggings and a fleece. There was frost on the cars and her breath smoked in the air.

I kissed her on both cheeks, one hand light about her waist. Her cheeks were cold. Her smile was a little strained.

Elise had followed me to the door. I introduced them. 'Elise, this is Kate,' I said. 'Kate, Elise.'

They shook hands and Elise did that thing that proprietary wives sometimes do – she checked Kate out. It's very quick, but it is a full glance from head to toe.

Kate seemed oblivious. We stood there in the hall.

'It's freezing, isn't it?' Kate said.

'Perfect training for the Sahara,' I said.

'Would you like a coffee?' said Elise.

'I'm fine.' Kate said. 'I'm drinking water.'

'She takes these races very seriously,' I said. 'Unlike me.'

I shouldered my bag and was about to leave when I remembered yet one more thing that I had forgotten. Vaseline. It keeps us chunky runners smooth and prevents chafing in all manner of unmentionable places.

I found some Vaseline in the bathroom and headed back downstairs. Elise and Kate had been chatting by the door, and they both looked at me as I decended.

Kate gave Elise a wave and walked out. I kissed Elise goodbye.

'She's pretty,' she said.

'Yes – I told you she was pretty.'

'You didn't tell me she was *that* pretty.'

'How remiss of me,' I said. Elise kissed me again. That does not happen so often these days. 'I'll see you tomorrow; I may be some time.'

I slung my bag into the back of Kate's car. It was a sexier version of the Mini, a dinky, pastel-blue Fiat.

Kate was sitting in silence in the car. The engine was running and her hands were tight on the wheel.

I got in beside her and looked at her.

'So what's up?' I said.

I didn't really need to ask, because I already knew. After four months of running with Kate and talking to Kate, I knew of only one shadow in her life that made her miserable: the boyfriend.

(Well, of course she had a boyfriend. Beautiful, sparky women like Kate are snapped up very, very quickly.)

Though from all I'd heard, this boyfriend, Edward, should have been dumped out with the trash long ago. Not that I'd met him, but it certainly felt like I knew him better than his own mother. Edward was good-looking; Kate had left me in no doubt on that point. He did something in politics, though don't even get me started on that one. I have worked in the Lobby in Westminster, and despite all their high-flown hollering, it is nothing short of a rat-infested pit.

The pair had met at journalism college in Cardiff, but after a year or two on an evening paper, Edward had given it all up to be a bag-carrier for some Labour MP.

There were a number of things that irritated me about this po-faced young man – not least that he was very dismissive of the *Sun* and Kate's job there. Of course I am *also* very dismissive of the old Soaraway *Sun*, but I do at least work there. Edward, on the other hand, was for ever droning on about when Kate was going to work on a – how I *hate* this phrase – 'proper paper.' But she was learning the ropes, she was enjoying her work. And she was pretty damn good at it too. What more did he want?

Other irks about Edward: he was jealous and intensely suspicious. Kate and I had barely managed a single run with each other without him calling to check in; she would always take the call. And amongst other things, he thought that Kate's paunchy middle-aged running mate had developed a very large crush and wanted nothing so much as to jump into bed with her. *As if...*

Kate eased us onto the Hammersmith roundabout. It was a Saturday morning, barely past 7 a.m., and there was hardly a car to be seen.

'It's Edward,' she said.

In the past, when the matter of the doltish boyfriend had come up, I had tried a number of different tactics, initially the concerned solicitous friend who listens long and hard, hem-ing and hah-ing in all the right places and never, ever offering any advice. I wasn't sure how effective it had been, so more recently I had been injecting a little levity.

'Oh!' I said in mock surprise. 'It's Edward! You were so hangdog I thought it was going to be something *really* serious. So what's the young scamp done now?'

That at least got a smile, the first genuine one I'd seen from her all morning.

'He wants me to come back to London this evening. He's got some dinner with his boss and he wants me to be there.'

'That's irksome,' I said. 'I mean we've only had this in the diary since Christmas – but dinner with the MP? Really no contest, is it?'

'He'll be so annoyed.'

To which, of course, the correct response should have been, 'Well screw him.'

But that's not how it is when you're in your twenties in love, and when you can't imagine a life without your lover and you think that all this horrid *Sturm und Drang* is actually normal.

'We're staying in a school hall in South Merstham tonight,' I said. 'I hear the mobile phone reception is not too good.'

We were heading south now. It was going to be a lovely day, cold and crisp and just perfect for running. Kate laughed again. 'Oh, no?'

'Actually I hear the phone reception is pretty lousy along the whole route of the Pilgrim.'

'That'll be terrible.'

'Terrible?' I said. 'It's not terrible – it's a complete and utter disaster! I mean, how on *earth* is Edward going to get his hourly updates?'

'Maybe the organisers could text him as I go through each checkpoint.'

'That's a great idea,' I said. 'I'm sure that'll keep him very happy.'

Kate stretched behind her and picked up a large bottle of water. She held it between her knees and unscrewed the cap, chugging back the water as we breezed over the river. She drank well over a pint, then smiled as she let out an almost soundless belch. She offered me the bottle and I took it. I could taste the aloe vera from the Vaseline on her lips.

'Sometimes I think things might be easier if we were married,' she said.

I twitched in revulsion.

'Let me tell you one thing, Kate – I've lived this one. This time, for once, I know what I'm talking about. All marriage does is concentrate what you already have. If there are any cracks, a marriage won't paper over them – it'll magnify them.'

'We've talked about it,' she said. 'I can't imagine life without him.'

There were many replies to that.

For once, I shut up.

On the outskirts of Farnham, Kate pulled out a map. Quiet, sleepy byroads, with hedges and trees thick with frost. We parked up in a field, registered and dumped our bags into the back of a lorry. We began to immerse ourselves into the world of the ultra runner.

They are an odd lot.

It was cold and the water had turned to ice. We huddled in a marquee and I stared at the other runners and I listened. Most ultra runners are men, very lean and earnest, with craggy skin that comes from being outside in all weathers. They had all the latest kit – shoes, trousers, fleeces and gleaming rucksacks. They talked about runs they'd done or runs they were going to do, and they talked about their training programmes.

And they watched Kate. And I watched them watching Kate, side-long appraisals and great double-takes. She was in the zone, sipping from her water bottle and lightly shimmying on the spot; you could tell she was a good dancer.

I liked the look of an affable moon-faced guy in the corner. His name, I later learned, was Lawson, and apart from me, he was the shabbiest runner in the race. He was dressed in a baggy blue tracksuit tucked into greying socks and dirty old trainers, as if he was about to spend the day at Ikea. But most striking of all was his hat, a woollen Viking helmet with two huge grey horns.

He had a paper cup of coffee in one hand and a jam doughnut in the other, which oozed over his fingers. He would lick his fingers and stolidly continue to eat the doughnut, sugar flecked around his mouth. It was then that I noticed the grubby buff around his neck. They call them buffs these days, but until recently they were always known as snoods, tubes of thin fabric that most often go round your neck like a scarf, though you can also turn them into beanies and pirate hats and balaclavas.

Lawson's buff was orange and black and faded by the sun. I recognised it immediately. It was from the MdS. It was hard to believe that he had completed it, but appearances can be deceptive. The MdS is a test of inner steel, and that's not so easy to discern. It's the eyes that show everything. They reveal fear and excitement, nerves and rage. They can also show a very quiet confidence.

We had our pep-talk from the event organisers, Extreme Energy. Drink water, we were told. It's cold out there, we were told. Don't slip, don't get run over, don't have a nasty accident – and see you all at the finish line.

And that's another reason why we do the MdS: We instinctively hate, detest, all this health and safety mollycoddling that is part and parcel of the twenty-first century. All these constant admonishments not to hurt ourselves, not to kill ourselves and above all to *Take Care!* Is it any wonder that there has been such a surge in endurance races and dangerous sports when we spend our entire lives having our hands held by nursemaids in Hi-Vis safety jackets...?

I went out with Kate to the line of Portaloos. Runners drink at least two litres of water before a race, so there is always a rush for the loos. The toilets were not for the squeamish – though compared to the windy flapping cubicles of the MdS, they seemed quite luxurious. On these long races, a runner very quickly overcomes their inhibitions. In normal life, it would be unthinkable for a woman to just drop her trousers in public. Yet on the MdS, it becomes just a part of everyday life. Within three days, men and women are happily performing their ablutions in full view of the bivouac. Runners become as unselfconscious as beasts of the field and pee and parp without the slightest hint of restraint. Not all runners, of course; even to the last, Kate always needed her privacy.

The first person to vacate one of the Portaloos was Lawson. He still wore his Viking hat, and was tying up the front of his tracksuit. He looked at Kate, saw that this beautiful woman was heading straight to his loo and then just gaped at her. 'I...' he said. 'I'm so sorry.' His fingers were constricting into knots.

I wondered what on earth he'd done.

'I'm sorry,' he said again. 'It, ahhhh... it wasn't all mine.'

Kate went into the toilet. The door hadn't even closed before she came out again. 'You don't want to go in there,' she said. 'I'll find a hedge.'

Later, I noticed Lawson standing at the start line.

How could I resist?

'How were your morning toiletries?' I asked.

'Vile,' he said, and then he looked past me and recognised Kate and was once again covered in confusion. 'Oh, it's you,' he said. 'I, I'm sorry about that. The flush had frozen and—'

Kate laughed. 'Don't worry about me,' she said. 'I'm surprised you could even go in there.'

'Never been very good at doing it *al fresco*,' he said. 'Blame it on my mum – poor potty training.'

'You've run the MdS?' I said.

'I am running it.' Lawson plucked at the buff around his neck and smiled. 'It is quite distinctive, isn't it? It was my dad's.' With a sad little sigh he raised his eyebrows, and I realised that, for Lawson, the MdS was a memorial to his old man. The desert can forge the most strange connections – not just with the living, but also the dead.

'Your dad ran it?' I asked.

'Years ago – and since he, ahhh...' he tugged again at his buff, easing his finger around his throat. 'Since he passed away, I've always wanted to give it a try. Don't know whether I'll finish it. But in April, I'll be there on the start line.'

'And us too,' I said.

'I'm liking it,' he said, before looking Kate up and down. 'You've been in training.'

'Just a little,' she said.

'Who the hell cares about training?' said Lawson. 'It's going to be great!'

We laughed as the other runners were stretching and staring out over the field, getting their heads round the 33-miler ahead of them.

One runner had been listening to our conversation. Tall, craggy and with an almost permanent air of aggrievement.

'You running the Marathon des Sables?' he asked.

'I don't know about running it,' said Lawson. 'Competing in it. That sounds better.'

'Need to lose seven or eight kilos, won't you?'

'Only seven or eight?' said Lawson. 'Ten at the absolute minimum!'

The abrasive stranger went back to his business.

His name, I soon find out, was Derek 'Del' Esbit.

Now, in trying to give you a fair and objective portrait of Del Esbit, I will concede that he had a number of fans. I have met them, and they rave about his acerbic style and his training methods.

But Del also had his detractors – many of them.

Del polarized people. You were either for him or against him; no one ever sat on the fence. Some people liked to label him a 'Marmite guy' – but that would be quite wrong. I would describe Del as more of a 'Tripe guy' – there might be a few people who quite like tripe, but at least nine out of ten people can't abide the stuff and retch at the very smell of it.

I shook hands with Kate and Lawson. The gun banged and we were off through the frozen fields, with Del hurtling off to catch up with the front runners. You see all sorts at these ultra events. Some start out at almost a flat-out sprint, going hard for the first two minutes before grinding down to a lumbering trot. Others are fully intent on walking the whole thing. And then there are the vast rump of runners who jog along as best they can, who run when they can and walk when it gets tough, and who are just hoping to finish the damn thing in the daylight.

The first ten minutes are always tough. They're not necessarily the toughest – that will probably come when you've got blisters and your blood-sugar levels are low and you've still got another ten miles ahead of you. But the first ten minutes are always a slog. Your body is wondering whether it can sustain this sort of pace. That first mile takes much more effort, as your body gripes at the unexpected exertion, and your heart rate soars. But then, after a bit, you level off and your body just knuckles down and gets on with it – as we all do in the face of adversity.

But the bigger question is this: what do we do in the face of *sustained* adversity. Do we doggedly continue on the path that's been set us, or do we weigh it all up and think to ourselves, 'This is one of the most pointless things that I have ever embarked on, so why don't I give up now rather than putting myself through another moment of this torture?' It is this perpetual question that we are faced with daily as we arrive at the next bridge – so do we cross it or do we burn it down?

And we take the next step.

Even with ten kilos on her back, Kate was looking strong. While I was panting like a dog, she was skimming through the frost, barely even out of second gear. She made it look effortless.

'Hey Kate,' I said. 'Don't hold back for me. You go on ahead. You shouldn't be with the goats.'

'Shut up,' she said.

'That's the spirit – anyway, any time you feel like sprinting, just go for it.'

'I'm enjoying myself.'

'Glad to hear it.' I looked at my watch. We'd barely been out five minutes. And we had another 33 miles to go. In these situations, it doesn't do to get too far ahead of yourself. You take in the scenery, the crisp rolling countryside and you imagine all the tens of thousands of pilgrims who have walked this route before you – and how utterly bizarre they would find it to see these nutty runners trekking out for 33 miles on the Pilgrim's Way, only to turn round the next day and come all the way back again.

And this is supposed to be fun?

You look at your watch and you find that you have run another half-mile and that now it's only 31 miles to the finish line, and you realise, to your amazement, that your body is once again knuckling under, and that the aches and the tightness are beginning to recede.

After 15 minutes, you sip some water. It's easiest if you stick to a routine, otherwise before you know it you've been running for an hour and haven't touched a drop. A lot of casual runners only drink when they feel thirsty, but you only start to feel thirsty after your body has already run dry. It's like the warning light on your car's fuel gauge – it only turns on when you're down to the last half-gallon.

Runners often forget to drink when it's cold. In the desert, when it's 52 degrees and you're losing a litre of sweat an hour, it's pretty obvious that you're going to have to drink a lot; and take salt tablets; and electrolytes. It's not the same when it's dark, overcast and the temperature is falling through the floor.

In the Sahara in April, it's dark by 7 p.m. and it gets very cold very quickly – and yet even seasoned campaigners on the MdS forget they're still running hard, still sweating hard, and that they still need that water. Before they know it, they're stumbling into the next checkpoint and, as the French commissaires check them over, they can barely even say their own names. They usually end up on an intravenous drip.

We trotted past a large vineyard on an expansive south-facing hill. Lawson had been more or less tagging along with us. 'The Romans used to make wine here,' he piped up.

'What do you reckon it tasted like?' said Kate.

'Good question,' Lawson said. 'Probably about as disgusting as most British wine these days.'

'All they wanted was the alcohol,' I said. 'The taste was irrelevant.'

'Sounds just like me,' Lawson said. 'Are you taking any booze out to the Sahara?'

'I hadn't thought about it,' I said.

'It'll be a whole week without alcohol! I haven't done that since I was 16!'

'What about a bottle of Absinthe?' I said.

'I've been thinking about raw alcohol,' he said. We were going uphill now and our gentle trot had eased to a walk.

'You could try wine crystals,' Kate said.

'Wine crystals?' Lawson said.

'Just add water. The water turns into wine.'

'I'm liking it!' said Lawson. 'It'll be a miracle!'

'The miracle will be if it's even drinkable,' I said. 'Though since you're not picky, that shouldn't matter.'

We'd reached a T-junction and it was not at all clear which way to go. The Pilgrims Way is well signposted with large white acorns pointing the way, but at this junction there was nothing to be seen. We looked to left and right and eventually saw what we took to be some runners at the bottom of the hill. We followed them.

Just as in the desert, it doesn't do to spend too long admiring the scenery – invariably, within two seconds, you'll have stubbed your toe on a rock or caught your shoe in a gnarled tree root. So as we ran down the hill, I would only fleetingly look up to admire Kate's back. (Men love to run behind women, dawdling off in this hazy daydream while gazing at legs, backs, hats, bums). But for the most part my eyes were glued on the ground two or three yards in front of me, my mind fully focused on nothing more than the next step. It is the perfect training for 'Be Here Now' – because if you've spent too long on that outrageous bedroom fantasy, then the next thing you're flat on your face.

We'd trotted half a mile down the hill and there was still no trace of a white acorn. We'd gone off course and we didn't have much option but to retrace our steps; a very minor setback. And a very minor test of character. Not a massive test, but nevertheless indicative of how somebody will act when the going gets tough.

'This can't be right,' Kate said.

'Let's go back to where we saw the last sign,' I said.

'I liked that hill,' Lawson said. 'I want to see those views again.'

Three other runners had joined our conflab and followed us back up. It's galling when you have to retrace your steps, but if it has to be done, I try to do it with good cheer; no good ever came from whining.

We trotted very slowly past the original junction and continued up the hill. At the top, we ran through a clearing. By now there were about 20 of us all blindly following the front runner. You always hope the front runner knows what they're doing.

After another half a mile without acorns, we realised we still weren't on the right track. Time for another conflab.

Del Esbit was haranguing a cyclist who had a map and a phone. The cyclist was from Eastern Europe and his English was limited.

'It can't be this way!' Del said. 'Why can't they bloody sign this thing properly? It's pathetic!' Some of the runners were, like Del, mightily pissed off. I didn't care much either way, though I did hope I'd get in before dark.

We went back down the hill again – back to the original junction which I was now visiting for the third time.

Time for another team talk. 'It's got to be that way!' Del said, pointing downhill.

'I think it's that way!' said an Irishman. He was pointing through the woods.

There was a delicious pause as we all wondered what to do next – and then for the first time, Lawson decided to throw in his ha'penny-worth. He was standing right on the edge of the group, and spoke with a high sing-song voice.

'Me no like-eee!' he said.

The reactions were varied. Most of the runners turned to inspect Lawson. They must have thought he was on day release; he was so not like your usual ultra runner. Kate started laughing, girlish fingers across her mouth as she chuckled. Del scowled.

I loved it.

'Me no like-eee!' I said.

The sign turned out to be a few yards away. It had been hidden by an overhanging branch. We trotted on; it got colder and the miles slowly clicked by, but it's not really helpful to think that you're 17 down with 17 to go.

Kate, as ever, looked like she was out for a morning jog. Going up the steps up Box Hill, the toughest hill of the day, she was so strong she could have probably sprinted it. When I caught her at the top, she was putting on some black gloves.

'You sure you don't want to head on?' I said. 'You could bag us a couple of decent spots in the gym.'

'I'm in no hurry,' she said.

'What's it like having your phone turned off?' I said.

'I should do it more often.'

Lawson stuck with us. At the checkpoints he would wolf down the malt loaf and the sweets and the stale sausage rolls. He ate the food completely at random, savoury followed by sweet, followed by another mouthful of cheese sandwich.

The problem with stopping is the cold. At the last checkpoint, we had to wait five minutes for Lawson, which is when your warm sweaty shirt quickly turns to an ice blanket.

As with everything about the Pilgrim, it was a foretaste of the Sahara.

★

On the double-marathon day in the desert, I got very cold.

I had been walking in the dark by myself. It's too easy at night to turn an ankle and put yourself out of the race, so I didn't run.

There was a green glowstick every 500 yards or so to mark the way, and the competitors all had glowsticks on the backs of their packs. Ahead of you, miles ahead of you, you might see a glowstick or two, and when you look back, there is this line of white head torches. It looks incredible, grand, even magnificent, and there you are, right in the middle of it. You may be just another glowstick and just another head torch, but you are a part of this insane, glorious race.

I'd had a minor setback and had got into the fourth checkpoint quite late, at around 11 p.m. I still had a long way to go, at least another 20 miles.

I hadn't planned on hanging around for more than five minutes. If you wait for too long, your muscles start to seize up, and suddenly your dormant blisters come to life and you can feel every one of them, raw, pulsing, screaming for attention.

I'd topped up my water bottles with the fresh 1.5 litres I'd been given. I dropped in an electrolyte tab to help replace some of the salts I'd been sweating out.

I swayed up my rucksack. It was the fourth day of the race and so it was nearly four kilos lighter than it had been at the start. But it was still way over 10 kilos.

I checked my straps, my gaiters, adjusted my head torch. The wind was bitingly cold and my wet shirt was wicking the heat from my core. I'd swapped my casquette for a beanie to try and keep the heat in and I gave the zips a final check to see they were secure. If you take a tumble down a dune, it's tough retrieving your kit from the sand.

I unwrapped a Nutri-Grain bar. I'm don't really like them but my body was crying out for more energy, so I managed to wolf it down in three brisk bites.

And then, just as I'm about to plug in my headphones, I hear her. Or at least I hear a scream – and I know it's her.

I don't know what she's still doing at the fourth checkpoint. She should have been long gone.

But it's her, it has to be.

I'm not exaggerating – the only time that I have ever heard anything like that was on the maternity wards.

The shrieking went on and on, barely human yet recognisable. I tucked my headphones into my front pocket and went over to the medical tent. It was like the low-slung black Berber tents that we slept in, very harshly lit, with a rug on the ground. One side of the tent was down to keep out the worst of the wind.

The screaming tailed off to a whimper. I unbuckled my rucksack and went inside.

Kate was lying on the rug with both her feet up on a little low stool. I couldn't see what the doctor had been doing, but there was a lot of blood and several soiled bandages on the floor. Kate was silently weeping, hands pushed into her eye sockets as the tears poured down her cheeks.

'Hi,' I said. I squatted next to her.

She took her hands from her eyes and looked at me and tried to smile. 'Hi,' she said.

Now that woman, that night – Let me tell you, she showed more grit than anyone else I've ever met.

'What can I do?' I said. 'Can I cook you some food?'

'I'd be sick on the spot.'

'A cup of mint tea?'

'Just water – please.'

I was holding her hand. It was quite wet.

The doctor was not nearly finished. He was a young Frenchman, pudgy and bearded, and probably sick to death of this never ending stream of foot-sore lunatics. He was fiddling around in a large plastic medical box and eventually produced an intravenous needle. It was almost as thick as a knitting needle.

'I will use this,' he said.

'That?' Kate said. She wiped the tears from her face and pushed herself up onto her elbows. 'Can't you use a scalpel?'

'No,' said the doctor. 'This is what I have to use.'

'Jesus,' Kate said and she lay back on the rug.

I gave her a water bottle and she took a couple of sips.

'What's he doing?' I said.

'He's going to pop my blisters,' she said. 'They're underneath my toenails.'

'Ouch,' I said.

'Tell me about it.' She had her white beanie tight down over her head. Her nose was red and wet. She wiped it with her sleeve.

'I'll be outside,' I said. 'No hurry.'

'Don't wait for me,' she said. 'You go on.'

'You must be joking! I'll be out here.'

'Well – it might be a little…' She shrugged helplessly. 'A little noisy.'

'Call if you need anything,' I said. 'Anyway, I need a rest. I could do with putting my feet up. Shall we spend the night here?'

'No – God, no,' she said. 'I want to get going.'

'I'll be over by the Land Rovers.'

I had put my coat on the ground and was lying on the coat with my feet on the Land Rover's front bumper. It's much better than just sitting down, as it drains your swollen legs and feet. Not many people know that. If you ever see the elite runners immediately after a race, they're always either eating or they've got their feet up. It's called the golden hour, and it is far and away the most important time in a runner's recuperation.

The screaming started again. The rest of the checkpoint was quite quiet, just a few people talking to each other. Her shrieks cut straight through the silence of the Sahara.

I tried to block out the noise by plugging in my earphones, but even over the loudest Van Halen, I could still hear her.

And that's when I started to get cold. My shirt was wet through and my fleece was also damp. Within a few minutes, the chill had enveloped me.

I didn't know how long Kate was going to be. Would it be ten minutes? Half an hour? Or would she be in for the full two-hour session that some of the runners endure at Doc Trotters?

If I'd had any sense, I'd have taken off my top and towelled myself down. I could have packed the sodden shirt and just worn my coat and my fleece. But I delayed and I delayed, always thinking she couldn't be much longer. Kate had stopped screaming by now, and I presumed the doctor was bandaging up her feet so that she'd at least have a chance of finishing the stage.

I got colder and colder, until I was so cold I was thrown into this dull lethargy. I'd wrapped my coat about me, and it helped if I didn't move. Parts of my wet shirt seemed to retain a grain of heat.

And – of course – just at the very moment when I'd finally had enough of it all and was about to climb into my sleeping bag, Kate shuffled over.

I rolled onto my front and creaked to my feet.

'Lookin' good!' I said. The words had become our MdS mantra. No matter how sick and how shabby we looked, our default was always to revert to those life-affirming words.

She made the correct reply. 'Feelin' good!'

'Me too!' I said, my teeth chattering. Little lancing stabs were dancing up from my toes as my blisters began to reassert themselves.

'Sorry about all the screaming,' she said. 'Needed a leather belt to bite on.'

'Had my headphones in,' I said. 'Were you very loud?'

We shuffled out of the camp and into the darkness. It takes great force of will to leave the snug of a camp at midnight and to pitch yourself into the vast void of the desert.

We were both of us laced up to our eyeballs on Ibuprofen and Paracetemol, though in those first few minutes we were like a couple of old crocks – not even fit for a walk to the shops, let alone 20 miles in the Sahara.

And what a night it would be: without doubt the most memorable night of my life. It would be long and it would be miserable. But if there'd been one lesson I wished I'd learned at the Pilgrim, it was to keep moving, especially if you're cold and wet. And if, for any reason you do have to stop, then you've got to get out of those wet clothes as quickly as you can. Otherwise... well, otherwise you will be, as an old friend of mine used to say, Fouquet in Le Touquet.

CHAPTER 4

We were in a vast school gym, bare striplights overhead and a winter wind slipping in underneath the fire doors. The room hummed with this rank mix of sweat and wet socks and deodorant and Deep Heat ointment. The monkey bars on the walls were festooned with wet clothes and the floor was littered with suitcases, rucksacks, inflatable mattresses and a ton of muddy kit. The swing doors banged constantly as yet another bedraggled latecomer limped into the room.

We were sat right in the middle of the gym, stretching out on the ultra runner's version of a Lilo, the more durable Thermarest, and dotted all about us were the scores of runners who'd finished the first day of the Pilgrim. Some stretched, some downed their protein shakes and some just stared up at the ceiling from the luxury of their sleeping bags. There was a quiet chatter about the gym, as runners compared notes of the day's run.

It was spartan. It was the sort of place that would have had my wife Elise spinning on her well-shod heel and heading for the exit door.

And yet it's all about perception. For after a chill day on the Pilgrim's Way, it was absolute heaven. It always is, after you've stopped running for the day.

The last few miles had been cold and pretty hellish, and my feet hurt and my knees hadn't been up to much either; but that moment when you cross the finish line and realise that, finally, you can stop – it's lovely. You stretch and you shower and then, even though your joints are all starting to seize up, you're filled with this glow of satisfaction as the day's pain and all that constant grinding is forgotten.

Kate was sitting next to me on her sleeping bag. Her hair was still wet from the shower, sleek about her shoulders. She was wearing a white hoodie and baggy blue tracksuit bottoms. I've said it before and I'll say it again: she just looked so damnably wholesome. She was a real keeper. There she was, fresh, pink and cheerful after a day of running with me – and happy about it! I don't know many other women who'd be happy to spend the night in a gym with a gang of grunting men.

I was lying on my sleeping bag, feet off the ground on my North Face. I was watching her very closely.

She got a stainless-steel clasp knife out of her rucksack and flicked it open. The blade was wickedly sharp. She stroked it against her thumb.

'Is this really the best way?' I said.

'It works for me,' she said. 'Some people make a crescent-like cut to let them drain. The French swear by a needle and cotton thread. But I believe in the power of the Compeed.'

'Okay,' I said dubiously.

On her heel was a blister about the size of a 50p piece, and there were similar blisters on the balls of her feet.

'I always get blisters,' she said. 'Anything over a half-marathon.'

She sprayed some antiseptic onto her heel and, without pausing, cut right into the blister. Clear serum dripped from it onto her Thermarest. I winced as she cut all the way around. She put the round piece of skin into a plastic bag and then carefully placed the knife on her small first aid box. The glistening wound was raw and red. I inspected it from a few feet away.

'That looks like it hurts,' I said.

'Not too bad,' she said. 'The pain comes from having a swollen blister rubbing against your shoe. But once they're drained and you've got the Compeed on, then it's like having a second skin,' she laughed to herself as she pulled out a small green box of plasters. 'Only they're much tougher than my skin.'

She held the Compeed plaster tight between the palms of her hands, warming it up so that it would form a tight bond with her skin. After a minute, she peeled off the backing tape and slapped it onto her heel. Not a single wasted movement. It was a master class in how to apply a Compeed.

'That's that,' she said. 'Give it a few hours and it will have formed it's own little comfort bubble.'

'And you leave it there how long?'

'A week or so, until the new skin's formed underneath.'

'And they don't rub off?'

'Never.' She jabbed her knife into another blister. It squirted across her Thermarest. She ignored the serum. 'You can go for showers, run with them. They're brilliant.'

Even though we were talking about blisters – bloody blisters! – I had not been so happy in a long time. The simple pleasure of putting my feet up. Lying there chatting with Kate. Just a couple of mates yakking to each other – it was all so easy, so effortless.

Ultra runners may have their faults, they may be boring and blinkered and the most abject compulsive obsessives, yet they do have one great quality that redeems them to the full. They never complain. It doesn't matter that their feet have been chopped to pieces and that the weather is just awful – they quietly soldier on. And at the end of the day, they certainly won't be whining about their billet or the foetid bathrooms, and they will be more than grateful for whatever food you see fit to feed them.

It's such a refreshing attitude. The number of times I have stayed in quite classy hotels... We've gone up to our room; a comfortable bed, reasonable view... and yet still it lacks that certain something, and within two minutes I'm having to call up the reception to find out if there's anything better on offer.

When you stay in a hotel or a B&B, then you have a level of expectation. There are standards of cleanliness and hygiene which have to be met. But go on an ultra, and you won't care about the smell or the filthy floors. You'll be just delighted to have a shower and a hot meal.

And on the Marathon des Sables... why, on the Marathon des Sables, just a single can of Coke can turn into one of the most magical moments of your entire life. I remember it well. In fact – I will never forget it. I have had many memorable drinks in my life, and with many memorable drinking companions. But that can of Coke in the desert takes the absolute top spot.

After the long day on the MdS, runners are issued with new race numbers so that sponsors' names can be clearly seen in the finish-line photos. When you receive your new race number, you also receive a can of absolutely ice-cold Coke. It is so cold that the condensation gleams as it drips down the side. They also give you a small savoury bar of tomato and nut.

I sat on the rug with Kate and Lawson. We'd dragged the rug out of the tent to dry. The endless desert shimmered in the afternoon heat, bubbling all the way to the horizon. I pressed the cool can to my forehead. It was so cold that I could not hold it against my skin for too long. And then I flicked the can open and sipped, and the cold Coke touched my tongue, and in that moment, in that desert, I would not have been anywhere else, or with anyone else, in the whole world. We sat in the most perfect silence grinning at each other, almost sheepish at our astonishing good fortune as we slowly sipped at the Coke and munched our tomato bars.

Kate was wearing her sunglasses. I noticed a tear rolling down her cheek. When she saw that I was looking at her, she smiled. 'Who would have thought it?' she said. 'Heaven and hell in one day.'

I have never had a drink to touch it; I doubt that I ever will. That is what the desert does to you.

But it's not the Coke itself.

It's what you've been through to get it.

*

I went through to the other hall, where I'd booked myself in for a massage. The Pilgrim organisers had got in a couple of sports masseurs, and for £10 they would knuckle and grind your legs until every last drop of lactic acid had been squeezed out of your aching muscles. Thumbs are squeezed into your knotted legs, and if the masseur finds a really tough spot, then he'll go in with his elbows. Now *that* hurts. Those rinky-dink massages you can get in the top spas may leave you feeling blissfully relaxed – but they are not going to give you fresh legs for a 33-mile run the next day.

Serious ultra runners don't drink alcohol during a race. They say it dehydrates them and marginally affects their performance; they have obviously forgotten the huge medicinal powers of a glass of beer. After a long run, the first sip of cold beer is always nectar.

I bought myself a bottle of Stella and sat on the school stage as the masseurs pounded and flexed. They were young men, students with huge muscles, and they worked over the runners' legs like bakers kneading dough.

Two Irishmen were sitting next to me. They were only wearing shorts and T-shirts. One of them was also drinking a beer.

I overheard the smaller, leaner one talking about contact lenses. 'I'm on the monthly lenses,' he said. 'Think I might use the daily disposables.'

The other one, bigger, sturdier, sipped and belched. If the ultra races did have a motto, it would be, 'Better out than in'. Belch and fart just as you please, no one ever takes offence. 'Going to be a lot of sand,' he said. 'So there will.'

'A lot of sand,' repeated the slighter one, and they were lost for a moment in a thousand-mile stare as they gazed across the hall, the drab walls suddenly turned into a million miles of sand and heat.

'You're running the MdS?' I asked.

'More fool us!' said the bigger one. 'Crazy isn't it now?'

'It's not crazy,' I said. 'It is absolutely, clinically, certifiably insane.'

I was introduced to two doctors, Martin and Carlo. They were outraged that I couldn't tell they were from, not Ireland, but Northern Ireland.

'Can't you tell from our accents?' said Carlo. 'Do we sound like we're from the South?'

'Haven't got a damn clue.'

They'd left Northern Ireland and moved to England, to the soft South. Carlo was a knee surgeon, a hearty rascal; Martin was more precise, clinical, and specialized in hands and boob jobs.

It had been snowing since dusk and, as we walked to the canteen, there was a good six inches of snow on the ground. We'd watched as one of the last Pilgrims had shuffled over the finish line. He was a butcher, I later found out, with wattles of fat about his neck and legs the size of huge hams. His skin was quite white from the cold and he looked dead on his feet.

There'd been talk that the next day's run might have to be cancelled, and a part of me longed to be whisked back to Farnham in a coach; but there was that other part of me, naturally enough, that wanted to get on and punch out another 33 miles. This is the endless dichotomy that goes on in the ultra runner's head.

'Here's to the Marathon des Sables!' said Carlo. We clinked our plastic glasses. We each of us looked each other in the eye, sizing the others up, wondering what sort of tent-mates they'd make. Wondering, also, if they'd got the grit to see out a week in the desert. But it's difficult to tell. A guy can look as fit as the proverbial butcher's dog; he can be honed and muscled. But ultimately there's only one way to find out whether they can do the desert, and that's to see them walk the walk.

We had spaghetti bolognese for dinner. Pasta. That's all ultra runners ever want to eat in the evening.

'Won't be the same in the Sahara,' Martin said. He was one of the slowest eaters I've ever seen. He would toy with his food, prodding it around his plate before eventually popping it into his mouth, when he would chew on it like a cow at the cud. 'Proper roof over our heads. Showers – even a cooked dinner.'

'And they carry our kit,' Carlo said.

'And it's minus four degrees outside,' Kate said. 'And it's snowing.'

'Though I was told that snow is very similar to the dunes,' Martin said.

'Bollocks,' I laughed. 'Snow's nothing like sand. It'll be slushy and slippery and our socks will be soaked in minutes.'

'That's what I read,' Martin said, and I'm sure he had. He seemed like a guy who was most meticulous with his research. Though the practicalities of an event tend to be a little different from what you might have gleaned over the internet.

'It'll be similar because it's similarly awful to run through,' Carlo said. 'More wine?'

He went to get another two bottles of red. We were joined by Lawson, who stood by the table and declaimed: 'This mortal frame grows weak. I require sustenance!'

Kate and I chuckled. We recognised the line. A few months earlier I'd taken the girls to see Thor at the cinemas, and doubtless Kate had seen the film with her Edward. A swashbuckling Nordic God comes crashing down to earth; the film has some cracking lines.

Lawson placed his tray on the table and grabbed my plastic cup of wine. He downed it in one. 'This drink... I like it! More!' He hurled the plastic cup at a pillar. Kate was spattered with wine.

Martin was watching in the most repelled horror. His eyes twitched from Lawson back to the wine on the floor – what sort of madman were we dealing with?

Lawson slumped into a chair, oblivious to the wine stains on his trousers. 'Spag bog!' he said. 'Going up Box Hill! What a killer!' He champed into his pasta. 'And we've got to do the whole thing again tomorrow!'

Carlo came back with more wine. 'Is it the living legend who's giving tonight's talk?' he said.

'It is,' Martin said.

'I don't know why you like him.'

'We bonded.'

I looked over, eyebrows raised in query.

'The living legend?' Carlo said. 'You'll see him soon enough. He's a character. He's a character-and-a-half.'

'That's an interesting turn of phrase,' I said. In my experience, 'characters' are mildly eccentric and should only be taken in small doses. But as for 'a character-and-a-half'... well, that generally indicates that they're a complete pain in the neck.

Carlo beamed, thick eyebrows raised, as if there was some delightful treat that awaited me.

We talked about gear and training plans and we all of us agreed on much the same thing. We'd have loved to have been putting in 90 miles' running a week, but somehow there were always these things called 'family' and 'work' getting in the way. Like me, the others had slotted in their training runs wherever they could, with a few miles at lunchtime and then maybe a longer run at the weekend.

Kate's phone rang and she took it. I don't know why she did. Apart from the fact that we were all having supper, it was only going to be her boyfriend, and he was only going to be bending her ear. 'Hi,' she said. As she got up to leave the table, I could see the jollity drain from her face.

She spent a good ten minutes on the phone, and when she came back her pasta was cold. She seemed to have shriveled; my beautiful, lithe runner had shrunk into a down-trodden girlfriend. I didn't know what Edward had said to her, but I was pretty sure that it wasn't good news. He had some extraordinary hold over her, Svengali-like, which I was never able to fathom.

I bought more wine for Carlo and Lawson, and we munched on Kit Kats after our cardboard plates were practically licked clean. It didn't matter how much we ate that night – we would be running it all off the next day.

I don't know quite what I'd expected from the living legend. I thought he would probably be small and wiry, with the sort of slight, compact physique that you often find in SAS soldiers. They have that glint of steel in the eyes that means they'll keep on going until they drop dead.

What I hadn't expected was Del Esbit.

He swaggered to the front of the hall. He liked being the centre of attention.

'Evening all,' he breezed. He was wearing baggy jeans and a tight white T-shirt. He took a sip from the small water bottle and then looked about the room. He was taking his time. Quite the showman. 'Nice to see so many ladies here tonight.'

And another sip of water and another pause, his mouth down-turning at the edges.

'My name's Del,' he said. 'Del Esbit. My grandad invented the Esbit stove – you may have heard of it. You may have heard of me too. Just in case you haven't, let me tell you a little about the Del-Meister.'

And *another* dramatic pause as he now sought eye contact with every woman in the hall.

'I've run over 1,000 marathons,' he said. 'I've bagged ten Guinness World Records. But no one's interested in that. No one wants to talk about that. No.' A beat for the punch line, and then: 'Not even with me.'

Kate and I simultaneously glanced at each other. I wrinkled my nose. She almost cracked up.

Del took another tiny sip of water. 'The only thing that anyone wants to talk about is the big one. The toughest footrace on earth. The Marathon des Sables. One week in the hottest desert on earth. Yeah…' He trailed off, and this time he had a far-off look, like a gunslinger before the shoot-out. 'That's all they ever want to talk about. But I can tell them about the toughest footrace on earth. And I can tell you too. Because I've run it and I know it. I know the Marathon des Sables. Life is about stretching yourself. And the Marathon des Sables. Now that's a stretch. I've run it eight times. This April, I'll be running it again. And that, I guess, is why they call me the Endurance King.'

Lawson was drinking wine and he paused mid-sip to look at Del; a look of slight quizzical surprise. Kate screwed up her face in distaste. Carlo was chewing a fingernail and wasn't even listening. Martin, though, seemed absolutely entranced. As for me… I found him just bizarre. I hadn't come across this type of man in a long time. There are many strange people in the world of the ultra runner – but none quite so odd as Del Esbit.

I could not work out how he'd won all his Guinness World Records. He was fit, but he was a big man and at least 50 years old. Had he smashed the same quirky little World Record over and over again? Or had he garnered a whole glut of records when he'd been in his prime? I could not fathom it.

'I haven't always been the Endurance King,' Del continued. 'Fifteen years ago, I was a slob. A fat alcoholic in a boring job with a boring life. My wife was bored too. But thanks to running, I turned my life around – and you can turn it around too. I am never bored now – not for a moment. My life isn't boring. It's wonderful. And those people who can't keep up with me... well, I move on. I move on and I move out. I don't have time for time wasters.'

I nudged Kate. 'I didn't know we were coming to an Alpha meeting,' I said.

'He's got a few fans,' Kate said. And there were – ardent devotees, seemingly mesmerised by the Del-Meister.

Del clapped his hands. 'So how many of you jokers have signed up for the MdS?'

About 40 of us raised our hands.

'And how many of you reckon you're going to finish it?'

A few hands waved. One of them was the butcher who we'd seen at the finish line an hour earlier. And I might as well tell you now that he never did get his MdS medal; but his exit was far and away the most spectacular of the entire race.

Del cackled. 'You just don't know,' he said. 'Until you've done it, until you've walked the line, you just don't know.' He looked again around the hall, searching out any dissenters. There was a pulse ticking on his straining neck. 'You just never, never know.'

Normally, I would have left the room. But this man was *so* awful that I found myself drawn to him – if only to find out what happened next.

He told us we had to train hard, much harder than we thought we ought to train. And we had to pack light, because otherwise we didn't stand a hope in hell. And of course we had to have all the right kit. Basically it seemed that, unless we had some mind guru like Del to hold our hands, we were more or less screwed.

He clapped his hands together. 'If you've got questions,' he said, 'then I've got the answers. Gimme your best shot.'

Somebody asked a question about food on the MdS. What was the best dehydrated pap to take in your pack? Another question about the best electrolyte to keep you alive. Another question, altogether more abstruse, about how best to train for the searing heat.

I bided my time.

I teach trainee journalists about press conferences. Outside the harum-scarum world of tabloid journalism, most people believe that the point of a press conference is to impart information to the public.

This – at least for a tabloid hack – is not the case. For a hack, the point of a press conference is to cause havoc and mayhem by asking the most difficult question that they can dream up. We are not rude or disrespectful, but we strive to stir things up for the greater glory of our newspapers.

It's an old habit that dies hard, and these days, even if I'm attending a friend's lecture, I will still do my best to lob them a hand grenade.

I raised my hand.

Del pointed towards me. 'Yes,' he said. 'The girl in the tight white hoodie. You an ultra virgin?'

I looked over. It was Kate. She was ready for him. 'Since nobody ever asks you about your World Records, I'd like to ask about them. Tell us about your ten World Records. What are they for?'

She looked like she was enjoying herself.

'Good question,' I said.

Del smiled and nodded. 'They're for running,' he said simply.

'Wow! You've got ten World Records for running?' said Kate. 'Can you tell us a little more?'

'I got them a few years ago.'

Kate was relentless. 'What sort of distances?'

'Spot running,' he said.

'What's spot running?'

'Running on the spot,' he said. 'It's tough. Much tougher than actual running. Each stride your knees have to touch your hands. Otherwise it doesn't count.' A frisson rippled around the room. People looked at each other in bemusement. 'Anyone else? Any other questions?'

I raised my hand. He beckoned to me. 'Let's hear it.'

'I think it's incredible what you do – amazing.' I soft-soaped him before delivering the sucker punch. 'You say life's about stretching yourself. How much of a stretch is it for you to be doing one ultra after the next? Wouldn't it be more of a stretch to do something different, like rollerblading or surfing, rather than just banging out another marathon?'

He forced a laugh. 'If you're saying the MdS isn't a stretch, then just give it a try.'

'Thank you. You've been most helpful.'

He sniffed and glowered, like a bristling pit bull. But it's always a tricky one to answer. If life is about stretching yourself, then running endless ultras becomes as much of a routine as popping down to the golf club for the weekly medal.

As we left, Martin and a few others went up to Del to pay their respects to the living legend. 'Tripe guy' – even though tripe both smells and tastes disgusting, you will still find the occasional oddball who yearns for it.

I had not slept in a room with over 100 people before. The main lights went out at 10 p.m., and the head torches went on, like miners in the pit.

Kate was lying close to me. She stretched over and squeezed my hand. No one had done that to me in a very long time.

'Good night,' she said.

'Good night.'

'It's been fun.'

I gave her hand a squeeze. 'It has.' And to my amazement, and despite the skanky showers and the carnival house atmosphere of the hall, it *had* been. It was all so very different from my genteel world in London, with its plumped pillows and its well-ordered routine. And even though bedding down in a bare hall with all these strange runners would not have been my first choice for a weekend's entertainment, I was enjoying myself.

The company helped.

Kate was a trooper.

I realised that, unwittingly, I had found the perfect place to take a woman who you might like to marry. When most people are in love, they tend towards luxury. We whisk our lovers off to chic country hotels, or glitzy city hotels, or – my least favourite place on earth – the five-star spas.

But is that really the way to find out if a woman is your perfect life-partner? For what we want in our life-mate is somebody who's going to be by your side in the ditch when the bullets are flying; who's cheery when things go wrong; who won't whine when everything is not to their complete satisfaction; who shares our passions, whether it be for tabloid hackery or something as abstruse and obscure as endurance running; and, who above all – at least for me – is just that little bit of a mischief maker.

I wondered how Elise would have fared if I'd asked her to bed down with this horde of snoring, grunting runners. I knew exactly what she'd have done. She'd have taken one look at the hall and then she would have called up a cab to take her straight back home.

And I thought, also, about how Kate's boyfriend would have got on. I knew the type. So jealous. So very introspective. And so desperate to cling to the thing he loved that he'd sucked every ounce of joy out of the relationship.

CHAPTER 5

In the desert, the runners' tents are in two circles, about 200 yards in diameter, one inside the other. The tents of the 200-odd French runners were in the inner circle, while in the outer circle, directly adjacent to them, were the 250 Brits: noisier, more coarse, not as well groomed and generally just that little bit more odd.

Most nights, Kate and I, and sometimes Lawson, would go for a little promenade. We would amble in the dark on the circular track between the two tent circles. It was like peeking directly in to a stranger's bedroom: runners washing, runners reading, runners brushing their teeth and runners stripping down as they prepared for another night in the desert.

The tents were traditional black Berber tents, made of very coarse wool which kept out the wind and a certain amount of rain, though they would leak in a downpour. They were held up in the middle by an X-frame of two three-metre long branches, while each end of the tent was propped up by a couple of short sticks. Most evenings we would collect rocks to weigh down the ends of the tent. The tent's sides could be left up, but we would normally leave one down to block out the worst of the wind. You could never get the side properly down, even when it was weighted with stones. We would try to block the gaps with our rucksacks and coats, but the wind always found a way through.

One night, there was such a gale that Kate and I couldn't go for our evening walk. The air was thick with this light orange dust. It coated everything, got in everywhere, working its way into cameras and iPods, blocking ears, gunking up eyes, gritting our teeth, and forming this thick brown crust in our noses. We had collected a lot of rocks and both sides of the tent were down, but it did no good. There was sand and dust everywhere, in everything, coating our sleeping bags and our clothes and our skin. The dust spangled in the air, swirling and bright; I thought of Zeus turning himself into a shower of gold as he seduced the beautiful Danaë.

I had been reading *The Cruel Sea.* Apart from talking, there is not much else to do at night. The book was heavy, well over 300 grammes, but I liked the thought of reading about the freezing North Atlantic while out in the heat of the desert.

I was sandwiched between Kate and Carlo. She was reading too, tucked deep into her sleeping bag with just her head out and one hand holding onto her book. Her entire face was coated with this layer of red dust, as if she had covered her face in thick foundation. Her eyes were small black gimlets, lashes almost closed to keep the dust out; camels, you know, have evolved the perfect filter for these dust storms. They have three sets of eyelids. The first two eyelids have a double row of long, wavy lashes to screen out the sand, while the third eyelid is thin and transparent; it even blinks sideways, clearing dust from the eyeball like a set of windscreen wipers.

Most of our tentmates were asleep, or trying to sleep, though it was difficult with the roar of the wind and the constant flapping of the guy ropes. Kurtz, being canny, had brought sleeping tablets.

I'd thought Carlo was asleep, but suddenly he got up. 'Sod it,' he said.

'When you gotta go, you gotta go,' I said.

He was wearing black long-johns and a fleece. He put his head torch on top of his hat, slipped on some flip flops and picked up his roll of toilet paper and his brown latrine bag. The latrine bags were being tested for the first-time on that year's Marathon des Sables and, although they took a little getting used to, they were very effective. In years past, the MdS runners had just made their ablutions by digging a little hole and then burning the toilet paper. But the toilet paper never properly burned away, and for years afterwards, blowing about in the desert, there would be these little scraps of white paper, pecked quite clean by the desert insects. It was also the cause of a lot of illness. If there are over 1,000 ablutions lying all about the bivouac, then runners will be treading in it and trampling it into the rugs.

The more tired the runners became, the closer they moved their toilets to the tents, relieving themselves just a few yards from their running mates. In past races, you were lucky if you didn't go down with a severe stomach bug.

There was one other reason why the organisers had abandoned *al fresco* toileting, and this was over the small matter of leaving all this muck lying in the Sahara. It would all eventually be eaten up, of course, but nevertheless it did not sit well with the MdS philosophy of leaving the desert just as we found it.

Instead, on the edge of the bivouac, a number of white canvas latrines had been placed – three side-by-side for the men, and single toilets, aloof and alone, for the ladies. And since some ladies like peace and tranquillity as they go about their business – not least Kate – there was a 20-metre exclusion zone around these single toilets.

The toilets were basically a sort of open stool. You placed your brown plastic bag over the frame, and when finished, you tied off the bag and dumped it in a dustbin beside the toilet. You were supposed to pee beforehand.

It took some getting used to. Not as zen as *al fresco*, but not nearly as repellent as an open pit.

Carlo pulled back a couple of the rucksacks and crawled out of the tent. The wind was ferocious, and the side of the tent flapped like a loose sail. I got out of my sleeping bag and blocked up the side of the tent. It was turning into a full-on sandstorm. With a duststorm, it's just windy enough to blow the lightest dust off the surface of the desert. But when the wind reaches a critical velocity, the sand itself is lifted off the desert, literally sandblasting your face and throwing up a haze as thick as any London fog. I have known it so bad that you can barely see a yard ahead of you. When that happens, you have no option but to hold hands and hunker down.

I continued to read. My heroes in the Cruel Sea were taking a pasting – though the worst of it for the sailors was not from the Nazi U-boats, but from the weather and the sea itself.

Kate continued to read. She was reading *The English Patient* by Michael Ondaatje, and she would occasionally treat me to Ondaatje's epic descriptions of the wind and the desert. I liked the book, though I always thought it was a bit of a cheat. Ondaatje wrote it from his researches. He never actually went to the desert. In journalist jargon, we'd call it a 'cuts-job' - a story that's been written from newspaper cuttings.

The gold dust continued to hang in the air, neither moving up nor down, as if suspended, and the wind continued to roar with this constant low-level thunder. It felt as if, at any moment, the tent was about to take off. You can probably guess what happens when that happens – as indeed it did to a few tents that night. Do the Berbers and the race organisers come scurrying over to help sort things out? Oh, no. No, in time-honoured MdS fashion, you're expected to sort it out yourself, and if you are not capable of re-erecting your tent, then do please enjoy your night under the stars.

Kate broke off from her book. 'Carlo's been gone a while,' she said.

I put my book down. 'He has.'

'Do you think he's okay?'

'Imagine trying to organise a search party in this,' I said.

'How long's he been gone?'

I checked my cheap plastic digital watch. 'Maybe ten minutes.'

I was not at all enamoured at the thought of going out into this sand blizzard to search for my tentmate. It was possible, I supposed, that he might have wandered off in the wrong direction, but how far would he have to go before he realised he was heading into the wilderness? Once he made it back to the bivouac, he couldn't go wrong. All the tents had numbered tags on the outside.

I couldn't work out what was keeping him. If I'd been out in that sort of wind, I wouldn't have even bothered with the latrines.

Kate looked at her watch. Her white beanie was quite orange from the dust.

Eventually Carlo returned. But he didn't come into the tent. He just poked his head in.

'Got any wet wipes?' he said.

'How many do you want?' Kate said.

'A few,' he said. 'Could you throw me a bottle of water?'

'Why don't you come in?' said Kate.

'Not a good idea.' It was then that I noticed something glistening on his hat. 'I could do with a plastic bag. Any sort of bag.'

I poked around in my billycan and tossed him one of the brown latrine bags. 'What the hell's happened?' I asked.

'I'll tell you in a few minutes,' he laughed, already aware, perhaps, that he had a story for his grandchildren. 'You'll like it.'

He disappeared for five minutes, and then wormed his way back into the tent. He was only wearing his shorts and his head torch. From head to toe he was covered in sand and dust. Despite the wet wipes, he had a lingering smell.

Our books long forgotten, Kate and I watched as Carlo put on his North Face coat and then inched his way into his sleeping bag. There is a certain etiquette when somebody has a story to tell. The storyteller has the floor. And until they are ready to tell their tale, it does not do to badger them with questions.

At length, Carlo was snug in his sleeping bag. He stared up at the roof and let out this colossal sigh. 'Jay-sus!' he said.

'You finally copped off with the pretty girl from Mauritius?' I asked.

Carlo turned to us, his grimy face wreathed with this big smile – and it was quite impossible not to smile with him. 'It was a bit breezy,' he said. 'A little bit breezy, so it was. Maybe I should have had a piss beforehand, but I didn't. So there I am, and there's sand everywhere, blowing all over the place, and I'm quietly trying to do my thing but I'm also thinking the toilet is going to lift off the ground.'

'It was windy,' Kate said.

'One hell of a wind. Finally I'm done and I've just stood up. I'm just about to grab the bag and tie it up when the wind gets in under the flaps and the bag's blown off the toilet frame.'

I sucked my teeth. I could picture the scene. The sand, the wind, the extraordinary shadows cast by the head torch – and then this primed bag of excrement.

'The bloody bag is spiralling around the toilet like a punctured balloon and I'm trying to grab it, but I've still got my shorts round my ankles and the next thing the stuff is spraying all over the shop.'

Kate was weeping with laughter, the tears cutting through the dust on her cheeks.

'By the time I got a hand to it, the bag was empty and…'

'Its contents all over you,' I said.

'Yep,' he said happily. 'Covered in it. Hat, face, fleece, trousers – everything. I've left it all outside. Have a go cleaning it tomorrow.'

We went to sleep, though periodically throughout the night, there would be another detonation of laughter as one or other of us pictured Carlo in the toilet trying to chase down his flying shit bag. We laughed because we were reliving the moment; and because we already knew that we would remember these moments for the rest of our lives.

★

The toilet facilities on ultra races are always repellent. There's never enough of them, half of them are blocked, the toilet paper runs out and everyone always want to use them at exactly the same time, which is precisely 30 minutes before the start of the race. Sometimes the toilets are unisex, sometimes not – though everyone prefers single sex – and the smell is very roughly on a par with an open sewer; it is best to breathe through your mouth.

I, being cheeky, had got up early in the South Merstham school hall and had used the pristine disabled toilets. You do not see many disabled people on ultra races – in fact I have never seen a single disabled person – but, British sensitivities being what they are, the able-bodied are still loth to use a disabled toilet.

The breakfast on the Pilgrim was fine enough – porridge and cereal and bananas, as well as tea and instant coffee. You don't really care much about the taste; it's just about getting the fuel in for the day's run.

For some weeks, I assumed that this sort of reliable, undistinguished food was just the standard fare on an ultra race. Well it is – on a *British* ultra. But then you join the MdS and you suddenly appreciate how the French cater for these events. For the two days before the race, the MdS chefs were cooking for well over 1,400 people, and they did it with panache. Fried eggs, ham, cheese, fresh Moroccan flatbread, fresh butter, jam, decent coffee; the sort of food that you would be delighted to eat in a Montparnasse café.

The stark striplights in the South Merstham school revealed the full carnage of over 100 mucky runners overnighting in a dank sports hall. I was taking a cup of tea and a banana through to Kate. She was lolling on my Thermarest reading a book as she twisted a kiss curl of blonde hair around her finger. She was happy, oblivious to me, and for a while I just stood in the doorway and watched her. She was lying on her front, legs bent at the knees, her bare feet paddling in the air; I wish I'd taken a picture.

'Some tea,' I said, putting the cup beside her. 'And a banana.'

'Don't I get some tea?' Lawson asked, still curled in his sleeping bag.

'I got you some water and a couple of bananas. How about that?'

'Handsome!' he said, propping himself up on an elbow as he took the fruit. 'I'm liking it!'

'Sleep well?' I asked Kate.

'Very well.' She gave me a peachy cheerleader smile. 'And you?'

'Like a baby,' I said, which I suppose was very near the truth, in that I was woken up at least a dozen times by the snoring and cannon-like flatulence of my fellow Pilgrims. But no one ever admits weakness on an ultra. The very moment you admit that you're feeling a bit rough, your mental defences seem to collapse, and your feet and your legs are all suddenly screaming that, actually, they're not feeling too good at all. Just like with a hangover.

'I'm going to go for it today,' said Kate.

'About time too. What's the point of a thoroughbred like you hanging around with a donkey like me?'

'I'll wait for you at the end.' She peeled her banana and took a bite.

'You'll be waiting for hours,' I said. 'There are any number of people who'll give me a lift back to London.'

'No,' she said. 'I'll be there.'

'Cool.' I turned to Lawson. 'Fancy starting with me?'

'Love to!' he garbled, his mouth half-full.

Kate's phone went and she looked at it and watched it ring.

'Not even 7 o'clock and he's calling to wish you good morning,' I said. 'That guy is keen.'

'Let me answer it,' Lawson said. 'I'll tell him you're otherwise engaged.'

The phone's ring continued to drill through the hall. 'I'll take it,' she said. She left the room, furtively muttering into her phone.

'Boyfriend sounds a bit clingy,' said Lawson. 'He needs a quiet word from Uncle Lawson.'

'What would Uncle Lawson tell him?'

'Uncle Lawson would tell him to back off. Give her some space. She's great, isn't she? Not as great as Ginny, obviously, but then Ginny does happen to be perfect in every way. But Kate's nice – very chirpy—'

'At least when she's not being hounded by Edward.'

'Well, he's young, he's an idiot, what the hell does he know about how to please a woman?'

'What do I know?'

'You probably don't know very much either, but if you stick with your Uncle Lawson, then you might actually learn something.'

Running on snow, I can report, is nothing like running on sand. It's a little similar, I suppose, if you're running downhill and it's fresh, but on the second day of the Pilgrim, as we trudged in each other's footsteps, the snow had compacted into icy brown slush.

We'd started out wrapped in fleeces, hats and gloves, with spare clothes in our rucksacks. I had more clothing – by far – for the two-day Pilgrim than I had for an entire week in the desert. Spare socks, spare shorts, extra shirts and thick dry fleeces. At least with the Pilgrim, the conditions were going to stay roughly the same. It was going to be cold, and it was probably going to be wet. But with the MdS, you have to cater for the most extreme heat; and the most spiky rain; and the cold. At night, you can be wearing every item of clothing you possess and you'll still be left shivering in your sleeping bag.

Lawson and I had given Kate a hug before she had edged her way through to the front of start line. Martin was fiddling with his GPS; a lot of runners, especially the Army and Navy boys, like to distract themselves with endless kit checks. Carlo chomped on a Pepperami. It was so cold that there was only the briefest of pep talks: If we pulled up, we were to head for the nearest station.

We ran through the town, abandoning the iced pavements to weave through the dawdling cars. We had run this route just the previous afternoon, but it was unrecognisable, transformed into a white moonscape, the snow thick in the fields and bowing down the branches. There wasn't the same air of excitement as there had been on the first day. Instead it was like this long chore that had to be endured; let's get this damn thing over with.

'So what other mindless displacement activities have you got in mind after our run in the desert?' Lawson asked. We were jogging along a bridleway, following the footprints through an avenue of white trees.

'Mindless displacement activities?' I said. 'Perhaps not mindless. That would mean that I haven't thought about the complete ridiculousness of the displacement activity. And I have thought about it long and hard. What about pointless?'

'All right. What other *pointless* displacement activities have you got in mind?'

'That's better,' I said. 'Might try skating. My technique is lousy. There's a huge skating race in Holland – Elfstedentocht, 120 miles along the frozen canals. Anything at all except another ultra.'

'How not to face the issues in your life – by undertaking a series of ever more pointless challenges.' Lawson laughed as he skipped over a branch.

'Though sometimes these pointless activities can be the very solution to the problem. The answer comes at you side on, obliquely, from where you least expected it.'

And this is sometimes the case. It's like sleeping on a problem, letting your subconscious snip through the tangled threads so that, by morning time, there is the answer, burnished and clear.

This is why I like long runs. And it's why – in part – I fell in love with the desert. It clarifies. Where all has been milky and opaque, the desert shines a bright light on those dark seamy corners of your life that have been left unwatched and untended.

CHAPTER 6

In the desert, a particular Frenchman had been irritating me for some days. He was tall and burly, and he was a liability. He had long walking poles which flailed about him as he went up and down the hills. He did not care very much who he poked along the way.

At the start of the long day, we had been going up a hill, or *jebel*. It was the biggest hill of the race with a 17 per cent incline. Some parts were so steep you had to use your hands, stones clattering all around you. I wondered how the camels, Charles and Camilla, would ever get up the *jebel*. Perhaps they went around the side.

Some smiley faces had been painted onto the rock in bright orange paint, as if to cheer us up. They amused me, though I know they irked some of the runners, who thought the faces were making light of our pain and our misfortune.

We were going up very slowly, in fits and starts, expanding and constricting, just as a worm moves on the grass. We would wait for ten or twenty seconds, catch our breath and then move on up again. A South African yelled out, mock serious, 'Come on, pick up at the back there!' Some of us laughed. We were all in this hot hell together.

The rubber tips of my walking poles had worn right through and the titanium tips tapped on the rock. That also irked some of the runners. When you're tired and you have blisters, even the tiniest things can irritate after a while – a runner's rasping breath; the voice of a chattering Yorkshire woman; a jaw moving up and down, up and down, as chewing gum is chewed for hours on end.

I had marked the Frenchman's card a couple of days earlier. He'd run past me as I was tentatively edging down a rocky hill, his poles held wide out to the side. I'd nearly tripped, skipping and jinking to keep my balance. After that, I'd given him a wide berth.

On *Jebel Otfal*, I had listened to the Frenchman muttering and cursing to himself, as he heedlessly dislodged stones onto the people beneath him. When he stopped to catch his breath, I quickly went past him.

I do not like stopping on hills. Some people like to stop and gloat at the long line of runners in the distance who have all this yet to come. But I like to get into a rhythm, poles clattering, one-two, one-two, with my head down as I focus on the moment; I don't like to look up very often, as it is easy to get dispirited when you see all that is ahead of you.

Finally, at the top of the hill, there lay the biggest sand dune I had ever seen. It stretched almost to the bottom of the hill. It was so steep at the top that they'd set ropes into the rock. I watched the runners as they tackled the sand. Some took it slow, methodically placing one foot after the next, and some would schuss the hill like a downhill skier, racing down in great bounding leaps.

I posed for a couple of pictures. Those sort of pictures turn out okay, but they're never keepers. The best pictures are the action shots or the moments of quiet contemplation; the times when you're not even aware of the camera lens.

I caught sight of Del at the top of the hill, mugging for the cameras. He was shouting, his face just two feet from the lens. 'Call that a hill, Patrick Bauer?' he screamed. He put his fingers up to the lens, just an inch apart, to show how small he thought the *jebel* was. 'That wasn't a hill, that was a molehill. Make it harder next time, Patrick! Make it harder!' He lunged at the lens like a wild dog, his open mouth wide about the lens.

I sipped my water, took my salt pills and my sports bean. I was about to tackle the dune. It looked excitingly dangerous.

The sound of a helicopter came suddenly from behind us. I stopped to watch. If there is any sort of drama, I will always stop and see what happens.

The helicopter isn't going over the hill. It's landing right by us, right at the top. After the still silence of the desert, the noise is enormous. I guess that one of the runners has hurt themselves, tripped on a rock, maybe, on the climb up.

A Commissaire gets out of the helicopter and makes his way to a runner sitting on a rock nearby. I recognise the Frenchman with the long walking poles. He gets up and walks over to the helicopter. He's not limping, he looks fine. There's a brief discussion. The Commissaire gives a shrug, one of those wonderful Gallic shrugs that carries such a wealth of different meanings, and then the sour Frenchman climbs on board the helicopter.

We watch as he is whisked out of the race.

'What the hell was that all about?' I asked a cluster of runners.

'He had had enough,' replied Oskar, a German. 'He did not want to go down.'

'Feeble,' I said. 'The dune's going to be the best bit.'

'We still have another 70 kilometres today. He thought he was never going to finish. So why go any further?'

The Frenchman had made the fatal error of looking too far ahead. The enormity of the task had overwhelmed him. Not that you can't look ahead – you need to be mentally psyched for the next day's terrors. But you must not dwell on them, otherwise you start to add flesh to the monster. It will develop claws and glinting teeth, and before you know it, you are imagining all kinds of terrible wounds that it will inflict.

Yes, the Frenchman let the bogeyman get to him: the whole thing was simply impossible, so what was the point in taking another step?

He had forgotten to take the next step.

But if the Frenchman had wanted to listen, I would have told him what to do. I would have told him how to get down the hill – and how to finish the rest of the race.

What he needed was food. Everything in the desert seems better and rosier and just more doable if you've had something to eat, especially if it's hot. The lukewarm powder-mixes are okay for recharging the batteries, but it's a hot meal that's going to bolster your mental armour.

So: if it had been Kate, this is what I would have done. We would have taken a stroll around the top of the *jebel* and I would have found a comfortable spot for us in the lee of a rock. My sleeping bag would provide us with a pillow to sit on, and within two minutes I'd have lit some hexamine tablets and half a litre of water would be coming to the boil. And I would talk. I would talk and talk without stopping, about anything except the desert and the race; I would do everything in my power to distract the woman from the sheer hopelessness of her position.

And the water would come to boil and I would stir in one of my dehydrated favourites, chilli con carne, and to show Kate that she was special, I'd pep it up with Tabasco sauce. Maybe a lot of Tabasco sauce.

I'd stir up the chilli and, while still merrily chatting away, would hand over the billycan and would watch in delight as the Tabasco blew the roof of her mouth off, eyes watering like a baby's. *That* is how to take a runner's mind off the desert.

And after that, well, it would all be perfectly simple. We would go down the hill, one step at a time, never once getting too far ahead of ourselves. We would go to the checkpoint and we would keep shuffling on. And above all, we would not allow our imaginations to dwell on the horrors that lay ahead of us.

Yes – that is how to nursemaid a friend through the Marathon des Sables. You feed them up. You don't stop talking. And you don't allow them one single second to dwell on the misery of their blisters and their bandaged feet.

But as it was... well, as it was, the Frenchman had no nursemaid and he was out of the race. And since I did not like the man, I was pleased to see him go. There are runners you like and runners you don't out here – and those who we do not like, well, it would be mealy-mouthed to pretend that we're not thrilled to see the back of them. Another one bites the dust.

As for me on that *jebel*, on that monster dune – I went at it like a tiger, and it was far and away my most exhilarating minute of the entire race. You go through a lot of emotions trudging the Marathon des Sables, but this was my first moment of genuine physical enjoyment. When I reached the end of the rope, I launched myself into the abyss, poles high in one hand, jumping and sliding, dodging the rocks that lay in the sand, and skirting the slowcoaches who dickered in the middle. I let out these demented shrieks of utter ecstasy, though I was also aware of the sheer recklessness of what I was doing, and that only the slightest slip would send me tumbling a long, long way. And even as I was slip-sliding through this deep, floury sand, I wondered if there would be a camera to catch me cartwheeling 300 metres down this sandy Black Run.

At the bottom, the adrenalin was scorching. To think: the Frenchman had jacked it all in just before the very best bit.

*

Going down Box Hill, on the Pilgrim, was treacherous in a different way. The steps were high and slick with ice, and there was no hand rail. I took them very gingerly.

I was wondering how the front runners had tackled the hill, and in the same moment I saw a large splash of blood in the snow, deep crimson against the stark white. It dripped on for a few more yards.

And we trudged on, for ever looking at our watches as we tried to estimate what sort of time we might cross the finish line. It's not a good mind-set. The pleasure, the only pleasure on an ultra, is the moment, the here and the now; as soon as you start thinking about finish lines, it's a short switch to, 'Only another three hours and this bloody thing will be over.'

It was late afternoon, very grey overhead, when we tramped into the final field. We picked up the pace. That's what the finish line does for you: it gives just enough of an energy boost to cross the line at a smart clip. Though this is misleading in the desert, where you can very often see the finish line from four, five miles out, see the white city of the Commissaires' tents and the huge white inflatables, like two blimps on end. In the desert you don't get your hopes up, can't ever get your hopes up – all you know for certain is that it's still a long way off.

At first I couldn't see anyone at all on the finish line, as if the organisers had just packed up and gone home. But then we saw a hunched man with a clipboard and standing next to him was Kate. She started hallooing us in from 200 yards out, calling out and clapping, and even the clipboard man managed a cheer. Though it may have been small, it was heartfelt. Kate hugged me and kissed me, one of those clumsy ones where you slightly mistime it, each going for the wrong cheek and somehow end up practically kissing each other on the lips. We laughed awkwardly, and then Kate chivvied us into the tents for tea and cake.

'Kim, I'd like you to meet Edward,' said Kate.

Trying to mask my astonishment, I shook hands with the boyfriend. 'Edward – how nice to finally meet you,' I said. 'I've heard so much about you.'

His grip was a little too tight, a knuckle-crusher. He was quite handsome in a preppy way, with floppy blonde hair, chiseled cheek bones and a prominent chin with a perfect dimple in the middle. He wore jeans and a blue v-neck and the sort of immaculate black overcoat that made you just yearn to spatter it with a snowball.

'Hi Kim,' he said, giving me the once over from the top of my wet beanie to the tips of my muddy shoes. 'You're older than I thought you'd be.'

'I just look old,' I said. 'All this running has done wonders for my wrinkles. I'm actually the same age as you.'

I looked over at Lawson. He was inhaling chocolate brownies by the cake table, and was starting on his third. It's normal to get swept up in this special kind of famishment after a long run, when you will devour anything that comes to hand, whether pizza or cake or your children's left-over fish fingers; it's all wolfed down so fast that it barely touches the sides.

'You a bit of a runner, then, Edward?' I asked. 'What's your sport?'

'Gyms are my thing,' he said. 'I try and pop in most mornings. Got to look my best for my girl.'

He gave Kate a squeeze round her waist. She faked me a smile, and it all struck me as rather awkward, as if they were playing at being boyfriend and girlfriend. There was none of that unquantifiable, undefinable essence that we call Chemistry.

'Yeah, gyms are good fun,' I lied. Gyms are my personal hell on earth. Since I'd started training for the MdS, I'd joined a gym and two or three times a week would pop in during my lunch hour. But it was only ever a means to an end, which was to try and slightly improve my core strength before the race. But grunting away in the gym over bits of ironmongery? Now *that* is a displacement activity that's both mindless and pointless.

'How did you get on?' I asked Kate. 'You look like you've been back at least a couple of hours.' She had been. She'd not only changed, but she'd showered too, and with time enough for her hair to dry. She was an ultra-running pinup.

'I did okay,' she said.

'None of this false modesty, Kate – what was your time?'

'Around six hours.'

'Six hours! Fantastic!' I was pleased for her. 'You must have been one of the first through the gate!'

'Second lady in,' Edward said. 'If you hadn't dawdled yesterday, you'd have been in the overall medals.'

'That was me, I'm afraid,' I said. 'Despite my urgings, Kate took pity on the geriatric contingent. How was your dinner last night, Edward?'

'It went okay.' Edward primped his hair, sweeping it back off his forehead. 'I'd have liked my Kate to have been there.'

Kate was a changed woman now that she was with her boyfriend. She looked rather uncertain, with this strained smile on her face; I had the sense of a spaniel that does not know whether it is going to be stroked or kicked.

'And you're enjoying Westminster?' I asked.

'It's where all the action is.'

'Certainly is,' I said, lying again to be polite. Westminster is a goldfish bowl, dull as can be.

Lawson came over with a cup of tea in one hand and another piece of cake in the other. His shoelaces were undone and he looked a total ragamuffin.

'Had any of the cake yet?' he asked, still happily chomping away.

'Edward, this is Lawson,' said Kate.

With both hands full, Lawson nodded to Edward. 'All right?'

'Hi.' A tight smile.

Lawson shifted his feet. I don't quite know how it happened, but he must have stood on a shoelace. He stumbled and the cake and cup went flying, upending all over Edward's black coat. He swore and started to pat pathetically at his coat while Lawson squawked the most abject apologies.

I moved over to the cake table to give Edward and Lawson some room. Kate came over too. I guess there's only so much you can do when your partner has suffered some slight mishap.

'I want to do this fundraiser,' she said.

'You want to have that charity film night?' I said. 'Sure. What's the movie going to be?'

'Something appropriate for the desert. *The Mummy*?'

'*Ice Cold in Alex*?'

'Never heard of it. *Sahara*?'

'Never heard of that either. *Lawrence of Arabia*?'

'Bit long,' she said. 'And it's the only film that doesn't have a single line from a woman.'

'*Flight of the Phoenix*?'

'No – not heard of it.'

'This is not easy.'

'Is *Casablanca* any good?' she asked.

'Of all the gin joints in all the towns...' I gave her a moody Bogart stare and scratched at my chin. 'I've never seen the thing from start to finish. I don't think anybody's ever seen the whole thing – leastways not on a big screen. But I do know that it's short and it's packed with great lines, so... *Casablanca* would be ideal.'

'Done,' she said. We shook on it.

'How's the coat?' I said.

She helped herself to a flapjack. She said nothing.

'Not sure Edward's got quite the robust nature required for the MdS,' I said.

She smiled at me, rather disarmingly. 'He has other qualities,' she said, and then she winked.

I looked over at Edward, who was now mopping at the hem of his coat with a white handkerchief. I couldn't believe Kate had ended up with this prinking poodle-faker. Well, actually… I *could* believe it, because the only thing I do know is that there is no accounting whatsoever for sexual chemistry.

CHAPTER 7

Elise never really understood the point of the running the Marathon des Sables. Not many people do.

No, the 150 miles and the heat and the general discomfort means that the race tends to be labeled with that catch-all phrase, 'Mid-life crisis,' dumped in with that long list of unsavoury things guys are allegedly prone to do when they hit 40: have an affair, buy a (red) sports car, take up motorbiking, basically do anything at all that's even remotely different from the daily drudgery.

For months and months I had heard my little MdS jaunt dismissed with the ol' 'Kim's having a mid-life crisis – and it's a big one.' Of course I would laugh it off. Entering the Marathon of the Sands leaves plenty enough doubts in your own mind without having to listen to the derision of your family and colleagues.

But I don't like the term 'mid-life crisis' – and nor does anyone who signs up for the MdS. It smacks of a certain sad desperation, of middle-aged men dressing like teenagers, of pathetically clinging to what remains of your youth.

The MdS *does* hold a certain fascination for men, particularly British men, over 40. When you're in your 20s, there is this infinity of time that stretches before you: you can still go where you want, do whatever you want, love whom you please.

But at 40, or earlier if you're lucky, there comes this dawning that there isn't much time left at all – indeed, it's a'flying. And if you don't do these things that you once dreamed, that you once set your heart on, then... well, in 30 years' time, you'll be just another guy sitting in front of the television mumbling that they 'coulda been a contender,' dreaming of what might have been.

There is, of course, one bonus that comes with reaching 40: You go for it. You grab every little sweetmeat that comes your way, and be damned to the consequences.

Whereupon...

The pain in my thigh was simply astonishing. It was like a red-hot brand was being pressed against my leg. And I held it, feeling the pain start to pulse, as I drew myself forward.

I was on the roller, squeezing the lactic acid and the knots out of my screaming leg muscles. As a rule of thumb, the more painful it is, the better it is for you.

Every day for the past four months, I'd spent ten minutes torturing myself on the roller. The roller is like a large rubber rolling pin, about four-feet long and eight inches in diameter. You lie on top, rolling backwards and forwards, as your full bodyweight bears down on your legs. Muscles are kneaded and stretched. It's a cheap sports massage.

I was lying on my side, rollering the long IT bands in my thigh, while Dolly sat on my hip, humming. At least she was enjoying herself.

'I'm loving it,' I said through gritted teeth.

'Do you really love it?' Dolly said. 'Why are you breathing like that?'

''Course I'm loving it!' I said. I looked over my shoulder. Dolly was walking a small plastic doll up my leg. 'One of the high points of my day, doing this with you.'

'So why is your hand so tight?'

'I just like clenching my fingers. It's good for them.'

I liked stretching with my daughters. It's tactile and it's different and it's a good time for easy chat.

'Daddy, are you going to die in this race?'

So much for an easy chat. The conversation had shifted onto a subject that I had been dwelling on for some time. Though up until now, I had not been aware that my daughters had even given it a moment's thought.

'I hope not,' I said. 'I'd be very annoyed if I did.'

'But you might die.' She looked at me with a small serious face.

'Well, I might die. But I certainly don't intend to die. Where would that leave you?'

'Has anyone ever died in this race?'

'Yes.'

'How many people?'

'Two men, as far as I know. And...' I did some brief calculations in my head. 'I guess around 20,000 people have done the race. So it's odds of 10,000: 1. Not too bad.' I grabbed her, held her upside down and swung her up over my shoulder. She squirmed and laughed and in seconds my death was forgotten and we had moved on.

'What's *Casablanca* about? Will I like it?'

'You might like it,' I said. I put her down onto the ground and sat on the floor, leaning forward to touch my toes. I am not as supple as I used to be. 'It's about a guy, Rick, and a woman, Ilsa. These two, they really, really love each other.'

'And it all ends happily ever after?'

'No – no, it doesn't. She's married to Victor Laszlo. But she thinks that Laszlo is dead and she falls in love with Rick. Then she suddenly learns that Laszlo is so *not* dead – and Rick gets dumped. Ilsa is the love of his life, and he has to let her go.'

'That's sad.'

'Yep – it's happily never after.'

'It's not like the stories you read to me.'

'No, those are fairy stories. This is more like real life. You can be deliriously in love. But that doesn't mean you end up together.'

'Why not?'

Dolly got off me and I creaked to my feet. Even my spine was starting to seize up. 'Don't know. But most love affairs end badly.'

'But that's not you and Mummy?'

''Course it's not me and Mummy,' I laughed, lightly skimming over some marital blips that we had had along the way. 'We're still head over heels. What are you wearing tonight?'

'My blue dress.'

'The perfect outfit for a waitress.'

Elise came into the bedroom, languid and sleek as a cat. She'd been to the hairdressers that afternoon and was wearing a little black dress and a black silk tuxedo jacket. Her makeup was immaculate. After all these years together, I still find her very beautiful. I fancy her; I fancy her rotten. I'd like to have sex with her before we go to the cinema, quick and urgent and so very life-enhancing for the fact that, out of the humdrum, we have snatched, seized, these golden moments of ecstasy.

Elise appraised me in my boxers and T-shirt, eyes taking in my gnarled toes, my sinewy legs, my slouched posture.

'Most love affairs end badly?'

'You overheard us?' I said, giving her a hug. 'Sad, but true.'

'Mummy,' said Dolly. 'How can you be in love – and not be together?'

Very graciously, considering all that had gone between us, Elise laughed. 'And what does Daddy say?'

'Daddy says it happens all the time.'

'Did he now?' she said, and what a wealth of meaning there was in those three words. 'Off you go.'

Dolly left the room, and there we are, finally alone in the bedroom, and I look at her, and I know that she knows just exactly what is going through my mind.

And then – or at least in my most vivid imaginings...

I clasp Elise around the waist. She pauses, looks at me in mock surprise, and then drapes herself around me, one leg curling between my knees.

'I like the new you,' she says.

'You, however, always look fantastic,' I say and I give her a long, moist kiss and the lipstick smudges on her lips, and the sight of her lipstick combined with her dress and tuxedo makes her look quite astonishingly wanton. This erotic thrill fizzes up my spine. My hands roam down her back. I inhale a breath of her perfume. She glances at me, glances at the door, and then with a languid hand, slips the bolt shut.

'Do we really have time?' she asks, and I lean into her, pressing her hard against the wall.

'I don't think we do,' I say, stroking the tops of her silk stockings. I love the texture of a woman's skin; I love the texture of Elise's skin. She is wearing black stilettos with towering high heels and she looks strong, powerful. There is something fantastically sexy about seeing your partner dressed to the nines – and then, with just one single kiss, watching them transform into a lover, hungry and reckless. Elise has one arm about my neck. Very deftly, very quickly, she pulls off her knickers. I have a glimpse of red silk as the knickers are tossed to the floor.

'I've often wondered, if, now that we're married, we could ever make love in two minutes flat.' She smiles as she pecks me on the lips.

'I'd been wondering that too,' I say. My voice is hoarse with desire.

'I know you have,' she says. 'But I don't think it would be possible.' Though she speaks in a very calm, matter-of-fact voice, the effect is spoiled rather by the little gasp that she breathes right into my ear.

'And having to do all your makeup again?' I say – and Elise is now matching me, word for word, kiss for kiss, action to reaction.

'I don't know why,' I continue. 'Having sex with you makes me feel rather chatty.' She grins. It is one of the great delights of my life to see Elise laughing as we make love.

'You are a chatty lover,' she says. 'In fact there are very few ways of shutting you up.'

'Like what?' I say.

'This,' she replies, and kisses me, soundly, roundly, lips smacking against mine, and her lipstick is now smeared all about her mouth and her chin. Very sexy. Much sexier than when her lipstick is limited only to her lips. And so very different from the well-ordered, well-groomed PR woman that I am normally married to.

'We should do this more often,' I say, and Elise mewls in my ear: 'Do you ever shut—'

Her voice trails off as the very breath catches in her throat, and for five, ten seconds we are locked tight like statues of shivering stone; she has melted, liquid, beside me.

And in reality…

Dolly leaves the room, and there we are, finally alone in the bedroom, and I look at her, and I know that she knows just exactly what is going through my mind. I stretch my hand out, stroke her hips and she moves away, ignoring my hand completely as she looks at her watch.

'Taxi's here in 20 minutes,' she says. 'Have you even shaved yet?' She leaves the room and I can only follow her with my eyes.

★

No need for fantasies when you're on the MdS. Your libido falls through the floor out in the Sahara, a combination of the heat and the exercise and the lousy food. You can go for hours at a time, days at a time, without once thinking about sex.

Del, of course, was different.

From the first, he was very keen to show that he was on the top of the heap. He did this in typical Neanderthal fashion.

The day after we'd flown to Ouarzazate, we were shipped out to the desert. Five white coaches, with a full military escort of trucks and Jeeps and God knows how many soldiers. We gazed out at mile after mile of rock and sparse scrub, all the while wondering what it would be like to run through it. Outside the city, by the road, were littered tens of thousands of plastic bags. I had not seen a desert for a long time. You forget its vastness.

We drove past scree mountains and long-dead volcanoes, where the layers of lava were quite distinct, as if sliced with a knife. And brown – every variation of brown, from tan and ochre to coffee and the richest auburn. As we drove, the houses became more primitive, built from dried mud instead of brick. And oases, little verdant hubs of the most brilliant green, with palm trees, prickly pear and marshy rushes.

We weren't hungry, since we'd only just eaten a gargantuan breakfast at the Berbère Palace, but with nothing better to do, we ate our packed lunches. As ever, the food was delicious – peanuts, crisps, dried apricot, a tin of tuna and tomato, mini salamis no bigger than your pinkie, crisps and fresh bread, yoghurt and an orange and a chocolate crêpe. Kate chewed slowly on a salami as she gazed at the desert, alone with her dreams. She had not spoken for some time.

Del was a few seats ahead of us, raucous, like the class clown. I did not know him well then, but from the little I had seen of him, I did not like him.

We stopped for the pee break known as The Hundred Man Piss.

The five buses pulled over by the side of the road, and 250 Brits all trooped out to relieve themselves. The men were on one side, and Kate went to join the women on the other.

All of us faced the horizon, scores of men in little lines gazing out at the desert.

Del was one of the last off the coach. I noticed him stride past all the lines of peeing men. He walked right to the front, turned to face us and, happy now that he had our attention, unzipped and started to pee.

'Look at FIGJAM,' said Lawson, using the nickname that Del had acquired the previous night. It comes from Australia: Fuck I'm Good, Just Ask Me.

'He's pissing all over us,' I said. 'Though he's quite well hung.'

'It looks like a piece of Italian salami.'

'A slightly chewed piece of Italian salami.'

I'd seen this sort of behaviour before on safari – lions, wildebeest, big, hefty hippos. But I had never seen it before from a guy. Perhaps I had not been around enough locker rooms.

I wish we'd jeered and started laughing, done anything at all to mock the willy-wagger. But we did not.

★

It was Del, naturally, who – at least so he claimed – had had sex on the MdS. Though it did directly lead to one of the most unforgettable experiences of my life, so for that I am grateful.

It was Easter Saturday, the day before the race. The first bivouac was in Ammouguer, flat, dusty desert, thorny scrub, and surrounded on all sides by hills and mountains. The sheer scale of it all always takes you flat aback; you have no idea of the distances, but they always seem immense. The heat also takes some getting used to.

It saps your energy, so that all you feel like doing is flopping onto your Thermarest and having a sleep. The thought of actually running in this heat, for hours on end, seems just fanciful.

We'd spent the morning in this endless round of queues and form-filling and health checks and kit checks. Though we already had doctors' certificates and electrocardiographs for our hearts, the on-site doctors still liked to check that we were in good order. One poor Mexican discovered he had a heart problem and was turned back before he even made it to the start line.

Then, after all the queuing, and after we'd been given our race numbers and flare and salt tablets and the Tag Heuer Asbo tag that strapped to your ankle, there wasn't much to do except sit around in the tents. Children from the local village would wander over to look at these strange beings who had flown thousands of miles to run through this wasteland.

Martin, already dressed in his race gear, was lecturing us on some of the mishaps that might befall us.

'You've got to knock your shoes out in the morning,' he said. 'Scorpions love to bed down in them.'

'Do you reckon these venom pumps actually work?' I asked. There were various bits of compulsory kit that we had to take with us, including a syringe-like thing that you placed onto a bite or sting, and – at least according to the theory – sucked the venom out.

'They're no bloody good at all,' Carlo said. He had his feet up on his rucksack and was eating an orange as you would an apple, peel and all. It was bizarre, yet oddly fascinating. 'By the time you've started sucking, the venom will be all through your body. To do any good, you'd have to chop your leg off.'

'So what's the point of carrying the venom pump?' Kate asked. She was wearing her red shorts, her white race shirt and her Oakley sunglasses, a picture of tranquillity as she leaned against her rucksack and gazed out to the endless desert; it was in those moments that you had a chance, a small chance, of truly being able to see the world in a grain of sand.

'Insurance,' said Carlo, taking another bite of the orange, oblivious to the juice dripping down his chin and onto his shirt. 'We're never going to use any of the kit they make us carry. But it keeps the insurers happy.'

'Got any other top tips, Martin?' I asked.

'If you're going to squat by a rock, then give it a kick first,' he said. 'Just to check there are no nasties underneath it.'

'Imagine getting stung on the bum,' Carlo said as he spat out a pip. 'That'd be annoying.'

'Sandflies are also bad,' Martin said. 'No bigger than a grain of sand, and they stay very low to the ground. They can give you some really nasty diseases.'

Kurtz, the ex-para, cocked a leg and farted. He never spoke much; in fact he probably farted more than he talked. It was a useful piece of punctuation, and could be used either as a full stop, an explosive exclamation mark or sometimes even an interrogatory.

'Avoid swimming in the *wadis*,' Martin said. 'The water can carry anything from bilharzia to leeches.'

'I'd like a paddle after a day in the desert,' I said.

'Risky.'

We lapsed into silence. The medics who run the MdS almost have too much knowledge. They know of every disease and every ailment, and throughout the race they seem to be forever terrified of being laid low by some exotic illness. They do not stop to smell the flowers along the way for fear of being stung by a rogue insect; they do not touch the Berber children's hands for fear of picking up a bug; and never in their wildest dreams would they take off their shoes and their socks and lie back in the dunes as they bathe their feet in the fine, hot sand of the desert.

I looked at Simon, smooth Simon the accountant, who was over in the corner doing one of his Sudoku problems. He was in his 50s, a sleek grey wolf who was running the MdS for the second time, desperate for a top-100 finish. The madness of the MdS takes on many forms: Many runners set themselves these entirely random goals, like finishing in the top quarter, or the top half, or beating a certain person. Then there are a few, like me, who would be quite content just to finish the damn thing.

'It's like the set from *Star Wars*,' Carlo said, still gazing at the desert.

'That's because it *is* the set from *Star Wars*,' Lawson said.

'What do you mean?'

'They filmed it just near here – in Tunisia.'

'Did they now?' Carlo said. 'Well fancy that.'

I remembered a school poster of the two *Star Wars* robots, C-3PO and R2-D2, roasting in the desert. Now it was me out roasting in the Sahara.

Kate took off her sunglasses. She squinted out into the glare of the sun. 'Is that Del?'

'Where?'

'Over there.' She pointed. About 200 yards away, distant yet also very prominent, a couple were stripping off. I recognised Del's blue singlet. I did not recognise the woman. She had dark cornrowed hair.

Del helped her out of her clothes and, naked, they stood in front of each other. Del poured bottled water over the woman.

'They certainly want to be seen,' Carlo said.

'Don't they just,' Lawson said.

The woman poured water over Del. He flicked it over her. They kissed and when they had finished, they walked off into the desert before disappearing from view behind a little hillock.

'I do hope Del's remembered to put on the factor 50,' Carlo said.

'It'd be such a shame if his privates got frazzled to a crisp.'

'Couldn't happen to a nicer chap,' Lawson said, and with nothing more to see, we turned to our books and our kit checks and our desert meditation. Mobile phones are banned on the bivouac, so there is no chance to call home or to check emails. A full ten days without hearing a single bleep or ring of a mobile phone is fantastically liberating. When I rule the world, mobile phones will be banned for at least one day a week.

After about 15 minutes, Del and the woman emerged from behind the hillock. They had another wash, dressed and walked back to the bivouac. The woman was kissed and sent on her way.

'When he comes back,' I said, 'nobody mentions the shower or the woman.'

'Choice,' Carlo said.

A minute later, Del swaggered into the tent. He was grinning and he looked round the tent, trying to make eye contact.

'All right mate?' Carlo said.

'Never better.' Del stretched up and held onto one of the tent poles. He was right in the middle of the tent. 'That was fun.'

Kate polished her sunglasses. I filed my toenails. Martin was immersed in his MdS roadbook. Nobody said a word.

'Just had a shower,' said Del. 'Very sexy.'

Carlo was watching the throbbing pulse in his ankle. 'Will you look at that?' he said. 'Seventy beats a minute.'

I leaned over to him. 'Can I have one of your oranges?'

'Sure.' He dived into his bag and tossed me one.

'Thanks. I won't be eating the peel. Do you want it?'

'I'm good.'

Del was stretching on his toes, still desperate to tell his tale. Kate blew onto her sunglasses and continued to polish. I peeled the orange and took a bite.

'There's nothing like desert oats,' Del said.

I wanted to let Del continue floundering on by himself, but Martin had to go and ruin it all.

'What are desert oats?' Martin asked.

'Getting your oats. In the desert.'

There was a leaden pause. We digested Del's clunker.

'Sounds a bit messy,' Lawson said.

'Can you imagine the sand?' Carlo said.

'Painful.'

'Not very romantic.'

'Not very sexy either,' I said. 'I guess some guys might consider it quite classy.'

'Can you imagine the chafing?' Lawson said.

'Bet Doc Trotters don't see those sort of injuries very often.'

Kate maintained a fastidious silence. She gave her shades one last polish and put them on.

Del pulled on the tent pole, stretching up. I don't know what response he'd expected, but he hadn't expected that. 'You guys think you're funny,' he said, before ambling off in his Speedos and singlet and his little MdS slippers.

Lawson and Carlo high-fived, and though Kate said nothing I could see her smirking.

'The shower looked good though,' Carlo said. 'Fancy giving it a go, Kate?'

'No,' she laughed. 'I'm not an exhibitionist.'

'Are you chicken?'

'No – I just don't want to have a shower with you.'

She looked to the left. She looked to the right. And at length her eyes slid sideways and she looked at me.

CHAPTER 8

I try to be generous. When people ask me for something, whether it's money or possessions, or even that much more valuable commodity, time, I try and give it to them.

But there comes a time when, eventually, you start to think, 'Oh for God's sake!' It's called charity fatigue, and if you work in a large office, sooner or later you will succumb to it. Colleagues asking you to sponsor them for their first marathon? That's fine. I don't have any problem with that. Colleagues asking you to sponsor them for a half-marathon or a 10K or even a 5K. I will happily reach for my cheque book and wish them *bon voyage*. Colleagues wanting to spend the entire day working with their head in a bucket of baked beans? Well, it's not exactly my thing, but I will duly hand the money over.

I get more huffy, however, when I realise I'm actually helping to fund their trip up Kilimanjaro or the Great Wall of China. Call me heartless, but the only things that stir me are the events and the causes that I could not do myself: the epic runs and the monster swims – in essence, the sort of events that are so grueling, they leave its participants absolutely shattered and weeping with relief and ecstasy when they've finished. I suppose the Marathon des Sables might qualify.

So when it came to sponsorship for the MdS, Kate and I were laying on a film night for our friends. And even though I was taking part in this scorcher in the Sahara that just might end up finishing me off, I was still loath to tap up my colleagues and my friends. It makes me feel squeamish. My psychotherapist would doubtless say that, through low self-esteem, I had issues over accepting gifts from others. Whatever.

We had booked the Ciné Lumière in South Kensington, and for £20 a ticket, colleagues and friends could come drink our wine and see our film, *Casablanca*.

I was nervous. I always am before a speech. I had written it out in full, honed my gags, practically memorized the thing. But I was still edgy at the thought of standing in front of 240-odd people.

Kate was also nervous. Her hands were shaking as she poured out the wine and she was constantly fidgeting. She was wearing a blue dress, shortish, lovely.

'You're going to be fantastic!' I said. I was on my third glass of red wine and drinking fast. I need alcohol to perform in public. Not sloshed, but tiddly.

The boyfriend, Edward, was twitching. He'd come straight from Westminster, still in his grey pinstripe. We were standing in the foyer, just the three of us. From behind the padded door we could hear a hum of expectant chatter.

'Darling.' Edward plucked at Kate's elbow. 'You don't have to do this.'

'Don't touch me like that,' she said, shrugging him off. 'You're like a vicar.'

Edward swept back his hair. He rolled his eyes at me in exasperation. I smiled, but I was actually thinking about his tan. It's difficult for a guy to spend time in a tanning salon without seeming faintly ridiculous. Women can do it, just as they can apply makeup and hair spray and all the other artifices that make them look so beautiful; a man cannot. *This* man cannot.

'We could leave it to Kim?' he suggested.

'I'm doing it – and I'm doing it because I've never done it before.'

'Good.' Edward fluttered and twitched. I know that he meant well but he was only feeding her anxiety.

I couldn't restrain myself any longer. 'It's a doddle, Kate. Listen to me – do you know what you want to say?'

'Yes,' she said, and then she spoke again, much stronger. 'Yes.'

'You've got a joke to warm them up?'

'Yes.'

'A quip for the end?' I looked at her, waiting for the nod. 'And you've got some heartwarming stuff in the middle and the whole thing is not going to take more than two minutes?'

She nodded again, squared her shoulders.

'Want a drink? Triple vodka here if you want it.'

'No. I want to feel the fear.'

'Okay.' I decided to try an old Samurai trick that speakers sometimes use to prepare themselves for the bear pit. A lot of speakers don't bother to warm up. They just mooch onto the podium, and suddenly they've got to go from 0 to 60 in five seconds flat. But if you know anything about public speaking, you know to do what the Samurai do: shout out loud; wet the lobes of your ears; and snap a pencil in half. It energises the senses.

I took an ice cube and dabbed it on Kate's ears.

'Now punch my hand,' I said.

I held up my hand. I was dressed in true *Casablanca* style in a white tuxedo and black bowtie – a little showy, perhaps, but I've never had a problem making a fool of myself.

Kate nodded and shook her head a little, like a dog as it gets up. She set her feet, boxer-style. I gave her the nod and she jabbed at my hand.

'Is that it?' I said.

Edward was writhing next to us. 'Do we have to do this?'

I didn't bother to look at him. 'And again – harder.'

Kate set herself again, took a deep breath, and gave my hand a good thump. I could see the power pumping into her.

'Both hands now. Give me a one-two. Tell me what you're thinking.'

She was getting into it, as all good speakers eventually do. She danced a little shimmy, and then jabbed, one-two. 'Bastard!'

'I'm not hearing you.'

'Bastard!'

I could see the nerves and the frustration oozing out of her pores. There was even a glaze of sweat on her cheek. 'Harder.' Bam-bam. Bam-bam. A skip to the right. As she danced, I moved my hands with her.

'You liking it?'

'No – I'm loving it.'

'I can't hear you.'

Bam-bam; bam-bam-bam; her knuckles fairly stinging my fingers.

'I said...' Deep breath. She gave me another two hits. 'I'm loving it!'

'That's what I thought you said.' I dropped my hands and took Kate by the elbow. 'You, my dear, are going to blow these bastards right out of the water.'

I wheeled her into the auditorium. The cinema was large, with a high rake which gave it the air of an old-style amphitheatre. It was heaving, though with an air of jollity that I had never seen before in a cinema. A lot of friends and, surprisingly, a good turn out from our colleagues on the *Sun*. Even a few of the mad masters were there. Bottles of wine were doing the rounds.

I saw Elise over to the side with the girls. She beckoned to Edward, who she had just met that evening and seemed to take a shine to. He sat down next to her and Elise kissed him on the cheek, her hand lingering on his chin. She patted his arm and they started to talk. For whatever reason, Elise was giving him everything she'd got.

Cheers and wolf-whistles as Kate and I walked to the front of the cinema. I'd not had that sort of reception in a long time. It felt like we were a couple of gladiators about to embark on some extraordinary venture. And so we were. In certain circles, at least, the Marathon des Sables is like a mythical monster – people may have heard of it, but they know of few runners who have actually tangled with it.

The music faded. Kate was still pumped. We biffed knuckles and she bounded onto the stage, and suddenly there she was, front and centre and in the spotlight. And no microphone. The cinema was purpose-built for Kate's voice to carry right to the last tier.

She waited – and she waited. She waited until the talking and the rustling had completely died, until there was not a sound to be heard. I was standing unobtrusively to the side, feeling that pit-of-the-stomach queasiness that a parent feels as their child takes to the stage for the first time.

'Hi,' Kate said, hands clasped in front of her. 'Thanks for coming tonight. Despite Kim's fears that we wouldn't even fill the front row, it looks like we've got a sellout.'

A slight rumble of laughter. The audience started to relax; we were in safe hands.

'So a few days ago, the *Daily Mail* – wonderful paper…' She paused a moment to ride the cat-calls. '…ran a feature on the ten things *not* to do when you're having a mid-life crisis. Top of the list? The Marathon des Sables.'

Laughter, genuine laughter, and enchantment too, at how this pretty young woman had them in the palm of her hand. She rubbed her hands together, palm to palm, and I realised she was enjoying herself.

'Some people might think I'm too young for a mid-life crisis. I can't wait to see what happens when I hit forty. But let me tell you why I'm doing it. I'd never even heard of this race until a couple of years ago. I'd run marathons and I'd done triathlons, and I was looking for something just that little bit different. And I wanted to raise a lot of money – and I mean a LOT of money – for my favourite charity, so I Googled the words, 'Toughest Foot Race on Earth.' Up came the Marathon des Sables – and that's why I'm here today. That's why I've been running 90 miles a week. And that's why I may seem to have gone a little mad over the last few months.' She smiled – now she wasn't just eyeballing the audience, she was milking it, hands alive as she sauntered across the stage. 'I'm sure it's only temporary. At least I hope it is.

'So thank you all so much for coming. I'd like to thank the Ciné Lumière for staging this show; and Edward, who's had to put up with my endless months of training; and I'd also like to thank Kim for being… for being such a good sport.

'I've already paid my MdS entry fee, so tonight, all the money I raise, every penny of it, will go to the Marie Curie Cancer Care. It's a charity that does wonderful things, and it has touched my life in many wonderful ways. It's a great cause – and it's a great movie too. So I hope you can dig deep – because if you don't, then next year I might just have to go in for the world's second toughest footrace.'

A slight lull as the audience realised she was done, and then came the applause, huge applause, and wolf-whistles, and it wasn't just for the speech but for the task that Kate was undertaking. She bowed, arms sweeping in from the side. She gave a little wave as she walked off stage, face wreathed in this huge smile.

I clapped and I whistled, and when she came over to me, we high-fived.

'Sensational!'

'Really?' she laughed.

'Best I've ever heard!'

Even as I was walking onto the stage, I was already mentally tearing up my speech. When I'd been working on it a week earlier, I'd presumed that Kate would be my warm-up act.

She'd only gone and stolen the show.

I waited for the hum to die down. But this time it was different. They didn't want me. They wanted more of Kate.

'Wow!' I said. 'Top that!'

That got a laugh. I decided to get out fast.

'Well, in the immortal words of Humphrey Bogart – if she can stand it, I can! Play it again, Sam!'

I gave them an even more elaborate bow than Kate's and quit the stage. Mild surprise that my speech had only lasted ten seconds, followed by a wave of laughter.

Kate was waiting for me at the front, arm ready to high-five.

'How was that for you?' I asked.

'Brilliant!'

'A little shorter than yours, but that'll come with experience,' I said. 'Yours certainly wasn't a bad effort. For a first attempt.'

She laughed and cuffed me on the arm. It was all so matey, so natural; I felt like an older brother joshing with his kid sister.

And as for the film: the film was just great. It was short and pithy and poignant and no one had ever seen it before, and, just as they had been with Kate, they were absolutely charmed.

The Epsteins' screenplay has so many cracking lines that, minute-for-minute, it must be the world's most quoted movie – 'Here's looking at you, kid'; 'A hill of beans'; 'We'll always have Paris'; 'I think this is the beginning of a beautiful friendship'; and, of course, 'Play it, Sam.'

But if I had to pick a single line, it would be the one that comes right at the end. Most of *Casablanca*'s great lines go to Bogey, but Claude Rains doesn't do too badly. He's got this absolute belter that taught me a useful literary device which I occasionally use in my columns: the legendary 'double shocked.'

Rick's great love affair has finally come to an end and it's the end, also, for his nightclub. As the club is being cleared and closed down by Captain Renault, our world-weary Rick watches as his world is dismantled, and Claude Rains delivers *the* line. He lifts himself up and says with a straight face, 'I am shocked, *shocked* to find that gambling is going on in here!' The very briefest of pauses and then one of Rick's waiters sidles up. 'Your winnings, sir,' he says.

Cracking lines aside, there are so many reasons why we love *Casablanca*: the utterly gorgeous Ingrid Bergman; a bittersweet storyline where the guy so does not get the girl; and a hero who never once complains. Right from the gun, he takes it all on the chin. When asked what in heaven's name brought him to Casablanca, Rick could go into some long-winded explanation about losing the love of his life. Instead he just shrugs and says, 'I came to Casablanca for the waters.' ('The waters? What waters? We're in the desert!')

Bogey's rueful smile is the only hint of all the heartbreak he's been through. 'I was misinformed.'

Isn't that what we want in our heroes, and our anti-heroes, and even those raddled old hacks in the desert who find that things have not quite turned out how they'd expected? Stoicism, a little shrug, perhaps, and not one single word of complaint.

★

Even though I am a Late Charlie, there were some bits of MdS kit that I'd had to sort out a few weeks early, like my running shoes and my gaiters.

You will see all manner of running shoes and every type of gaiter in the desert, with shoes ranging from thick, chunky trainers designed specifically for the desert to the average road-running shoe that you might see in Hyde Park. And there are the oddballs, too, whose footwear you look at and you just think, 'Wow!'

At the startline on the first day, I saw a Japanese man who was wearing very thin Injinji running shoes and no socks. I'd seen these shoes before in the gym – they were made of thin grey rubber, a very snug fit, with each toe having its own little compartment. Like toe socks. I nudged Lawson. 'Check out those shoes.'

'Ouch!'

Later that day, I saw the Japanese man limping to Doc Trotters. He was wearing flip-flops and his feet were swollen and bloody, his soles and heels covered in blisters. He was carrying his Injinjis. They looked like they had been chewed by a wild dog, with ragged holes at the toes and all along the sides. You don't realise how many rocks there are in the desert. Your shoes take an absolute battering.

I had spent some time researching desert footwear on the internet, but there's so much advice out there, it's impossible to know who to listen to. I eventually plumped for a pair of my regular Mizunos, though a size bigger so there was room for my feet to swell. This is another of the MdS imponderables that you will really only find out once you're in the Sahara. Some runners' feet won't swell in the heat at all, while others find that their feet are suddenly two sizes bigger and swelling fast. In the end, a lot of these runners have got no option but to remove the insoles.

My gaiters were the best I could find, orange parachute silk, and I'd paid a cobbler £40 to sew them to the soles of my trainers. Other runners, like Kate, Carlo and Lawson, looked quite cool in their gaiters, as if they'd been wearing them all their lives. I don't know why, and I don't know how. I looked like a complete weirdo.

There were a few other things I hadn't been able to leave to the last minute, like the £100 medical check with my doctor. Half my chest-hair had been shaved off, and my fine rug now looked as if the moths had been at it.

And instead of showering, I'd been having baths – long, hot baths, with a book and a glass of red wine. The first time I'd tried it, Elise found me at 11 p.m.

'It all looks very cosy in here,' she'd said. She was wearing a cream silk nightgown that I'd brought her back from Paris. 'What are you doing?'

'What do you think I'm doing?'

'You never have a bath.'

'We used to have baths—'

'That was different.'

'It's a good way of training for the heat. Or so I'm told.'

She raised her eyebrows at that. 'I thought you were off to one of those heat gyms.'

'Waste of time. If you want to acclimatise for the heat, it's just as effective to have a long hot bath.'

'Is that so?'

'Care to join me?'

She picked up my glass and took a sip.

Now: it's not that men in their forties are obsessed by sex. But when it comes to sex, our love lives are probably not as varied as they once were. And we wonder, wistfully, whether we're still capable of climbing a fresh peak, our partners by our side, loyal Sherpas to the end.

Most people, I believe, have bedroom fantasies. I do. Most of my male friends do. I think Elise does. But do you want your bedroom fantasies to come alive, or is it best not to go there? Do you ever tell your partner? Do you say it like it is?

Let me tell you one thing: if you don't ask, you won't get. Or, to put it another way, how ever can your beautiful wife make your fantasies come true if she doesn't know what they are in the first place?

I wanted: more sex outside the bed; and outside the bedroom; and outside the house. I wanted to have sex in restaurants and theatres and cinemas and places where it would be embarrassing if we were caught in the act. I wanted: sex with food; and drink; and pretzels; and wine; and tumblers of whisky. I wanted: sex in the countryside; on a long walk, as you're overswept by this urge to stop for a while and linger in the hedgerows; on a picnic, with a blanket and strawberries and ice-cold Prosecco. And on a yacht, as the wind sighs off the sea and the boat bobs upon the tide. And in the car, with the music playing and the front seats eased forward. And perhaps in a tree, an oak or a broad beech, cleaving to some golden bough as you are brought to the brink...

Basically I wanted variety in our sex life. Short couplings and long seductions, with clothes on and with clothes ripped off, when the children were at school and we had the whole morning to ourselves... but also when the girls were prowling about the house and we had but five minutes to lock the bedroom door and sate ourselves upon each other.

And I wanted sex in the bath, as the warm water lapped about my shoulders.

Elise's nightgown slips to the floor. I eye her up and down. It's not so often that I see her naked these days. She keeps herself in great trim. I sometimes wonder how many men make passes at her. I've never asked, but I reckon quite a few. She dips one foot into the bath.

'This is hot!' she says.

'I told you it was hot,' I reply.

She gets in, kneeling in the water, and then lies back, our legs intertwining, knee to knee. My hand slips through the bubbles and I stroke her thigh, and her knees part a little.

'Lucky we're not trying for more children,' she says, her hand stroking my knee before it glides into the water.

'It's all frying nicely down there,' I reply.

And in silence, we stroke and we tease, though our eyes never once leave each other. She leans forward, kisses my knee, and continues pressing towards me until she is lying on top of me.

'It's good to practice though,' she says, 'just in case...'

And Elise does this because we are married, and because – at least I hope – she still fancies me a little. And because we are generally aiming to please our partners. We like to do things that make our partners happy. We like, within limits, to bring their fantasies to life.

Maybe we'd have made love in the bathroom, maybe we wouldn't – but as it was, well, we'd never had the conversation. I'd never told her about my fantasies. For some reason I had not found it easy to broach the subject. We can share the most amazing intimacies with strangers in the Sahara – and yet it is often so much easier to continue blithely skating over the surface with our loved ones. Don't ask, don't get.

So, in reality…

I asked Elise if she'd care to join me in the bath.

She sipped the wine. She looked at me. And then without taking off her nightgown, she dipped her toes into the bath. She has beautiful feet. The nails are perfectly shaped and have been painted a glossy burgundy. Though sadly not for me.

'This is hot!' she said.

'I told you it was hot.'

'It's too hot for me.'

'I can put in cold if you like.'

She smiled. And then she said the phrase that I have come to loathe over the years. She would use it when I offered her a glass of wine or a piece of toast or a cup of tea or even crispy bacon in the morning.

'I'll sort myself out later.'

Perhaps Elise did not realise that these little offers are merely light strokes, a small acknowledgement of what you have and what you share – and so they should be accepted, whether or not you want to drink the wine or the tea, or eat the toast or the bacon. By turning down these blandishments, you are keeping a person at arm's length.

But then again, perhaps Elise realised exactly what she was doing.

CHAPTER 9

With terrifying efficiency, Kate had bought all her MdS kit weeks ago. I'd ask her to send me her kit list and she'd sent me the whole spreadsheet, all organised and divided into various sections.

I bandited a lot of my MdS kit from around the house: a compass, billycan and Esbit stove from the girls' camping kit; a signalling mirror from Elise's makeup bag; a spoon and fork combo – the spork – from the junk drawer in the kitchen; a Swiss Army pen-knife that my dad had given me; trendy white sunglasses courtesy of Elise, which would have to do me until I could buy a proper pair out at the first bivouac; and a solid silver lighter, rather fancy, that I guess one of Elise's old boyfriends had given her.

I found wet wipes and TCP in the bathroom, as well as paracetemol and ibuprofen, which, as we ultra veterans know, can be taken together to give you a double hit of pain relief. And Vaseline, and a toothbrush and toothpaste, and of course not forgetting my roll of soft white triple-ply toilet paper.

I am not good at these sorts of jobs. After a very short while, I become fantastically cavalier. I start to think, 'Oh well, we'll sort it out on the day.' And this is generally true – one way or another, most things *can* be sorted out on the day, and if not, they can be bodged. Until there's a crisis, and then...

That's when you think that, if you had your time over, you might have done things just a little bit differently.

Not that I am in any way blaming Kate; I am a cretin and I know it. Well, maybe not a cretin, but I do at least know that I am capable of the most cretinous behaviour.

But the problem with Kate's MdS kit list was that she was intent on taking at least 90 different items, and I had no sort of indication as to which items were luxuries and which were *essential.*

For instance, Kate had included on her list: 'eight poo bags,' 'zinc oxide tape,' 'duct tape,' 'spare batteries,' 'lock for bag,' 'soap concentrate,' 'constipation relief' and 'diarrhoea relief.' How was I to know that the whole lot could have been merrily binned – except for the one vital one, the one that, without, could have you damn nearly drummed out of the race?

I browsed through the family medicine cabinet and found a small packet of supermarket brand diarrhoea relief. I'd never come across them before. They were chalky and blocked you up in the old-fashioned way, but they looked fine enough. I popped them into my bag.

Should you ever undertake one of these mad events, here is a word of wisdom: The organisers will have enough medication and pain relief to cater for a small war zone. They'll have miles of tape and bandages and gallons of antiseptic. They will have painkillers, too, ranging from ibuprofen to the heavy-duty opiate tramadol. And there will certainly be more than enough poo bags to go round.

But when you get diarrhoea in the desert, you need to knock it on the head quickly, before the fluid has started to drain out of you and the sun has sapped your strength. By all means, skimp on everything else – but don't stint on the Imodium.

I was pleased with one of my compulsory items – the safety pins. We needed 12 to attach our race numbers to the front of our shirts and the back of our rucksack, and I'd looked all over the place and couldn't find any. Then, to my delight, I discovered a few while rummaging through an old box of cufflinks. They were 18-carat gold.

I gleefully seized upon them, wondering what my grandfathers would have made of me using their favourite tie pins for my MdS race numbers. I liked the link it gave me to them. Not that the MdS was ever going to compare with my grandfathers' activities in the First and Second World Wars, but it was still going to be a battle. Like my grandfathers before me, I was going off to war.

Back in my snug, Dolly and Marie were trying on my clothes. My kit was lying all over the floor, and there seemed to be masses of stuff;

I wondered how on earth it would all fit into my rinky-dink 32-litre Inov8 rucksack. Dolly was wearing my cream-coloured 'eco-mesh shirt,' breathable, expensive. It looked like a farmhand's smock. Marie had my Injinji socks on. They were black and long and stretched all the way up her legs. The girls were laughing at her toes.

'I'd like socks like these,' she said.

'Sure – have them when I get back.'

'Can I have a pair?' asked Dolly.

'If you want, you can have every single thing here.'

'What's this?' said Marie, twisting in my chair as she stooped for something from my food pile. I would need 2,000 calories a day, which weighs in at about 1 kilo, so I had decanted my dehydrated meals into thin zip-up bags. This saved a bit on weight, but the bags were not nearly so hard-wearing and tended to split.

I squinted at the bag. It contained about a pound of muddy brown powder. 'Might be spaghetti bolognese,' I said. 'Or possibly chilli con carne. Might even be lasagne. I don't know.'

'What's this one?' asked Dolly, holding up a smaller bag of creamy powder.

'That's Peronin – like custard powder. It's going to be my lunch.'

'Yuk!'

'Every day for six days.'

'And this?'

'That one?' I opened it and sniffed. 'Smells like spaghetti carbonara. Could be chicken and rice.'

'Are these jelly beans?'

'They're sports beans.'

'What's the difference?'

'Sports beans are twice the price.'

'Can we try the spaghetti?' Dolly said.

'Do you have noodles? I like noodles!' Marie said.

I dithered. It would mean another shopping trip the next day.

The girls saw my weakness and struck.

'Please!' Marie said. 'It'll be our tea.'

'And you have to taste the food before you go, Daddy,' Dolly said. 'You might not like it.'

'We want desert food!'

'Very well,' I said. 'But I don't think you'll like it.'

We went to the kitchen. The girls ate their sports beans as we waited for the kettle to boil. Dehydrated food is fantastically simple, and perfect for the MdS. Just add water – either hot water for breakfast or supper, or cold water for lunch or the golden hour refresher. The freeze-dried spaghetti bolognese has the most calories per kilo, and Lawson had taken this knowledge to heart – his every evening meal consisted of spag bol. He never tried it before he got out to the Sahara. He hated it.

I made up bowls of spaghetti bolognese and Lancashire hotpot, pepping up both dishes with Tabasco. Dehydrated food is bland.

'What do we think?' I asked.

Marie warily sniffed at the hotpot. Dolly ate a spoonful of spaghetti. 'This is spaghetti?'

'It's spaghetti.'

'Why isn't it long? Why isn't it like normal spaghetti?'

'This is special MdS spaghetti.'

'What's so special about it?'

'You have to be really, really hungry to eat it.'

'I don't think I'm hungry enough.'

'I don't like this,' Dolly said. 'Can I try the custard?'

'Sure – but it won't taste any better.'

'Do you like eating any of the things you're taking to the desert?'

'Good question.'

MdS food was never supposed to be enjoyed. It's just energy, stuff to power you through the next day, and since you're carrying all your food on your back, it has to be the lightest energy going. So there have to be compromises, and that compromise is usually taste. And texture, too. After a few days of eating pap, you dream of all kinds of food – chicken or fish, or eggs and bacon. My ultimate fantasy was a cool, crisp and tart Braeburn apple.

Most runners would bring a few little treats, which they would suck and chew in the evening, or when they needed a pick-me-up in the middle of the day. Pepperamis were quite popular, though they were not favoured by the elite runners because of their poor calorie-to-weight ratio. Al had fruit pastilles; Simon had Tic Tacs; Lawson had biltong, very spicy, made from the eland antelope. MdS treats were rarely shared, but Lawson gave me some. I would take a small shard of biltong and savour it for a minute before swallowing.

And there was one guy, a Brit, whose treat consisted of a bottle of Heineken. His dream was to trot over the finish line and crack open his bottle of lukewarm lager.

There'd been no mention of treats on Kate's kit list, so I hadn't given them a thought. But when I arrived in the desert, I found that my darling daughters had packed me some presents for Easter Day: a small box of Lindt Easter eggs. They had melted to mush by the time I found them, and my beanie hat was covered in chocolate. Carlo, Kate and Lawson and I sat on the rug in our tent, licking the silver paper clean, scraping it against our teeth and jangling our fillings.

*

Our first fight was over food. It is often the way. Preparing food, even though it's merely a matter of boiling up some water, can be tricky. The Hexamine tablets are not easy to light and the Esbit stoves were precarious. It was often windy and, on top of all of that, you were probably hungry, hands possibly not as deft as they might be… Oh, and you were hugger-mugger with seven other people in a tent while trying to cook…

As ever with the MdS, it was a good test of character. You find out who can roll with the punches and who's as brittle as a cast-iron pot. Like I said, if you are in any doubt whatsoever about your choice of life-partner, take them on the MdS. You learn some pretty useful stuff.

Kate had definitely passed the marriage test. Not that I'd ever be marrying Kate, but if I'd been 15 years younger… and single… and if my aunt had indeed been my uncle… then by the end of Stage Two, I would have had no qualms whatsoever in popping the question.

But before that fight and before that test of character, we first had to get through the second day. The second day had been just hellish. It was bad at the start, bad in the middle and with the fight in the tent, bad at the end.

Kate had stuck with me for the whole of the day, as my guts rumbled and we bumbled on through the dunes and the endless desert. At least I didn't have the runs. After about a mile together, Kate was beginning to really stride out.

'Feel like doing a bit of running?' she asked.

I laughed at her mirthlessly. 'You can run all you want, Kate. I'm just walking this one. Don't wait.'

'I'm happy. Gives us a chance to chat.'

'I can certainly do that – I can chat till the cows come home.'

The miles go by more quickly if you're talking. I remember my father telling me about his early days in the army, when he'd been a young subaltern. The whole platoon had been on a six-mile route march, walking as fast as they were able. My father had been striding out front, side by side with the Regimental Sergeant Major, and the pair of them had talked every step of the way. When the route march was over, my father and the RSM had barely broken a sweat, but the troops who'd been marching silently in the ranks were blowing and panting as if they'd run a marathon.

Monitoring water intake is one of the major difficulties of the MdS. Drink too fast between the checkpoints and you'll run out; drink too slowly and you start to go woozy and lightheaded, which by then is too late as you're already severely dehydrated. A good rule of thumb, Kurtz told me, was to aim for a light tingle in your bladder – not enough to make you want to pee, but just a slight pressure. It lets you know there's water to spare.

It hit 52 degrees on the second day. I had not appreciated how much I had been sweating out, until I realised that I had drunk a full 11 litres of water since breakfast and had not once stopped for a pee.

My bladder had never once felt full – just, as I say, slightly stretched and tingly.

Kate and I took more than three hours to walk barely eight miles on the second day. You can tell it's noon because the sun is almost directly overhead and you are walking on your own shadow. The heat pounds at you, relentless, and you wonder just how much longer this hell is going to continue; how much more of it you can take.

The Commissaire at the first checkpoint clipped the water ration card on my lanyard while another wrote my race number on the top and sides of my water bottle. Any loose bottles found in the desert can be traced back to the individual runners, who will then be docked a time penalty.

I stumped over to one of the white MdS Land Rovers, heaving a sigh of relief as I unclipped my rucksack and swung it to the ground. My shirt was sopping and had turned blue at the shoulders where the dye from my bag had started to run. I took my shirt off and hung it out to dry on the front bullbars of the Land Rover. I sat down on the car's foot plate and tried to stay in that moment, tried to enjoy taking the weight off my feet, and tried, above all, to avoid thinking about the 14 miles of desert that still lay ahead of me.

Kate, being lovely, filled my water bottles. This needed care, as they were easy to knock over. I watched her as she removed the first one from the bag's shoulder holster. She unscrewed the top and held it between her teeth as she carefully filled up the water bottle. Then, the tricky part – she dropped two electrolyte tablets into the bottle, which fizzed like Alka Seltzer. She screwed the top on tight and returned the bottle to its holster.

'This what you expected?' she asked. She was squatting beside me with the second water bottle. So young and full of energy. Quite dispassionately, I looked at her tanned legs. They strained against her red shorts. She had taken off her *casquette* and her blonde hair gleamed, burnished.

'I don't know what I expected,' I said. 'I knew it was going to be so outside my experience that I didn't have any expectations. And you?'

'I hadn't realised it would be so beautiful.'

'It is that.' I sipped some water, swirling it around my mouth, washing the grit from my teeth, and stared at the desert. It can be quite searingly beautiful. Not that you'd notice if you were driving it or flying it. But when you are on foot, and when you are not in too much pain, the sand can be quite stunning.

'It's funny,' I said. 'I'm finding it much easier to carry on walking. The moment I stopped, I started to feel faint.'

I had not realised that one of the Commissaires was in the Land Rover. At the checkpoints, especially on the first couple of days, the Commissaires check you out as they talk to you. They look into your eyes to make sure they're not yellow or bloodshot and they watch to see whether or not you're slurring your words or wobbling on your feet. Basically they watch to see if you're lucid and in control. She had been listening and she came out to talk to me.

'You – Kim,' she said. She was one of the French medics. She was sizing me up, looking at my feet, my bare chest and my haggard face. I don't know what I looked like then, but I was probably quite a state. 'How are you?'

'I'm loving it.'

'Have you been taking your salt tablets?'

'Two an hour, on the hour.'

'You are fine?'

'Yes, I am fine.'

'Do you feel faint?'

'No I do not.'

The woman did not bother to ask how Kate was, because Kate was looking fit and fresh, and just about the best advertisement for the Marathon des Sables that Patrick Bauer could have ever hoped for.

Kate finished my water bottles and made my lunch. She tore the top off the silver Peronin pouch with her teeth and poured in a little water. She mixed it up thoroughly with her spork and handed it over.

'*Bon appetit*!'

I took a spoonful and nearly retched. It was like very sweet lukewarm custard. 'Lovely!'

Kate grinned at me as she made up her own Peronin. 'Beats the hell out of that shit they serve up for lunch at News International.'

'Maybe we should suggest it to the catering committee.' I had another spoonful. It really was disgusting, cloying, so, so sickly sweet. I forced myself to swallow. 'For the journalist who's really in a hurry – a pack of Peronin. The perfect meal to keep you going for the rest of the day.'

Kate didn't even bother with a spoon and was pouring the Peronin straight into her mouth. She scooped out the dregs with her fingers, licking them one by one. Five hundred calories ingested in under one minute. She burped, giggling as she automatically put her hand in front of her mouth.

'How are those blisters of yours?' I asked.

'Blisters are good. Compeeds are doing what they're supposed to do.' She tapped the end of her shoe against the Land Rover's wheel and winced. 'You don't have any paracetemol, do you? I've got ibuprofen but I could do with a double hit.'

'They're in the top pocket. Take as many as you like.'

It was the first inkling I'd had that all was not well with Kate's feet. She'd had blisters the previous day – we'd *all* had blisters the previous day. But if her feet were already causing her pain after only 32 miles, it did not bode well for the rest of the race.

Kate came over and stood beside me with her hand on my shoulder. 'Try this.' She took off my *casquette* and poured water down the back of my head. I felt it trickle down the nape of my neck. The water was cool, reviving, delicious. One of the great pleasures to be had in the heat of the MdS is to have water poured down your neck by a beautiful woman.

I hoist my rucksack onto my back. It is so heavy, at least 15 or 16 kilos, and the straps feel like cheese wire. My shoulders are sore and the skin is grazed and the salt from my sweat is rubbing into my wounds. I try to make the straps more comfortable, but it still hurts. I saw a guy two days later who had snapped the straps on his cheap rucksack. For the rest of the race he carried his rucksack in his arms, clasped to his chest like a small child.

I remember the *Lac Ma'der El Kebir* on that second day. It was a dried-up lake, the route stretching six miles, straight as a die, between the second and third checkpoints. We walked over these flat shingle-fields where the parched mud had set into mile upon mile of grey crazy paving. The runners' tracks had turned the mud to fine dust, and there was not a plant nor animal to be seen. I walked for an hour over the lake, but the next checkpoint did not seem to be one jot closer.

Sometimes Kate would move ahead and talk to other people; she was popular and people always wanted to talk to her. But periodically she would look back to check on how I was doing. I would give her a wave with my poles and she would wave back.

Towards the end of the lake, I saw my first plant. I felt like Noah on the Ark when the dove brings back the green twig of an olive tree. It looked like the samphire that grows on the Norfolk coast, and I was soon wandering through fields of scrub. My step-mother Edie should have been there; she would have identified the plants, probably by their Latin names too, but I could not name a single one, not even the pretty white flowers and lush thick plants that looked like brussel sprouts. I came across a muddy pond, the first water I'd seen in the desert. I was tempted to dip my feet in, but there was still a long way to go, and I didn't want the hassle of cleaning my feet and redoing my bandages.

We were given two bottles of water at the third checkpoint. I checked my watch.

'Another two hours and we'll be there,' I said.

'Easily make the cut-off,' Kate said.

'At a canter.'

She looked at me, momentarily taking her eyes off the track, and in the same instant she stubbed her toe. She let out a short, sharp swearword, hobbling for a bit before finding her stride.

'Got to keep your eye on the road,' she said. 'I was getting ahead of myself. Already thinking about the finish.'

'Have you noticed the dunes are much easier on your feet? The sand has got a bit of give.'

Kate checked her watch and stretched behind to unzip one of her side pockets. She pulled out a pack of ibuprofen. 'My feet have swelled up so much. My toes are being squeezed.'

'Want to stop and change your socks? Ease off your laces?'

'Let's press on.'

A Commissaire drove past in a sandbuggy, a Polaris RZR S. They were very fancy machines, and cost 20,000 Euros each. They were Patrick Bauer's vehicle of choice, with huge thick Maxxis Bighorn tyres and superb suspension. You revved them up the side a dune and then eased off the gas as you flew off the top.

'Only four kilometres to go!' called the Commissaire. We waved and, because we did not know any better, we believed him. It was a mistake. Once you start thinking about the last few miles, you are no longer in the moment and you start dreaming about getting back into the tent and putting your feet up. The Commissaires invariably underestimated the final stretch by at least a mile, if not two.

We realised as much when we reached another plain. Far off, at least an hour away, we could see the lights of the finishline winking in the dusk. 'Thar she blows!' I said.

There was a fortress, abandoned long ago, its walls falling into disrepair as it slowly turned back into desert dust. I thought of Beau Geste and his grand gesture, and a moment later I was thinking about the French Foreign Legion. The MdS was made for Foreign Legionnaires. They know how to deal with heat and sand and long distances, and above all they know how to deal with pain. The Marathon des Sables is, in large part, an exercise in dealing with pain.

Four young boys appeared out of the middle of nowhere. They'd ridden out into the desert on a single adult-size bicycle. '*Vous êtes fatigués*?' they called.

'*Bon soir*!' I said.

They wanted sweets. Kate patted their outstretched hands and I tossed them a bag of sports beans.

Behind us, out in the darkness, I could see two head torches. I couldn't tell how far off they were, perhaps half a mile, perhaps two. I wondered if they would make the cut-off. It would be harsh to disqualify them if they were just a few minutes past the deadline. But then again the MdS thrives on its reputation for harshness; otherwise it wouldn't be the toughest footrace on earth.

We finally wandered over the finish line. Our Tag Heuer anklets set off a double ping and our names would now flash up on the MdS website, letting our friends know we'd made it through the second stage.

I bowed to the webcam. Kate just kept on walking straight to the tea tent. We eased our rucksacks off our wet backs, savouring a hard-earned cup of tea.

We chinked, though I could not see her face because of her head torch.

'Cheers,' she said.

'Two down – four to go.'

'You said it!'

I took my first sip of Sultan tea. It's served at the end of each stage of the MdS, sweet and without milk. It is the most perfect tea on earth and I don't think I ever want to drink it again. It would be such a shame to discover that it wasn't the tea at all, but rather the wonderful associations that came with it, and at knowing that another day in the desert was done.

I had spent over ten tough hours with Kate that day – and over that stretch of time, a person's looks are about as relevant as their hair colour. Character is all, and the MdS is such a massive mental test. And hadn't she just delivered? She was thoughtful, upbeat, considerate – all you could ever want from an MdS runner. And a soulmate too, come to that.

I finished my tea and asked for another one. '*Shukran bezaf*,' I said – thank you. I sipped and wallowed in the ecstasy of the tea and the relief of having a rest, and the sheer pleasure of Kate's company. Ecstasy is always best when it's shared. And I realised that, in the last few years, there had been very few ecstatic moments in my life. I'd had good times with my family and even, on the odd occasion, at work. But moments of true, heavenly ecstasy, when it was just thrilling to be alive? Hardly a one.

'I'm not looking forward to taking my shoes off,' she said.

'Doc Trotters will sort you out.'

'I thought the ibuprofen would stop the swelling.'

'See what the doctors say.'

We each picked up our three bottles of water and walked to our tent, Tent 71. Coloured lights guided us to the bivouac.

Our tentmates were all in long ago, hosed, watered and in their sleeping bags. Some were reading and some were asleep. They'd left a small space for us in the middle. The first people in tended to bed down at the ends of the tents, which were shielded better from the wind.

I tossed my sticks and my water bottles onto the ground outside the tent. The wind was really picking up and everything was coated in a fine layer of orange dust.

'You've made it!' said Carlo. He was pleased to see us. Well, Kate. 'How was it? How are you?'

'Brilliant!' said Kate.

With a slight lack of grace, Martin moved his kit over to give us some more space in the middle.

I sat down on the rug, untied my gaiters and unlaced my shoes. There were a couple of hot-spots on the balls of my feet, the prelude to a blister. I pulled off my socks and a fine mist of sand fell from between my toes. I had a few more blisters to go with the ones I'd garnered on the first day, particularly on my toes. My little toe was double its normal size.

I mixed myself a REGO recovery drink. Yet more vanilla. I wish I'd thought about that before I'd gone out to the desert. Vanilla for lunch and vanilla at the end of the day. After four days of it, I was so sick of vanilla that I never wanted to touch the stuff again.

I pulled out my sleeping bag. It was wet, completely soaked through, and I thought for a moment that a water bottle had leaked over it. But it wasn't water – it was sweat, litres of it, that had wicked into my rucksack. I hung the bag out to dry and lay on my Thermarest with my bare feet raised up on my rucksack. I was engulfed by this feeling of general well-being. I was in a filthy tent in the middle of the Sahara, my muscles were aching, my toes throbbing and the wind was blowing hard. It was heaven.

Kate had taken off her shoes and gaiters, but still had her socks on. She also had her feet up and was chatting to Lawson.

'Did you see those kids near the end?' asked Lawson. 'Where did they come from? Do they live out here?'

'I bet they love seeing us,' Kate said. She was on her side, stirring water into her REGO powder; always elegant.

'But you didn't touch their hands?' said Martin.

'Sometimes. They like it.' She took a spoonful of REGO and continued to stir. 'I like it too.'

'You know what they do with their left hands? Covered in bugs.'

'I thought that was just another one of the urban myths of the MdS. Anyway, I've got plenty of antiseptic.'

I got out my Esbit stove. It was so windy, I had to set it up right in the corner of the tent where Simon was sleeping. Simon was an odd one – well, we're all odd ones, but Simon never much enjoyed the camaraderie of the tent. He never slummed it with the rest of us. Every night, he was the first in and would set up his stall in the least windy corner of the tent. If it had been an option, I think he would have much preferred to have been by himself.

I piled ten Hexamine tablets onto the Esbit and huddled down to try and light them. I don't know why I put on so many. Three at a time is normal. Ten is a lot.

It took ages. My thumb was sore from striking Elise's lighter so often. It was a Cartier lighter, burnished silver, and on it were engraved the words, *Für Elise*. I could play that Beethoven sonata once, but not any more. As I held the flame to the tablets, I whistled the tune. The Hexamine tablets caught, were ablaze, and then a moment later a gust of wind blew the flame out.

Another test of character. We do not swear. We do not moan. We dust ourselves down and we start all over again.

It took me at least 15 minutes to light the stove – though it's true that I am particularly cack-handed in these matters. I admit it. I am a bodger. No – worse than that: I am a liability.

Still trying to shield the flame, I put the billycan onto the stove. It contained a litre of water, half for me and half for Kate, and it was all very rickety. The ten Hexamine tablets produced a huge flame which licked up the sides of the billycan. I was concerned that the fire might blow out, and there was every chance that the billycan would fall over. I watched over them like a mother hen.

The water was just beginning to simmer, bubbles seething at the bottom of the pan. I remember feeling quite pleased with myself. I, Kim, had single-handedly lit an Esbit stove and, without screwing up once, had brought a litre of water to the boil.

Then there was a sudden random gust of wind, the flame blew out to the side and the next thing I knew, Simon's fleece had caught fire. It went up very quickly. The flames were spectacular.

'Shit!'

I did the only thing I could think of. I hurled the hot water over the burning fleece. The flames were dowsed. Simon twitched and then shrieked, tearing himself out of his sleeping bag.

'What—' He looked at me and looked at his charred, sopping fleece. It looked expensive. Tendrils of smoke eddied into the dusty air. 'What have you done?'

'Sorry, Simon. I'm very sorry.'

Simon looked from the blue fleece to the billycan still in my hand. The flames from the Esbit stove were still roaring.

'You idiot!' he said. 'You're a bloody idiot!'

'I'm sorry, Simon,' I said. 'It was an accident.'

'You're an idiot!'

Far from calming down, Simon seemed to be working himself up into the most complete rage. His face had gone quite white. He clenched and unclenched his fingers. The whole tent was wide awake.

'I'm sorry – look, use my fleece if you want.'

'I don't want your bloody cheap-shit fleece.'

'Okay – well, I'm sorry.' I wondered how else to mollify him. 'Can I make you a cup of mint tea?'

A puff of wind caught the stove's flame. It darted towards Simon's sleeping bag.

'Get that bloody stove away from me! Get it away! Just stay away from me!' He threw a punch, cuffing me on the shoulder. My mood switched. I went from apologetic to very annoyed.

'Calm down! It's not the end of the bloody world.'

He hit me again, harder. 'Get that thing away from me!'

'Watch it!' I sized him up. I was bigger than him, younger than him. I could take him out easy. 'Don't you hit me again.'

He hit me again, catching me hard under the ear.

In that moment, I could gladly have throttled him. I was tired, I was hungry and now I was angry.

Kurtz, the ex-Para, stopped it from turning into an all-out brawl. He got up and stood directly between us. 'Excuse me, ladies,' he said. He held up his finger as if asking for silence, and then let out the most monumental fart, which was not particularly loud but which went on – and on – and on. It had the shrill whine of a wasp. It went on longer than seemed humanly possible. After a while, we could only listen in wonderment. Kate looked at me and gave a little shrug. It was incredible, amazing, the most effective method of finishing a fight that I have ever seen.

Then, without a word, he climbed back into his sleeping bag.

All at once we started laughing. Lawson was giggling, Carlo was roaring and Kate's stomach was heaving, her REGO recovery drink spilling all over her rucksack.

'Should we call the Guinness Book of Records?' Carlo said.

'Kurtz – you ever thought of turning professional?' Lawson asked.

And Kurtz just smiled, rolled onto his side and let off another ripper.

There was one last drama that night before we went to sleep.

Kate took off her white Injinji ankle socks, the toes and the heels brown from dried blood. She tried to ease off the first sock, teasing at it like a plaster, but it wouldn't come, so in the end she just tugged it off.

She had her head torch on and the light was focused on her foot. She picked at a piece of dead skin, rubbing it between her fingers before she flicked it out of the tent. 'This does not look good.'

Her trusty plasters, the Compeeds, had come off. The previous night, just as at the Pilgrim, she'd cut off all her blisters. She had sprayed them with antiseptic and slapped on at least seven Compeeds, including a couple of large ones on the balls of her feet. But the dust and the sweat had got in at the edges of the Compeeds, and the plastic plasters had slipped and wrinkled into sticky balls of blood. Her blisters had been squeezed for 11 hours into too-tight running shoes while being abraded by sand and sweat. In fact, they were no longer blisters. They had turned into great angry blotches, red, raw and weeping. Some of them were the size of an old penny.

Kate sighed and pulled at her other sock. She didn't waste any time and just tugged it straight off. It was the same story. Her white feet were covered in red dots of raw, bare flesh. There were a few fresh blisters too, puffing up her toes and forming odd-shaped lumps on the soles of her feet.

She cocked her leg up and examined her blisters, one foot, then the other. 'I don't like it.'

I stroked her shoulder. 'You'll be fine.'

For a time, she stared out into the darkness, wondering what on earth she'd let herself in for. Forty-six miles down, over a hundred to go.

'You better change socks,' I said. 'Try a pair of my socks tomorrow.' If your shoes and socks weren't right at the start, then they certainly weren't going to improve midway through.

'Thanks.' She spoke in a soft, small voice. It was the voice of someone who was still in the process of resigning themselves to their fate. She was already envisaging the horrors that lay ahead of her. 'Can't be any worse. Thank you.'

'It must have been walking with me,' I said. 'You had too long on your feet. I'm sorry.'

'It was going to happen whatever.'

'Let's get you to Doc Trotters.'

'Yeah.' She set her shoulders back. I could see the steel in her face. She had already moved on. It would hurt, probably hurt a lot. But she would deal with it. 'I better get going.'

'I'm coming too.'

'No – please don't.' She winced as she got to her feet. Blisters can be endured in a race, but when the running is over, they're unbearable.

'Let's go.'

She slipped on her flip-flops and I picked up a bottle of water. There was a chance that we might be some time. We limped out of the tent. I held her hand, fingers interlocked. We'd get through this. We'd get through this together. Very briefly she brought my hand to her lips and kissed my fingers.

CHAPTER 10

Signing up for the MdS is a little like being on Death Row. It is this huge, foreboding thing that hangs over your head, and for a long time, for months, the event seems so far off in the future that it's barely worth contemplating. Even when it's a month off, it's still way ahead of you. Then it's only a week to go, but that's seven whole days – and anything could happen. You might stub your toe on the sofa and end up in hospital, or get laid low with gastric flu, or pop your Achilles running for a tennis drop-shot. Not that you want to get injured, of course…though it does give you a 100 per cent legitimate excuse to pull out of the race.

Then, suddenly, time starts to contract very, very quickly, and you've only got one day left, one night left, and before you know it, time's up and you're on your way.

I was at Victoria Station catching the Gatwick Express. I had a wheelie bag, packed with at least 20 kilos of non-essential kit which I'd tossed in the previous night, and on my back was my Inov8 rucksack, packed with all my essential kit – passport, paperwork and running shoes. At least a couple of runners every year lose their bags in transit. If they asked nicely, they could usually scrounge all the kit from the other runners out in Morocco, but if you'd lost your running shoes and gaiters, it was going to be more difficult. And painful.

My rucksack came complete with shoulder holsters for my two water bottles, and they're very unusual. They're only ever used by ultra runners, so it was easy to spot the other head cases. There were a few of these head cases wandering around Victoria Station, with Raidlight and Inov8 rucksacks on their backs, bottles of water in hand. They were predominantly men, lean, with crew-cut hair and a slightly mad look in their eyes, though they seemed quite an affable bunch. Our rucksacks and our shoulder holsters were like this secret Masonic sign; we knew, though nobody else did, that we were all off to the Sahara. We would spot each other in WHSmiths or at the ticket machines, or in the queues for coffee, and we would smile as we sized each other up. As I looked at them, I realised I was completely underprepared for the task ahead of me.

It was on the Gatwick Express that I met Kurtz, the ex-Para. He'd flown down from Scotland the previous day and spent the night in London.

'Been enjoying your training?' I asked as we got on the train.

'Bloody hated it.'

Kurtz had a huge khaki kit bag, which he effortlessly pitched onto the overhead racks. We sat opposite each other at an empty table. Kurtz surveyed me, pursed his lips, and after deciding I'd passed the test, he started rummaging in the top of his rucksack. There was something in each other that we both recognised and liked.

He pulled out a couple of Courvoisier miniatures and placed them on the table between us. I was enjoying the show. Kurtz was interesting to look at – his face had been ravaged by sun and scarring, and he had a prominent eye patch, black leather, strapped about the top of his shaven head. On his cheek, there was a puckered round scar, perhaps a bullet wound. His nose had been broken a few times and a thin white slash of a scar stretched from his mouth to underneath his chin. I think he'd lost a lot of teeth; white implants were set against greying gums.

I didn't know then that he was an ex-Para, but he was undoubtedly a very hard man.

He delved into the rucksack again and plucked out a small leather cylinder. He popped the cylinder's top. It contained six stainless steel stirrup cups.

He placed two cups onto the table and, still without a word, emptied each Courvoisier bottle into a cup. I waited for him to pick up his cup, then picked up mine and gave him the nod as I toasted him.

'*Slàinte*,' he said. He spoke with a thick Scottish brogue, and the more he drank, the more impenetrable he became.

'Cheers.'

He sipped and swirled the brandy in his cup, and all the while his single black eye had never left mine. 'I'm Kurtz,' he said.

'Kim.' We shook hands.

'Why did you sign up for this piece of shit?' he asked.

'I'm certifiably insane.'

His laughed at that, his lips down-turned in a little moue of a smile. 'I *was* certified insane.'

'Padded cells? Straitjackets?'

'Yep.'

He noticed two young men sitting near us. They had long black hair, denim jackets, earrings and tattoos. They ached with cool. The pair of them lounged in their seats, their new Nike trainers up on the chair in front.

'You two,' Kurtz said. 'Feet off the seats.'

They stared at him, but didn't move. Kurtz held up his hand and rubbed the tips of his fingers together. I had seen Spaniards do it before, as they say the word '*Puta*!' You don't quite know what it means, but you know that it's obscene. Then he smiled at them. 'You want some?'

The men took their feet off the seats. They stared at him, surly, and Kurtz stared right back. 'D'you want some?'

They lowered their eyes like whipped curs.

Kurtz turned to me. 'I don't hit people any more,' he said. 'All I have to do is look at them.' He upended his cup and gargled the brandy before swallowing. 'Hooo-Haaaa!' He went back to his rucksack and pulled out two more miniatures – this time of Glenfiddich. 'You're having another,' he said, as he twisted off the first top. It wasn't a question.

'I'll stick to brandy.'

'There is no brandy.'

'Why are you called Kurtz?' I asked. 'Anything to do with *Heart of Darkness*?'

'Aye,' he said. 'I have a volcanic temper.' He wafted the glass under his nose, inhaling the whisky fumes as his one good eye stayed riveted on me. 'And a very short fuse.'

After two more miniatures, I was merrily on my way. Kurtz did not talk about any action that he'd seen with the Paras, but I did learn that he had a family up in Aberdeen. After leaving the Forces, he'd become an oil lawyer; he must have been a terrifying negotiator. If things ever got testy, he said, he would take off his eye patch. I saw it several times and it was quite gruesome to behold. Kurtz seemed to revel in his own hideousness.

'So what do you do?' he asked bluntly.

'I'm a journalist.'

'Who for?'

'The *Sun*.'

'Yeah?'

'Yeah.' I pushed him a copy of that day's paper. The MdS column that I'd been writing with Kate had been ticking over nicely, and now that we were flying off to Morocco, our mad master had given us a centre-page spread. The feature was dominated, naturally, by a photo of Kate in her kit, while I lurked in the background. We'd posed for the picture on the sand at Rotten Row in Hyde Park. Kate looked beautiful; I just looked rather strange. I think it was a combination of the orange gaiters and my smock shirt.

Kurtz looked at the feature. 'You wrote this?'

'I did.'

He nodded and started to read. He read the whole feature from start to finish. It wasn't half bad; I don't write those sort of articles very often these days, but I enjoy it when I do.

'Choice.' He left the paper on the table. 'Never met a *Sun* journalist before.'

'Not just the scum – we're the crème de la scum.'

'Good line for the Paras.'

'I'm full of them.'

He opened another two miniatures, this time Grand Marnier.

'*Slàinte!*'

'Cheers!' The Grand Marnier was sickly orange. I normally drink it at night when I'm completely senseless. 'Where the hell did you get all these miniatures?'

'Cleared out the mini-bar.'

'As you do.'

By the time we reached Gatwick, we had agreed to be tentmates. I told him about Martin and Carlo and Lawson. And I told him about Kate.

'A girl in the tent?' He turned and glowered at the two young men who'd had their feet on the seats. We hadn't heard a squeak out of them for the entire trip. 'It'll be different.'

'How's that?'

'Not so much swearing. Not so much farting. A few less fights – sometimes. Though the girls can cause fights too.'

'I guess so.'

'Guys don't like to back down in front of a woman.' He tapped Kate's picture in the *Sun*. ''Specially not a looker.'

'You'll be all right in a fight.'

'Me?' He laughed, the skin crinkling around his scars. 'It's you I'm worried about.'

There were many more MdS competitors at Gatwick. Unusually for a Late Charlie, I had arrived early. This was one flight I did not want to miss – though if you did miss it, there was a very expensive contingency plan.

Kurtz went shopping for flip-flops while I tried to sober up in one of the coffee chains. I took a couple of paracetemol and drank water and double espressos.

Elise had given me a package before I'd left. 'Might be useful if you get bored,' she'd said. It was small, barely bigger than a packet of cigarettes. She had wrapped it beautifully, just as she always did, with striped paper and a green ribbon. I shook it but it didn't make a sound. I thought it was probably going to be something expensive and useless from Tiffany's or Asprey.

But actually... it was cheap and brilliant. It was a tiny little iPod, barely the size of a postage stamp. I had not originally planned on taking any music out to the Sahara. I thought that it might detract from my commune with nature – and it's true that after a while the music can become an aural comfort blanket. It can be a subtle barrier that stops you from connecting with the desert, but it can also power you through the tough times. She had taken some thought and care in choosing it. I was touched.

★

The first time I used the iPod was on that grim second day, when I'd been suffering from the runs. Kate and I had just gone through the first checkpoint, it was hot, I'd had my disgusting vanilla lunch and the desert was just about the very last place on earth that I wanted to be.

'I'm going to give the iPod a go,' I said.

'Whatever gets you though the night,' Kate said. We walked on. We could be together for hours, quite companionable, without ever having to say a word. I have never known that before with a woman.

I plugged the headphones into my ears and fiddled with the iPod. It was idiot-proof and I worked out how to use it in under a minute. I stubbed my toe, too, banging another blister. I remember that.

I turned the music on and I was suddenly three thousand miles away, in an old scout hut in London, where Marie had been putting on a show with her dance mates. One of the numbers was a very simple tune by Snow Patrol - 'I Am an Astronaut'. It brought tears to my eyes.

Elise had ranged far and wide as she made her selection of tracks. She had a few old favourites, Beethoven's 'Pastoral,' Bach's 'Well-Tempered Clavier,' some Vivaldi and some Van Halen. But there were a number of tracks that amazed me. She must have quizzed the girls about the music videos that we'd been watching on YouTube.

My favourite, by far, was Kelly Clarkson's 'Stronger' – it's a play on Nietzsche's line, 'That which does not kill us makes us stronger,' though Kelly was singing about her life after being dumped by her boyfriend.

Within a minute of hearing this song, I got stronger with every step – my feet and my stomach pains were forgotten, and I drove my poles hard into the ground, yowling to myself as I pounded through the desert. And when I got to the end of the track, I clicked back and played it again – and again. Five times on the trot I listened to it, each time nearly as good as the first. I didn't want the song to become stale, like so many David Bowie and Fleetwood Mac songs from my youth, now reduced to homogenous stodge. So I limited my time on my iPod. Whenever I saw another runner, or if there was anything different to be seen or to be heard, I would pull out my headphones. The iPod would also come off whenever I saw a checkpoint. In those moments, I wanted to revel in the event and the anticipation rather than allow myself to be swaddled in music.

There were other more serious problems with iPods, as I witnessed on the fifth stage after the double marathon.

*

It was my old friend the butcher, who I had first seen in the snow in February on the Pilgrim. He was a very big, very strong man, and he had far and away the heaviest rucksack of any of the competitors in the race. He had pots, he had pans, and – most amazing of all – he had fresh meat.

We'd first encountered him on Easter day, when Kate and I were on our evening walk. We were very content. We'd had our food, we'd treated our blisters and we had each filed our 1,000-characters of scintillating copy to the *Sun*. It was night-time and the harvest moon was just past full, low and orange against the stars. When we walked together on those nights in the desert, I liked to shamble, very slowly, dawdlingly slow. I savoured the scents of the desert. And I loved the quiet companionship of this woman.

We had started holding hands when we walked.

As we'd gone out for our evening stroll, Kate in her longjohns, her fleece and her stained white beanie, she had quietly slipped her hand into mine. It was small and warm and dry, and I gave it a squeeze. It was an acknowledgement of… I don't really know. I was in the moment, and that moment was about nothing more than having Kate's hand in my own.

'Happy Easter,' she'd said.

'It's been different. Stuck in the Sahara.'

'Jesus would have felt right at home.'

We'd done one circuit, about 600 yards, and had arrived back at our tent. Neither of us wanted to stop. 'Shall we do another?' I asked.

'Let's.'

It was on this second circuit that we came across the butcher. From some way off, we could see him squatting over his stove.

'That smells different,' I'd said.

'It smells like sausages,' Kate said.

And it *was* sausages. Not content with bringing every conceivable bit of clobber, the butcher had bulked out his huge Bergen rucksack with several kilos of meat. Not freeze-dried meat, but fresh meat: sausages, steaks, bacon, even chops. It was even said that he had a few eggs for his morning fry-up.

We ambled over to the jolly butcher. He'd only just got in to the bivouac an hour earlier and was now cooking himself up six fat pork sausages. He sat crosslegged on his sleeping bag and was poking at the sausages with his tongs. He was bald and sweaty, the Friar Tuck of the Sahara.

We stopped by his fire. He looked up and smiled as he took a bite out of a sausage.

'You must be the only person who's brought along sausages,' I laughed.

'Like as not,' he said. 'Though I'll bet the Commissaires have got a load. Have you seen the food they're on?'

'Some of it.'

'They eat like kings.' He took another bite of sausage, meditating over it for a moment. 'They drink like kings too.'

'There have to be a few perks for coming out here to look after our blisters,' said Kate. She stooped and warmed her hands by the fire.

'And they party,' said the butcher. He gave the pan an expert flip and the sausages rolled onto their backs. 'They'll be at it like knives.'

Since the butcher was not running the race, he'd figured it didn't make much difference whether his pack weighed 15 kilos or 25 kilos. And since he loved his meat, what were a few more kilos of sausages here or there?

'Like one?' he asked.

'Yes please!' Kate said.

He pronged a sausage on a stick and we ate it together as we continued our walk. The sausage was crispy black, deeply charred, and so hot that I could barely take a bite.

We came across the jolly butcher again the next day as he was getting rid of some of his kit. The second day tended to be when runners started to pare down their rucksacks. Mostly they'd be throwing away food, particularly puddings. After a day of sugar and vanilla, the very last thing you want to eat at night is yet more sweet stuff.

The butcher was dumping clothing too, though he was still carrying quite a weight. I'm not sure if he'd packed his Bergen wrong. As all boyscouts learn, the heavy stuff should be packed into the middle of the rucksack rather than at the bottom. It settles more easily on the shoulders. The butcher's rucksack seemed very top heavy.

Then, on the fifth stage, we saw him, clattering along through the dunes. He'd clipped his frying pan, billycan and stove to the back of his rucksack, and they continuously clinked together. The sound of it started to get on your nerves after a while.

He was some way ahead of us but we eventually caught up with him.

'How's the jolly butcher?' I asked.

'Wishing he could get his iPod to work,' he said, without looking up. He was fiddling with it, smashing the buttons with his fat thumbs.

'Sand got into it yesterday?' I asked.

'What a storm!' he said.

We mooched on. We were skirting along the crest of a steep-sided dune, sticking to the ridge where it was easier to navigate. A third of a sand dune is made up of air, which is why you sink so much.

We hadn't gone far when we heard a bellow. The butcher was teetering on the crest, and then his massive Bergen took him right over the edge. He cartwheeled through the sand, rolling and rolling with his great rucksack still tight to his back, kicking up a small dust cloud. Even from a distance, I could see random bits of kit spraying across the sand. He landed in a heap at the bottom of the dune and did not move.

We jogged over to him. My feet were suddenly loose and easy as I slid through the sand.

The butcher was lying on his side, his damp clothes and red sweaty face dusted with sand. He'd lost his sunglasses and his cheeks had been grazed. Blood trickled from his nose.

I'd thought he might be unconscious, but his eyes were open and he recognised me.

'Help me off with this,' he said.

I unclipped the Bergen and Kate helped me tug it off his shoulders. It was still very heavy, nearly 20 kilos.

Kate gave him some water. He sat in the sand and poured the water loosely over his face, letting it trickle over his mouth and cheeks.

'Are you okay?' I asked.

He put down the bottle and started to twist and flex. It was then that I saw his ankle. His foot was kicking out at a sharp 45-degree angle.

He noticed it then too.

'Bugger,' he said. We stared at it. It looked horribly painful. There was nothing much to say.

'I'm sorry mate.'

'That's me out.'

'I'm sorry.'

He blew out his fat cheeks and sighed as he stared up at the sky.

'Shall I set off a flare?' I offered.

'No, I'll do it,' he said. 'Always wanted to set off a flare.'

'Are you sure?'

'First though – time for a fry-up. The buggers'll take all my food off me when they pick me up.'

He looked around for his stove and his frying pan. The pan was halfway up the dune. Kate went to retrieve it, and I chatted with him for a while.

The last we saw of him – the last we ever saw of him – he was sitting there at the bottom of that dune, all alone, frying sausages in the heat of the desert. I wish I'd taken a picture. He had quite filled the pan with sausages and steaks, and the smoke and the sizzle drifted straight up to the noonday sun. I waved to him from the top of the dune, and the butcher waved back with his tongs still in his hand. It's tough getting drummed out on the fifth stage, especially after you've broken the back of the beast.

'Did he say what happened?' Kate asked when we were back on our way.

'Fiddling with his iPod.'

'Poor sod.'

I offered her one of my caffeine gels. I only had a few of them; they were little luxuries for when the going got tough. No – that doesn't quite do them justice. They were little luxuries for when the going got *really* tough.

Kate sucked on the gel and squeezed out the last drops with her fingers. It perked her up. Caffeine is always in very short supply in the desert.

She sucked up some water and we walked on in silence as we thought about the butcher. 'Remember that sausage he gave us?' she said.

'Delicious.'

She smacked her lips and then licked them with the tip of her tongue. 'It was the best sausage I've ever tasted.'

'Must have been an MdS sausage then.'

She laughed and slipped her arm through mine. We walked a ways in the sun like that, hip to hip, her warm arm pressed lightly against my elbow.

CHAPTER 11

I was in the queue for the charter flight to Ouarzazate. There were well over 150 of us, skittish, like horses before the Grand National.

Kate was standing next to me while her boyfriend Edward got a coffee. He had taken the day off work to take her to the airport.

There was a weight limit of 20 kilos for our larger bags, though this was only enforced by one of the check-in staff. Kate and I waited for Zara, who seemed more amenable and less strict with weight requirements.

'What do you think we're doing?' I asked Zara when we got to her. 'Who are we?'

Zara looked from me to Kate, and then her eyes glided over the rest of the MdS competitors. She had a homely face and was happy to chat.

'And you're going to Ouarzazate?' she said. She pronounced it correctly. It's not 'Ooo-arr-za-zarte' or 'Ooozzza-zarte.' The city is pronounced 'Wazza-Zatt.'

'Are you police?' she asked.

'Does she look like a cop?' I gestured to Kate.

'She could be.'

'No, we're not cops.'

'Forces?' Zara tagged my bag without even looking at the weight.

'No – we're going off for a race in the Sahara.'

'One of those, eh? Which one's this one?'

'The Marathon des Sables.' I hefted Kate's bag up onto the scales.

'Another marathon, is it? Those sort of desert marathons are becoming quite popular, aren't they? We had some lads going off to do a really long one…' Zara paused as she clipped our tickets together. 'Might have been the Gobi. What's it costing, if you don't mind my asking?'

'With kit? At least four-and-a-half grand.'

'Four-and-a-half thousand pounds!' A look of absolute incredulity passed over Zara's face, tinged almost with horror at the sheer wastefulness of what we were doing. 'You could spend a fortnight in any five-star hotel in the world for that! You could go to that spa in Thailand my mum's always talking about, Chiva-Som.'

'Chiva-Som or the Marathon des Sables?' I said. 'No contest.'

'I know where I'd prefer my boyfriend to take me.' She laughed and handed over our tickets. I looked back as we were walking away and caught Zara rolling her eyes to her colleague. I don't know exactly what the look conveyed, but it was something along the lines of 'Mad as March hares'.

Kate was sniggering as she put on her rucksack. 'Did she just imply that I'm your girlfriend?'

'Either that or you're my daughter.'

'I'll go for girlfriend any day.'

'Quite right too – I give my daughters merry hell at home. They think I'm an absolute tyrant.'

We were still laughing when we found Edward in the café. He was disconsolately drinking a cappuccino and twitching over his mobile phone, though every ten seconds or so he would look up to catch sight of us.

He smiled and stood up.

'Beyond the call of duty, delivering your girlfriend right to the airport,' I said.

He shook my hand. 'You're going to take good care of her?' he asked.

'It'll be Kate who's taking care of me.'

I like my goodbyes to be very short; in fact, I have no problem not even saying goodbye at all, just disappearing quietly from the party without any hoo-ha whatsoever.

One thing I particularly dislike is having to hang around while other people say their goodbyes.

'I'll see you at the gate,' I said to Kate, and I clapped Edward on the shoulder as I left the pair of them to it. How I remember my goodbyes with girlfriends past. We would eke out every last minute together, until the train doors were all but being slammed in our faces. I never enjoyed it, but I did it all the same; the long and sometimes tearful goodbyes seemed to be all part and parcel of being 'a boyfriend.' Not now though. Now, with Elise, it's a dry peck on the lips, and a 'Have a great trip, and see you when you get back.'

There were over 200 of us at the gate. It was the first time that we'd ever been together. For months, years, we'd been training in quiet isolation. Now at Gatwick there were suddenly scores of us; we might have had different dreams and different motivations, but every one of us was similarly driven and similarly deranged.

I had spotted Del Esbit very quickly. He was talking to three men, hands on hips, a touch of a swagger about him. He was the top dog already making his mark. He wore a very tight white T-shirt with the words, 'Fit. For. It.'

'I don't need to prepare for the MdS,' I overheard him saying. 'I'm marathon-fit. Any day, every day, I'm ready for it.'

On the flight, Del switched to the role of court jester. When the stewardesses came round with the duty free, Del pretended to steal a carton of cigarettes from the front of the trolley.

I admit it now: I found him extraordinary, in the way, perhaps, that a naturalist might be enthralled by the antics of some freakish throwback. I had never come across anyone like him and – at least in small doses – his primal behaviour was utterly compelling.

In small doses.

The aircraft crew were interested in their odd assortment of passengers, asking about our training and our kit, and taking good care of us. We ate every scrap of food that they gave us, all but licking the polystyrene plates.

There was a queue for the aircraft toilet on the plane. Lawson was at the front; I had not seen him since the Pilgrim. He was very excited.

'I heard some great advice for the Marathon des Sables,' he said.

'Let's hear it.'

'"There are times in the race when you may experience joy and even extreme elation."'

'Oh yeah?'

'"Do not worry. This feeling will soon pass."'

'Thanks for that,' I laughed. 'Really useful to know.'

The toilet door banged open and out came Del. There was a horrible smell. Lawson put his head into the toilet and immediately ducked back out again. 'I'll pass for the moment,' he said.

'Frightened by a bit of shit?' Del said. 'Better get used to it if you're doing the Marathon des Sables.'

'I'm not frightened of shit,' Lawson said. 'I'm just phobic about shits.'

Del took off his sunglasses to reveal craggy grey eyes. 'Where have I seen you two before?'

'The Pilgrim,' Lawson said. 'You gave a very fine talk there.'

Del clicked his fingers, and his index finger turned into a gun pointing at Lawson. 'That's right. I thought I told you to lose a stone…' He broke off and grabbed Lawson's midriff. 'Not put it on!'

'He should have gone on one of your training courses, Del,' I said, sipping my water.

'I'd have told him not to waste his time,' Del said. 'People like you really make me laugh. You turn up without any training, without any kit… and then on about day two, you realise the MdS isn't so funny.'

'It must be a bit funny,' said Lawson, 'Why else do you keep coming back?'

'Done any other ultras apart from the Pilgrim?' Del asked Lawson.

'I've done the West Highland Way.'

'That's not a proper ultra.'

'Would it qualify if I'd lost all my toenails?' Lawson asked.

'You're funny,' Del said. 'You two are so funny. Let's see if you're still laughing in the middle of the race. Let's see if you're still laughing when you've run out of water and your feet are killing you.'

'I'll certainly be laughing,' said Lawson. 'Haven't you worked out yet that the MdS is all in the head?'

Del realised he was not going to get the better of us with this verbal jousting. He stood there, brawny arms folded across his chest in the manner of a Sergeant Major with a new recruit.

'I am so looking forward to seeing you on day six,' he said.

'The pleasure will be entirely mutual, Del,' Lawson said. 'Tell me – do you already have a boyfriend?'

I laughed and I did the nose trick, water snorting out of my nostrils. It was not an auspicious start for our relationship with Del, but it was fairly indicative of how things turned out between us.

Out of the window, I could see the desert, endless, featureless, hot, bleak and treeless. In the distance, still holding up the sky, was the long snow-white strip of the Atlas mountains, stretching the length of the horizon, 1,600 miles all the way from Morocco right through to Tunisia. I pointed them out to Lawson.

'That's a dead giant,' I said.

Lawson stooped to squint out of the window. 'It is?'

'Atlas, biggest of all the giants,' I said. 'It was his job to hold up the sky.'

'What happened to him then?'

'He thought he was immortal. He thought he was the guy who could never be beat. And rather to his surprise, he discovered he was just as mortal as the rest of us.' I looked at the mountains and tried to imagine Atlas, bent down by the weight of the firmament above his head. 'He had an argument with Perseus and looked into the face of Medusa the Gorgon. He was turned to stone.'

'Turned to stone, was he?' Lawson said. 'Looking a bit weather-worn now, isn't he?'

'Probably the best thing for him. Must have been a tough gig holding up the sky.'

When we stepped off the plane, it was like opening the door to a blast furnace. The heat hit me like a wave, and I couldn't imagine doing *anything* in this temperature, let alone running through the desert.

I made the mistake of writing down 'journalist' as my occupation on my immigration form. I didn't think it would make any difference, but for ten minutes they grilled me about my intentions in Morocco. When I got through to the baggage reclaim, Kate was already waiting with my bag. She laughed when she saw me. With every minute in Morocco, she was growing in stature and confidence.

'So what did you write on your immigration form?' I asked.

'I said I was a project manager.'

'Cute.'

We got on the last of the five Brit buses and were driven through Ouarzazate, Morocco's Hollywood. No one talked much on the coach. We devoured the city with our eyes, staring at the red terracotta new-builds, all in the same Moorish style, low-slung and crenellated. Dogs wandered the streets. There were few people about in the heat of the day.

I liked the Berbère Palace. It was an old hotel, dark and opulent, and littered all about with film props. At first – until I learned of Ouarzazate's film status – I could not understand why these bits of movie bric-a-brac were littered along the corridors. There were two Egyptian Gods from *Asterix and Obelix*, Caesar's throne from *Cleopatra* and a monkey's cage, the size of a large barrel, from the film *David*. They looked impressive, as if they were carved from marble or hewn from stone, but they were all made from either plastic or polystyrene; all style and no substance. And there were posters too, as well as one of our old favourite *Casablanca*. 'Here's looking at you, kid!'

Kate and I were the last in the queue. We'd never discussed the matter; we'd both just automatically assumed we'd be sharing a room together.

And though nothing was said, I was aware of a certain tension in the air as we dragged our bags to our room. It was not like anything was going to happen. It was not that anything *could* ever happen. But we were going to be alone at night for the first time.

I wondered what it would be like to kiss her.

Outside the hotel proper, there was a warren of ochre hotel rooms, hundreds of them, all paired up in little cottages. I could smell jasmine and orange blossom. Compared to rain-swept England, it was idyllic, with fountains and palm trees, sysel, roses and mimosa, and new vines climbing up the sandy walls.

I stopped and plucked a ripe orange from a tree. I cut it into quarters with my pen-knife and gave Kate a piece. We stood in the sun in silence and each bit into the orange. It was disgusting, sour as hell. I laughed as this look of revulsion spread across Kate's face.

It helped, a little, to break the ice.

We found room 429 and walked through the vestibule. I fumbled with the keys in the lock. The room was dark and smelled of fresh paint. I dropped my bags on the floor and swept open the shutters. Light flooded in. There was a TV, a wardrobe, a bathroom, a small single bed and, over by the window, a large double bed.

Kate dropped her rucksack onto the single.

'You have the double,' I said.

She looked at me. Did I imagine the hint of a wry smile on her face? 'No, you have the double.'

'Honestly, Kate – you have the double.'

'No, you have it.'

I shrugged. 'Okay I'll have the double,' I said. 'You'll be in it after the race.'

'Will I now?'

Just the merest whiff of innuendo. I observed it, wondered whether to ignore it, and then decided not to. 'Yes, you will.'

I nodded at her, and all the while I was so aware of these swirling undercurrents, of tides and riptides, surging and eddying this way and that, yet not quite discernible on the surface. I wished I were a mindreader, that I might have been able to fathom just what it was she was thinking.

'Let's have a swim,' she said.

'Sure,' I said.

'Race you. Four lengths.'

'Let's make it ten.'

'Breaststroke?'

'Of course.'

Runners were milling all about the pool and by the bar – though, oddly, there was no one actually in the pool. I wasn't sure why.

Kate peeled off her khaki shorts and her white T-shirt to reveal a blue one-piece swimsuit. It was elegant, functional, the swimsuit of a woman who does a lot of swimming. As she put on her goggles, I tugged off my shirt and tossed it onto a sun lounger. I was aware that we were being watched; or, rather, that Kate was being watched.

I was just the guy in the faded pink shorts standing next to the beautiful woman.

I put on my goggles, squeezing them tight onto my eyes.

'Ten lengths?' Kate said. She was bending over, one leg in front of the other, hands on the edge of the pool. 'Go!'

The water was freezing. It was as cold as any pool that I have ever been in, the water hitting me like a physical punch, spiking through to my core. I swam two strokes under water and came up for air. My skin tingled. I could not believe such a cold pool could exist in sun-blistered Morocco.

Kate was a little ahead of me on the second length. She reached the end and got straight out of the pool. Without a word, I followed her.

'Ouch!' she said. Her hair was sleeked back. She had goosebumps on her legs and I could see every taut, tight curve of her body underneath her swimsuit. 'That wasn't pleasant.'

'We need a hot shower.'

We went back to our room, two pairs of wet footsteps on the peachy tiles.

I was fiddling with the TV when Kate pulled off her swimsuit. It was nothing overt.

I didn't look, but I could see her in my peripheral vision. Just as she was wrapping herself in a white towel, I turned towards her. I caught a glimpse of breasts and of leg.

She was watching me. She gave me the most disarming smile. 'Better get used to it,' she said. 'You'll see much worse in the desert.'

'Is that a promise?'

'If you like.'

*

We only had one other shower together, if you can call it that.

But it was far and away the most memorable shower of my life.

It was on that extraordinary second day in the desert, the Saturday before Easter. We'd registered, done all our checks, and now there was nothing to do but loaf.

From Tent 71, we'd watched as Del had showered with his groupie, where they could be seen by the entire bivouac. Carlo had chafed Kate, asking her if she fancied having a shower too.

'Are you chicken?' he said. I think he fancied her. I'm sure he fancied her. We all fancied her. She was beautiful and she was lovely. And she was more than a little feisty too.

'No,' Kate said. 'I just don't want to have a shower with you.'

She looks to the left. She looks to the right. And then she looks at me, and I know for an absolute certainty that my number is up.

'Kim,' she said. 'I'll have a shower with you, Kim.'

'Me? You don't want to have a shower with me.'

She raised an eyebrow. 'Are *you* chicken?'

'Chicken?' I said, and at that moment I did not even have to pause for thought. 'Let's go, Kate.'

'Have you got enough water?' she asked.

'Couple of bottles. You?'

'Same.'

'Let's do it.'

I was just wearing shorts and a T-shirt. I slipped on my black leather sandals, cheap holiday shoes, though they had a thick sole and they were comfortable enough. Kate was putting the water bottles into a bag.

'I'll take that,' I said, slinging a towel round my neck, and we left the tent's shade to go out into the baking heat of the afternoon, just when the sand and the rocks were beginning to roast.

'Since they're all watching, we might as well make it look good,' said Kate and she took my hand. Our fingers interlocked. I gave them a squeeze.

'That's the spirit.' We swung our hands like a couple of children on the way to the beach.

'Done this before, have you?' she asked.

'Once – half a lifetime ago. Used to work at a hotel in Dorset. We all went skinny-dipping on the first day. God it was cold.'

'As cold as the pool at the Berbère Palace?'

'Not quite that cold. It was only the Channel.'

She looked so happy. She had begun to soar since we had arrived in Morocco. With no job, no boyfriend and nothing but her and the desert, she did not have a care in the world.

'I never dreamed I'd be stripping in the desert,' she said.

'Another rich new experience provided to you courtesy of the Commissaires of the Marathon des Sables.'

'Though I have always wondered what you'd look like with no clothes on.'

'I fear you have a very big disappointment ahead of you.'

She laughed and exhaled. 'I love it out here. I can do what I want, be what I want. It's—'

'Fun?'

'It's brilliant.'

From out of nowhere she kissed me on the cheek. 'That's for the guys in the bivouac.'

'They'll have the binoculars on us by now.'

'And this one's for you.' And she kissed me again on the cheek. And I ignored it, feigning the most complete indifference.

'You're a brazen hussy Kate,' I said. 'What would your boyfriend make of such behaviour?'

'What happens in the desert stays in the desert.'

'Quite so.'

We had walked through a sunken dip in the ground and past some thorn trees, which were dotted throughout the desert, thin and gnarled, with little green leaves and the most vicious thorns imaginable – over an inch long and as hard as nails. The thorns tended to fall in clusters and were like caltrops, spiked iron balls that could bring down a horse. Whichever way they fell, one spike was always left pointing vertically upwards. And even when the tree itself was long dead, the thorns would still linger in the sand for years afterwards, like uncharted mines, stabbing their jags into the feet of the unwary.

'Is this all right?' she said.

I looked back at the bivouac. It was some way off, our black tents rippling and shimmering in the heat.

'This'll be just fine.'

'Did you bring any sunscreen?'

I waved my blue bottle of Factor 50 spray. The girls used it on holiday. It was not the usual cool kit that was used on the MdS, but it did the job.

'Perfect.'

Without another word, she kicked off her shoes and pulled off her top. She wore a grey sports bra underneath, which she unclipped and tossed to the ground. It was all done in a very matter of fact way, as if there was nothing surprising or awkward about her taking off her top like this; as if we had been undressing in front of each other for years. I was suddenly aware that she was topless. I didn't really look.

I kicked off my black leather sandals and hauled off my shirt, exposing my pasty white flesh to the sun. I did that pathetic thing that middle-aged men do and sucked in my stomach.

I looked at Kate and Kate looked at me.

'I'll show you mine if you show me yours.' She wiped the hair out of her eyes, smiling at the challenge.

'I haven't heard that line in a while.'

What was I frightened of? Was I really embarrassed at the thought of being naked in front of Kate? That it might suddenly dawn on her that I was not quite the buffed Adonis that I appeared to be in the *Sun* newsroom... Well if there was one thing I was reasonably certain of, it was that Kate was not, nor had ever been, remotely interested in my looks.

I dropped my shorts, kicked them away and then, without looking at Kate, I opened a bottle and let the water trickle over my hair and face, eyes closed, basking in the warmth. The water trickled down my nose and cheeks and into my open mouth. I had not washed in 36 hours. With the sun on my dusty skin, the water was just beautiful.

'Let me help.'

I passed her the bottle.

'Got to give the guys in the tent something to look at.'

She had a tube of dehydrated wemmi wipes, each about the size of a fruit pastille. Just add water and they grow in your hand, turning into a small soapy flannel. Still not looking at Kate, I offered her my back and, as I stared out over the desert, she sponged my shoulders and the back of my neck. She was humming Fred Astaire, 'Dancing Cheek to Cheek'.

Her hands worked lower down my spine. She broke off to open another bottle of water, drizzling it over my shoulders. She was standing in front of me, flannelling my chest. I shut my eyes, revelling in the sun and her humming and the light movement of her hand. I longed for it to continue.

'Didn't expect to be doing this when I woke up this morning,' she said.

'It was always on the cards.'

'Yeah?'

'That's the point of the MdS – anything can happen.'

I felt the last of the water being poured over my head. I opened my eyes and there she stood in front of me, naked and grinning. Her eyes were vividly blue.

'The sand brings out the colour in your eyes,' I said.

'Pah! My turn?'

She knocked out a couple of wemmi wipes from the tube and gave them to me. I poured on water, watched them grow and, for the first time, I looked at Kate properly. She was pulling off her hairband and her hair fell loose about her neck. She looked at me over her shoulder, smiled, and stood there quite calm, feet square on the ground, hands loose by her sides.

Her hair turned sleek and brown when I poured on the water. I could see the white of her scalp, and I noticed a scar, long and deep, that stretched around the back of her head. Her hair did not grow on the scar. It slashed through her hairline like a white cut.

I wondered what had been the cause.

I could never ask her about it.

I stroked the wipe on her shoulders, very business-like. Her skin was so incredibly smooth. It spoke of daily lotions and nightly grooming. I was aware that I had not touched skin like this, a woman like this, in a long time. It was almost impossible to believe. I was naked. Kate was naked. I was flannelling her down.

'Gently,' she said.

I eased up, stroking the flannel over her skin as if I were waxing her back.

'Where did you get this all-over tan?' I asked. 'I thought you never stripped in public.'

'Best way to get ready for the heat.'

'I hope the guys in the tents are getting some pictures of this.'

'The perfect picture by-line for our next column.'

I laughed. Throughout the MdS, we were writing a 'His n' Hers' column for the *Sun*. Our mad master had wittily entitled it 'Beauty and the Beast,' and our joint picture by-line had lived up in full to all of my most gruesome expectations.

I poured water down her back. I was cool, dispassionate, just a guy pouring water over this bronzed statue, interested in the way the water eddied through the white dried sweat on her back. I watched it drip down her perfect runner's buttocks and then to her legs and then to the ground.

She turned to face me. Her eyes had been closed, but she opened them and looked at me. This haze of unspoken thoughts crackled between us, flickering like static electricity. Nothing was said.

I took another wipe and soaped her shoulders and her chin. I soaped to her collarbone. I looked at her breasts, though I did not go any further down.

'Shall we explore a little?' She sipped from the water bottle, breasts jutting, one hand artlessly on her hip; I wish I were a sculptor, that I could have captured her in marble.

We put on our shoes but left our clothes on the ground, more comfortable now with each other's nakedness. We walked to the same little hillock where Del had been earlier, and I flopped out the towel. We each took an edge of it and I passed Kate the sun lotion. She sprayed it onto her legs and chest, smoothing the lotion onto her skin in long languid circles. I put some on too, and then we lay back on the sand, almost shoulder to shoulder but not quite. I was not going to kiss her. That would have been taking advantage of what had just started out as a little dare.

And yet what we were doing seemed far more intimate than a mere kiss.

I thought about my girls, sitting tight at home as they wondered if their dad was going to pull through. At that moment, the girls might have been a million miles away, but they were still the very bedrock of my life. And though being in the MdS with Kate seemed beyond miraculous, I was also aware that, when compared to my family, it was nothing more than a mirage. Enticing. Alluring. But ultimately no more substantial than a desert dream.

'I wish I'd brought a camera,' I said. I spoke very softly. It was so still, no wind, no cloud, not a sound, nor a smell, just this epic arc of wilderness.

'What happens in the desert is supposed to stay in the desert.'

'It's not for anyone else,' I said. 'It's for me.'

We were both leaning back on our elbows now, studying the infinity of the desert, and it somehow seemed right and appropriate that we had nothing on. The hot sand lapped at my feet and my thighs. I looked over at Kate. She was studying my body, my chest, my legs, everything.

'Nice,' she said.

'You'd never guess I used to be a supermodel,' I said.

She laughed, and purred that one word that has such a wealth of meaning: 'Hmmm.'

Slowly, inexorably, I was falling in love.

CHAPTER 12

The more neurotic MdS competitors take along their own food to Ouarzazate; they're terrified of picking up some bug from the hotel vegetables. So, while the rest of the runners dine like kings in the Berbère Palace, the fastidious types eat rehydrated pasta in their rooms. Other runners wouldn't touch alcohol either, as if a few beers on the Thursday night would drag down their performance three days later.

But as for my little team, well, on that last night in the Berbère, we drank hard. The bar was cool and dark, with high ceilings and low, comfortable sofas. It was extremely busy, as, for the first time, the Brits came together. We would meet the other nationalities the next day in the desert, but that night was a night for the Brits. And a few Canadians, I remember them too. One man in his fifties had spent four days travelling from Canada to Morocco – and had been dressed in his full race kit throughout. It was mildly bizarre, but then that's the way of the MdS and all the sorry souls who choose to run it.

Kurtz was at the bar. With his scars and his eye patch, he looked hard as teak. He drank and he listened, and then he would drink some more. We drank straight from the beer bottles.

'Here's tae us,' I said, chinking.

'Wha's like us?'

'Damn few, an' they're aw deid,' I said, completing the ritual.

Martin was indulging in one of his favourite occupations: telling MdS horror stories. I had heard several variations of them before.

'Some people use methylated spirits to toughen up their feet,' Martin said. 'But there are certain problems concomitant with that—'

'Concomitant!' said Lawson. 'Get you!'

'Like what?' I said.

'Well,' Martin said, taking a long pull on his beer. 'We had one guy in the hospital. He'd been soaking his feet in a bowl of meths, sitting in the garden, drinking a beer and reading the paper – as you do when you're enjoying yourself out in the sun. He gets it into his tiny head to have a cigarette. He lights his fag and... Ba-boom!'

Even I hadn't heard that story before. The ending was so unexpected that we exploded with laughter.

'You ever see the feet?' Lawson said.

'I did, as a matter of fact,' Martin said. 'He won't be running the Marathon des Sables for a long while yet.' He chuckled as he scooped up some peanuts. 'There was another guy who also went down the meths route a few years ago: every morning, the month before the race, he would dunk his feet in meths. On race day, the skin on his feet was so hard and so thick, it was like shoe leather. Know what happened to him?'

Martin paused, looking us all in the eye as he ate one peanut. We all dutifully shook our heads. 'Your feet grow in the heat,' Martin said. 'They can grow by as much as two sizes. And that's what happened to this guy. His feet swelled up. The only thing was that his thick soles didn't grow by so much as a millimetre. They couldn't grow, they were so hard and they'd lost all their suppleness. The soles of his feet just broke off. They peeled off his foot like the sole of an old shoe.'

'So did he make it?' I asked.

'No,' Martin said. 'You're more or less buggered if you've lost your soles.'

'Or your soul,' piped Lawson.

Kate joined us at the bar. She sure was a head-turner. It was one of those moments when every single man was aware that an absolute beauty had walked into the room. Discreetly and not so discreetly, they checked her out, taking in her hair, her clothes, her disposition and, last but not least, the company she was keeping.

Kurtz had 15 beers, ice-cold, already lined up in front of him at the bar. He offered her one and she took it. 'Thanks,' she said. 'Cheers!'

She took a delicious swig from the bottle and we basked in her reflected glory.

'Have you seen that guy with the ironing board?' she said.

'An ironing board?' Simon said.

'He was taking it to his room.'

'Maybe he wants all his clothes pressed before the big day,' Lawson said.

'No he's taking it with him,' she said. 'He's running the race with it.'

'Boll-*ocks*!' said Martin.

'It's true,' she said. 'You'll see him tomorrow. I had a chat with him. He got it for £10 off Amazon. Together with the iron—'

'He's got an iron too?'

'With the board, it weighs about five kilos.'

Maybe it was the booze, and maybe we were just wired at the thought of our desert endeavour, but we were off again, howling with laughter at the thought of this madman with an ironing board strapped to his back – though, of course, he was no more mad than the rest of us.

And best of all, it was true. There was indeed a man who ran the sands with an ironing board. He was one of these 'extreme ironers' who take their ironing boards up mountains and to the bottom of the deepest oceans. The photographers and the TV cameramen just loved this prime exhibit from the 'Crazy Brit' camp.

'Apparently there's a guy here who's suffering from extreme agoraphobia,' Carlo said. 'He hates wide open spaces.'

'It'll be kill or cure,' Lawson said. 'How did he train?'

'I'm told he did it on a running machine in his house,' Carlo said. 'He's a computer wonk, so doesn't have to go out to work. And then he spends two or three hours a day on his running machine, so he does.'

'And now he's come out to the Sahara?' Kate said.

'Quite a good story,' I said. 'If it's true.'

'I haven't seen him,' Carlo said. 'Just heard that he's with us.'

'Yeah,' Lawson said. 'He'll be the guy quivering in the corner.'

I never did find out if there was an agoraphobic on that MdS, but it's one of those stories that's too good to question – part of the MdS lore. We went through for supper, walking past Ramses II's throne from *The Ten Commandments*. It seemed to be made of white marble and looked very imposing. But, like the story of the poor old agoraphobic runner, it did not do to touch it, or to probe. Just look, and enjoy, and then move on.

The dining room was large and well lit, filled with round tables covered in white tablecloths. Down the middle of the room, they had laid on a buffet that would have fed a battalion. A long table was set up with a score of different salads, fish and fruit and other dainties. At the end of the room, the head chef was slicing into a vast haunch of beef, about the size of a drum, the biggest I'd ever seen. There were stews and tagines with lamb and apricot, and great trays of chicken drumsticks. We swarmed over the food like locusts. The seven of us loaded up our plates with salad and sat at one of the round tables. It was the first convening of what would be Tent 71.

We ordered red wine and toasted each other, all the while wondering how on earth this adventure would turn out; who would thrive, and who would crumble, and just who we would be on speaking terms with at the end of it all. I think the guys liked Kate being in our tent; she added a touch of class.

She was tucking into a huge plate of sardines and salad and pasta. I remember the relish with which she ate her food. I also remember thinking: over 250 Brits staying in a foreign hotel, and not a single complaint about either the bedrooms or the food. Can you imagine? (Well, except for those two guys who'd lost their bags, complete with shoes and gaiters – disaster).

Simon and Martin, meanwhile, were vying with each other over the extremes they had gone to in order to lighten their packs.

'Did you repack all your Mountain Meals?' Simon said.

'Get rid of all that tin foil?' Martin said. 'Of course. They're all packed in sandwich bags. It saved 350 grammes – I weighed it.'

'I cut the end off my toothbrush last night.'

'Check,' Martin said. 'That was 17 grammes.'

I looked over at Carlo, who was on his second plate of pink beef. He tapped the side of his head with his finger and rolled his eyes. We were witnessing yet another form of desert madness.

'What about your zips?' Simon asked. 'Have you changed your zips?'

'My zips?' Martin said. 'What about the zips?'

'Most zips are made of metal. I changed mine for plastic.'

'Ohh,' Martin said, slightly crestfallen. 'Didn't think of that.'

I felt a presence behind me. Somebody was holding the back of my chair.

Martin looked up and, zip woes suddenly forgotten, he beamed with delight. 'The last of our tentmates!' he said. 'Good to see you Del!'

I turned in my chair and looked up, Martin's words only just beginning to register: Del was going to be our tentmate.

'All right, lads?' Del said. He was wearing baggy blue jeans and a grey T-shirt. He gave us all a little nod, pulling up a chair and squeezing in between Kate and Lawson before helping himself to the red wine. He slurped and sighed and then looked round the table. 'Any of you lot done this race before?'

'I have,' Simon said.

''Course you have. I remember. You know what it'll be like,' he said. 'And as for the rest of you – who knows?'

I watched the others. Kurtz spat out a bone from a chicken wing. Lawson mopped up some mayonnaise with a piece of bread and Carlo poured himself more wine. Simon and Martin looked at Del with what might have been awe. But Kate did it best. She pulled out a notebook from her back pocket and started scribbling.

Del peered at her. 'What you writing there, love?' he asked.

'Just stuff,' she said. She continued to write.

'Funny sort of writing.'

'It's shorthand. Teeline.'

'Are you a secretary?'

The notepad was returned to her pocket. For the first time, Kate looked at Del and smiled. 'Something like that.'

'You can take *dick*-tation from me any time,' he said, hitting the first syllable and winking.

'That's very funny, Del,' she said. 'Are all your jokes like that?'

Lawson patted his mouth with his napkin and then smiled. 'If so, we might have to *dick*-cline your request to join the tent.'

Carlo ran with it. 'Which would pre-*dick*-ate you having to sleep elsewhere.'

'You might even have to sleep on a *dick*-chair,' I added.

We laughed at this preposterous man who had just been foisted on us by Martin and Simon. He was awful. Martin was desperate to change the subject.

'Tell me Del,' he said. 'Should I take along a Thermarest?'

Del grimaced, as if about to deliver some great wisdom from on high. 'Wouldn't bother,' he said. 'They weigh at least 400 grammes. It's not too uncomfortable sleeping on the ground.'

'I didn't think they were for comfort,' Carlo said.

Del chuckled. 'The voice of experience speaks.'

'The Thermarests keep you off the ground,' Carlo said. 'They stop your body heat leaching into the sand.'

'Sounds like you know all about it.'

'I know it's going to be freezing at night.'

Del plucked a drumstick from Lawson's plate and took a bite. 'Seen the forecasts, have you?'

'I have, as it happens.'

*

Carlo was right. It was cold at night.

Some nights it was almost balmy, so hot that we were out of our sleeping bags. We would drowse for a little while and then wake up, too hot to be comfortable. Even after a week in the Sahara, the fluctuating temperatures would still catch you unawares. Sometimes, if you were lucky, it would also be cloudless, and you would be able to see the gibbous moon, just past the full; I would put on my glasses, so that the blur of stars became suddenly brilliant.

But most nights it was just cold, unbelievably cold, so cold that you could not imagine how just a few hours earlier you had been sweltering in 50 degree heat. It starts to get cold soon after sundown, and, because there is no television to watch and no alcohol to drink, most of us would turn in for the night; by 8 p.m., almost all of us would be asleep, apart from the late birds like Lawson and Kate and me, who would read into the night, occasionally whispering, as we did our best not to wake the others.

The coldest night was on Easter Saturday, the night before the start of the race. It's a more intense kind of cold, too, because the air is so dry. I had put on my socks and my black longjohns, my thermal vest and my fleece, but it was not nearly enough. If I didn't move, I could trap some warm air in my sleeping bag, but I could not get to sleep. Your mind twitches between wanting to stay in your sleeping bag and wanting to put on more clothes, and usually general inertia wins through. But eventually you come to realise that you're so uncomfortable that doing anything at all is better than doing nothing.

I searched for my headtorch, but could't find it. It could have been anywhere – perhaps at the top of my rucksack, perhaps lying in one of my shoes. Along with being a Late Charlie, I am also spectacularly, chaotically untidy.

I was making a lot of noise, crashing about in the dark as the others pretended they were asleep. Eventually, I gave up looking for the torch and dived straight into the rucksack. I found my cagoule, but couldn't find my hat. I had to do it all by touch. I would pull some garment out of the sack, feel it, and then discard it to the side. Clothes and food packages were littered all around my sleeping bag, and it was only when my rucksack was empty that I remembered leaving my hat by my shoes, just in case I needed to go out at night. More noise, more squirming, as I pulled on my crinkly coat and my hat, and if there was anyone still asleep in the tent, they'd be able to sleep through a hurricane.

I pull the hat down tight over my ears and curl up into a crinkling ball; and even though I've now got my coat on, I'm still cold. I close my eyes, but with the race about to start in a few hours, it's impossible to sleep. My mind is churning over so many things. I think about this monster that lies ahead, and whether I will make it, and how badly I'm going to be injured. I know it's going to hurt. I know it's going to hurt a lot – and to think I'm paying for the privilege of putting myself through it. And, of course, because she's lying right next to me, I'm thinking about Kate; in particular about the shower we shared in the desert just a few hours earlier, and the way that we had basked naked in the sun, with the hot sand lapping at our feet.

She's awake too, I know she is. I can hear her teeth chattering. She has no meat on her, not like me, so she must be really feeling the cold.

I'm turned away from her, curled up on my side, fingers tight around the opening of my sleeping bag, trying to keep in all the precious hot air.

I hear Kate rustling. She's wriggling over towards me in her sleeping bag.

'Are you awake?' she whispers.

'Of course I am,' I say. 'I'm frozen.'

'So am I,' she says. 'Budge over.'

At first I think that she's going to snuggle next to me in her sleeping bag.

But she's not.

She gets out of her sleeping bag.

And she gets into mine.

It is a very tight squeeze. I can't quite believe it, but Kate and I are in the same sleeping bag. I thank my stars that it's so cold outside - and that I had the immense foresight to bring along such a huge sleeping bag that could, at a pinch, accommodate two people; Martin and Simon would have been horrified at having to lug this thing round the desert.

I'm still facing away from Kate and she snuggles in behind me, her body melding to mine, knees pressed hard against my knees, her front pressed to my back. Her arm immediately snakes about my waist and I hold onto her hand.

'That's better,' she whispers, her lips barely inches from my ear.

'Much better.' I say. 'Your teeth have stopped chattering.'

'I've never been so cold.' She gives me a squeeze, and though the whole thing is so downright strange, it also suddenly seems like the most normal thing in the world, to be snug next to her as we share our body heat.

I would like to turn round, so that I'm facing her. But it was quite tight just for Kate to get into the sleeping bag, and there's not much room. But it doesn't matter. I'm pretty damn happy with how things are turning out. There's nowhere else in the world I would rather be. And perhaps it's for the best I can't turn to face Kate; there's only so much temptation I can resist, and if we were face to face, I might have kissed her. And that might not be the best start to the Marathon des Sables.

Or it might be the most perfect start imaginable.

'Night night,' says Kate, her lips on my ear.

'Night.'

She hugs me, and her hand worms its way underneath my coat, my fleece and my long-sleeved thermal vest. She presses her palm against my stomach, skin to skin.

I lie quite still, wondering what she will do next.

There is a pulse as, momentarily, she presses herself hard against me. Her hand strokes my stomach, and as I ponder all that this means and all that I shouldn't do, and all that I would like to do, I hear the soft sound of her heavy breathing. Kate is asleep.

CHAPTER 13

We left the Berbère Palace straight after breakfast. We had gorged ourselves as if we were about to start some monumental fast. I had had coffee and an omelette, orange juice that I'd squeezed myself, then cheese and fruit and hams, and another coffee, and another coffee, and by the time I was climbing on board the white coach, my stomach felt as tight as a gourd. And yet, within minutes of us setting off for the desert, they'd be handing out our packed lunches and we'd all start grazing, nibbling on dried apricots and mini salamis.

Del provided us with a small but interesting little cameo as Kate and I boarded the coach. He was one of the first on, Kate and I right behind him. The drill was to put our main bags in the luggage bay under the coach and keep our rucksacks with us.

All perfectly simple, and yet...

Del's bag is large, at least three feet by two feet, and made of durable grey plastic. He squats down, pops the bag into the bay – and then leaves it there, right at the front, blocking any further bags from being put on.

I actually have to climb inside the bay to push Del's bag out of the way.

Kate gives me my rucksack.

'Tosser,' I say.

'You said it,' she says.

We already knew he was a sexist oaf, but this small incident told us, clear as a bell, that he was also an inconsiderate shit.

There was not much talk on the coach. We were all dwelling on the ordeal ahead – for there it was right in front of us, the MdS Road Book. Soon after we'd left Ouarzazate, they'd handed out the Road Books, A5 in size, about 100 pages, with maps and regulations and detailed itineraries for every stage.Mario Angel, a runner from Argentina, was on the cover; he'd been in the 2011 race. He looked rugged, hard, the very epitome of an MdS runner.

There are about five or six different courses for the race, and the runners don't know that year's course until they're actually on the way. There was talk that the 2012 course was a real backbreaker, the better to weed out the weak, but that might have been another desert myth. Some said the MdS Commissaires revelled in running the toughest footrace on earth and they'd set the most gruelling course imaginable in order to ensure a good percentage of dropouts.

We'd be heading east, it seemed, following the sun. I leafed through the maps, mouthing the names of these exotic places I had never heard of as I traced a route – from Ammouguer to *Oued El Aatchana*, on to Taourirt Mouchanne and El Maharch, and then the big one, stretching 51 miles to *Jebel El Mraïer*, and after that there was just the small matter of a marathon to Merdani. The last day, Stage Six, was barely a ten-miler – ten miles! I remember wondering at the time why the last stage was so short. It went through some sand dunes, but that was all I could see.

There were several pages of rules and regulations, as well as advice written in both English and French. I read it all in rather a half-hearted fashion. Just as with the equipment that you take out on the trip, it was difficult to tell what was important and what was not.

I nudged Kate. 'Listen to this,' I said. '"In the event of a serious sand storm when visibility drops to almost nil, it is imperative that competitors stop immediately. Do not panic!"'

'I'll try not to panic,' she said. She was eating an orange, her shoulder nestling comfortably against mine. We were off to run the world's toughest footrace and I was sitting next to Kate. I was so happy.

'"Use your common sense,"' I quoted from the Road Book. '"And No Heroics!"'

'I'll leave them to you.'

'"Do not walk bare foot in the bivouac area, in order to avoid thorns in your feet or being bitten by insects."'

Kate placed the orange peel in one of the bin bags in the aisle. 'Tell me something I didn't know.'

'"The use of mobile phones in the bivouac and along the route of the MdS will not be allowed and will be subject to a penalty."' I pointed out the paragraph in the Road Book. 'Edward's not going to like that. He'll just have to write you lots of lovely emails.'

'That'll be a first.'

'"We remind you that over 40,000 emails are received during the race and distributed to participants in their Berber tent each day. This form of communication with the outside world is more in line with the MdS spirit."'

'Is there much more of this?'

'"Any runners with skin lesions may not use the swimming pool at the end of the race."'

'And I'd really been looking forward to another dip in that pool.'

'"We wish you an excellent Marathon des Sables and look forward to sharing a week of adventure with you!"'

After five hours, we were dumped out of the coaches and into the desert proper. It was hot and bleak and inhospitable, just sand and scrub stretching to the horizon. There were lorries to take us the last few miles to the bivouac – not flatbed trucks, but rugged high-sided lorries with great belching exhausts. They were better suited to carting quarry ore than carrying humans. We threw our cases on board and I helped Kate up.

Del was already there, sitting on his case. He was the old pro who knew all the dodges.

'Now you're going to wish you'd brought your buffs,' he said, laughing as he pulled his MdS buff right over his face. A moment later the lorry clunked into gear and we were enveloped in a cloud of dust and sand.

We did not see the bivouac until the lorries had parked up. We were like children on their first day at school, gradually finding our feet as we took in the two circles of black tents and the Commissaires' pristine white city. It was daunting, so very different. It was one of those times where, like it or not, you just have to get on with it.

The Brits were the first to the bivouac and had been assigned around 35 tents on the outer ring; the French, who had been staying in a different hotel, were camped next to us in the inner circle.

I dragged my wheelie bag through the dust, and within a matter of moments the wheels were jammed with sand. I also had six bottles of water, nine litres. There's always plenty of water to spare before the race, but come Sunday morning, your water is rationed and every drop you're given is docketed on that infamous plastic tag.

Martin, out front, bagged us a tent about 80 yards from the entrance to the bivouac, Tent 71, situated at about nine on the clockface. We followed him in. There was a thick rug on the ground and both sides of the tent were open. We dumped our bags at the side of the tent and lay down, resting against the rucksacks. We looked at each other and, gradually, we got our bearings, taking stock of our tent and our tentmates. Little by little, the grandeur of it all started to seep in.

We sipped water and watched the other nationalities drift in. It was only then, I think, that we realised how cosmopolitan, how multicultural, this whole extraordinary adventure would be.

'Shall we go for a walk?' Kate asked, and, with Lawson, we had our first stroll around the bivouac, like boulevardiers taking the air. There were flags everywhere and each nationality had a different flavour. The French were already gathering twigs and wood for their communal fires and there was an air of *joie de vivre* as old regulars were reunited. The Germans, who had only a few tents, were much more earnest about the task ahead of them; and the swaggering Americans who'd worked out so hard in the gym, as if large biceps were of any use in the Sahara.

You could also spot the thoroughbreds.

'See that guy?' Lawson said, pointing to a wiry man, slim, smiling and confident. 'I've been reading about him – Salameh Al Aqra. He's one of the frontrunners, a Jordanian cop. He's 42. I can even tell you what he eats.'

'What does he eat?' I said.

'Well...' said Lawson. 'He'll have potatoes for breakfast, dried dates and rice and raisins for lunch, and then for dinner he'll have noodles and veg.'

'No protein?' I said. 'How do you know all this?'

'Read an interview he gave. He also gets the runs, so his trainer has to carry a sachet of wet wipes.'

'Thanks for that,' Kate said. 'That's a really useful piece of information which, I'm afraid, I will not be able to forget.'

'He's sponsored by some Jordanian company,' Lawson blithely continued. 'The prize money is just gravy. Guess how many miles a week he does?'

'A hundred?' I ventured.

'Just fifty miles – that's all he does.'

'Lucky bastard.'

A few minutes later, we saw the favourite, Rachid el Morabity. He was the king of the MdS, had won the race the previous year. Though not this year. This year it would all end in disaster.

*

On the fourth stage, the long stage, the frontrunners played a splendid practical joke on Patrick Bauer and all the Commissaires – a joke that had Patrick absolutely popping with rage until he had the good grace to start laughing.

The bulk of the ne'er-do-well runners had the usual 9 a.m. start, with all the noise and the heat and the sweep of the helicopters; the fifty fastest men and the five fastest women started three hours later. A few tents were left up for them so they could stay out of the heat. They lounged and chatted and felt the adrenalin start to churn, and it was during this three hours that they cooked up their extraordinary plan.

Patrick, meanwhile, was haranguing us about a rogue runner from the Eurosport team who had accepted a can of Coke from one of the Commissaires. This was against the entire ethos of the MdS being a self-supporting race; the Eurosport team was docked three hours. (This would prove fatal. They came second in the overall standings, losing to Scotta Roata Chiusani by 2 hours, 59 minutes and 20 seconds. Ouch!)

I did not start out with Kate on the long day. I trudged alone instead, eight minutes of jogging and two minutes of walking, during which I would take my four sips of water and eat my single sports bean, and tug at my shirt and wriggle my shoulders and paint my lips. I like my lips to be moist.

It was the first time I came across a river. Over the previous two days, I'd seen a few patches of mud, and foolhardy runners would occasionally take off their shoes and socks and cool off their steaming feet in the thick sludge; I have no idea how they cleaned their feet afterwards. But this was not mud, but a genuine river, shallow and flowing quite fast, and I skipped over the rocks like a squealing deb, petrified of getting my socks wet.

Two men were actually swimming in the river, floundering around in the shallows, aping the crawl for the photographers. I was so tempted. The water looked cool and clear and wonderful, and the heat that day was pushing 50 degrees; my rucksack was already soaked through. But then I thought about my feet and the hour-long performance I'd been through that morning as I'd lanced my blisters and strapped up my soles. It seemed like a better idea just to get on with the job.

While I was skipping over the river, the frontrunners had gathered at noon for the start of their race. Even though there were only 55 of them, the visiting dignitaries were all still there, and the runners were given the full send-off, complete with pep talk and music.

ACDC's 'Highway to Hell' was blaring, quite deafening as the helicopters thundered overhead. The countdown was on. And Patrick sends the runners on their way.

Nobody moves.

The two leaders, Rachid el Morabity and Salameh Al Aqra, contemplate the horizon; the rest of the elite study their nails. They stretch. They contentedly chat.

Patrick, standing on top of his white Land Rover, can't believe it. Why aren't they obeying his orders?

'*Allons*!' he yells. '*Allons! Allons-y*!'

The runners continue to chat. They pass the time of the day. Rachid stares up at the sky. Patrick, who is more than a little used to getting his own way, becomes agitated. But he also knows he can't lose his temper or he would lose face with the dignitaries.

'Go!' he says, though this time with a smile. 'What are you doing? Go!'

Then, as one, the elite runners turn to Patrick, point at him and start roaring with laughter. The dignitaries join in the joke. Patrick shrugs and laughs, for what else can he do?

Rachid and Salameh look at each other and then, after a nod and a smile, the pair sprint into the desert, and the rest of the pack follow, snapping at their heels. For the first time, the runners had showed that, though the MdS was Patrick's race, they were not his hirelings. This race belonged to them.

Rachid caught up with me a few miles after I'd crossed the river. He took a different path from the rest of the runners, a good 15 yards off to the side, so that he could see where he was heading and would not be felled by any mulish stragglers. He was running very smooth seven-minute miles, which is fast. If I don't have a rucksack, I can keep that up on the flat for about five miles. It didn't seem possible that Rachid could keep that speed up through the heat of the day.

At least 15 minutes later, I was overtaken by Salameh who was running with his coach. 'Looking good!' I called. Salameh waved at me. I liked that.

What happened next was the talk of the MdS.

Rachid was coming into *Jebel El Mraïer* at the end of the fourth stage. He had run right through the heat of the day and had covered 51 miles in just over six and a half hours.

It had gone 6.30 p.m. by the time Rachid caught sight of the two white blimps on the finish line in the distance. It was dusk and though he was in some pain, he just wanted to get the damn thing over with and get some food inside him. The mile or so before the finish line was moderately flat, but was strewn with rocks and scrub; one moment Rachid was flying through the desert, truly the fastest man in the Sahara, and the next he was in agony. He didn't know what was wrong with his leg, but as he writhed about on the ground, he knew it was bad. He was only half a mile from the finish line. He set off a flare and that was Rachid done: he was out of the race with a severe muscle lesion to his left quad.

It was a shock when we heard the news. There was endless talk laced with *schadenfreude* as we speculated about how the mighty are fallen. But sometimes it's just bad luck and there's not much to say about it.

Later, like the ghouls that all journalists are, Kate and I went to inspect the list of '*abandonements*,' as they're called. There, at the top, leading the list of the 23 abandonees from Stage Four, was Rachid, runner number one.

Though I did wonder if it was entirely down to bad luck. He'd pushed himself hard in the day, and I'd heard that he might have slipped on a rock. Perhaps a more cautious soul might have eased up, or taken more care at dusk when the rocks turn to black shadows.

But that would be like asking a leopard to change his spots. The Marathon des Sables is not for the timid. The more cautious souls, they stay at home and play golf, sip gin and tonics in the evening and shake their heads at the sheer folly of all these mad men and women who have shipped themselves out to Morocco to run through the Sahara.

I, however, know a little of what it's like to be driven through the heat, driven by the race. So, to all those Mad Men and Mad Women of the MdS, I salute you. And to the leader of the pack, to Rachid, I say: You may not have won it. You may not even have completed it. But you're a champion. Better by far to go for it, to run through the pain, than to be bound by this constant clucking fear of having to play things safe.

CHAPTER 14

There's actually a lot of sitting around in the Marathon des Sables. It's like the army: Hurry up and wait!

Queues for the medical checks, queues for the admin checks, queues for food, queues to send email, and immense queues, more than an hour long, for Doc Trotters.

But some people are not good at hanging around, at queuing. They lie in their tents, they stare out at the desert, they whine about being bored.

Kate was not like that – and that was one of the reasons why I fell in love with her.

'I've seen a camel spider!' she announced to the tent after her admin check.

'What's that when it's at home?' Lawson asked.

'It's about three inches across, sandy coloured.'

'How did you know it was a camel spider?'

'One of the Commissaires pointed her out to me.'

Carlo joined the conversation. 'They can run at 10 miles an hour,' he said. 'They love the shade, that's why the little devils run at you – all they want to do is get in your shadow. If you run away, they'll chase after your shadow. You can never outrun them. And they scream, you know. They scream when they run.'

'What sort of scream?' Lawson said.

'More like a shriek,' said Carlo. 'When you're asleep, they can suck your face off. They can grow to the size of a sheep. And they like to hang from the bellies of camels – where the shade is. That's why they're called camel spiders.'

'And how do you spot them?' asked Lawson. We were enjoying Carlo's tall tale.

'Very tricky to spot a camel spider,' Carlo said. 'Usually the only thing that gives them away is their scream as they're running up to bite your face off. Believe it or not, it's not even a spider. It's a type of scorpion.'

'Is it really a scorpion?' asked Kate. 'Or did you make that up too?'

'I didn't make any of it up,' Carlo said stoutly. 'It's as true as I'm sitting here.'

Kate was entranced. She looked girlish and beautiful. 'Do you think we'll see any scorpions?' she said. 'I'd love to see a scorpion. I've never seen one in the wild before.'

Martin looked up. He was rearranging the kit in his rucksack again. It was one of his obsessions; at least three times a day, he would be checking over his rucksack. 'If I see a scorpion, I'll put him in a matchbox and give him to you.'

'That would be lovely,' said Kate. 'Though please don't kill him. I'll take him out into the desert and release him under a nice rock.'

'And you could leave him some bread and a saucer of milk,' said Lawson.

'That would be very thoughtful,' said Kate. She dropped down onto the rug and, like a puppy, lolled back, using my stomach as a pillow. 'Though I think he'd prefer a fly, or perhaps a little dung beetle. And then I would wave him on his way, and he would scuttle off to tell his family about his adventure on the Marathon des Sables.'

'And we could give him a medal too,' Carlo said.

I laughed and Lawson laughed and, quite naturally, quite easily, I stroked Kate's hair. I had not done that before; in fact, Kate had not used me as a pillow before, but it felt natural. Everything felt natural in the desert with Kate. Her hair was sleek and bleached and soft. I examined it closely in my fingers.

Del was picking his nose with edge of his thumb as he watched us from the corner of the tent.

'Are you two lovers?' he asked.

'Can't you tell?' I said. I brought Kate's hair up to my nose and I smelled it. We had been out in the desert for over a day and her hair smelled of sand. I started to plait three locks.

'She your bit of stuff, is she?'

'She's certainly not my bit of stuff, no!' I said. I could feel Kate giggling, her head wobbling on my stomach. 'She is my love, my muse, my life, my everything. You, Del, may have bits of stuff, but I would not touch them.'

'You certainly wouldn't want to touch Del's bits of stuff,' said Carlo.

'I would not want to touch any bit of stuff anywhere,' I said. 'Bits of stuff do not do it for me.'

'Bits of skirt on the other hand—' said Carlo.

'Ohhh, a bit of skirt?' I said. 'Bits of skirt are quite different matters altogether. Far superior to bits of stuff, and if you were to offer me a bit of skirt, I would jump on her immediately.'

Kate still giggled. 'And bits of fluff?'

'Somewhere between bits of stuff and bits of skirts, a little higher than bits on the side, and perhaps a little lower than bits of all right.'

Del chewed his thumbnail, staring at us in bemusement. He turned to Martin, who was now hanging his rucksack on a compact weighing machine.

'Nine kilos!' said Martin. 'Check it out!'

'Let's have a go,' Del said. He took off his MdS slippers and tucked them into his rucksack. They were special MdS slippers, very thin, very lightweight, like the white slippers you wear in upmarket spas. I remember thinking at the time how flimsy they looked; the soles were barely thicker than a piece of cardboard. 'Eight kilos,' Del said triumphantly. 'No Thermarest, see?'

'Why don't you dump the bear?' said Carlo, pointing at a white bear that was tucked into one of the mesh side pockets of Del's rucksack. 'That must be at least 100 grammes.'

'Fred Bear?' said Del. 'He hasn't missed a race.'

Kate cooed. 'That's nice,' she said.

We took it in turns to weigh our rucksacks. They all came in at around 10 or 11 kilos. Then it was my turn. I hadn't actually packed my rucksack before. I had just thrown all my kit into my suitcase.

As I lifted the bag up to hang it on the scales, I knew it was going to be heavy.

'Seventeen kilos!' crowed Del. 'You are one dumb bastard!'

'That's quite heavy,' sniffed Martin. 'What have you got in it?'

'I don't know,' I said. 'Just the same kit as you. Except you've gone for the most expensive kit around, and I've gone for the cheapest.'

'Look at those sandals!' said Del, pointing at the clumping leather boats on my feet. 'Those have got to be half a kilo before you've even started!'

'I like them,' I said. 'They're my lucky sandals.'

Del shrugged and shook his head in weary amazement. 'Well, when you do get drummed out of the race, can you put me down for your spaghetti carbonara?'

'You can have all of my food, Del – though I do hope it's reciprocal. I'd love to get stuck in to your pepperamis.'

'You just don't have a clue,' he said. 'You have no idea.'

'Well maybe that's a good thing,' I said. 'Look at Simon over there, quietly minding his own business. He's done this race before – and he knows exactly how horrific the long day is going to be. He knows what's ahead of him. But me – all I know is that it's going to be a bit tough. What position would you rather be in?'

'Not one with seventeen kilos of shit strapped to my back,' said Del.

'Language please, Del – there's a lady present.'

'Do you ever shut up?' He stooped down to leave the tent. 'I'm going off to get some lunch.'

'Enjoy!'

Such were the conversations that we used to have in the tent, freewheeling from one loopy subject to the next, and some people like Del and Simon absolutely hated them, and some people, like me and Kate and Lawson and Carlo, would jabber and riff about any footling subject that came into our heads and we absolutely loved it. And then there was Kurtz, listening and quietly smiling to himself as he farted away in his sleeping bag.

We ate like absolute kings for the first two days of the MdS. It was an extraordinary contrast to our own rehydrated food. The catered meals were unforgettable. The best one, of course, was our last, on the Saturday night, with a full moon just beginning to creep above the mountains.

The cooks were catering for over 1,400 people and their food was so good you could have served it in a restaurant; the French queue-barged with aplomb. We lounged around low round tables, lolling like the ancient Romans as we ate with our hands. Because we were with the French, there were four courses: delicious potato and leek soup, Waldorf salad, lamb tagine, thick, rich and juicy, and fresh flat bread on which you smeared two perfect mouthfuls of warm, ripe camembert. And, to finish, a tarte tatin and a cup of decent coffee. We couldn't get over it. Had they really shipped all this extraordinary food out from France? They even served us wine with dinner – after all, what self-respecting Frenchman could possibly have dinner without a glass of wine? – and we each of us were given a small 185cl bottle of claret.

Del devoured his food very quickly. He drank the soup even as we were walking to the table. He put his food on the table, squatted, and immediately wolfed down the tagine. The whole lot had gone in under two minutes. I watched, fascinated, as he drained the wine straight from the bottle.

'Wow,' said Kate. 'You were hungry.'

Del burped and, wiping his mouth with the back of his hand, stood up. 'I'm going back for seconds.'

'Cheeky,' I said.

'You got to know the game.'

'I suppose you do.'

The rest of us took our time. We placed the food on the table and poured our wine, and when we had sat on the mats, Lawson told us an old African fable.

'When a gazelle wakes up in Africa,' he said, 'it knows that it must run faster than the fastest lion or he will be eaten. And when a lion wakes up in Africa, he knows that he must run faster than the slowest gazelle or else he will starve. So in Africa, it does not matter whether you are the lion or whether you are the gazelle. What matters is that when the sun comes up, you'd better be running.'

We raised a toast to each other's desert dreams. The atmosphere was good-natured, easy; we looked about us at the other competitors and laughed at a crazy guy who was wearing nothing but a lime green mankini, Borat style. We wondered if Patrick Bauer would have thought the man 'looked good.'

That had been one of Patrick's chief concerns when he'd given us the team talk an hour earlier: 'Look good!' he'd said, as he stood on top of his Land Rover. 'If only for the sponsors. Keep looking good!'

Most of the runners stood for Patrick's talk, but Kate and I had gone to the front and sat down on the sand. I looked around and saw some of my tentmates. Del, I noticed, was just off to the side, leaning against one of the vans.

Patrick was in his sixties, I guess, ebullient, charismatic. He stood on the Land Rover with Sarah, his translator.

'We know the preparation's been hard, but we are so excited to see you here today. We can't quite give you the exact number of runners, but there's more than 850 of you, with 48 different nationalities – that's a record!' We cheered and Patrick waved and his translator smiled. 'About 12 to 14 per cent of the people here are women – and the rate of women giving up is much lower than the men. So go, go girls!' Patrick looked straight at Kate and gave her a little nod.

We were told about the 20 salt tablets we had to eat every day, and that stomach cramps were a sure sign of dehydration, and that we had to keep drinking our water in the evening. Then a flare was set off. It went impressively high, burning red against the blue sky as it slowly descended on a parachute.

We were introduced to the some of the stars of the show. There were 11 French firemen who would be pushing a relay of four disabled boys through the Sahara; a father and a son; a mother and a son; a grandfather and grandson; Joseph, who was 79 and the oldest man in the race; Michael, from France, who was 18 and the youngest.

And we were introduced to a grizzled grey veteran who had run 25 of the 27 Marathon des Sables. We gave him a cheer and we clapped. I happened to glance over at Del, who was still slouched against the van. He did not clap and kept his arms crossed. He hocked and spat on the ground.

And to end the show: Queen's hit, 'We Are The Champions,' blaring out from the speakers, even though we hadn't started yet. Even though we weren't yet champions.

*

Kate was still in my sleeping bag when I woke up. It was 6am on Easter Sunday. I don't know how it happened, but I had turned in the night and we were now facing each other, Kate's head tucked under my chin, her arm about my waist.

She looked so contented, so beautiful. Without even really thinking about it, I leant down and kissed her forehead.

She woke up, blinked a couple of times, and looked at me.

'Good morning!' she purred, giving me a terrific hug, her body pressed tight to mine. She looked at me slightly quizzically.

'Is that what I think it is?' she said.

''Fraid so,' I said. 'Morning Glories do tend to crop up in… in the morning.'

'I'd have been disappointed if it hadn't.'

'It's nothing personal, you know.'

'Of course not.' She deftly slipped her hand into my longjohns and gave my Morning Glory a light playful squeeze with her fingers.

Now that: that had a very unusual flavour indeed. I guessed that it didn't mean anything, that Kate was just larking around. For her, it might have been much the same as flicking my ears.

Or it might not.

I didn't know.

'Did you do what I just thought you did?' I asked.

'I did,' she said. 'Felt like it.' And she did it again. Her fingers lingered.

'And do you do that often?' I said.

'All the time,' she said, smiling at me. 'With my boyfriend.'

'He's a lucky guy.'

'We've got a race today, you know.'

I laughed. It was so out of this world to be lying tight in that sleeping bag with Kate's face just a few inches from my own, her hand...well...

'Is that the Marathon des Sables? I've been looking forward to it.'

'Well, let's get going!'

She gave me a quick hug and slipped out of my sleeping bag, and for a while I just lay there, head against my rucksack, staring out at the desert with this lazy smile upon my face as I thought about Kate and absorbed the sounds of the bivouac as it came to life. I heard a cow mooing and then a cock crowing; it was the bivouac's alarm call, waking up the slug-a-beds. Yes indeed, after months and months, the Marathon des Sables was upon us.

It was all very relaxed that first morning. We were all well fed and well rested and there were no blisters or wounds to be tended. I put on some water for our porridge. Del was already up. He'd been off to the latrines and was making coffee; coffee was his one luxury.

'Morning Del,' I said, yawning and stretching. 'How we doing today?'

'You all looked very cosy last night.'

'Damn cold, wasn't it?'

'Cold? That wasn't cold! That wasn't even close to cold. I've had nights where the water has frozen in the bottles.'

The Berbers started taking down the tents, crying 'Y'Allah, Y'Allah, Y'Allah' as they knocked out the tent pegs. I was still stirring the porridge when a Berber looked into the tent. He grinned at Kate and then the whole tent was swept over sideways and dumped on the ground. Kate and I were suddenly sitting on a rug out in the open desert. Carlo was still in his sleeping bag.

'That was quick!' Lawson said. He was fiddling with his socks, getting his toes right. Any sort of seam or wrinkle in a sock would be magnified tenfold during a day in the desert.

'Happy Easter,' Carlo said, wiping sleep from his eyes. 'Where's my egg?'

'I was saving it till the end of the first stage.'

'It better be a good one.'

And the banterers bantered with each other, and the more serious folk like Del and Simon and Martin packed and repacked their rucksacks, and checked their zips and their sunscreen. And while we squabbled and jittered, Kurtz sat on his rucksack, quite tranquil, and looked out to the east. There were hills to the left and right, a sandy valley running right through the middle – and that, in a couple of hours, was where we'd be running.

I pinned on my race numbers with my grandfathers' gold tie pins. I wondered what the old boys would have made of it all. A few decades back they'd have worn those tie pins to work and to their London clubs and perhaps to their own weddings. And now their maddest grandson was wearing them once again in a strange little jaunt across the desert that, if they'd known of it, would have had them rolling their eyes.

Our race tags were pinned to the fronts of our shirts and the backs of our rucksacks. They were a great leveller. They had just our numbers, our first names and our nationality. It didn't matter who you were or what you did or how many races you'd run. Today I was just Kim, the chatty man from GBR, who happened to be a good friend of the beautiful Kate, also from GBR.

The lugubrious rep came over to check we were all set. We called him Eeyore. I don't think I ever saw him smile.

'So what's it going to be like today?' asked Martin.

'Hot.'

'What about that hill at the end of the stage?'

'It's high.'

'Is that it?'

'That's it,' he said. 'Oh, one more thing. Make friends with pain – and you will never be alone.'

'Make friends with pain? ' queried Martin. 'What's that mean?'

'How do you make friends with pain?' asked Lawson. 'Do you take her out for a beer? Do you cook her a nice dinner?'

'What about make friends with the desert?' said Carlo.

'This is the one,' said Kate. 'Make friends – and you will never be alone.'

I filled up my two water bottles, one with electrolytes and one without, and for the first time I shouldered my rucksack. Full weight, with water, it must have been well over 18 kilos.

'Christ!' I said.

'Now that's what I call a man-sized rucksack,' said Lawson.

'He's a big boy,' I said. I jumped up and down. The rucksack felt like a huge sack of potatoes on my back. I tightened the straps around my chest and waist.

'You don't have to run it,' Lawson said. 'Let's just walk the first checkpoint. Take it easy. It's a holiday, not a route march.'

We laughed as the sheer enormity of it all began to sink in. This was the Marathon des Sables. And we were a part of it.

We posed for pictures and group shots, and then drifted over to the start line to gather for the traditional MdS photo. They herded us into two separate pens that, from above, would spell out the number '27.' A helicopter clattered overhead. Most of our team were inside the pen, but Kate and I insisted on stepping outside the ropes. We held hands and waved, a small but perfect full stop at the bottom of the '7.'

Everywhere was colour and excitement and sweat and nerves and testosterone, as hundreds upon hundreds of runners gathered into the two pens. The 11 firemen, the Pompiers, dressed in red, with one of their handicapped boys in the dune buggy, like a sedan chair with a single wheel at the back; the extra-tall Dutchmen, all of them 6'4" at the very least; Joseph, the oldest man in the race, French, always with a smile playing beneath his moustache; Didier, the blind man, stocky, tanned and tattooed, and attached to his guide by a short lead; the Brits, noisy and raucous as we bawled out 'Happy Birthday'; Del, ineffectually trying to pass his teddy bear up to Patrick on top of the Land Rover; the camels, Charles and Camilla, waiting at the back to mop up the stragglers; and, above all, Kate, deliriously happy, like a rock groupie as she danced, beautifully, to Laid Back's 'I'm a Happy Dreamer.'

In these kind of situations, I am usually quite detached. Though I can register the atmosphere and the energy, it does not touch me. But there, then, I was genuinely enjoying myself. I was enjoying

'Happy Dreamer,' and was even dancing to it in my own middle-aged manner. This was the toughest race on earth. And I, amazingly, was a part of it.

Lawson was next to me, burbling on about I know not what, until he grabbed me by the arm. 'Let's run it,' he says.

'I thought you wanted to walk it.'

'You've got to be joking!'

I turned to Kate. 'Good luck!' I had to shout to be heard over ACDC and the two helicopters.

She gave me a hug. I could smell the sunscreen on her cheek. 'We,' she said, 'are in the Marathon des Sables.'

'You better believe it!'

And with a sudden surge, like a wave sucking back into the sea, we were shuffling over the line, and then trotting, and before I even knew it this insane lemming-like madness had swept over me and I'm charging off with the rest of the horde, not walking, not jogging, but sprinting with my rucksack banging at my back, and it seems that everyone, every single runner in the race, has been possessed by this same madness, for we're all running like fury. And laughing, for we know it's an insane way to start a race.

We blew up after 400 yards. For most runners, that was about the point when the breathless madness started to wear off and we realised that, actually, there was still 150 miles to go, and even 21 miles in that sort of heat was going to be a stretch.

Lawson stopped and tugged out his walking poles. We waved to the helicopter that was flying back towards us, enveloping us in its dust and its backdraft.

'Are we liking it?' Lawson said, as we struck out into the wilderness.

'No!' I said. 'We're loving it!'

'Has Uncle Lawson ever told you about walkie-runnie?'

'I don't know if he has.' I looked about me, marvelling at this great spectrum of endurance runners, some peeing, some eating, and some so winded they couldn't even walk. 'But I think he's about to tell me.'

'Uncle Lawson recommends jogging for eight minutes, then walking for two.'

'When are we going to do that?'

'After the first checkpoint,' he said. 'But for this first nine miles, we are going to enjoy ourselves. We are going to soak it up. We are going to immerse ourselves in the sights and sounds of the Sahara.'

'Let's give it a go.'

Kate caught up with us a minute later. She was going at a nice easy trot, the same sort of pace that she'd been doing out of Wapping that first day I'd run with her. She looked strong, like she could keep it up for another 20 miles easy.

She waved as she ran past. 'Go, Kate!' I called, and Lawson waved his sticks and hollered. We were not just a part of the race; we were a part of a team, a great team, on this magnificent but insane adventure together, and Kate, above all others, was our mascot and our champion.

'Lovely woman,' said Lawson.

'Really?' I said. 'I'd never noticed.'

'You sure you're not lovers?'

'Quite sure.'

'You're showing a lot more self-restraint than I would under the circumstances.'

'The Pope's already been notified.'

Lawson took a suck at his water and stumbled over a rock. 'Don't worry though – that rampaging libido of yours will soon be shot to pieces. By the end of today, sex is going to be the very last thing on your mind.'

He was not wrong.

I very quickly worked out a drill for the rest of the MdS runners. When I passed someone, I would, fisherman-like, cast a fly over their nose. 'Looking good,' I'd say, or 'How we doing?'

And sometimes the fish would not move. I would just receive a sullen reply, or even no reply at all, but that wasn't a problem. I would just move on. If you're in a lot of pain, the last thing you want is to be accosted by chirpy strangers.

But sometimes the fish would move, and for the space of a few minutes, or an hour, or perhaps even an entire stage, you would keep each other company, chatting about anything and everything that came to mind.

The Commissaires gave us a thorough going-over at the first checkpoint, asking us how we were, asking us if we were taking our salt tablets, sizing us up, checking to see if we'd already been undone by the desert madness.

It was the first and only checkpoint where I didn't take off my rucksack. Lawson and I stood there in the shade of a truck, sweat pouring off us, and we were so eager to get moving that we didn't even sit down to fill our water bottles. By the next checkpoint, we had learned wisdom. A checkpoint is a time to take stock and regroup. Usually I would take off my shirt and hang it out to dry on the bull bars of one of the Land Rovers. I would sit down and relish the shade; and eat and sip water; and would try not to dwell on the many miles ahead, but rather would savour having the weight off my feet and the wind on my bare back.

After the first checkpoint, we started to jog, one in front of the other. You can't talk when you're jogging, and you can hardly even think because you're concentrating so much on where you're heading and where you're next going to plant your feet. The idle thoughts that had been drifting through your head are replaced by constant and urgent orders to move to the left, and to step out wide, and to jump that rock. And then you check your watch and discover to your absolute relief that your eight minutes are up and that you are now allowed to walk, to have your four sips and to chew, slowly, on your sports bean.

These were the moments when you look about you and see the wild open spaces, when the cynicism would drop to be replaced by awestruck wonder at the sheer beauty of it all, at these incredible sights that we had been gifted. There was also that special delight in knowing they were just for us: it felt as if, the whole world over, no one would ever see these things but us.

The most spectacular view by far was at the top of *Bou Laihirh Jebel*, about 200 metres high, trotting along this mile-long ridge with a precipice just a few feet to the side of us. The view, whenever we looked up to see it, was a breathtaking panorama. If you stared hard, you could see this long line of ants stretching into the distance. There was pleasure in knowing that, in time, it would be you trotting along the flats, or struggling up that killer hill at the end, *Tibert Jebel*, which did for 15 runners on the first day.

I assumed that those extraordinary views would always be with us, that every new mile would bring some fresh delight to the eye. But this was not the case. Nothing ever topped the sweeping panoramas from the top of *Bou Laihirh Jebel*.

We were surprised to catch up with Carlo halfway up *Tibert Jebel*. He had stopped on a rock and was frying in the heat as he untied his shoelaces. His feet had swollen way beyond what he'd expected and he was hoping to stave off blisters by putting on fresh socks. Sometimes this works and sometimes it doesn't; in Carlo's case, changing socks was actually the cause of his blisters. Once his feet were out of his shoes, they swelled so much he could hardly put his trainers back on again. Those last three miles absolutely flayed him.

It's very unsettling when you get blisters on the first day. You know, for a certainty, that something's wrong with either your feet or your socks, or perhaps both. You also know that if you don't do anything, don't change anything, those blisters are going to get bigger and will start to multiply. The worry is that even if you do change your socks, it still might not make any difference.

It's the fleeting pleasures that make it worth it, like the ping of the timer as you walk over the finish line, that first sip of Sultan tea, that welcoming hug from Kate, who's been in for hours and has already butchered her blisters, and eaten her supper, and is now just itching to get to the communications tent and start filing her breathless copy for 'Beauty and the Beast.'

CHAPTER 15

The MdS Commissaires' small tent, snug and smelling of joss sticks, could have been specifically designed as my personal heaven. It was the communications tent, with four phones and about 20 keyboards, from which we were each allowed to send a single 1,000-character email.

Lawson and I had stumbled back into the camp, revelling in the sheer bliss of not being on our feet. Now that sex was no longer uppermost in my mind, I can safely say that lying there in that windy tent, feeling the blood gradually ebb from my feet, was close to ecstasy. Kate, being lovely, mixed our revival drinks and boiled us water, and the ecstasy rolled on and on, lasting until long after I'd eaten half my lasagne. It was like an orgasm, only better, for it went on for a full hour. It may have been the endorphins, but more likely it was down to the total relief of not having to walk and not having 18 kilos pinned to my back.

And when my hour was up, Kate and I wandered over to the communications tent. I was hobbling. They have a couple of names for this particular gait: The Sahara Shuffle or, sometimes, The MdS Mince, and I would see much of it over the next week.

'Is that what I think it is?' said Kate. We were queuing outside the communications tent.

'Sounds like bird song,' I said.

'That is one thing I never thought I'd hear in the desert,' she said.

It was indeed, and it was another wonder of the MdS, that as we all quietly tapped out our emails in the communications tent, there was bird song piped through the speakers, and occasionally even Gregorian chant; I would close my eyes and imagine myself as some humble monk scribing away at the Bible in a Cistercian Monastery.

Kate and I were colleagues, and tentmates and running mates, but I knew that there would still be a certain amount of rivalry when it came to our copy. Words were our business, and we both wanted to shine. I wrote about the heat and the sweat and the blisters, and the food and the views. It is difficult to distil the MdS into 250 words, but if anyone was up to the job, it would be a journalist from the *Sun*.

I wrote my copy and checked it, and when I'd filed, I read my book.

Kate had been typing for a long time. She was smirking to herself, reliving the moment as she wrote about it.

She gave it a last read-through and filed and then, deliciously, she took my hand and we left the bird song and joss sticks, and walked out into the wind and the dust.

'You were writing a long time,' I said.

'I was,' she said. 'Del and Kurtz aren't sending any messages. They've given me their race numbers. They said I could have their quota.'

'Jesus!' I said. She'd been filing 750 words to my meagre 250. 'That's good. That's clever! You sly dog!'

She squeezed my hand. 'I may have more words, but I don't have your gift with them.'

'I very much doubt that,'

She wriggled her shoulders, swinging her arms backwards and forwards. 'I'm so stiff,' she said. 'Kurtz suggested shoulder massages.'

'He may not say much, but when he talks, he's worth listening to.'

Then and there, Kate stopped, halfway to our tent. 'Do me now.'

She stood directly in front of me. I placed my hands on her shoulders and, gently at first, began to probe with my fingers. Her muscles had turned to tight knots.

She was leaning forward a little, hands braced on her knees. 'That's good. Firmer.'

I pushed with my thumbs, harder and harder, working away at the knotty mass of muscle.

She screeched, and I let off, but she gestured for me to carry on. 'It's good. God it hurts.'

So I continued, digging and probing with my thumbs and with the blunt ends of my fingers, forcing the lactic acid out from her shoulders. Sometimes she whimpered, but if I laid off, she peremptorily ordered me to continue.

And then it was my turn. I leaned forward, hands on my knees, and Kate gave me a couple of preliminary strokes before going straight in with her thumbs. It felt like she was drilling me with a blunt skewer.

'Ow!' I yelled, taking an involuntary step backwards.

'I thought you'd like it,' she said, forcing my head down as she started again on my shoulders.

I tried to be stoic, but still I squealed and still I yelped as Kate lanced with her thumbs, probing away at new knots and new nerve endings.

'This is more painful than blisters!' I hissed. And it was, much more painful, another exquisite session with my new friend pain.

'The way you're bent over like this.' She started to chop my shoulders with the blades of her hands. 'And all this racket you're making. It sounds…'

'Like I'm being broken in?'

'That's it. Though quite sexy. I don't think I've ever produced these sounds from a man before.' She pressed her thumbs tight into the side of my neck. 'At least not outside the bedroom.'

'Oww!'

'You liking this?'

'No,' I said. 'I'm loving it!'

And, thanks to one of those weird tricks of the mind, the moment I said it, the pain eased. Once you tell yourself that you're happy, you're halfway there.

She gave me a quick hug and took my hand and we wandered on our way again.

'Much better,' I said.

'You'll thank me in the morning.'

I wiggled my shoulders. They were already feeling much lighter. 'I'm thanking you already.'

'A pleasure.' She gave my fingers a squeeze. 'Shall we do a circuit?'

I felt a twinge in my guts. It was only a tremor, but I knew immediately what it meant, and what I'd been in for in the next half hour.

'I'd love to.'

So we walked the camp. Having Kate by my side numbed the pain in my feet and even, for a while, stopped my thinking about my spasming stomach. We were like lovers who had sated ourselves on each other, so shattered that sex was the very last thing on our minds. And once that happens, once you are spent, there comes this easy lightness to a relationship when there is no side, no demands to be met, and when you can say it how it is.

We saw a Frenchman standing by a fire drinking tea. The French did things with much more style than the Brits. Every tent had a proper wood fire with stones at the edge. Most of the French wore baggy white jumpsuits. They were made of paper, very light, very snug, and were usually daubed with goodwill messages. The man was tanned, with long curly hair, and he was wearing shorts and a T-shirt. I noticed his glass and, for the first time, I felt envy. Most of the MdS hackers drank from their bottles or their billycans; this man was drinking his tea from a goblet of cut-crystal glass. If there is one thing I adore, it is antique glasses; I like to drink my wine from a cut-crystal glass, swirling it slowly in front of the firelight. I coveted that glass, and if ever I ran the race again, I would have to have one for myself.

It was quite dark beyond the bivouac, and cloudy too, and we could see nothing of the desert or the wilderness; we could have been anywhere.

'Imagine being lost in this,' said Kate.

'I wouldn't fancy it,' I said.

'What do they say in the Road Book? "No heroics!"'

'And "Don't panic!" Though you'd have to try quite hard to get lost in the MdS.'

'You think so?'

'Yeah.'

But actually, you don't have to try quite hard at all. It can happen quite easily. You just take your eye off the ball, and your mind wanders, and before you know it, you are way, way off piste and there you are: alone and lost in the Sahara. It is all a little unnerving.

★

I blame, of course, myself. I know a little about compasses and maps, but like a lot of men, I prefer to bodge it. I will try to flounder out of the morass rather than admit defeat.

Though, to be fair, the Berber kids didn't help.

But they were merely the cause. It was me and me alone who managed to turn it into one of those oh-so life-enhancing situations where the hair crackles at the nape of your neck and this quiet, insistent voice starts to whisper in your ear: 'Take a care, my lad.'

It was on the long day, the double marathon, and it happened in the night. At the third checkpoint, they had given us yellow glowsticks to attach to our packs.

Del was there too, hamming it up for the cameras. He twirled the glowstick like a cigar, rolling it between his fingers and putting it into his mouth before asking the cameraman, 'Have you got a light?'

I went on my way. Most of the runners prefer to stay clustered together at night, but I liked going solo, the cat that walks by himself. I was walking through dunes and camel grass, and with the wind sighing in the air, I could have been at home in England with the beach just over the next hill.

At 6.30, I put on my beanie and my head torch and snapped my glowstick. It came to glimmering life as I tied it to my rucksack. I had a map and I had a bearing, but I did not need them, because every few hundred yards there were wayside markers, with glowsticks attached; and there were the winking glowsticks of the people ahead of me; and the white lights of the head torches of the people behind; and, if all else failed, there was always the actual tracks in the sand, the thousands of footprints that marked out the route of the MdS.

I was walking fast, driving my poles into the ground, twisting them as they hit the sand. I would spy a group ahead of me, nothing but a twinkle of yellow light, and within minutes would have overtaken them.

'How we doing?' I asked Paul, a Brit.

'Do you have to be so bloody chirpy?'

And on I went, my world reduced to the five yards of light that were thrown up by head torch.

I came across a couple of small shacks and wondered about the lives of the families who lived there, what they lived off and what they drank. There were five or six kids, quite young, who were very excited by these weird folk walking past their door step. They chattered away in French and I gave a handful of sports beans to a small boy. He shook me by the hand. It was only as I watched him disappear into the night that I saw that his back pocket was stuffed with glowsticks.

I carried on walking, rubbing disinfectant gel into my hands. I realised I hadn't seen any markers for a while; the kids had obviously taken them.

I could have stopped. I could have got out my Road Book and my compass, and taken a bearing. But, of course, my compass was stuffed right at the bottom of my rucksack. It had never occurred to me that I might actually have to use the thing.

I knew I was still on the right track. I was following the footprints, hundreds of them hammered into the sand. And ahead of me, way off, I could see the twinkling white lights of the fourth checkpoint.

I continued on my way. I soon got into a routine, pounding my way through the sand. I was eating up the miles.

I was thinking about Kate. What I would have done with that girl if I'd been single; if I'd been a few years younger. Those pitiful thoughts of what might have been.

I wondered what it would be like to kiss her. I bet she was a good kisser, a historic kisser. And she looked like a great lover too. You could see that just from the way she danced. And, not a few days earlier, she'd only just climbed into my sleeping bag; and then, at first light, had given me that light playful squeeze. I laughed at the thought of it. And just what would she have done if I'd returned the compliment? And there was the hand-holding, that was nice; I hadn't held a woman's hand so much in a long time.

Oh yes – and she was fiery, too. By God she was fiery. One way or another, I find I am often attracted to fiery women.

But it could never work. I was a good 20 years her senior, was married with children, was a paunchy middle-aged man. In every conceivable way, I was a decidedly bad bet.

If I were kind, if I had a heart, I would discourage any further advancement in our relationship. Hand-holding was fine; hugs were fine; pecks on the cheek were fine. But anything more than that, and I'd fall more hopelessly in love than I already was. And she might fall for me (stranger things have happened) and we might make mad, passionate love – and that would probably turn out to be one of the most fantastic experiences of my life. But it would all end in disaster, and so better by far not to go there. Certainly a lot better for Kate. Better to stick with this extraordinary thing that we already had. And, for a cast-iron certainty, better for my daughters. I wondered how they were all getting on with Elise.

I wondered what it would be like to kiss her.

What on earth did she see in that bloody boyfriend? What Svengali hold did he have over her? Was it sex, or was it something more? But if he was out of the picture... And if Elise miraculously decided to trade me in for some younger model... I envisioned a little flat near Wapping, lined wall upon wall with books, making love all day on our days off, drinking white wine by the river...

The footprints had petered out. I'd been walking for 15 or 20 minutes, heading towards the lights of the fourth checkpoint when I suddenly realised there were no footprints. Maybe the other competitors had taken a slightly more direct route. I supposed it didn't make much difference; if I just kept on heading towards the lights, I'd soon be there.

And still no sign of a way marker.

The kids must have been very industrious when they'd been stripping off all the glowsticks.

I wondered what it was like to kiss her.

This lethal combination of beauty and brains and wit. And she laughed at my jokes too. I always fall head over heels for women who find me funny.

What a temper she had, though – *what* a temper.

But didn't she have just the greatest body. I mean *the* greatest body. Tall and toned, with beautiful hair; those legs, those breasts… had she *really* thrust herself against me when she'd snuggled into my sleeping bag?

What was that scar about on the back of her head? Probably a car crash or some other brutally mundane horror. And she liked her lipstick, almost as much as I liked my Vaseline. Together, we would have the moistest lips in Christendom.

And on, and on my thoughts would burble. For a few moments I might spare a thought for my other tentmates, but always my default was Kate. I loved her.

And the minutes ticked by, and the kilometres passed, and it was perhaps a little strange that I hadn't seen a single other walker for quite a long time, but anyway… the checkpoint wasn't far off, not far off at all now, barely a few hundred yards away.

And that's when I squint at it properly for the first time. A jolt of alarm ripples through me. It was definitely not the checkpoint. It didn't look anything *like* a checkpoint. There were no banners, no arc lights, no marshals, or Land Rovers, or Berber tents. It was just a cluster of two or three tents, with some kerosene lamps hanging outside.

This is bad, I thought. This is very bad. I pulled the Road Book out of the back of my rucksack. It looked like I'd gone off way to the west, and was now in some wasteland called *Iferd Nou Haouard*. I checked my watch. Nearly an hour. Nearly an hour! How could I have been such an idiot? I must have walked well over three miles.

I took off my rucksack and burrowed right to the bottom to retrieve my compass – not that it was going to do me any good. If I was to go off on the correct bearing, 118 degrees, I'd just be taking a parallel route to the main course. I'd miss the checkpoint by miles.

I pulled out a Nutri-Grain bar, eating it slowly, trying to calm myself down. The bar was nutty and chewy and very dry. I sucked on one of my water bottles and realised it was empty. I looked at the other water bottle; it held barely half a pint.

I must have been insane!

If I'd had more confidence in my map-reading skills, I might have tried heading direct to the checkpoint. But that would have been sheer folly.

So my only option was to try and retrace my steps. I'd been walking in a straight line. Or at least I hoped I had. I took a very careful bearing of the route I'd just come. If I stuck to it, it ought to be a simple matter of walking for an hour before I cut across the correct MdS path.

I hoped.

I hoped I'd recognise the route when I came to it – see some footprints or a glowstick, because if I didn't... I was going to have a problem.

Maybe not as much of a problem as the Italian Mauro Prosperi, who in 1994 got lost in a sandstorm and managed to blunder 130 miles in the wrong direction. It's said he survived by eating a snake and drinking his own urine. So things weren't that bad. But I did have to take a care. I double checked my compass and checked my watch again. One hour of walking, steadily and easily, and there would be the MdS trail. And wouldn't Kate just be howling with laughter when she heard what an idiot I'd been. And God I wanted to kiss her...

I shook my head and slapped myself twice across the cheek. There would be plenty of time for lusting after Kate later. For the moment, I had to concentrate on trying to get myself out of this ridiculous mess.

After 15 minutes, I lost track of my own footprints. A lone walker leaves very little trace in the desert, especially in the deep sand.

I checked my bearing again, trying to sight it on something, anything, on the horizon, but there was nothing but darkness, not a light nor a headlight to be seen. The wind was starting to pick up. My mouth was dry. I was trying to conserve my water.

Never again! How could I... how could I have been so fantastically stupid? Not that I was in any danger, not yet at least, but this was most definitely not a time for more mistakes. I still had my flare, of course, but I never considered using it. I'd work my own way out.

Besides, wasn't this now turning into a genuine A-grade adventure? Wasn't that one of the main reasons why I'd signed up for the MdS in the first place?

I skittered down the sides of dunes and clawed my way up the other side, fingers thrust deep into the camel grass. After 50 minutes on the same bearing, I started casting around from side to side, searching for footprints or any trace of the MdS. There was nothing.

I carried on walking. After an hour, I stopped. I took off my rucksack, ate a sports bean and, as I stared at the Road Book, I tried to understand where the hell I was.

After an hour out and an hour back, I had to be close to where I'd originally blundered off course. But I couldn't decide whether I'd already crossed the MdS route – or whether I'd yet to come to it.

Should I retrace my steps, or should I carry on walking in the same direction?

I scratched at the fine piebald beard I'd been growing and decided to keep on walking. If I'd already passed the MdS trail, then I'd have seen someone or something.

And I looked at my watch again and realised that, apart from being lost and apart from not having much water, there was a matter of even more pressing urgency: I only had two and a half hours to get in to the fourth checkpoint before I missed the cutoff.

I couldn't... I couldn't be kicked out of the MdS for that. It would be a disaster. I could live it down if I'd lost all the skin on my feet, but to be drummed out of the race because I'd got lost? What a clown!

I was bristling to get on, fumbling with my belt buckles. I took another bearing and set off once more into the darkness. Every couple of minutes it would hit me anew: I was lost in the middle of the bloody Sahara! It seemed so extraordinary, so unbelievable. I was getting increasingly nervous about the time, but at least I managed to laugh at my own predicament. The whole thing was so utterly ludicrous.

I kept searching the ground for any sign of a footprint, but there was nothing, nothing at all. On every hilltop, I would stop and turn 360 degrees, looking for anything, a torch, or even a beautiful glimpse of the checkpoint. In that desert darkness, it seemed as if I was the only human being in existence.

After another 20 minutes I stopped again. Had I crossed the MdS route? Or was it just ahead of me? Perhaps it was just over the next hillock.

I'd give it another five minutes, or maybe ten, and if I still hadn't found anything, I'd retrace my footsteps, and then... well, we'd deal with that one when we came to it.

I wished I had more water.

I wished I had more time.

I wished Kate was with me.

I sat down, leaning against a tuft of camel grass, looking for lights. There had to be hundreds of headlights in the desert. If I kept looking, I'd *have* to see one.

I couldn't be that far off course.

Could I?

From behind me, over my left shoulder, I heard a whistling shriek and a bang. I twitched with surprise.

And I turned and I saw it – and I said to myself, 'Oh you little beauty.'

Somebody had let off a flare. After the darkness it seemed fantastically bright. It was about a mile away, and as the parachute drifted down, I took a bearing and started running as hard as I could towards my pulsing red pole star.

I didn't know who it was or where they were, but the one thing I knew for certain was that, any minute now, a helicopter would come clattering into view. My big fear was that the flare might have been set off by some solo runner who was pulling out of the race. If that were the case, the Commissaire would just pick him up.

I did not want to be forlornly looking up at the helicopter as it pounded off into the night.

So I ran as hard as I could. My blisters and my aching legs and my dry mouth were all forgotten as I ran my fastest mile of the MdS. The flare had gone out by now, but over from the north, I could see the flashing lights of a helicopter. It swooped in low, once, twice, and then landed, and by the time I got to the top of the next dune, I could see a Commissaire jumping to the ground.

I eased up a little. There were five of them, all huddled together; they couldn't all be pulling out.

The sheer relief of it. I wasn't lost in the Sahara. I was now just another MdS runner who'd strayed a little along the way, but who was now firmly back on track. And who now had a great story to tell.

They were only a hundred yards off now, and the Commissaire was standing with his back to the helicopter, hands on his hips. He did not seem happy.

'These are for emergencies!' he was saying. 'This is not an emergency.'

'But we were lost,' said a woman, Sue. She was British and seemed to be the one who'd set off the flare. 'We couldn't find any way markers.'

'You are not lost,' snapped the Commissaire. 'The lights have been taken by the local boys. Do you not have maps and compasses?'

I sauntered over. The six of them were standing in a pool of light by the helicopter.

'Evening all,' I said, very breezy. 'Is there a problem?'

The Commissaire turned to me. I recognised him from Doc Trotters. He was one of the French doctors. 'Where have you come from?' he said.

'Just having a little wander,' I said, suddenly feeling ecstatically jaunty. 'How far to the next checkpoint?'

'It is four miles away,' he said. 'You are on the route.'

'Thanks.' I looked at the five other MdS competitors. After setting off the flare, they all seemed a little shamefaced.

The Commissaire climbed back into the helicopter. 'You people,' he said. 'Why do you come on the Marathon des Sables if, when the adventure starts, you have to be rescued?'

'I'm sorry,' said Sue.

'This is the Marathon des Sables!' said the Commissaire. 'This is the Sahara! Being lost – it is all part of the fun!'

The Commissaire's good temper had returned. He waved to us as the helicopter lifted off.

'Let's be getting on then,' I said, and this time, after taking a very, very careful bearing from the Road Book, I went on my way. Behind me, I could hear Sue bickering with a man. 'How was I to know?' she squawked. 'I thought we were seriously lost.'

But the Commissaire was right. Being lost is indeed all part of the fun. It's even more fun if you can find your way out again.

CHAPTER 16

The reactions of my tentmates, when I got the runs on the first night, were varied. Kate and Lawson were solicitous: 'How are you?' 'How you feeling?' 'Everything okay?'

Kurtz and Simon just hunkered down in their sleeping bags and tried to shut out the sound of me clattering around in the dark as I searched for my head torch and my roll of toilet paper.

As for Martin and Del...

'How's it going over there?' Martin asked. He was on the far side of the tent, about as far away from me as he could get. It was Easter Monday, the morning of the second stage.

'It's going fine,' I said. 'How about you?'

'You were up a few times, weren't you,' Martin said.

Del stirred his porridge. 'You never washed your hands.' He looked at me out of the corner of his eye, like some malign toad. 'You don't wash your hands, you only got yourself to blame.'

'Actually Del, I've been scrupulous about washing my hands.' My guts gave another heave and, quick as I could, I darted off to the latrines. What had happened to me? How could I have picked up this bug on the very first stage of the race? The second stage was another killer, 24 miles; I thought it might do for me.

'I'm worried about you,' said Martin when I got back. 'You've been taking the pills?' Martin and Del had obviously been discussing me.

'I have.'

'We think, though...' Martin was checking the pockets of his rucksack. He liked to keep his snacks in the right-hand pocket, compass in the left-hand pocket and his flare at the back, next to his race number. 'We think you should see Doc Trotters. Get some proper drugs to treat it.'

'I'll think about it.' I was applying bandages to the first of my blisters. It would become part of my morning routine. I'd cut the blisters and air them overnight, and then in the morning I'd tape them up with broad bandages that almost covered the sole of my foot.

'You ought to,' he said again. 'I'm a doctor, I know about these things.'

'You ought to get it seen to,' Del said. He had his billycan very close to his face and was shovelling porridge into his mouth.

'I'll think about it.'

'These things can get really bad if they're not treated properly,' Martin said. 'You've got to knock it on the head quickly.'

'Or you'll be out of the race,' Del said. He wiped his chin, smearing porridge across his beard.

I wondered why Del and Martin were so concerned about my health. I sat down outside. I dickered: should I see the doctors? What would be the harm in going to Doc Trotters?

Kurtz was nearby, sitting on his rucksack. He'd taken out his glass eye and was poking around in his eye socket with his little finger. 'They're terrified they're going to pick up your bug,' he said, still poking around. I tried not to watch too closely. 'Bunch of old women. But it isn't a bug. It's your body getting used to the heat and the shitty food. Give it one hour in this heat and you'll be tighter than a gnat's chuff.'

'Really – yomping in this?'

'It's not a yomp. Marines yomp.'

'Is it a TAB?'

'Tactical Advance to Battle. That's army. They haven't got a—' He never finished what he was going to say. He was staring at the end of his finger. 'Myst all chucking frighty!'

He flicked something onto the sand. 'There was a bloody spider in my eye socket! The bastard!' He started probing again with a wet wipe. 'Think he's laid any eggs in there? I've had an earwig before, couple of maggots. But never a spider.' He gave his glass eye a polish. It was black, like a large black marble. He popped it back into his eye socket. 'Better.'

'So don't bother going to see Doc Trotters?'

'Waste of time.' He rolled over onto a buttock and let off a stupendous fart. 'Give it 24 hours and you'll be farting with confidence.'

My stomach did sort itself out and as it happened, it was Kate, my nursemaid on the Second Stage, who was off to see Doc Trotters that evening. I went with her.

I'd already seen her blisters. They were now nothing but open red wounds and looked astonishingly painful. After the first stage she'd cut off all her blisters and planted warm Compeeds onto the skin, but they had come off in the heat and the sand of the second day. For the last four or five hours of the stage, Kate had been walking along with dirt and dust being rubbed into her raw wounds. It must have been agony.

We went first to Triage, just next to the communications tent. This was where runners' injuries were assessed. If you had just a few small blisters, you were given a scalpel, iodine and some bandages, and told to sort yourself out. But if your blisters were large, or if you were squeamish, you would be sent to the main Doc Trotters tent.

The nurse took one look at Kate's feet and sent us to Doc Trotters. We joined the queue.

'What are you in for?' asked Oliver, a Brit with a crew-cut and feet that were swathed in bandages.

'A few blisters,' Kate said. She showed off her feet. Her soles were covered in angry red blotches; you couldn't tell immediately that there was no skin there.

'That?' said Oliver. 'I'll see your blisters, and I'll raise you the king-sized blister on the ball of my foot! It's swelled up so much the fluid has gone all the way round the side and up to the top!' He let out a merry peal of laughter.

Kate smiled. 'You win.'

'These blisters are a bugger. We've got one woman in our tent, a chiro... chiropo...'

'A chiropodist?'

'Yeah – a foot doctor. She's spent months on her feet, getting them all just perfect for the MdS, toughening them up, you name it, and she's already starting to feel her toenails move.'

'How bad is that?' I asked.

'They'll be off in a week.'

There were two bowls of disinfectant at the entrance to Doc Trotters. Kate had taken off her flip-flops and was about to dip her feet, when Del stepped in front of her. He was holding his teddy. 'Won't be a moment,' he said. He kicked off his MdS slippers and stepped into the bowl of disinfectant.

It was the first time I'd ever really noticed his gnarly white feet. Each toenail had been painted with a different flag – the Union Jack, the Saltire, the Cross of St George.

'I thought you never got blisters,' I said.

'I don't,' he said, giving me a playful punch to the shoulder. 'I know how to play the game. This is more than just an ultra. It's about foot management. They've got the disinfectant. I use it every night.'

We went inside. Doc Trotters must surely have been one of the most bizarre medical centres on earth. Over a dozen doctors and nurses treating nothing but foot injuries, every one of which had more or less been self-inflicted. In the middle of the tent, there were 20 or so runners lying in two lines on raffia mats, heads in the middle and their feet facing outwards raised up on little 18-inch tables. Some of the runners had silver foil blankets to keep warm. Each doctor had a box, like a large toolbox, filled with all the tools of their trade. The room stank of disinfectant. The noise was awful. In the main tent there would be the occasional yelp, but off to the side there was an annexe for the IV drips and the really bad cases. There was a man screaming in there. He was screaming as if his foot was being sawn off. Then, quite suddenly, he stopped. For a while there was a silence, and then we could hear him weeping.

The doctors were very professional and polite. They were all volunteers who had been shipped out to the MdS with the lure of the Sahara and carefree sex in the sand, and wonderful food and sensational wine. It was said that there were two huge stainless steel cases inside the Commissaires' bivouac, each about the size of a small car, containing all the cheeses, the condiments, the vittles and the wines that would fuel the Commissaires through their week in the desert.

Kate lay down on the floor. She said a few words to the doctor, but there wasn't much to say. She was hurt, and she needed fixing up so she could hurt herself some more the next day.

I'd brought my book, but there was no way I could read. Instead I watched Kate and the other runners. She was staring straight up at the ceiling and holding her hands so tight that her knuckles were white.

Oliver was also being treated. He had his headphones on and his eyes closed, and as the doctor bled his blisters, he conducted an imaginary orchestra.

There was a woman near me whose toes were being treated. At first she whimpered, but then she put her Road Book into her mouth and bit down on it. She caught my eye and I looked away.

It seemed unbelievable that so many feet could have been so badly injured after just 42 miles in the desert. It seemed unthinkable that these runners could ever complete the race.

The doctor gave Kate's feet a preliminary inspection before trimming off the dead skin with a scalpel. He was a young man with a wispy blonde moustache, barely out of medical school – though these days I am hopeless at guessing people's ages. The doctor was very methodical, taking his time. None of the doctors were in a hurry, and would spend as long as they needed with a runner. After he'd finished with the scalpel, he meticulously disposed of it in a yellow bin; tread on a loose scalpel and your MdS would be over. The doctor squeezed on some disinfectant, bright red, the colour of blood, which made Kate wince and after that he put on some brown iodine, which was even more painful. With great care, he stuck on plasters before swathing her feet in white bandages. He was a master. It was wonderful to watch.

'Thank you,' Kate said, slowly getting to her feet.

'You will come here tomorrow,' the doctor said. He was gathering up the waste paper from the table and the trimmings from the bandages.

'I don't know,' said Kate. 'Will I need to?'

'That was not a question. You will come here tomorrow – you will have to.'

'Right,' said Kate. I could see she was taken aback.

'Your feet, they are not going to get better. They are going to get worse,' said the doctor. 'You have not done a third of the race.'

I did not like the sound of this talk at all. The man may have been telling the truth, but after a hard slog in the desert, who wants to be told that there's much worse to come – that it'll be much more painful?

'Thanks for that,' I said, taking Kate by the arm. 'Tell you what Kate – you can cry at every checkpoint.'

I waved and, before the doctor could detail any more of the nightmares that lay ahead of us, wheeled Kate out of the tent. She was hobbling badly and was leaning heavily on my arm.

It was dusty, bitter and windy, and the end of the race still seemed a long, long way off. 'Get some painkillers inside you and you'll be fine,' I said.

Kate hobbled on for a while. She was favouring her right foot. 'I don't know,' she said. 'I don't know if I'm going to make it.'

'Don't talk bloody nonsense! Of course you're going to make it. If needs be, I'll drag you.'

'What about the long stage?

'I'll drag you through that too,' I said in my breeziest, most confident voice. 'It'll be fun. I'm looking forward to it.'

'What painkillers have you got?'

'Ibuprofen, paracetemol… Look, if the going gets really rough, I'm sure our chirpy doctor friend has got some tramadol. But let's not get too far ahead of ourselves – tomorrow we've got our jaunt to El Maharch. Cheer up, chicken! There'll be a canyon and an oasis! And a dried-up lake! Think of that – a lake that does not exist any more! It's dried up!' I ruffled her hair, just as I like to do with my girls when they're in a pet.

And eventually, after I'd clucked her under the chin, Kate started to perk up. 'Oh there's a dried-up lake, is there?' She clapped her hands in mock delight.

'I think there's a little restaurant in the oasis too, and if we were very, very daring, we could sneak in there and I could buy you a coffee and a bun.'

'Chicken,' she said. 'That's what I want. Roast chicken, with crisp salty skin.'

'I'll see if I can call in ahead and order you one.'

A walker, Peter, tall and angular, had come up behind us. I'd seen him at Doc Trotters. 'No food talk in my hearing,' he said.

'What are you looking forward to at the end of the race, then?' I asked.

'When I get back to the hotel…' Peter trailed off as he pondered the delights of the Berbère Palace. 'I will go straight to the bar and I will order an ice-cold bottle of Champagne. I will take the bottle to the pool. I will sit in the shade, and I will drink half of it.'

'Aren't you going to share it?' Kate asked.

'I'll share it with you,' Peter said.

'And me?' I asked.

'More doubtful.' He mimed drinking a glass of Champagne and went on his way.

As the mood lightened, so did Kate's feet, and within a short while, we were swinging our hands and concocting the most fantastical dream dinners for ourselves.

'I haven't even pulled the girly card yet,' said Kate.

'What's the girly card?'

'Start crying. Say I'm hungry and that I can't carry my rucksack.'

'Kate, dear, you don't have to start blubbing. It'd be a pleasure to carry your rucksack. I'll just pop it on my own. It barely weighs the same as my front pouch.

'Thanks.' She slipped her arm around my waist and I put my hand about her shoulders, and as we walked back to Tent 71, I was as content as I had ever been.

*

The next day, we had not one, not two, but three rows in the tent. I don't know if these spats were common in other tents; it may well have been something to do with me, because somehow I always seemed to be very near the epicentre. I couldn't have cared less about the first two. But I hated the last one.

I'd started the morning with debris from my rucksack strewn all about my Thermarest. As my tentmates gave me more room, my kit seemed to spread along with it. Carlo was similarly chaotic; I'd always thought surgeons were neat and tidy, and perhaps they are, though maybe only in the work place.

The Berbers had already peeled off our tent, but had left us with the rug. Carlo and I were squatting on our Thermarests, in a nest of our own filth. I remembered how Patrick had urged us on the first day to 'look smart'; we looked absolutely filthy. White shirts turned brown from the sand, so saturated with salt that they seemed to have been starched, and black trousers turned grey from the rivers of sweat.

I'd already been out to the Doc Trotters' morning station at the centre of the bivouac and had picked up some large strips of bandage. They were much more substantial than the puny little bandages I'd brought out from Britain.

'Got a bit of a Groundhog feel to it, this race, so it has,' Carlo said. He'd brought out his own set of scalpels and was carving a crescent cut into a blister on his big toe.

'Groundhog Day?'

'Yep,' he said, leaning back to admire his handiwork. He stretched for some antiseptic. 'Doesn't matter what we do – every single day starts the same way. The desert. The porridge—'

'And bandaging our feet while everyone else gives us a very wide berth.'

Carlo chuckled. He was looking for somewhere to put his scalpel while he wiped on the disinfectant. Without really thinking about it, he popped the scalpel into Martin's Thermarest. The Thermarest let out a little hiss of complaint and started to deflate.

'Feck it!' he said.

Carlo looked dumbfounded. Kate came over, and when she saw Carlo sitting there with the scalpel still embedded in Martin's Thermarest, she burst into laughter.

'We'll mend it,' I said.

'I'm such a feckin' eejit.' Carlo shook his head and laughed.

'I've got a repair kit. We've got five minutes till he gets back with his water.'

The repair kit was very simple, similar to a bike repair kit. You just wiped the puncture clean and then stuck on a self-adhesive patch – and it should all have been fine, except Martin returned before I'd finished.

'What the hell are you doing?' he said.

'Oh – Hi Martin.' I turned to face him and the patch popped off the Thermarest.

'You've bloody burst my Thermarest! I knew you'd do that! I knew it!' He bubbled with rage. 'You are such an inconsiderate wanker – look at all this shit of yours!' He kicked my billycan, which was half-full of tea. It skittered across the sand.

'Do you have to?' I sighed and leaned back on my sleeping bag.

'Well if I don't tell you, then who the hell will?' He was getting more and more hysterical as the vexations of the previous four days suddenly came to a head. 'You leave your shit lying everywhere, you infect everyone with your foul diseases, and now you've gone and bloody butchered my Thermarest.'

Carlo was scratching at his beard. 'Martin...' he said.

'Let me speak. This English twat—'

'Do you have to call me an English twat?' I asked.

'All right – this English prick has to be told when he's out of line.'

'Martin,' Carlo said. 'I popped your Thermarest. I'm very sorry.'

'Oh,' said Martin, slowly digesting what Carlo had said. 'You burst it. Why the hell is he—'

'The English prick,' I interjected.

'—mending the thing?'

'He had the repair kit,' Carlo said.

'Oh,' said Martin. He started inspecting his Thermarest. 'I wish people would leave my stuff alone.'

He mooched off to talk to Del and I thought that was going to be that, but he came back a few minutes later to apologise. 'I'm sorry,' he said. 'Been getting a little tense, that's all.'

I looked up from my bandages. 'That's all right,' I said. 'I'll just have it on credit for the next time I really do irritate you.'

Lawson came over. 'Hey – English prick. Are you ready to go yet?'

'If I'm an English prick, what the hell are you?'

Lawson thought for a moment, twirling his walking pole like a majorette. 'I'm an English knob,' he said. He lost control of the pole and it spiralled into the air.

'I'm an Irish prick!' Carlo said.

'Well can you pricks please avoid stabbing my Thermarest,' said Martin.

I smeared on some Vaseline. I'd been warned before the race that Vaseline was a disaster in the desert, that the dust would work its way in and would stick to it, and would turn to a gritty sandpaper. But after a couple of days, my skin was so chafed and painful that I had nothing to lose. I put on a liberal coating; and I can report that it worked like a charm. Vaseline works just as well in the Sahara as it does on the ice-cold paths of the Pilgrim's Way.

'What's it going to be like today?' we asked Eeyore, the rep.

'Hot.'

'And any hills?' Lawson said. 'What will they be like?'

'High. Very high.'

It was the one day that there was a real glut of water - bottles and bottles of mineral water going spare. Kate had gone out ahead of me, hoping to finish the stage before the real heat of the day had kicked in. It was just over seven miles to the first checkpoint on that third day, and for the first time I was going at a modest – well, a very modest – clip. I was trotting along, feeling not too bad, thanking my stars that my guts had stopped rumbling. At the checkpoint, I took my 1.5 litre bottle of water, went through my water bottle routine and had a bite of Nutri-Grain.

As I was leaving to head north up a high sandy hill, *Jebel Zireg*, I saw all the discards. Empty water bottles were usually screwed up and tossed into a white canvas bin about the size of a hot tub. But the bin wasn't at all full. The first leg had been so short that nobody had wanted any of the water, so they'd left their half-full bottles by the bin.

I looked at them longingly. I wondered whether to take an extra litre with me. Just in case.

'Will you just look at that?' Carlo said. He'd come up behind me and we stood together by the bin. Carlo looked in good shape. After five days in Morocco, we'd both adjusted to the heat; we still sweated a lot, but the heat was not nearly as gruelling as it had been on the first two days.

'You could have a bath in there,' I said. 'Though the Commissaires would probably start whining.'

'So they would.'

We looked again at the water bottles. There must have been 200, maybe 300 litres of bottled water going spare. We wondered what they'd do with it all. It seemed such a waste to leave it.

'We could at least have a shower,' I said.

'Feck it, let's do it,' Carlo said, unbuckling his rucksack. 'Shorts on though. I can't be doing with any of that nuddie showering like you had with Kate.'

'It just won't be the same.'

We took off our shirts and poured bottle after bottle of mineral over each other, rubbing it into our faces, wringing it through our hair. It was magical, a beautiful break from the sheer grind of the MdS.

Other runners gawked at us, wondering whether to try it; but, ever mindful that this was the Marathon des Sables, they ruefully went on their way. And we laughed and we poured more water, and this was not some rationed shower like I'd had with Kate, this was bottle after bottle of cold clear water, cascading over my face and into my mouth, and the sheer ecstasy of turning my face to the sun, eyes closed, with the white heat and cool water, the droplets dazzling like diamonds. My shorts and gaiters and socks and shoes were all saturated, and I didn't give a damn. I washed away the salt sizzle on my shoulders and the tired tide-lines of salt on my cheekbones. I felt as if I had been reborn.

'Look at those poor saps,' I said. Up ahead of us was *Jebel Zireg*, at least half a mile of deep sand, and on it was a long line of trudging walkers, who had only stopped for a few moments at the checkpoint, had taken their water – and had forgotten to smell the flowers before they'd continued with the race.

'Tough hill,' said Carlo. He had soaked his shirt in water and was tugging it on. In ten minutes, it would be bone dry. 'What comes after this?'

'Best not to know.' I emptied a bottle on my *casquette* and the water dripped deliciously onto my face and down the back of my neck. 'We don't mind what's ahead of us, because we, here and now, are enjoying this labour of love in the sand.' I tossed the empty bottle into the canvas bin and shortened off my walking poles for the hill.

'You and your fancy talk,' he said. 'Is this how you sound on the *Sun*?'

Up ahead of us the 11 Pompiers were manhauling their dune buggy through the deep sand. We overtook them very quickly and I peered inside the dune buggy. There was a teenage boy on a comfortable chair and in complete shade. He was one of the four boys who took it in turns to sit in the buggy. He was surrounded by water and snacks, though he looked very hot. I wondered if he was enjoying himself. The Pompiers weren't even towing him now, they were carrying him, silently trudging up that hot hill.

'Know what the Pilgrims say on the route to Santiago de Compostela?' I asked.

'I don't think I do,' he said.

'*Cállate y camina*,' I said. 'Shut up and walk.'

'Is that right now? Shut up and walk?'

I was driving my poles into the ground, using my arms to power me up the hill. I liked having people ahead of me. I liked overtaking them.

'You hear how many people dropped out yesterday? Only five.'

'Is that so, Kim?' He tugged his *casquette* down on his forehead so that he could only see just a few feet ahead of him. '*Cállate y camina*!'

*

And onto the second row.

I nearly stopped at the Camp Auberge site for a Coke and a sandwich, but by then I was by myself and, like so many things in life, it didn't seem much fun to go into the café alone. I could feel these two huge blisters developing on the side of each heel and I knew that if I stopped, even if I stopped for an ice-cold Coke, all my defences would go down, and when I started again it would be like trying to crank up the engine in an old rusting jalopy.

A little further on, I was daydreaming and I took my eye off the path and kicked a huge stone. It burst the blister on my left heel. I sat by the roadside, wondering whether to take off my shoe and examine my foot.

Patrick Bauer pulled up in his dune buggy, looking as happy as can be. He was like the happy dreamer from the song that we heard at the start of every stage.

'How are you, Mr Kim?' he asked.

'*Bonjour*, Monsieur Patrick,' I said, 'My blister's just burst.'

He bellowed with laughter. '*Bon courage*!' he roared, before driving off into a cloud of dust and hot sand.

As ever, I was one of the last into the tent. Before I'd got in to El Maharch, the tent had blown down. The wind was whipping the sand in through the middle of the tent, and it was making everyone tetchy. Most of them, including Kate, were in their sleeping bags, though Del was making himself some coffee. It was just brewing. He brought the billycan up to his nose and inhaled, a smile of pleasure on his face; it was the first time I'd seen his human side.

I drank my REGO recovery drink and steeled myself for pulling off my shoes. As I untied my laces, I could feel my feet starting to breathe again. The blister on my left heel had been obliterated, but, even before I'd taken off my socks, I knew the other one was going to be large and tender.

The sock came off in a shower of sand to reveal a blister the size of a golf-ball. I was surprised that it hadn't burst like the other one. The skin was stretched tight.

'That's a beauty,' Lawson said.

'Can you take a picture?' I asked, tossing him my camera. 'My daughters will be impressed.'

I got out my medicine kit and disinfected the blister with TCP before selecting a sharp clean needle. 'This should be good,' I said. I stabbed into the blister.

With most blisters, the clear serum normally just eases out. You make a cut and the serum drips down your skin. But if the blister is big and if it's tight, and there's a lot of pressure behind it, then…

The serum fountained out of my blister in a perfect arc before landing in Del's steaming coffee.

Del stared in amazement at the billycan and at the spray of gunk dripping from his fingers.

Lawson let out an involuntary laugh. 'Was that what I think it was?' he said.

'I'm not sure,' I said. My foot was still poised in the air and I still had the needle in my hand.

'You…' said Del, looking from me to his coffee and back again. 'Is that from your bloody blister?'

'I'm not sure,' I said. 'It might be.'

'You tosser! You bloody tosser!'

Lawson was not helping things. 'Guess what the English prick's done?' He gave Carlo a nudge. 'He's just squirted his blister into Del's coffee!'

They wanted to know all the details, demanding a re-enactment, laughing and laughing as Del slowly simmered.

'I'm sorry Del,' I said. 'Is there anything I can do to make it up to you?'

'Screw you.'

'I'm sorry,' I said again, rather lamely. I didn't know what else to say, or what else I could do.

'Extra protein in there,' said Lawson. 'Might even taste nice.'

Del wiped his fingers on his shirt and quietly studied his coffee mug. 'I'll get you,' he said.

'I'm sorry, Del,' I said. 'What do you want me to do?'

'I want you to stay the hell away from me.' He tossed the coffee out of the tent.

'I'd have drunk that,' Lawson said.

'Go screw yourself.'

So that was the second bust-up of the day. And then there was the third. It was this last one that was the most painful of them all. I couldn't have cared a damn about annoying either Del or Martin. But Kate? I cared about her a lot.

CHAPTER 17

Soon after I'd emptied my blister into Del's coffee, a Commissaire came by with printouts of emails we'd received. She gave a clutch of papers to Carlo who passed them around the tent.

'One for you,' Carlo said. He squinted at the single sheet of paper as he handed it over to me. 'From Human Resources. Nice to know they care.'

It was a single message, a very short one – though not quite from the Human Resources department. It was from my mad master, the editor. 'Keep it coming!' he'd written. 'We want all of the injuries and all of the pain. If you kick the bucket, I'll give you the front page!'

I laughed. The *Sun* has one great similarity with the MdS, in that its practitioners are morbidly addicted to gallows humour.

Elise hadn't written. Over the first three days of the MdS, Elise had chivvied the girls to send me little notes, but now – nothing. I wondered why. There would be a reason, I was sure of that, but I couldn't quite fathom it. Perhaps they'd gone off somewhere? It made me miss them even more. Martin looked over at me and my single sheet of paper with its few terse lines. 'Looks like your family's really missing you,' he said.

'Who needs family when you've got an army of *Sun* readers?'

'Have you mentioned me yet in your write-up?'

'Not yet,' I said. 'Though I certainly will after your little tantrum this morning.'

'Does that mean I get a mention too?' Carlo asked, looking up from his four pages of emails.

'You'll be getting star billing.' I neatly folded my email and tucked it in with my passport and money; every MdS competitor has to have 200 Euros in case of emergencies.

The emails prompted a range of emotions in the tent. Kurtz, tough old Kurtz with his scars and his eye patch, was openly crying as he read and reread the messages from his family. He wiped away the tears as they rolled down his cheek.

Lawson was crowing with laughter. 'Listen to what my business partner has written,' he said. 'I'll read it out to you! "Sounds like you're having a blast. I think I might give the Marathon des Sables a try next year." Well, my friend, bring it on!'

Kate was tucked in her sleeping bag and, with her head torch on, was reading and rereading two pages' worth of emails. I presumed that at least one of them was from Edward. She was quite inscrutable, her mouth set in a straight line.

'Everything all right?' I asked.

'Fine,' she said. She scrumpled up the two pages and tossed them into the top of her rucksack. 'I'm going to file my copy.'

I should have listened. I should have paid attention to what every one of my senses was screaming at me. This was a woman who wanted to be alone.

But I didn't listen. I was a love-struck fool and I wanted to be with her.

'Mind if I come too?' I asked.

'Sure,' she said, and even as she got out of her sleeping bag, I should have known to have stayed in the tent.

We walked to the communications tent in near silence. She was hobbling, even worse than the day before. I hadn't seen the state of her feet that evening, as she'd already strapped them up by the time I got in. But it didn't look good.

There were so many things I wanted to ask her, but I didn't really know how to couch my questions, so I said nothing at all. How had her day gone? How were her feet? How was she feeling about the next day's double marathon? And also – anything she wanted to tell me about those emails?

We queued, and Kate prickled next to me, glowering as she stared at her feet. I started talking to Denis, a Scotsman with a lined, corrugated forehead, a thick red beard and very burned skin. 'How's your day going so far?' I asked.

'Terrible,' he said. His fingers strayed to the peeling skin on his red cheeks. 'I was on a yacht once, sailing to Kintyre. I felt so ill, I was nearly suicidal. I'd have done anything to stop the pain; I'd never felt so awful. That's how it was today. I kept wondering, How bad would it get? Had I been through the worst? Or was the worst yet to come?'

I tried to be upbeat. 'We've nearly cracked it,' I said. 'Only tomorrow to go and that's it.'

'I don't know,' he said. 'After that heat today, I might take the seasickness.'

Bird song was playing in the communications tent as usual. Kate was a few yards away from me and I could hear her clattering at the keyboard, punching at the keys as if at an old-style typewriter. She had this look of concentrated fury on her face.

I should have left the tent once I'd filed my copy, but I didn't. Instead I sat down on a battered steel trunk and waited for Kate.

She had filed her first take of copy and was about to start on her next email when a Commissaire touched her on the elbow.

'You are only allowed one email a day,' the Commissaire said.

'I know,' she said. 'I'm sending emails on behalf of my tentmates. I have their race numbers.'

The Commissaire looked at Kate, sizing her up. 'Come back later,' he said. 'When there is no queue.'

Kate was enraged, but she didn't say anything. She picked up her water bottle and abruptly left the tent. I followed her out. There were a number of people clustered around the finish line. It was dusk and very windy. From way out in the wilderness, we could just make out a small white light.

'What's happening?' I asked a woman.

'The last guy's coming in,' she said.

I turned to Kate. 'We better cheer him in,' I said.

She shrugged. She couldn't have cared less. 'Okay.'

And slowly, so slowly, the headlight came towards us; the guy would make the cut-off by about ten minutes. His body began to take shape, a blur of grey against the darkness. I thought of *Lawrence of Arabia* and a scene that goes on for minutes on end, Omar Sharif on a camel, slowly, slowly ambling towards the camera.

I wondered what would happen if you were two miles out and you saw the finish line for the first time, realising that you only had 20 minutes to make it. Would the adrenalin kick in and give you enough of a fillip to get you over the line? Could you even break into a canter after ten hours of trudging on raw, blistered feet? Did the Commissaires have some degree of latitude? Could you stay in the race if you missed the cut-off by five minutes? Or could you, perhaps, abandon your rucksack and just sprint for the line?

Twenty of us cheered the Frenchman over the line. He'd picked up a couple of sticks and was using them as walking poles. He gave a tired wave and, without slowing down, went straight for his Sultan tea.

'Well done,' I said to him. 'Does it feel good?'

His face was coated with a thin layer of dust. He wiped the sand from his eyes, licked his lips and took a very small sip of tea. 'I am very happy,' he said. He took off his rucksack. With his hands on his hips, he arched his back and let out a huge groan. 'I did not think I would be here now.'

Kate was on the periphery, watching as the Commissaires dismantled the electronic strip on the finish line. I went over and took her hand.

It was a mistake.

Her hand stayed quite inert in mine, and then she broke off and put both hands to her face. She dragged her fingers from her forehead all the way down to her chin. She looked right at me, and I realised that she'd hardly looked at me all evening.

'I'm going to make a phone call,' she said.

'Oh,' I said, very noncommittal.

She looked at me again, more searchingly. There was an odd hardness about her face that I had not seen before.

'You think that's a bad idea?' We were walking back to the communications tent; she winced with every step.

'Calling up Edward while you're in the middle of the Marathon des Sables?' I said. 'Getting an earfull from him just a few hours before the toughest day of your life? Oh yeah, I think it's a great idea.'

She. Absolutely. Exploded.

'What the fuck do you know?' she screamed. 'You know nothing about this. You know nothing about me! Why the hell do you think I'm even calling up Edward?'

We had stopped walking. I was so shocked that I took an involuntary step backwards. It was quite dark now and the wind was blowing hard, lifting the sand off the surface.

'You know nothing,' she said again, her face a mask of rage. 'Who are you to tell me whether or not I can make a phone call? You who've been stuck at the *Sun* for nearly 20 years, writing rubbish that nobody reads. And you're married – you're married with beautiful daughters, so why the hell are you holding my hand? And what are you doing in this desert anyway? Just some sad man having a mid-life crisis, trying to get your leg over while you're at it. Is that what I am to you? Is that what I mean to you?'

Kate's voice had become quite shrill. She was pointing at me now. I remember how my shoulders slumped. I felt this overwhelming sense of loss – not so much at the insults, but that the idyll was over.

I took it. I can soak things up very well.

Kate was not nearly done.

'You talk about Edward with such disdain. You don't like him. You don't even know him. Well I love him. I have more love for him than you could ever conceive. Edward has more heart and more passion in his little finger than you have in your whole body. Everything is just one big joke to you. But that's not how life is. I fell for it. I so fell for it. But I don't want any of it any more. It's pathetic.' She looked at me, nodding; I would hardly have recognised her. 'You're pathetic.'

She was breathing hard, her eyes searching my face as she waited for my reply.

I wondered what to say. There were quite a few things I could have said, some amelioratory and some not, but I was sure that, whatever I said, it would only add more fuel to the flames.

The wind continued to blow and the sand started to pepper my hands and my face, the blimps at the finish-line bending and straining against their ropes.

'Good night,' I said. I turned on my heel and limped back to the tent.

It was a quiet, lonely night in the tent that night. My general good cheer had ebbed into the sand. I just wanted the race to be over; to have a bath and a beer; to never, ever have to see Kate again.

Many people think that, because I am imperturbable and rarely ruffled, their words and their insults have no effect on me. Most of it doesn't. I move on. I do not dwell on the insults and, in time, I forget.

But I knew there was more than a little truth to what Kate had said to me. I was indeed a sad middle-aged man who was frittering away my life on the *Sun*; and I was married with three adorable daughters; and there probably was more passion in Edward's little finger than in my entire lumbering frame.

So her words hurt. But what hurt most of all was that, quite clearly, my little desert dream was over. I didn't know if Kate and I would ever be able to recapture what we'd had. But even if we did, things would be different. There would be an edge, a wariness, to our friendship that there had not been before; anything I said, I would first have to edit and censor to check there was nothing too offensive. Our relationship, or such of it as remained, would be reduced to the trite and the bland, like the chocolate-coated froth on a sweet cappuccino.

Kate came into the tent, a great gust of sand blowing in behind her, and climbed into her sleeping bag without saying a word. I lay awake in the darkness, listening to the wind and the sound of her silent tears.

CHAPTER 18

The next day, I saw a man have a heart attack.

The fourth stage, the monster, had barely started and, compared to what we had been through, it was not that hot.

I had been walking along with Kurtz when suddenly, not 20 yards in front of us, a flare went off, screeching into the sky. Kurtz thought he was under fire. Much to my amusement, he dived to the ground.

The 11 Pompiers were clustered around a man, and I went over to see what was happening. He was a Frenchman, Albert, and he was sitting on a rock. His face was dripping with sweat and his eyes were closed. He looked wan and his skin was waxy and pale; he was all in. One of the firemen was taking his pulse.

Within seconds, a helicopter had flown in. It swooshed low overhead before bumping down next to us in a billow of sand. The Pompiers stretchered Albert onto the helicopter, and he was away in under two minutes. In all the wild world, you could not find a better place to have a heart attack than on the MdS – doctors and defibrillators are never more than five minutes away. If he'd been in the Highlands, he'd have been dead before they'd even dispatched the helicopter.

At the time I thought that Albert had heat stroke. It was only at the second checkpoint that I learned he'd had a heart attack and was being treated in hospital. I never found out what happened to him. Albert was like so many people on the MdS: the ends are always left untied.

It was a very sober and thoughtful Kim who was walking through the desert for the rest of the day, dreaming about death and blisters and the pain in my feet, which had numbed a little since I'd started alternating between ibuprofen and paracetemol.

And, of course, I was thinking about Kate a lot too. I wasn't sure if the previous night's explosion was about me and my general behaviour, or whether I just happened to have been the man who'd bumbled along and tapped the volcano. Was it personal? Or was it a much broader rage, crackling wild in the clouds until it found a lightning rod? Like the stressed-out businessman who soaks it up and soaks it up, and then bites his wife's head off at home for overcooking the dinner.

I didn't know. I didn't even know if Kate and I would manage to get back onto an even keel before the end of the race. Was she the sort to hold a grudge? Perhaps we'd go two or three days hardly speaking to each other, and then the race would be done, our desert dream would be over and we'd be on our way home. And after that – with no race looming and no reason to train together, it would be very difficult to pick up the pieces.

I wondered if she'd even want to pick up the pieces.

And on and on – through the midday sun, through the afternoon bake, mile after mile of desert, and checkpoints and more bottled water, and my feet aching, bad but not terminal, and those horrendous three hours after the third checkpoint when I got lost in the night.

That quite beautiful moment when, ecstasy upon ecstasy, I made it into the fourth checkpoint, a clear hour before the cut-off. I felt this ridiculous sense of elation. I wasn't lost any more, I'd made it out of the mire and I was still – just – a part of the Marathon des Sables.

And then, as I'm zipping up my zips and about to leave, I hear this screaming from the medical tent, and I know without a shadow of doubt that it's Kate. In a moment the great tirade from the previous night is forgotten – completely forgotten – and I am holding her hand and getting her water and offering to cook her food. And, seamlessly, without even the flicker of an eyebrow, we have moved on. Though there may have been a blip, it's simply what happens with a beautiful woman who is in possession of a temper. But you don't throw in the towel after the very first sign of trouble. Especially not when there's a crisis.

And this was some crisis.

The blisters had grown and grown until there was no skin left on the sole of one foot; it had been delaminated. Her other foot was in slightly better shape, but not by much. Blisters had been growing underneath her toenails, which was causing her the most pain. Losing the skin on your feet is, of course, going to be painful – but it can be endured. Having an IV needle jammed through your toenail, on the other hand, is not just a new pain – it's a different quality of pain, very different from the chafing that leads to blisters.

Kate was dosed up on painkillers, but they were taking a while to kick in, and each step was like treading on needles.

I was in pretty good shape compared to the others – my feet were blistered and my legs ached, of course, but I couldn't allow myself the luxury of even a word of complaint. I had to nursemaid my mate, my runningmate, through the rest of the stage.

I was worried about the cold for the next leg. I'd waited for well over an hour for Kate to get fixed up, and I hadn't bothered to get out of my sweat-soaked shirt and trousers, and gradually the cold and the wind had eaten into my bones. Just when I'd decided to take off my shirt, Kate had come up and we were on our way, and there wasn't much I could do about it from there.

No, for the next 20 miles, I had to be cheerful and kind and upbeat and at times sympathetic and at times quite militant; and, above all, I could not allow one word of worry or whining to pass from my lips.

I was damn well going to get her in.

'Lookin' Good!' I said, as we walked out of the snug security of that camp and into the dark Sahara.

She forced a smile, but then it turned into one of genuine warmth. 'Feelin' Good!' she said. We were on our way.

We were heading roughly northeast now, through low flattish dunes. You had the option of taking the direct route, straight up the side of the dunes through the thick sand, or you could try and follow the contours and weave around the sides. We had become experts on every type of desert terrain. Deep sand was softer on your blisters, as it had some give. Hard ground hurt your feet, but you could travel on it more quickly. Little thorn bushes had to be avoided or they would jag and rip your gaiters. Worst of the lot was trekking sideways across a dune. Ideally you want your shoe to land flat on the sand, but when you're walking across a dune, then only half your foot is striking the ground. This leads to shear, then to hotspots, and finally to blisters.

It took us a little time to notice it, but there was a green light directly ahead of us. We realised it was a laser, beaming up high into the sky. It was guiding us in. Though whether the laser was at the next checkpoint or whether it was at the finish line, we could not tell. It could have been a mile away; it could have been a hundred miles away.

'We could be the Three Kings,' I said.

'It has a religious feel,' Kate said. She had borrowed my walking poles as they helped take a little of the weight off her feet. 'We're following our star.'

'We could be going anywhere now. Maybe we're going to Shangri-La.'

'It'll be heaven when we stop.'

'And you know what comes before heaven?' I said. 'Purgatory.'

She laughed and for a while we were silent, with nothing but the sound of her poles clipping in the sand. I thought Kate was happy with her own thoughts, but then I heard this sound, low and long, and I realised that she was letting out this constant, soft moan. It was the sound of somebody forcing themselves to endure the unendurable.

'This is hell,' she said. 'This is hell.'

I realised that walking along in this companionable silence was no longer an option. If we were going to get through this together, then I was going to have to start talking and entertaining. I would have to chat breezily, humorously and insightfully. I would have to be versatile, too, because if Kate was to be distracted and taken out of her misery, then I would need to glide from monologues to the madcap. Since we were walking so slowly, and since we had perhaps ten hours ahead of us, I might even have to throw in some myths, some poetry, some personal anecdotes. I didn't know what I was going to say. But I'd keep on talking.

My love life was a very rich seam. I told her about my first great love, my piano mistress, and how we had made love in the spinneys and the brambles of Eton College. I told her about how I'd met Elise in New York and of the devil's own pact that I'd made with her when I'd been in the first flush of love. I told her about my elopement, and about the woman who knew what she wanted, and about my first marriage, madder than mad.

Kate did not talk while I was talking, and at first I thought she might have switched off completely, mindlessly putting one foot in front of the next. But she had stopped whimpering, so I kept on talking. Then, quite out of the blue, she asked me a question.

'Why did you marry your first wife?'

'Yeah – why did you marry your first wife?' I looked over my shoulder. It was Loren, a black American, huge and lovely; he looked like a retired linebacker. The white lines of sweat were quite clear on his cheeks.

'Hi Loren – looking good.'

'You look like a champ!' he said. He was moving well, using his walking poles very handily. 'So? Why did you marry her?'

'I've often asked myself the same question.'

'She was great in the sack?' said Loren.

'Not especially,' I said. 'I don't really remember. I can remember a lot about it. I can remember the rows and the interminable shouting. But I don't remember what happened in the sack.'

'There must have been something though,' Kate said. She turned her head to me. I could not see her face. All I could see was the dazzle of her head torch.

'We were very different,' I said. 'Polar opposites. And for a while it was all very exciting, and…' I drifted off. For a few months it *had* been so exciting, so different.

'And?' said Loren.

'It didn't end well,' I said, and there must have been some inflexion in my voice because Loren did not probe any further.

'I wonder if I should get married,' said Kate.

Loren let out this deep bass 'Ho-Ho.'

'Kate, honey, you don't get married unless you are one thousand per cent certain that this guy is the one. If you're not sure, if there is even the *slight*-est doubt in your mind, then don't do it!'

'Listen to the man,' I said. 'He knows his stuff.'

I gave Kate a caffeine gel and offered one over to Loren. 'You sure?' he asked.

'Enjoy every drop.'

We ripped off the silver foil tops and squeezed the gel into our mouths. It was pure energy and we could feel the hit in seconds. I'd warmed up a little by now and my feet were nicely numbed; I could have gone faster, but Kate was dictating the pace.

'Thanks,' Loren said. He tucked the empty gel wrapper into his pocket. 'See you at checkpoint five. Water'll be on the boil.'

I kept talking, about anything and everything that came into my head. As we followed the line of the laser, it really did seem like a pilgrimage, painful and hard, and with lessons to be learned along the way. I talked of the world's oldest pilgrimage, around Mount Kailash in Tibet, and I told her everything I knew about the epic pilgrimage to Santiago de Compostela.

And when I was spent with religion, I started on poetry. Not that I know much poetry, but I can still remember those poems I learned at school. I gave her Tennyson's 'The Revenge,' and 'The Charge of the Light Brigade,' and Lewis Carroll's 'Jabberwocky,' and then some Lear poems that I sometimes recite to the girls, and when that was spent, I started on Shakespeare, working my way through the highlights of *Othello* and *Romeo and Juliet* and even *Titus Andronicus*.

Kate did not talk, but she was not moaning either, and I took that to be a good sign. 'I know!' I said. 'You'll love this one. It's perfect for you. It's perfect for us. I'll give you some Samuel Beckett – *Worstward Ho*. I'll give you the best bit. You'll love it.'

Kate let out this snort of surprised laughter. 'Let's hear it.'

'"Ever tried. Ever failed. No matter. Try again. Fail again. Fail Better."' I paused and looked up at the laser. I loved it. I loved where

I was, and I loved what we were doing together: Ever tried. Ever failed. No matter. Try again. 'Like it?'

'I do,' she said. 'Very much.' And then she started to speak, softly at first, but picking up speed and growing in volume, and to my total astonishment, I realised that she was reciting some more of Beckett's *Worstward Ho*, but way beyond anything I'd ever managed to remember. '"No choice but stand. Somehow up and stand. Somehow stand. That or groan. The groan so long on its way. No. No groan. Simply pain. Simply up. A time when try how. Try see. Try say. How first it lay. Then somehow knelt. Bit by bit. Then on from there. Bit by bit. Till up at last."'

I was staggered. 'You know it?' I said.

'I know it all.' She spoke so quietly that I had to move closer to hear her.

'I'm impressed,' I said. 'That's a monster of a poem!'

'It is.'

'I wish I'd had that sort of dedication when I'd done my degree.'

And still we walked, and still we followed our green laser, which was the only star to be seen in the sky.

'I learned it when I was 17,' she said. 'It was a challenge I set myself. I thought that if I learned it, then I might live.'

I was about to say something, but I snatched back the words as they came out of my mouth. She didn't need me to talk; she needed me to listen.

'I thought I was going to die,' she said. 'The doctors said I was going to die. They said I had only two weeks to live. That was when I made this pact with myself, that if I learned the Beckett poem, I would stay alive. I'd heard it the previous week while I'd been in one of the Marie Curie care homes. And I made this deal. So I learned it – and I lived.'

I was riveted. We were walking shoulder to shoulder, arms and legs in silent synchronicity. I didn't say a word.

'I had cancer,' she said. 'Brain cancer. They'd operated on me when I was 13, and again when I was 15, and the next time it came back, I was 17 and they said it was inoperable. They told my parents that nothing could be done. They said I'd be dead in a fortnight.

'But it turned out that something could be done. It could be done, but it had never been done before. It was a very risky operation. My parents were desperate. They asked the doctors to try it, to try anything. The doctors told them it would be their responsibility if anything went wrong – as if that was going to make any difference. My parents gave their permission and the operation went ahead. They had a big team, doctors, anaesthetists, nurses. It went on all day. And the next day, because I'd learned my poem, I lived.'

'My… God,' I said. It was beyond conception. Years of going in and out of hospitals, years of treatment, and at the end of it all, being told that it was terminal. And after all that, to put your faith in a poem. How ever I looked at it, what ever I thought, I would never even come close to what Kate had been through.

'I've been left with a scar on the back of my head, and a hole in my brain the size of a grapefruit. It's now filled with fluid, so sometimes when I get tired I lose my sense of balance,' she said. 'But apart from that… there doesn't seem to be very much wrong with me. Though my mum says that if I hadn't had a fifth of my brain removed, I'd probably be the most intelligent human on the planet.'

I wiped a tear from my eye. I was intensely moved. I'd had no idea.

'Some people, after they've had cancer, they just lose the will. They turn to alcohol or drugs; they do what they can to get them through the night. But with me…' Kate winced as she kicked a rock. She bumped into my shoulder, and for a moment, it brought her back to the here and now, to the reality of the desert and her blisters. But after a while she continued.

'I went the other way. I had this hunger to grab life by the throat. Every day was a gift and I wanted to seize it and live it as if it were my last. So that's why I raise money for the Marie Curie Cancer Care –that's why I'm doing the race.' She laughed to herself. 'Funny to think that three years ago, I'd never even heard of the Marathon des Sables.'

'Was that a story for our film fundraiser, or did you really do it?' I said. 'Did you really Google the words, "Toughest footrace on earth"?'

'I did,' she said. 'And up came the MdS. As soon as I found out about it, I knew I had to do it.'

'And here we are, living the dream.'

'I just didn't know the dream was going to be this painful.'

'Compared to what you've been through, this is a complete snap.'

'Not a snap,' she said. 'But different.'

'And to think – all because of a poem.'

She took the walking poles in one hand and slipped her arm comfortably through mine. 'Fail again. Fail better.'

CHAPTER 19

The green laser was mounted on a huge truck, about the size of a dustbin lorry, and it was blasting its beam at a low, flat angle towards the previous checkpoint. Even when we were just 200 yards away, we still had no idea we were so close. And then suddenly we were walking past it. It could have come off the *Star Wars* set, a laser to blast Jedi fighters out of the sky. Half a mile on was the fifth checkpoint, and we both had that surge of relief that came from knowing that, for a little while at least, we could put our feet up.

Kate was all for taking our water and pushing on while the tide was still with us, but I'd eaten nothing but powders and gels since the morning and I needed some proper food.

'I could do with a break,' I said. 'Put your feet up. I'll make you some spaghetti bolognese. We'll have some food and a cup of tea, and then in half an hour we'll be on our way. Forty miles down. Only 12 to go.

'A cheeky half-marathon.'

There were a couple of tents for the runners to sleep in if they didn't want to walk through the night. The tents were very inviting, cosy and windproof, with lamps hung from the poles. The carpets looked rich and thick and I longed to lay my head down. We found Loren brushing his teeth. He'd taken off his shoes and socks and was about to get into his sleeping bag.

'I'm in no hurry,' he said. 'I'm savouring it.'

'I want to get it over with,' Kate winced as she pulled off her shoes.

'Can we do a bit of both?' I asked. I untied my laces, cursing at the double knot.

My feet started to breathe again and I groaned with relief. For a while Kate and I just lay there, side by side with our bandaged feet raised up on our rucksacks. She took my hand. We didn't say anything. It was blissful not to be walking any more, and to be holding her hand again, and to know that… that the previous night's spat might never have happened. Everything was all right.

I rolled onto my front and pulled my stove and billycan out of my rucksack, and in a few minutes the water was simmering. I cut a couple of empty water bottles in half and poured out the dehydrated spaghetti bolognese; it looked very similar to the desert sand that we'd just been walking through. I added the water, gave it a mix, let it stand, gave it another stir and handed a half-bottle over to Kate. She'd been lying with her eyes closed, though she was not asleep. 'Thanks,' she said, and turned onto her side and started to eat. We hadn't realised how hungry we were, and ate stolidly and in silence until there was not a scrap left. It was more than delicious. It was the best spaghetti I've ever tasted.

'Still hungry?' I asked.

'I am a bit.'

'Let's have another one,' I said and had another rummage around my rucksack. 'What about chilli con carne?'

'Go for it.'

And we ate that too, and then we had some mint tea, stiff with sugar, rocked by wave after wave of bliss at not being on our feet any more. The longer we spent in the tent, the more difficult it was to extricate ourselves. I sipped my tea and looked out into the forbidding darkness. Back in the tent, Loren was gently snoring in the corner in his sleeping bag, and Kate was humming to herself, feet up on her rucksack, and I wondered why I'd even considered going on any further that night. It wasn't as if we were in any hurry. It wasn't as if there were any prizes for walking through the night. And as for our tentmates, well, they'd certainly be happier if we spent the night at the checkpoint rather than waking them all up at dawn.

But I didn't know about Kate. If Kate wanted to keep on going, then I'd have to go with her.

I yawned. 'I'm tempted to spend the night here.'

She checked her watch. It was gone 2 a.m. 'It would be so good to get this thing over with.'

'Wouldn't an hour's kip be great, though? Warm sleeping bag. A full belly. The sound of Loren's snores. What more do you want?'

'Maybe an hour,' she said, and so we climbed into our sleeping bags, and I was asleep almost before I'd realised that she'd flung her arm around my waist.

We didn't have an hour's sleep. We woke at dawn, and it was windy and cloudy, and I had this horrible feeling that we might have missed our moment. A few hours ago, the walking conditions had been just perfect, cool and windy, and perhaps we should have cracked on while we had the chance. The weather in the Sahara is wild and can turn very quickly. And it never just rains in the desert – it rains hard.

I woke up with a sore throat, and I knew what that meant: I'd be going down with a cold or flu within the next day or so, with all the sneezing and shivering that that entails. My energy levels would fall through the floor, and I'd have all the drive of a sloth.

Loren had gone, everyone had gone, and we were the only people left in the tent. I made some tea and knocked out the sand from my shoes. My socks were starchy from the sweat. They felt like crinkled cardboard as I pulled them over my bandages.

Kate was waking up, her blonde hair matted and wild. She let out a groan as she realised where she was and what we still had to do. How we wished we'd gone for the sensible option and walked through the night to the bivouac. We'd be having a lie-in and we'd have a full day to recuperate.

And as it was, we still had 12 miles to go and, in that morning haze, as I sipped my peppermint, it seemed like a backbreaker. Most of the time in the MdS, I looked forward to what lay ahead of me. These last few miles seemed like the most tedious chore.

Kate was whimpering as she pulled her socks back on. She had so many blisters, on her soles, under her toenails, that each foot had become an open, seething wound. Eyes closed and with her mouth in this rictus of pain, she tugged at her socks. Getting her shoes on was another ordeal and, finally, when all was ready, she got to her feet and let out this explosive screech, the pain flooding through her legs, raw and ripe, as every enflamed sore found new voice.

She'd taken ibuprofen and paracetemol, but for that first half a mile, as we tottered out of the camp, she was in absolute agony. I did my best, but there was not much I could do to distract her.

'How far to the next checkpoint?' she hissed through gritted teeth.

'Not far at all,' I lied. We still had another five and a half miles, undulating through a series of small rocky valleys, and we were tired and clumsy. Every time we put a foot wrong, another shard of pain would lance up our legs.

It was so windy that we had our beanies on underneath our *casquettes*. And it only got windier. First came the dust, enveloping us in this red cloud, and then the sand itself was lifted off the surface. We were in a full-on sandstorm, the sand whipping up off the ground and scouring our skin. I pulled my buff high over my face and fixed Elise's sunglasses tight on my ears, but the sand and dust were everywhere, in our eyes and our ears. We couldn't see a thing, not even three paces in front of us. A sandstorm has its own incredible roar, almost like a firestorm. It is the genie of the desert, breathing its hot breath across the sands.

I grabbed Kate's hand. 'There's a rock there!' I shouted, and she said something to me, but I couldn't hear her over the wind. I dragged her to the rock, grey and craggy, about the size of a small car. We got into the lee of the stone and I kicked away some brittle scrub. We squatted down and rummaged in our rucksacks for our coats. My eyes were stinging and I had to find my coat by touch alone.

We sat crouched next to each other, knee to knee with our backs against the stone, and I had my arm round Kate's shoulders. Beyond Kate, I could see nothing, not a single thing. The sandstorm had reduced my world to just us. I found it strangely exhilarating. My worries, my job, my life and my wife back home had all been reduced to this magnificent void. I was not watching myself in the sandstorm, or observing the actions of others. I was in it. In it with Kate.

I was loving it.

She had her arm round my waist now and we were holding onto each other as if the very wind might blow us away. I nestled in towards her ear. 'At least this sandstorm has distracted me from my feet,' I said.

'Speak for yourself!' she shouted back, and we laughed and hugged each other.

'You know why I could never give up?' I said. 'We've got to find out how it all it turns out.'

'Find out the next bit of the story?' she said.

'Of course there's the sponsorship and the glory and all that,' I said. 'But I want to find out what happens next.'

Kate looked at me, her eyes so close to mine, and there was a slight upward flicker of her eyebrow, as if… I don't know. I didn't know what.

I had not noticed it at first. There was a spot of water on my arm. And then another, and I thought for a moment that Kate might have been crying. But she wasn't. She was looking at her hands, pecked by drops of water, and as I remember it now, the sandstorm gradually petered out into one of the most violent thunderstorms I have ever witnessed. Within five minutes, the little specks of rain had turned into a deluge. Sheet lightning crackled overhead and the desert boomed with thunder. The sky was an angry face, dark and livid as it scowled and roared, and it turned very cold. But sitting there with Kate, knee to knee, cheek to cheek, and with a little ledge of rock above our heads to fend off the worst of the rain, I would not have changed my position for anywhere else in the world.

Kate leant over. She had both her arms about me now. Her buff was around her neck and I could feel her breath on my ear. Her lips were nearly touching me. There was another boom of thunder, directly overhead, lighting up her face.

'I'm sorry,' she said. 'I'm so sorry.'

I pulled my buff down. 'What are you talking about?'

'I'm sorry about the other night – when I said those things to you. I was horrid. It was awful. I'm so sorry.' She held me, even tighter now, her cheek next to mine. I could hear her crying.

'Really, Kate – I have no idea what you're talking about.'

'Yes you do,' she said, and she gave me a little dig in the ribs. 'I was so stressed out. It was so unnecessary. And to you, of all people. I'm more fond of you than anyone else in the world. Will you forgive me?'

The rain stung, and above us a storm to end all thunderstorms raged, and then, as if turning on a sixpence, the weather changed again, and the rain became harder, firmer, more painful, and we found that we were being pelted by hailstones. They stung as they pinged off our legs and our arms. I moved my legs over Kate's to protect her and covered my own with my rucksack.

'There's nothing to forgive,' I said. 'And anything that might have needed forgiveness has already been forgotten.'

'Thank you,' she said, her lips all but touching my ear. 'I was so vile – and you're so kind. I think… I think it was my last stand.'

My cheek was pressed so tight to hers. Of all the many oddities of the MdS, this was the strangest by far, sheltering from this rippling hailstorm with Kate fast in my arms. 'Now I really don't know what you're talking about,' I said.

'I'm talking about this,' she said, and she moved her head slightly so that she was facing me, so that she was looking into my eyes, and, very slowly, very deliberately, she kissed me, soft, but quite firm. Her lips were moist from sunscreen and gritty from the sand and they moved under mine.

'I've wanted to do that for some time,' she said.

'Well, do it again,' I said, and she kissed me again, longer and harder.

The sound of the storm was enormous, the hail hammering down onto the rock and the sand, enveloping us in this wall of noise, and my legs were soaked as icy bullets drilled into my calves. I was quite delirious with happiness.

Kate pulled back and raised a finger as if to still me. She wiped her sand-specked lips with the sleeve of her coat and then, very gently, wiped my lips too. She pulled out some lip balm from her pocket, put it onto her lips and kissed me again, working the lip balm onto my own mouth. Her lips opened under mine, her tongue rolled and her hands slipped beneath my coat. Come join the Marathon des Sables, for all life is there.

We kissed each other until the hail stopped, and then we kissed some more, experimenting, exploring new smells and new tastes. Sometimes I would open my eyes and would see Kate's lips working languorously beneath my own, and it would hit me anew that here, now, on the MdS, Kate and I were kissing.

She kissed me again and held me tight, and then, quite naturally, I lifted off my rucksack. We extricated our limbs and hauled ourselves to our feet. We brushed each other down from all the sand and the hail that had lodged in our clothes and our gaiters. The storm clouds were fast being blown away, and in their stead was clear blue sky. In under an hour, we had gone from sandstorms to rain and hail and now to this most brilliant blue morning.

Kate and I clipped on our rucksacks, smeared on fresh sunscreen and, when we had finally adjusted our gaiters and our *casquettes*, moved towards each other and embraced. And, of course, there had to be a kiss, and if there was one kiss, there had to be another. And another. You forget, very quickly, what it's like to kiss a new love, and you're for ever wanting to kiss them again and again, just to remind yourself of that new exquisite pleasure. She laughed, such joy on her face, and she kissed me again, both hands clasping my stubbled bristling cheeks.

'Where are we going?' she asked.

'To hell in a handbasket.'

She brushed some of the wet sand off my trousers. 'That's where we'll end up,' she said. 'But do you know where we're heading now?'

We looked about us. The storms had obliterated every last trace of the race. There were no runners in front of us, not a runner behind us.

'Leave this to me,' I said. 'I have some experience of getting lost in the desert.' I studied the map in the Road Book. 'Thirty seven degrees,' I said, and took a sighting on my compass. 'Aiming for that little knobbly hillock.'

'The knobbly hillock it is,' and she kissed me again and we were on our way. I don't know whether it was the painkillers or whether we were just smitten with love, but the miles seemed to melt. We would sing and we would chat and we both of us would laugh until Kate had to hold her sides so that she could barely walk another step.

I liked that we didn't talk about the past – we didn't have that conversation about, 'When did you first...' And we did not talk about that acrimonious night, nor did we talk about the future and what might come of us. We were, like all the happiest MdS runners, living in that moment.

At the last checkpoint, we allowed ourselves another hug and another kiss. We were in the shade of a Land Rover. There were a few Commissaires milling about, but hardly a runner to be seen. It was a ghost checkpoint. We filled up our bottles, took a bite of Nutri-Grain and then, even as we were busying ourselves with our rucksacks, we caught each other's eye. We immediately knew what it was we most desired, and we stood up and held each other close. She kissed me and very delicately lifted her knee so that it was between my thighs.

'That feels good,' I said, in between kisses.

'Almost as good as you did when I was in your sleeping bag.'

'And you grabbed my Morning Glory.' I pecked kisses about her mouth. This was Kate – the unbelievable Kate who worked in my office and who I was now kissing.

'Why didn't you make love to me?'

I laughed, kissing her nose and her forehead, and burying my face into her hair. 'For a first outing, I'd prefer not to be performing in front of Del and Simon.'

'A first outing?' she asked.

'Of many – I hope.'

Very quickly she slipped her hand underneath my trousers and my lycra shorts. Ever so suggestively, she cocked an eyebrow. 'So we think alike, Kim,' she said.

Forty-six miles down and six to go, and we continued on our way through camel grass and small dunes. The sun stretched high overhead and the storms had blown away all the mugginess; the desert was clear and flat and bright, and the dust and wet sand were no longer kicking up under our feet.

The pain in Kate's feet seemed to build up very slowly. At first she was fine, and I'm sure that the elation of all those new kisses helped, but she still had to walk, and her raw skin still had to grind against her socks and shoes. Soon even the kisses were forgotten, and all that she had was the pain. She was whimpering again, soft groans with every step she trod, so once again I started to talk, talk and talk without ever stopping, like the biggest club bore that you could ever imagine. I had moved on to jokes that amused my daughters. 'What's the difference between a weasel and a stoat?' I asked her. 'Come on, what's the difference? Do you know?'

Kate shook her head, and though she did not say anything, she had stopped whimpering, and I took that to be a good sign.

'You don't know?' I said. 'You really don't know the difference between a weasel and a stoat? I am shocked, shocked that your father didn't think fit to tell you! It is so simple! A weasel is weasily wecognised, and a stoat is stoatally different.' I cuffed her shoulder. 'Admit it – you're likin' it, aren't you?'

'I'm not liking it,' she snarled, lashing the walking poles into the ground. 'I'm bloody loving it.'

'Excellent,' I said. 'Or as our revered mad master would say, "*Excellenté!*" I'll bet you'd like to hear a few more of my daughters' jokes. Like to hear the funniest joke that's ever been told?'

Kate's face was set in this mask of gritty pain. She nodded.

'Okay – now I hope you're ready for this. It's the best I've got. Right out of the top drawer. What noise annoys a noisy oyster? Know this?'

Briefly she shook her head.

'Don't know that one either? Well, Kate, I'll tell you. I will tell you! What noise annoys a noisy oyster? A noisy noise annoys a noisy oyster!'

And she smiled, and the miles clipped by. I would look at her and still marvel at the very thought that, not an hour previously, I had been kissing her. In time the finish line came into view, the white blimps quite breathtakingly beautiful, and we walked for half an hour and the blimps did not seem to be one jot closer, and then, eventually, the sand turned to rock, and we were walking through this field of stone. It turned to a dusty track, and the finish line was only a few hundred yards ahead of us. Kate was whimpering now with every step; her pace quickened, and these great choking sobs were coming from her throat and tears dripped from behind her sunglasses and down her cheeks.

We crossed the finish line, with that lovely double ping of the timer, and the moment we were over, Kate let out this shriek, a mix of agony and ecstasy, and buried herself in my arms. Three Commissaires clapped as they came out from behind their table. I had this lump in my throat that soon turned to a burning ball behind my eyes. What a day we'd been through. What a journey, with the pain and the heat, and the miles and the kisses. And we'd done it. We had shepherded each other over the line. I burst into tears. It was a combination of so many things – the euphoria that comes at the end of a long journey and the sympathy that springs from a lover's tears. For some time we clung to each other and we cried, our tears wet on our shirts, and the Commissaires looked on and listened and said nothing at all. This was new to us, but it was not new to them.

Another walker came over the line and broke the spell. 'Hi,' he said softly. Without another word, he joined our hug. 'That was some day.'

Kate and I stood in silence as we had our tea at the Sultan stand, trying to weigh up what had happened to us. We did not have the words.

I picked up our six bottles of water and we started the long limp over to the bivouac. Now that our tent was only 300 yards away, now that the job was done, the nerves in our feet were suddenly clamouring for attention.

We tottered over to Tent 71. The sun was high in the sky now and there were a few people about, hobbling to the toilets and to Doc Trotters, but for the most part, the bivouac slept. I tossed the water down outside the tent and stooped to peer inside. I couldn't understand what had happened. The tent looked half empty. There were some people sleeping on either side, but there was this huge empty space in the middle.

At first, I thought that some of my tentmates must have still been out on the course, and then as I looked and counted, I realised that all six of them were in there – three to each end, huddled up close together to get out of the wind and the rain.

In the snuggest corner, with the sides of the tent firmly down, were my three fastest tentmates, Simon, Del and Martin. They had done a good job of sealing their corner of the tent, weighing it down on the outside with heavy rocks. The side of the tent was propped up with three sticks so that it didn't sag during the storms.

On the other side were my three more affable tentmates, Carlo, Kurtz and Lawson. They had not managed to seal down their end quite so well. There had been no rocks to hand, and the tent flapped in the wind. The side of the tent was propped up with just the one stick, and after the storms it hung so low that it was all but covering Carlo's face.

And then there was the middle of the tent. It had been turned into an absolute wind tunnel, and there was so much sand I could not see the carpet.

Kate let out a sigh and sat down. She lolled on the sand with her feet on her bag. She was spent. I pulled out my Thermarest, blew it up and helped her onto it. I mixed up our recovery drinks and handed one to Kate. She drank it quickly, the REGO dribbling down her chin. She did not have the energy to wipe it off.

I tugged out her sleeping bag, zipped it wide open, and as Kate lay on top of it, I started on her feet. I had to steel myself before I took off the socks. As gently as I could, I eased them off her heels and over her bandages. Kate had been dozing, but with a great yelp she was wide awake. Her feet were swaddled in bandages. The bottom of the bandages was a reddish brown, a mixture of sand and sweat and blood. And then it was time for the grand reveal, and I knew it was going to be bad, very bad, but even so the sight that confronted me was so awful I had to turn my head away.

'How is it?' Kate said. She was staring directly up at the apex of the tent.

'Not too bad at all.'

She had lost the sole of one foot. It looked as if it had been neatly snipped away at the edges, and what was left was this red raw meat, angry and oozing and speckled with sand. The other foot was like a piece of Swiss cheese, her white sole pockmarked with these large round red holes. Half her toenails were black. There was not much I could do about them. They would all drop off within the week.

I got a couple of wemmi wipes and a bottle of water, and I started to clean her feet. It reminded me of bathing my daughters when they were young. I dabbed with my fingertips, trying to remove the worst of the sand, but it was still excruciating. I could see Kate clenching her fingers.

The wind continued to blow and the sand continued to scour the tent, and I found myself getting increasingly irked by my tentmates.

'You'd have thought these guys could have sealed the tent properly before they went to sleep,' I said. I had a couple of cotton buds and was trying to wash out the sand from between her toes. 'But no – they just think, 'I'm all right, Jack,' and they go to sleep. Look at those ones there – first in. They bag the best corner, seal it all down nicely, and then blow me if the tent isn't sagging a bit in the wind, so they pinch one of the sticks from the other side to keep it off their pretty little heads.'

I squeezed some antiseptic into my hands. 'This may hurt,' I said, and stroked the cream into Kate's foot. She said the efficacious word. 'Then the other lot come in – well they can't be bothered to find any rocks, so they just seal down their end with their rucksacks and off they go to sleep, so that's them sorted. And what do they leave us with? Wind and sand. We might as well be sleeping outside!'

I was getting quite raucous. If the others could hear me, they wisely pretended to stay asleep.

I zipped Kate into her sleeping bag. Her eyes were closed, and I kissed her on the cheek. 'Get some sleep,' I said. 'Then we'll get you to Doc Trotters. He'll fix you up for tomorrow. It's only a marathon, you know.'

Kate's eyes were shut, but she smiled. 'I know,' she said. 'I kissed you today.'

'So you did – it was perfection.'

She brought my hand to her lips and kissed my palm.

I was unspeakably tired but I could not sleep. I boiled some water and had some stew, and now there was nothing left to do but attend to my own injuries. For the first time in well over 24 hours, I had a look at my own feet. I let out a little giggle. If, a week before, I'd had a glimpse of those feet, I would have been absolutely horrified. But as it was – well, after five days of the MdS, I'd seen a huge array of injured feet and, in comparison, these blistered soles didn't look too bad at all. A little painful, especially the huge new blister that had grown on my heel overnight, but certainly good enough for another 40 miles in the desert.

I took my sleeping bag and went outside the tent. Lawson had wasted his money on a collapsible canvas footbath the size of a small basin. I poured in a bottle of water and some liquid soap. It was bliss to stand in the footbath and watch the bivouac as it came to life.

I sat on my sleeping bag, basking in the sun as my feet dried. I was still cold from the previous night and I still had my coat on. Some local boys had come out to investigate and the security guards chased them away.

An empty bottle was being blown away by the wind. Both bottle and bottlecap would be marked with the runner's number. When the bottle was retrieved, its owner would be docked half an hour.

Some thorn trees were nearby, and five goats had managed to climb them, avoiding the long thorns to nibble at the dusty green leaves.

A German bodybuilder, Florian, waved to me as he hobbled to the medical tent. I'd seen him about. After the long day, you've seen everyone on the MdS. Florian was tanned and tattooed and bald, and with his goatee, he would have looked quite at home in any gym. The MdS had knocked the stuffing out of him; he was suffering.

I lay back and I thought about the long walk, and I was swept with this feeling of total exhilaration, like Edmund Hillary after he'd climbed Everest: 'We've knocked the bastard off!'

I'd managed to get lost in the Sahara, that would certainly be something to tell the girls about; and Kate, she'd made it, she'd done the long day, and that was a miracle in itself. And then the realisation of what had happened just that morning took me so by surprise that I could barely believe it. We'd kissed each other, with love and passion and with tenderness, too, and now that she was lying asleep in the tent, it seemed like some extraordinary dream. She'd kissed me, had joked about making love with me…

But I didn't want to get too excited about it all. Maybe the kiss had been just the fillip she'd needed – I'd needed – to get us through the storm and those last 12 miles. It had come when we had both hit rock bottom, and when love and lust had completely outweighed any thoughts of obligation or fidelity.

And if the kiss did not lead to anything more, then, well, that would be sad, but… it would be realistic. Nothing could come of it. Nothing could ever come of it. She had her Edward, I had my Elise, my daughters, and I was married. It could only lead to that heartbreak hell I know so well.

But what a kiss – what a woman.

I wondered what it would be like when she woke up in a few hours time. Would it all be forgotten? Would there be a secret squeeze of my hand, perhaps a rueful look to my eye, as if to say, 'What happens in the desert stays in the desert'?

Or perhaps… Perhaps we might continue exactly where we had left off, and there would be more kisses and hot sweet words and all those other wonders that come with them…

We middle-aged blowhards must sometimes be indulged in our little fantasies.

And mine, that morning, as I drowsed in the sun, was the most extraordinary fantasy I had ever dared dream: a hailstorm, sheltered by a desert rock, with Kate tight next to me, love in her eyes and her mouth slick with balm as her lips rise up to kiss me.

CHAPTER 20

There was another fight in the tent that day. Of course there was another fight that day. With emotions running high, we did not need too long in each other's company before matters came to a bilious boiling point.

It was to be the last fight in the tent – and, as it turned out, the decisive one.

I woke at midday. The wind was still gusting and I was covered in sand. It was in my hair and plastered thick on my face; it had even blown into my sleeping bag.

Kate was already awake, her face a couple of feet away from me. I winked at her. She blew me a kiss. I was as smitten as I'd ever been.

'Good morning,' I said. I stretched my hand out and stroked her hair. It was thick and gritty with sand.

She clasped my fingers to her cheek. 'How are you?'

'In great need of a bath.'

'If only,' she said. 'One bath to clear off the dirt, then another to soak in.'

'With bubbles.'

'With bubbles and every oil they've got in the Berbère Palace. My skin's so dry!'

'Two days to go – you'll appreciate it all the more.' I continued to stroke her hair. It was one of those moments in life that is so extraordinary you can hardly take it in. I was lying next to Kate. I was stroking her hair. And we were talking like lovers.

'I'll be ever so appreciative.'

'I'll make you some mint tea.'

Lawson piped up. He was right in the far corner, and the side of the tent sagged over his sleeping bag. 'And me, while you're at it!' he said. Carlo wanted one too.

Still in our sleeping bags, we sat at the edge of the tent and drank tea and swapped stories about our long day in the desert. I told them how I'd got lost and they laughed. Del told us to be quiet, and we laughed even harder. I could feel Kate watching me as I sipped my tea. She was curled up close, head on her elbow, quietly taking everything in. I looked at her and she stretched out and touched my hand. I don't know what she saw in me, but I know for a certainty that it wasn't my looks.

'You look grubby,' Carlo said to me.

'I've got a photographer mate at the *Sun* called Grubby.' I scratched at my hair. It was thick and wild and hadn't seen a comb in a week. 'You sure I'm not dirty? It's a better word. Got a touch of desperado about it.'

'No – definitely grubby.'

The rain had soaked through the tent and there were large wet patches on the rug. The sand was everywhere, in everything; you couldn't get away from it. 'Can we get this rug out of the tent and clean it?' I said.

'It could do with a dry,' Lawson said.

Martin rolled over, surly and tired. 'Don't care.'

'Well I care,' I said.

'You care if you want to.'

I took Kate to Doc Trotters. She could barely walk, hissing with pain at every step. She had an arm round my shoulders and was hopping along on one foot. The medical tent was about 400 yards away and it took an age to get there. We both sat on the sand as we waited in the queue.

Kate was anxious. She'd taken off the blue plastic bag socks and was inspecting her feet. 'Do you think I'll be all right for tomorrow?' she said.

'You'll be fine,' I said, my arm around her waist. 'If needs be, our tentmates will carry you in a stretcher.'

'The Pompiers could give me a lift.'

'Give them a kiss and they'll put you in the back of their dune buggy.'

It took an hour to sort out Kate's feet, and while they treated her, I went off to file my copy to the *Sun*. There was no queue and no limit to the number of emails we could send, and for a while it was me and my keyboard and the sound of the bird song, and I was a million miles from the desert. I sent over 2,000 words to my mad masters, though much thanks I would get for it. I told them about getting lost and about the flare, and I told them about Kate's feet and the blisters under her toenails. I wrote, also, about our long slog in the morning, with the wind and the rain and the hail. I did not write about the kiss.

I felt a little like those sad people who go on Big Brother. They perform, they fight, they sing their little hearts out, but they do not have a clue how it's all playing out back home. They don't know if they're loved or hated, or if they're even making it onto the TV screens. Just so for all the copy Kate and I were filing; I did not know if it was making centre-page spreads, or whether it was just being sent straight to the spike.

When I returned to Doc Trotters, Kate was talking to Del. Her feet were covered in fresh white bandages and she was dosed up on tramadol, a synthetic opiate very similar to morphine. It doesn't just knock out the pain – it gives you a little high. They'd given her more tramadol to get her through the next day.

'How was it?' I asked, squatting down in the dirt next to her.

'The doctors are getting a little blasé,' she said. 'On the first day, they were all incredibly professional. Now they've seen it all. They're inured to it.'

'A little short on sympathy?' I said. I looked over at Del, who was sitting on the sand, legs outstretched. He was wearing his blue Speedos, groin pointing directly at Kate. His sunglasses were off. I'd never really noticed his grey dead-fish eyes before. He'd brought his teddy along too, which now had a silver foil cape tied around its neck.

'Fred's got a nice outfit,' I said.

'Made it this morning. Fred'll need it if there's more rain.'

Kate and I looked at each other, inscrutable. Our deadpan faces spoke volumes.

'What are you in for, Del?' I asked.

'Got a blister,' he said. He flicked off his white slipper. On his big toe was a small penny-sized blister. It nestled against the Saltire that had been painted on his toenail.

'Is that it?' I asked. 'You're going into Doc Trotters with that?'

'It's what they're there for.' He swigged from his bottle, gargled, then spat. The water flicked onto his legs and onto his Speedos.

'I guess it's all part of the game.'

'You're learning,' he said. He put on his sunglasses and crossed his arms.

Kate hobbled back to the tent. At least she was able to walk under her own steam, which was a good sign. I didn't know if she'd be able to keep ahead of the camels the next day.

After a lot of pestering, I cajoled my tentmates into pulling the rug out of the tent. Kurtz and Lawson lifted the two central poles while we dragged the rug out from underneath. I had a corner of the rug. There was a rucksack lying open, and I kicked it off the rug. I don't really remember how it happened but the rucksack tipped over and a couple of plastic bags fell out onto the sand.

The rug was long, at least eight metres, with a red and black pattern. The sand was embedded deep in the pile. Three to each end, we cracked the rug up and down. Lawson dived onto the middle and we gave him the bumps. He cackled as he flew up into the air. He laughed even louder when we dumped him on the ground.

Martin and Simon emptied their rucksacks onto the rug to go through another of their interminable kit checks, after which they didn't know what to do with themselves. Martin went off and got his new race number and his ice-cold can of Coke; he had drunk it even before he got back to the tent.

But Kate, and Lawson and me, we savoured our Cokes to the full, sitting on the rug, taking delicate little sips, revelling in our desert immersion. Kate was sitting next to me, her shoulder nestled against mine. Lawson was trying to mend his camera. Some dust had got into the works and the lens wouldn't open. It was hot, the sun blazed, but I still had a chill and kept my coat on.

'I had a friend in South Africa,' Lawson said. He was wiping the lens with a handkerchief. 'He was called Solomon. When Solomon was quite young, he had this rite of passage. He went up the mountain. That was what it was called: he went up the mountain. He would never tell me what happened, but I think it involved being cold and naked and hungry for three days. At the end of it all, they circumcised him. Without anaesthetic.'

Kate stared at Lawson. I let out a low whistle.

'It was so awful that every time he thought about it, he remembered what it was like to be in hell.' Lawson tossed the broken camera into his rucksack. 'I was thinking, though – the MdS is our mid-life rite of passage. You only do it the once.'

'And you never forget it,' I said. 'My dad always said that every year you should do something that you'll still remember in a couple of decades.'

Kate took a bite from her savoury tomato and nut bar. She chewed thoughtfully. 'I'll never forget this,' she said. 'Sitting here, drinking Coke with you two.'

'It doesn't get any better,' I said. Kate held my hand; Lawson burped.

'Got to go and see a man about a dog,' Lawson said. We watched him shamble to the latrines.

And in my mind's eye…

Kate turns to look at me. She smiles and I can see the tips of her brilliant white teeth, and she leans towards me and kisses me. I'm caught a little unawares. It is our first kiss since we'd got back to the bivouac and I had not really known whether to hope for another. Her face is clean and smooth, and flushed with youth, and I want her so much that the desire almost catches in my throat. Her lips roam about my mouth and my cheek and I have a glimpse of her, eyes closed, neck bared and tilted up towards me in the most wanton abandon. She draws back a little, her tongue tipping out from between her teeth and lazily she licks my lower lip. She gazes at me through half-closed eyes.

'You turn me on, Kim,' she says, and I kiss her neck, her chin, her cheek.

'I love your kisses,' I reply, and she lifts up her knees so that she is curled on my lap. And we kiss and we kiss, not caring who sees us, absorbed in nothing but each other's mouths. Flushed, she lies back on my legs, her face looking up to me and her fingers curling around my coat.

'Let's make love,' she says. 'Let's make love now. Take me to the desert,' and she kisses me again and giggles, 'Take me in the desert…'

And in reality…

We watch Lawson go to the latrines, and Kate tilts her head up towards me, and we're looking at each other, just a few inches apart, and she kisses me. She sighs with contentment and we kiss some more, and she is lying on my lap and clasps my head and draws me down on her, so that I'm all but leaning on her. I feel this little pulse, a slight thrust towards me.

'I want you,' she says. 'Am I turning you on?'

And I kiss her and I make a joke of it. 'Let's just say I'm glad I've got my coat on.'

'Imagine what we could do in a bedroom,' she said.

And I kiss her, because that's what you do when you are in love and when your beautiful lover is lying there in your lap. 'After we've had that bath?'

'After we've had that bath and after we've drunk that bottle of Champagne.' And she slips one hand into my coat and lightly rakes her nails across my chest.

'What did you have in mind?'

'I think, Kim…' Her hand slides up my leg. 'I think that, from dusk till dawn, I would like to make love with you. I dream of making love with you.'

I kissed her. Was this really happening? Could it be happening? 'We are in accord.'

This little switch flicks in her head and her eyes get this cheeky glint. We both stare out to the desert.

'What about here?' she said. 'Why wait for a bedroom? Let's do it here – now! I want you…'

I look at glistening lips and eyes that dance.

'You don't want to make love in the desert?' she queried. 'Don't you dream of having sex in the sand? Didn't you think of it when we were lying naked in the sun after our shower? I so wanted to touch you.'

Of all my most outrageous fantasies…

I felt like a fisherman with a very rare, very fine fish on the end of his line, who must now take immense care reeling it in. No slips now – please no slips now.

Sometimes it's best when you say nothing at all. I nodded.

'Over there.' Kate pointed and turned to me, kissing me on the cheek. 'Behind that little hill. Let's make love. Let's make love now.'

'*Carpe diem*?' I said.

'Seize everything,' she said. She was on her knees, pulling my arms. 'Seize you.'

'I'm in,' I said.

And suddenly there it is, in the very palm of my hand. We almost visibly relax. We have a meeting of minds.

Kate bit her bottom lip. So sexy. 'Come on, let's make love.'

I must have had the stupidest smile on my face in the whole of Christendom. 'Say that again,' I said. 'I still can't believe it.'

'You want to hear it again?' she whispered in my ear. 'Come on Kim – let's make love. I want to make love with you.'

I've never had a woman offer herself up to me like this; or a lover who was quite so much my junior; or so fantastically alluring. I am shaking, shaking, with excitement.

And as for my wife, Elise… I'm afraid I did not give her a thought.

What happens in the desert stays in the desert.

Kate kisses me again, more urgently now. I can feel her heat. 'Come on Kim,' she says, tugging me, and I start getting to my knees. 'Let's do it.'

'Let's fall in love.'

There was a bellow from the tent.

Kate sighed as she ran her fingers through my hair. 'Why him?' she said. 'Why now?'

'Why him?' I said. 'Because who else could it be? And why now? It's our destiny.'

It was Del – and he was shouting.

'What's happened to my rucksack?' He let out a shriek of rage. 'My coffee! Where's my coffee?'

Still entwined with each other, Kate and I looked over at Del. He was rampaging around the tent.

Martin was lying in the shade. He didn't say anything. He just pointed at me.

It could have been me who'd kicked his rucksack over; I don't really remember.

'You!' Del screamed. 'Of course it was you, you bloody shit!'

Del stormed out of the tent. He took a scything kick at my rucksack, spewing its contents out over the sand.

I don't know what made me do it. I don't normally react in a physical way. But it was almost instinctive.

Del was lashing out at my can of Coke, and as he did so, I leaned backwards and yanked his other leg. He was upended and landed flat on his back. I could hear the wind being punched clean out of his lungs. It all happened very quickly. It was quite comical. Kate started laughing.

'You bastard,' said Del. He got to his feet and stood over me, his fingers twitching. 'I'm going to have you. Stand up.'

I leaned back and gazed up at him. 'I'm not getting up for you, Del.'

'I'll kick you on the ground then.'

'Why do you have to do any kicking?' I said. 'I don't know who knocked over your coffee powder. If it was me, I'm very sorry.'

'Get up!' Del said. He grabbed the hood of my coat and forced me to my feet.

Now let me be clear: I am not a fighter. But I do not like to be manhandled. I especially do not like being half-strangled by my coat collar.

I was still bent over. I lashed out, driving my fists one-two into Del's stomach. He was solid, very solid, but I'd caught him by surprise. He let go of my collar and took a couple of steps backwards.

'We've got a fight,' he said. He beamed, the wrinkles on his face turning to solid lines of hate. 'I've been looking forward to this.'

He held himself like a boxer, hands weaving beneath his chin. He'd obviously had lessons.

'Stop that!' Kate said. 'Stop that now!'

'Not your fight, pretty girlie,' Del said. He skipped towards me, very light on the balls of his feet.

'I'm not fighting you,' I said.

'Fine by me,' Del said as he jabbed at my chest. I staggered backwards. It felt like I'd been kicked by a mule.

Lawson was trotting back from the latrine, billycan in hand. He was still a way off. 'Guys!' he called. 'Cool it!'

'I'm going to knock your head off,' Del said. He shimmied to the left, to the right and then threw this absolute haymaker at my head. I ducked and his fist thumped into my shoulder. I was already readying myself for the next punch when Del was suddenly screaming. He fell to the ground and was rolling on the sand clutching his leg to his chest.

Martin bustled out of the tent. 'What have you done to him?'

Del was lying stricken on the ground, his red face rippling with pain. Sweat was popping from his forehead, and over and over again he was mewling the same sharp swear-word.

'I didn't touch him,' I said. 'I don't know what's happened to him.'

'It's his foot,' Kate said. 'He's trodden on something.'

We all stared at Del's foot. He was wearing those very thin MdS slippers, and from the sole of one of the slippers was projecting a cluster of thorns; I remembered the thorn tree and the goats I'd seen in the morning. The thorns seemed to be embedded deep into the ball of Del's foot.

'Leave this to me,' Martin said.

'Shouldn't we take him to Doc Trotters?' Lawson said.

'I've got everything I need,' Martin said. He was relishing the thought of an operation. 'I'll get my kit.'

As Del lay face down on the rug, Martin returned from the tent with a small medical pack. It had iodine, bandages, scalpels, scissors and two pairs of medical tweezers. We all craned to have a look. Del was whinnying with pain, banging the palm of his hand onto the rug.

'This won't take long,' Martin said. 'I'm going to cut your slipper off. Is that all right?'

Del grunted and Martin snipped away the slipper. The sole was so thin that he could have been cutting through butter. He gestured for me to move backwards. 'Give us some light.' Del's five painted toenails seemed oddly pathetic now that they were splashed with blood.

There were six thorns, white and brittle, in Del's foot. One was so long that its sharp tip had even broken the skin on the other side of the foot. Martin pulled out the first thorn. It was nearly an inch and a half long. Lawson proffered a billycan and Martin dropped the thorn into it.

Martin dabbed on some iodine and pulled out three more thorns. 'This is more difficult than I perceived,' he said, sucking on his teeth. 'Two thorns have gone in at rather an oblique angle.'

'You sure about not taking him to Doc Trotters?' Lawson asked.

Martin was annoyed his skills were being questioned. 'I do this all the time.'

He pulled one more thorn. It had gone in quite shallow. The thorn was dropped into the billycan. 'And one more to go.' He was unable to get a purchase on the thorn with his tweezers. 'I'm going to have to cut in a little.'

Lawson caught my eye and gave a wide shake of his head – no, no, no.

Martin cut into the sole of Del's foot with his scalpel. There was suddenly much more blood. It dripped down Del's leg and onto the rug. 'Someone mop this blood up,' Martin said.

Lawson found a couple of wemmi wipes and washed the blood away. I didn't know what Martin was doing. If it had been my foot, I would have insisted on being taken to Doc Trotters.

Del was quieter now. He had a ripple of the rug in between his teeth and was biting down hard.

Martin poked into the wound with the tweezers. 'Nearly.' He gave a tug, though nothing came out. He made another probe with the tweezers. 'Got you!' he said. He gave a sharp, jerky pull and the thorn came out. It dripped with blood. It was much smaller than the other thorns.

'That's that then. Just get you bandaged up.'

Del spat out the rug. 'That hurts.'

'It will hurt for a while,' Martin said. He washed down his scalpel and his tweezers and returned them to his first aid box. I looked over at Lawson. He'd sluiced out the billycan with water and was peering at the six thorns.

Martin poured iodine onto the wound. Del spasmed; it must have stung like hell. Martin placed a gauze square over the wounds and wrapped a long strip of white bandage around the ball of the foot before securing it with tape. Martin seemed pleased with his workmanship.

'We're done,' he said. 'Very unlucky. Very unlucky indeed.'

Del groaned. 'I'll be good for tomorrow?'

'Of course,' Martin said. 'We'll get you some tramadol.'

Lawson gave a small cough. He had been examining one of the thorns. 'Excuse me,' he said. 'You sure you got all of that last thorn out?'

'Course I did,' Martin said. He was washing his hands with soap and water.

Lawson handed over the thorn. 'This thorn has been snapped in half.'

Martin took the thorn, scrutinised it and, with a sniff of disdain, flicked it with his thumb. The thorn arced into the sand. 'Old break.'

'Looked fresh to me,' Lawson said.

'I'm only a consultant surgeon, Lawson,' Martin said. 'I've been doing this sort of thing for nearly 20 years.'

'Only asking,' Lawson said.

'Well thanks for all your concern, Lawson, but if it's all right by you, I'm going to have my supper.'

We dragged the rug back into the tent and Del hobbled inside to lie face down on his sleeping bag. He took some ibuprofen. He had his head on his arms and was glowering at me as if I had personally placed the thorns underneath his foot.

I took Kate's hand and we walked, or rather hobbled, a little way into the desert. We sat on the hard sand.

'Poor Del,' she said.

'Del's a total shit,' I said.

'You wouldn't wish that on him though, would you?'

'I'm not nearly as nice a person as you are.'

I looked at her, she looked at me and we kissed, and as one we were struck by the sheer incongruity of it all and we started roaring with laughter.

'Talk about a passion killer!' I said.

'A bit of a turnoff,' she said. She stroked the stubble on my cheek. 'I can smell the desert on your beard.'

'Getting a bit chilly, isn't it?' I said, and she shivered.

'It is,' she said. 'But don't think you're getting out of lovemaking quite so easily.' She licked my ear, dabbing at my earlobe with her tongue. 'I can taste your sweat.'

'What's it taste like?'

'Salty. Like sea salt. If I ever ran out of salt pills, I could lick you all over.'

'Anyway – lovemaking,' I said, and we paused to watch a middle-aged French couple. They'd both worn turquoise throughout the race and they did everything together. They were holding hands. They had been off exploring – or perhaps something more exciting – and were walking back to the bivouac.

'Yeah – lovemaking,' she said. 'I'm looking forward to making love with you.'

I picked up some sand. It was still firm from the rain that morning. Was it really only that morning? I tossed the sand towards a dung beetle. It skittered into its hole.

'Lovemaking,' I said. 'Just thinking about it makes me lightheaded.'

'Maybe tomorrow,' she said.

'Or maybe the Berbère Palace,' I said. 'I don't care where, all I want is you.'

'Shake?' And we shook hands and we kissed. That spectacular mouth, once again opening up beneath my lips, a sight I could never tire of. We walked back to the camp, leaving our twin tracks in the hard sand. And so the deal was done.

CHAPTER 21

I have run a few marathons before, in New York and London. The night before the race, I'd usually have a large bowl of pasta and a single glass of red wine. Pudding too, probably. You're allowed pudding if you're running a marathon.

I would then, with luck, have a good eight hours sleep, would get up early on the morning of the race and would make myself a large bowl of porridge. The oats would be thick with full-fat milk and maple syrup and at least two chopped bananas. After breakfast, I would check that my toenails were clipped short and that I was slick with Vaseline. I'd pin on my race numbers, tie and retie my shoelaces, and check my gels and paperwork. And I would be drinking – drinking a lot, perhaps three litres of water. I remember the start of the New York marathon. It takes place in all five boroughs, starting on Staten Island at the Verrazano Bridge. This is a spectacular suspension bridge with epic views of downtown Manhattan, but all I can remember is the river of pee. The race had only just started and already hundreds of runners were stopping to relieve themselves. The men were out to the side, peeing away from the runners, and the women were lined up knee to knee on the pavement, and this rolling river of pee ran through the gutters. That's how much water you want to have inside you before the start of a marathon.

Before the start of the marathon stage of the MdS, I had a litre of water and some custard and some mashed potato. Now that I was through to the fifth stage, I was quite blasé about the prospect of a mere marathon. Not that I had any reason to be so cocky. They were only giving us 11 hours to complete the stage and I was well on the way to developing a full-blown flu. My nose was running and I felt weak and generally knackered.

Kate and I had slept as well as you can in the desert. We were each in our own sleeping bags, though occasionally stretching out to the other in the night. As soon as she'd woken up, she'd taken tramadol and ibuprofen and paracetemol, but she was really on the rack. I walked her two times around the bivouac. She had my walking poles, but every footstep was agony. She was gritting her teeth and shaking her head. It took an age for the painkillers to kick in.

Sometimes, if you're trying to cajole a friend through the merry hell of the desert, you have to be the Boot Camp Sergeant-Major; and sometimes you have to be Mr Sympathy; and sometimes the storyteller; and sometimes just the ear that listens. But you can't be the same thing all of the time; you have to mix things up. Only constant variety will distract a sick friend from their misery.

That morning, I decided to chance my arm with some humour; I was aware that this tactic could go dangerously wrong.

'You're looking good,' I said. We were on our second circuit of the bivouac. The tents were coming down and the bivouac rang to the sound of the Berbers' hammers.

'Feeling. Good,' Kate spat. Each word was an effort.

'Still up for it tonight, darling?' I said. 'Still looking forward to a little light lovemaking?'

Kate's mouth was open and her teeth bared. Her face was a mask of pain, and yet still she was stuttering forward. She was leaning heavily on the poles.

'Screw,' she snarled.

I was amazed she could even talk. If I had been walking on a delaminated foot, I would have been unable to say a word.

'Screw what, darling?' I said. 'Screw this whole farrago of a race that we've signed up for? Screw our inconsiderate tentmates? Screw our jobs on the *Sun* and screw our mad masters with it?'

'Screw. You. Senseless.'

'Oh – me?' I said. 'You were planning to screw me senseless tonight? That would be just… divine. You'll have to tell me later what you've got planned.' I laughed, and for the first time that day she raised a savage smile. I dared to hope she might just make it.

There were a few other walking wounded from Tent 71. Kurtz didn't appear to have anything too bad, just the same spattering of blisters that the rest of us had. But for a few days now, he had been suffering from IT band syndrome, which affects the long bands that run down your thighs. They were putting a lot of stress on the outside of his knees.

'How's it going?' I asked him. I was zipping the last of my kit into my rucksack. It was now a full six kilos lighter than when I'd started the race on Easter Sunday.

'IT bands have gone.' He was rolling a full water bottle on the side of his leg, trying to loosen up the knots in his thigh.

'Is that bad?' I said.

'It's going to be murrrr-derrr,' he said, rolling his Rs. 'I'll be on crutches when this thing is over.' Like all the best competitors, he blanked it out. He wasn't giving it another thought. Kurtz closed his eye, lifted his face to the east and basked in the sun's rays. 'It'll be cosy today.'

'Cosy – I like it.'

Kurtz sighed and then flipped up his eye patch to pull out a Trebor Extra Strong mint from his eye socket. 'Want a mint?'

'Thanks.' I stretched over and took it. 'Unusual place to keep your mints.'

'I get five in at a time. The kids like it.'

At long last, Martin had got the runs. He was fretting about whether he had enough water. He wanted another 1.5 litre bottle but didn't want to take the half hour penalty.

'I don't mind having a half hour penalty,' Lawson said. He was lolling on his Thermarest and trickling sultanas into his mouth. 'I'll get you another bottle of water.'

'Really?' Martin said.

'Be a pleasure,' Lawson said. He farted. After a week in the desert, the men in Tent 71 were without inhibitions and would fart and burp and pee just as and when they felt like it. Lawson flicked a sultana into the air with his thumb, catching it on his tongue. 'Just give me your two hundred Euros and the bottle's yours.'

'My two hundred Euros?' Martin said blankly.

'I'll do it for a hundred and fifty,' said Carlo. He was gobbling down jelly babies. First he would bite off the heads, then the legs and then finally the body. He never ate them any other way.

Lawson spat out a sultana. 'A hundred,' he said.

Martin was about to sit down on his rucksack. A look of mild consternation passed over his face and then he was off again, trotting to the latrines with his toilet roll.

Out of all of us, Simon was looking the best. He'd never got the hang of being able to drink while he was running. On the long day, he'd only had one bottle of water and had nearly blacked out. The medics had stuck him on an IV drip and pumped three and a half litres of saline solution into his body. It was as if he'd been given a full service and MOT. He was hoping to complete the marathon stage in under three and a half hours. That's good going, even for a road race; even if you're fresh.

And then there was Del. Del was not a well man. His foot had ballooned to double its normal size, and he was only able to squeeze his shoe on by taking out the insole. He'd got a cold from having no Thermarest to sleep on during the night and, combined with the infected thorn in his foot, he was becoming feverish. He was shivering, his face a frowning gargoyle of lines and hate. He blamed me for the thorns in his foot. He'd have done anything at all to have put me out of the race. I kept well out of his way.

The Eeyore rep came round, gloomy as ever. 'You know what,' Lawson said. 'I bet it's going to be hot today.' He was lying on his front, grunting as Carlo massaged his shoulders.

'It will be hot,' said the Eeyore.

'And the hills,' Carlo said. 'Bet they'll be high, so they will.'

'You are correct. There is a hill at the end, *Jebel Debouaâ*. It will be high.'

'Give that man a cigar!' Lawson crowed, stretching up to high-five Carlo's hand.

At 8.30 a.m., just as requested, we walked over to the start line; and, just as expected, the French were late. They were always the last to arrive, as they knew the show could never start without them.

We were introduced to some French journalists. Their mad masters had paid out 10,000 Euros for each of them to run the marathon stage. We were supposed to be impressed.

By now the men were looking like cavemen, bronzed and bearded, and with these wild, crazy eyes. The women, of course, looked as if they'd only just arrived in the desert.

Lawson was singing to himself, 'One wheel on my wagon – but I keep rolling along.'

I joined him, hollering like a cowboy. 'Them Cherokees are after me, but I keep singing my song!'

The Pompiers were next to us with their boy already strapped into the dune buggy, and all about us were these familiar faces. Didier the blind man, already strapped to his smiling guide; Paul, the mad Brit with the ironing board; Michael, the 18-year-old American who'd been treated to the MdS as a graduation present; Joseph, the oldest man in the race, still cheerful behind his drooping moustache. And there was Loren, too, the black American who we'd seen on the long night. I called to him. 'You look like a champ!' I said. He pointed his finger at me: 'You are a lion!'

Del was standing next to Martin. His face was pale and clammy. He'd tucked his bear into the side pocket of his rucksack, its silver cape fluttering in the breeze. Del seemed to be talking to himself. 'I am the Del,' he said. 'I am the Del, I am the Del, I am the Del. I am the Delmeister. I've got world records. I've got world records. I've run over a thousand marathons.'

Lawson whispered in my ear. 'Now he's going to say he's done eight Marathon des Sables.'

On cue: 'I've run eight MdS. And nothing, and nothing, and no one, and no one is gonna stop me. I'm gonna do it. I'm gonna, gonna, gonna, gonna do it.'

'Sad sod,' said Lawson. 'Does he do anything in his life apart from ultras?'

'When he's not running them, he's talking about them,' Carlo said.

Kurtz farted and pulled another mint from his eye socket. He offered it to Kate and, when she shook her head, he popped it into his mouth. 'Adds flavour,' he said.

'I've never seen anyone do that before,' Lawson said.

'Not many people have.'

And still we waited for the French. They arrived in small groups, ambling with all the urgency of a Parisian boulevardier on his way to the coffeeshop. The Berbers had all but taken down the bivouac, and in a few minutes we'd be running straight through it. I liked running over the bivouac. It gave the race starts a sense of finality, as dust was once again returned to dust, and the Sahara exhaled and breathed.

A Brit, Mark, came over to us. He was tall and friendly, and was re-adjusting his shorts. 'I'm pissing blood,' he said. 'Is there a problem with that?'

'Yes!' Martin said. 'Your kidneys are packing up!'

'Maybe I'll get it checked out,' he said. He started fiddling with his gaiters as if the matter was of no great consequence.

Carlo looked at his watch and realised the date. 'It's April 14th tomorrow!' he announced. 'Now that is one big, big centenary coming up.'

'It is?' said Lawson.

'Hundred years to the day,' said Carlo. He was obviously delighted with his little nugget of knowledge. 'Probably the biggest thing to happen in 1912.'

We looked at each other and shook our heads. I had no idea.

'Was it big?' I asked.

'So big you've seen the movie,' he said.

We thought some more, but I couldn't think of a single memorable event from 1912. Carlo started humming a tune; it was a little familiar.

'*Titanic*,' Kate said.

'The girl wins the prize!' Carlo said. He put his arm round her waist, hugging her as he crooned the *Titanic* theme tune. 'The *Titanic* was built in Belfast by Harland and Wolff, so she was.

My great-grandad was born in 1900, and every day he went to school, he watched her being built.'

'What an appropriate centenary for the Sahara,' said Lawson. 'Iceberg dead ahead!'

Patrick rattled through his race talk. Some 23 people had dropped out the previous day, taking the abandonees' total to over fifty. Patrick was still telling us to look good, but after a week in the desert, we were no longer quite so prepared to put up with his monologues. The grumbling was audible.

On came 'Highway to Hell' and Patrick was warbling over the soundtrack. There was a surge forward. I saw Simon hare away. Martin trotted over the start line, and despite his punctured foot, Del was intent on keeping up with him. He was jogging but he looked very uncomfortable. He obviously wanted to get the day over with. Carlo and Lawson gave us a wave and trotted off towards the hills of *Kfiroun*.

Everyone but the walking wounded had set off. 'And then there were three,' I said, and Kurtz and Kate and I had a team hug and we went on our way – and much to my surprise, it was a great day to be in the desert. It was a great day to be alive.

Kate started out very slowly. She had a slow arthritic gait, grimacing with every step; Kurtz went off by himself and after a few minutes was nothing more than a pinprick on the horizon. The sand was still hard from the previous day's rain, and Kate was smacking the walking poles into the ground. I hoped her feet would soon start to warm up. The camels, Charles and Camilla, wouldn't be out for a while yet. I wondered what I'd do if they were about to catch us. I might be able to carry her in a fireman's lift. For a short way. I hoped it wouldn't come to that.

'Do you like Oasis?' I asked, trying to keep Kate distracted.

'Some songs,' Kate said. For that first half hour, Kate could only talk in brief staccato sentences, no more than four words at a time. 'Hate the brothers.'

'One of their albums was called *Be Here Now*,' I said. I was watching the ground very closely and sort of slouching along, like a schoolboy, hands in my pockets, chin down. 'It also happens to be one of the Dalai Lama's favourite sayings. Though I doubt Oasis have even heard of the Dalai Lama. But it does happen to be the perfect motto for the Marathon des Sables – Be Here Now.'

'Thought it was…' She let out a gasp of pain. We were walking on a high plateau with ridges running through the rock. Kate was not able to place her feet squarely on the ground, and each little ridge was sending a new jolt of pain up through her feet. 'I thought it was…' she tried again. '*Cállate y camina*.'

'*Cállate y camina* is the pilgrims' motto on the way to Santiago de Compostela,' I said. 'Shut up and walk. But with the Marathon des Sables and its condensed week of pain, you need something to keep you focused in the moment. Be Here Now.'

'Be here now,' she repeated. 'My now is pain.'

'Do you like me talking?' I said. 'Or do you want my iPod?'

'Keep talking.'

So I told her the stories that I'd picked up along the way. I told her about the SAS in the desert during the Second World War, who would camouflage their vehicles with pink paint. I talked about the Berbère Palace and how the staff must be preparing themselves for this whirlwind of 250 Sahara-hardened Brits. I said it had been the longest week of my life; every day, every night, I'd lived every moment of it. And for a while, I talked about an old love, Cally. 'Do you ride horses?' I asked.

'No.' Kate shook her head. She had her cap low so that she couldn't see anything more than the ground two yards in front of her feet. It keeps you focused, stops you getting too far ahead of yourself; stops you thinking you'll never be able to make it.

'I'm going to give you a bit more of my wisdom then,' I said. 'I know you'll love it. If a guy is dating a horsewoman, he is never ever going to be able to compete against the horse. The horses are strong. They can carry you. And you know what else a horse does? A horse does whatever you tell it to do. What sort of guy does that?'

'I want a horse,' Kate said.

'No horses round here,' I said. 'They've got some camels though. If you just stay put for a little while, Charles and Camilla will be here.'

We stuttered along. After an hour, I watched as Kate worked her shoulders up and down, and for the first time she looked up, and she looked around her. 'That's better,' she said. 'My feet are numb. Really numb.'

'That's good news,' I said. 'Good news in the short-term. Though you're probably doing untold damage to your feet.'

'Let's make the most of it,' she said. 'I don't know how long it's going to last.'

'We jogging – or are we walking?' I said.

'A brisk walk.'

We came to an *oued*, a river gully. I liked the *oueds*. Like the hills, they gave variety to the grim plod of the desert. The water was deep after the previous day's storms. The Pompiers were there, lowering the dune buggy down the four-metre banks to the water. The boy was strapped in and holding on tight. It looked hazardous. Two of the Pompiers were already waist-deep in the river.

I slid down the bank on my back and waited at the bottom to catch Kate. She cannoned into my legs, and I staggered backwards and fell into the river. Even the Pompiers were laughing. Some branches had been ripped down from the nearby trees, and had been placed across the river to form makeshift steppingstones. We skipped across the water and scrabbled up the other bank, red clay thick in our hands. We stood at the top and watched the Pompiers. '*Magnifique*!' I called, clapping my hands above my head. The man in the middle of the river gave me a thumbs up. We did not wait to see how they dragged the dune buggy out of the *oued*.

The first checkpoint was in a little oasis. We clattered in and took our water, and were on the road again within five minutes. If your feet have stopped hurting, you can't afford to dawdle at the checkpoints. Mark was in the medical tent, the Brit who was pissing blood. He was lying flat on his back. We waved as we walked by.

We walked through dunes and stony plateaus, and undulating bumps of sand that were salted with camel grass. We took it all in while we were momentarily pain-free, this constantly changing desert that rolls on forever. Its beauty took our breath away.

Just before the second checkpoint, we caught up with Del. Martin had abandoned him and he was wandering along by himself. We could hear him talking in a sing-song voice.

'I'm going to do this,' he said. 'I'm going to do this. You can do this. Del, Del, you can do it, you can do it, you can do it. You are the Delmeister and you can do it.'

'Are you all right, Del?' Kate asked.

I'm not even sure he recognised us. He continued to stare at the ground ahead of him. The shoelaces on his injured foot were now completely loose, trailing along the ground. His face dripped with sweat. 'Me, I'm fine, I'm fine, I'm fine,' he said. 'I'm fine. I'm good, I'm good, good, good.'

Kate gave me a sidelong glance. 'What?' she mouthed.

The man was raving. I didn't know what to do. He had been reduced to this gibbering madness. 'Let's get him into the checkpoint,' I said.

Del hardly stopped talking. 'I'm going to get him,' he said, his voice low and gravelly. 'I'm going to get him, I'm going to get him, I'm going to get him. And when I get him, I'm going to knock his head and break his teeth…'

We let him walk ahead of us and when we reached the checkpoint, Kate took Del firmly by the arm and escorted him to the medical tent. He was still mumbling to himself, and his head had started to twitch.

'This is Del,' Kate said to the fat and happy Commissaire.

'Del!' the Commissaire said. 'I know Del very well!'

'Check him out, please,' Kate said. 'He needs help.'

'I see what I can do,' the Commissaire said. 'Del, come and sit down, please.' He took Del by the wrist and settled him on the rug.

I stayed outside, out in the full glare of the sun.

Kate placed Del's fresh bottle of water by his side, and then backed out of the medical tent. 'Be seeing you, Del,' she said. He'd taken off his sunglasses and looked at her blearily through bloodshot eyes.

'Yeah, see ya, see ya, see ya,' he said. 'I'll be seeing you soon, very, very soon. See ya later, see ya later, I'll see ya, see ya, see ya later.'

Mark was the first person to overtake us. He didn't just jog past us – he ran. 'All sorted!' he yelled. We gave him a cheer. Like so many of the runners, I never saw him again, never found out what happened to him. I hope he was all right. It's not uncommon for MdS runners to develop terminal kidney problems.

The second person to overtake us, believe it or not, was Del. We were about three miles out from the third checkpoint, and were walking through a low run of dunes in *Erg Znaïgui* when I heard the stamp of wild footsteps. I looked round and there was Del, trotting quite fast but moving very erratically. His cap was so low over his head that he could barely see a yard in front of his feet. He seemed to be following the trail of the MdS footsteps, though he was veering from left to right. He was mumbling to himself, and he suddenly let out this high-pitched cackle. Kate and I stopped and stood to the side. He didn't even notice us as he ran past.

'Del?' Kate said.

He heard her voice, and his head twitched to the side, but he did not stop, continuing on with his mad flight into the desert.

'I hope he's okay,' Kate said. 'Should we have gone with him?'

'I couldn't have kept up with him,' I said.

Kate bit her lip. 'Should we tell someone?'

'Check at the next checkpoint?'

'We'll do that.'

We continued on our way. I popped my ibuprofen and my paracetemol, Kate had her tramadol, and it was lovely. You don't often hear that word used to describe the MdS. For a time, we were just two friends, out together on a long walk. Who happened to be talking about sex.

'I'd like it tonight,' I said. 'But I'll probably be shattered.'

'I've always wanted to make love in the desert,' Kate said. She was gaily swinging her walking poles. Apart from her feet, her body was holding up well. 'Especially on the MdS. How many other runners have had sex on the MdS?'

'Del, obviously,' I said. 'Be quite a feather in our cap.' We were heading north through a rolling field of dunes. Way off to the east, my eye was drawn to an unusual rocky outcrop that rose sheer out of the desert – *Jebel Bega*, two tall stone clumps separated by a wedge-shaped cleft.

'But the hotel room will be fine,' she mused. 'Did you dream about making love to me when you were in that double bed?'

'I certainly dreamt about making love. I don't know if it was with you.'

She laughed and slapped her pole against my rucksack. 'When we get into that room—'

'Room 429.'

'Room 429, yes, you will have to carry me over the threshold as my feet will be so sore. Do you know what the first thing I'll do is?'

'Get into the shower?'

'I'll go down on you.'

'After a week of not washing in the desert!'

'What did Kurtz say? Adds to the flavour,' she said. 'I'll expect you to return the compliment.'

We walked past a runner who was lying in the dunes with his feet raised up on a little hillock. He might have been asleep. I waved but he did not move.

'You sure you don't want to make love here – now?' Kate said.

'I'm tempted.'

'So am I,' she said. She came alongside and gave me a quick peck on the cheek. 'Then, once I've finally got better acquainted with your Morning Glory—'

'Are we still in Room 429?'

'Yes – and then you will make love to me—'

'Covered in sand and muck and sweat—'

'And definitely with your shoes and your gaiters still on—'

'And you'll still be wearing your shirt—'

'Of course, as well as my shoes and my gaiters.' We held hands. 'And my *casquette* and my buff and my sunglasses. This talk is really turning me on. And as for my shorts, you will have pulled them off one leg, but you will not have had time to take them off the other.'

'Your red shorts, rumpled up around one ankle,' I said. 'What an erotic thought.'

'And I'll be lying there on the side of the bed -'

'With your knees wide—'

'And you'll be kneeling in front of me – and you'll still be wearing those stupid sunglasses of yours—'

'With my rucksack still on my back?'

'Yes, and your *casquette* and your buff, with your lycra shorts around your dirty knees on the floor -'

'Between your legs,' I said. 'Hold it right there. I just want to savour that image. I particularly like the idea of your red shorts around just one ankle -'

'It speaks of the most abandoned desire—'

'Aren't these miles going by quickly?' I said.

'And then, as I start to sing "Highway to Hell"—'

'In a French accent—'

'Yes, and as you start on zee countdown—'

'In French – *cinq, quatre, trois, deux, un*...

'And on zee zero, you will ease forward, so very gently, so smoozly—'

'Like a rocket edging off the launch pad—'

'And zen, as I continue to sing "'Ighway to 'Ell," you will make love to me—'

'Like the desert animal I am—'

'But not for so very long, because zis will be our first time, and since we want to make it zo special—'

'So special—'

'We will go to zee bathroom, where, as I bend over zee taps, you will rather sweetly take me from behind—'

'Still wearing my rucksack?'

'Yes, undoubtedly,' Kate said, kissing my knuckles. 'Zen you will lift me up onto zee basin—'

'Where we will continue to make love—'

'As you admire yourself in zee mirror in your oh-so-cool sunglasses, but your mind will not be altogether on zee lithe body melting to mush beneath you, because...' She paused. 'I want you.'

We stopped and I hugged Kate so tight, and for one brief moment it seemed as if we might add flesh to our extraordinary fantasy. She jumped up so that she had straddled me, her legs about my waist. We pulsed against each other. We kissed and, reluctantly, we continued to walk.

'So while I am on zee basin,' she said, still perfectly mimicking a French girl.

'And as I make love to you—'

'And as you are making love to me, you will undo my gaiters and untie my laces and take off my shoes and my socks.'

'And the bandages?'

'Not for zee moment,' she said. 'I would not want to put you off your stroke, cher Kim.'

I could picture it all. I laughed uproariously.

'And zen,' she said, 'you will peel off my red shorts—'

'That are still on your ankle—'

'Zat are still on my ankle, and zen my shirt, my sunglasses—'

'Until you're as naked as the day you were born—'

'But you must leave my buff around my neck, and zen, very carefully, you will lift me into zee bath—'

'Without slipping on a bar of soap -'

'And, as quickly as you can, you will take off all your clozthes and you will join me in zee bubbly bath—'

'Forget tomorrow's finish line,' I said. 'Forget Patrick giving me a smacker as he drapes the medal round my neck! This is what I want!'

We were following the tracks of the MdS along the gorge of an *oued* bed. The sides of the gorge were steep and we were tucked away from the wind. We could see nothing of the desert, just the gorge and the sky overhead, painfully clear and blue. Even after a week in the desert, the heat was still hitting us like a sledgehammer.

'But, cher Kim, I still want to make love wiz you in zee desert,' Kate said.

'What about our day off, on Sunday?' I said. 'Hire a Land Rover. A rug and pillows and Champagne and a roast chicken—'

'And a parasol,' she said. 'We must 'ave a white parasol.'

'And a windbreak.'

'We will drive out of Ouarzazate to zee top of a big dune,' she said. 'You will shake out zee rug and put out zee parasol—'

'And the windbreak—'

'And zee windbreak, and zen you will pop zee cork –not, of course, your own cork,' she said, tongue poking slyly out of the side of her mouth. 'And we will drink zee Champagne, and zen, as tenderly as you know 'ow, you will ease *mon petit derrière* onto a pillow, and you will lift up my dress, and zen, as I trickle warm sand down your neck you will make love to me—'

'Whilst at the same time peeling off your dress—'

'Which can only ever be done when we are joined at zee hip—'

'So to speak—'

'And zen we will be both be naked and making love in zee Sahara—'

'And wherever we look, there will just be desert—'

'And nothing else but you.'

We lapsed into silence, revelling in our fantasies as we dreamed of all that was to come. Even walking through the desert seemed like the most outrageous fantasy: Kate was holding my hand and she was smiling at me. The thought of actually making love with her still seemed like this mythical mirage on the horizon, and no matter how far I walked towards it, there it would be, still on the horizon, still a desert's distance away from ever becoming a reality.

We came to the third checkpoint. There were two boys selling fossils. They had sharks' teeth, 150 million years old and now turned to stone, all that remained of the sharks that once swam the Sahara. It needed the most complete mindshift to imagine this desert turned to sea.

I nosed through the boys' fossils, the ammonites and the sharks' teeth that were still embedded into rock. I bought two white triangular teeth, serrated at the edges, each like a short fat dagger.

'Present for you,' I said. 'Matching shark's teeth. One for you, one for me.'

Kate was filling her water bottles. She tossed the tooth lightly in her hand. 'I'll turn it into a necklace,' she said.

'A much better memento of the Sahara than an MdS medal.'

She tucked the tooth away into her rucksack. We were psyching ourselves up for the final stretch. 'What about Del?' she asked. 'Shouldn't we ask about Del?'

We went over to the check-in Commissaires. They checked their lists, but they had not seen Del.

'He might have strayed a little,' I said.

They promised to keep an eye out for Del. There was nothing more I could do. I remember looking out over the desert, to the east and west, as if there was a cat in hell's chance of me ever seeing Del. There was nothing out there – of course there was nothing out there. But then, from way out to the east, I caught a wink of light. It was nothing more than a flash, like the far-off flare of a match on a pitch-dark night.

'Excuse me,' I said to the greying, precise Commissaire. 'May I try your binoculars?'

He gave them to me. They were top-of-the-range Zeiss binoculars. I panned over to the east, looking for any sort of movement. I scanned from left to right and back again, and then I caught it, an absolutely miniscule flare of light coming from the two twin rocks that I'd seen earlier in the day, *Jebel Bega*. I focused the binoculars. Now that I knew where I was looking, I could see it quite clearly. Though it still took some moments to comprehend what I was looking at. I was staring at the shining silver cape of Del's teddybear.

I watched Del very closely. He was so far away that it was difficult to tell which direction he was heading in, but after perhaps a minute, I realised he had been jogging towards *Jebel Bega*. He started to climb. The rocks looked treacherously steep.

I passed the binoculars to the Commissaire. 'He's on *Jebel Bega*,' I said. 'He's got a bit of silver in his rucksack. It's acting like a shiner.'

As the Commissaire stared through the binoculars, I pointed Del out to Kate.

'That's a long way off,' she said. She drank water as she looked across the desert.

The Commissaire scanned with the binoculars and then was quite still as he focused on *Jebel Bega*. He quietly picked up his radio and started issuing curt, urgent orders. I could not understand his rapid French, but I twice heard him mention the *jebel*.

He snapped off from the radio and picked up the binoculars again, training them on the base of the rocks Del was climbing. 'Thank you,' he said. 'Your friend is in much danger.'

Nothing happened for a few minutes, but then we saw two white Land Rovers racing up from the south towards *Jebel Bega*. They were side by side and going flat out, long twin trails of dust in their wake. They pulled up at the bottom of the rocks. The Commissaire was watching it all through his binoculars. He was giving us a running commentary.

'They have got out of the cars,' he said. 'They are running over to him. They must be calling to him.' The Commissaire paused, scratching at his nose. 'But your friend Del. He will not come down.'

I could not see what was happening, but I could picture it all. Del, half-crazed from fever and whatever else was in his system, hell-bent on climbing the *Bega* rocks and nothing – but nothing – was going to talk him down.

Excited jabber came over the radio. The Commissaire gave us a Gallic shrug and sat down. 'This may take some time,' he said.

Kate and I watched *Jebel Bega* for another ten minutes, but it was not at all clear if anything was happening. It could have been minutes or hours before they ever got to Del.

Kate took my hand. 'Can we go?' she said. 'I'm tightening up.'

'Let's go.'

'*Bon courage*,' the Commissaire said. He picked up his binoculars and once again trained them on Del.

Jebel Bega was soon out of sight. We were walking a long sandy passage up through the hills of *Jebel Debouaâ*. We did not talk. Both our minds were on Del and what had happened to him.

'He was miles off course,' Kate said.

'He wasn't going to stop either,' I said.

'I wonder what he was going to do once he got to the top.'

Dead ahead of us we had our first glimpse of the glittering ochre mountains of *Erg Chebbi*, the highest dunes in North Africa. This was the Sahara of my imaginings – great undulating dunes of sand. The dunes did not stretch across the horizon, but took up a relatively small patch of desert, just 15 miles across. Where *Erg Chebbi* ended, the desert reverted back to its usual wilderness of stony scrub.

There were three dunes that were far and away taller than the rest.

'How high are they?' I asked.

'One hundred and fifty metres,' Kate said.

'And we're going over the top tomorrow?'

'Not over the top. We're running through the middle.'

'Shame,' I said. 'Would have liked to have schussed off the top off *Chebbi Erg*.'

We came across three men, Westerners, who were lounging around a deserted village, *M'Fis*. They were about my age, though much more heavy-set, and they were eking out their mid-life crises in the more traditional fashion. In the shade of a dusty tree were parked up three huge new motorbikes. I recognised the bikes, two Ducattis and a BMW. I knew them well; once upon a time, before my MdS epiphany, I had also dreamed of biking through the deserts of Africa.

The men were wearing white T-shirts, black leather trousers and biker boots. They were sat on a low wall by an old mineshaft. They seemed quite content to soak up the sun and watch this unending line of desert runners. After a while you forget that, to the outside world, you must seem like the world's biggest freakshow.

'How's the mid-life crisis going?' I called to the bikers.

The taller biker, bearded and with a bandana over his head, called back. He was German. 'Not as well as yours,' he said.

We'd travelled about 20 miles, which is about the distance that marathon runners often hit the wall. I've hit the wall once before. You feel so knackered you can't take another step; but it's primarily a mental block. I had heard no talk of walls on the MdS.

We could see the bivouac. It was the last time I'd be walking into it, and it already felt like it was over. I started to feel an enormous sense of loss. For all its insanity, the MdS had been my life for a week and I would miss it. The race had been so all-consuming that everything else in my life, my family, my job, had dwindled to specks of sand in the desert. I'd miss the clarity of the Sahara; I'd miss the routines we had when we got up in the morning and when we returned to camp; I'd miss the banter and the jokes; and Lawson and Carlo and their loving massages; and Kurtz and the Extra Strong mints he stored in his eye socket.

I'd miss Kate.

I looked at her. Her mouth was a small tight line of pain and her face was set on the bivouac three miles away.

I wondered if we would make love. Or was it all just so much badinage? Bravado is as good a way as any to tough out a hot day in the desert.

But those kisses we'd shared – I grinned at that treasure of a memory. Funny to think it was only yesterday, underneath that rock in the hailstorm.

I'd have done the whole of the MdS for just a single one of her kisses.

And all that talk about us making love together… that would be good. That would be amazing. The perfect end to this most perfect of weeks.

And I thought, also, about what was going to happen afterwards. Would it just be this incredible one-off? Would we return back to our mundane lives, me to my Elise, Kate to her Edward, and would all be just as it had been before? Would everything that had happened in the desert just stay in the desert, a magnificent moment now stuck in amber, becoming ever more burnished with age?

Or was it possible… Could it ever happen?

Was it an affair we had embarked upon?

Or did we really have a chance of it together? Would I swing the axe and cut loose from Elise and the girls, and perhaps, one day – pitiful, hopeless dream – Kate and I could live together and have a brood of our own…

I didn't know. I didn't know how it would turn out.

But what I did know was that Kate was walking by my side and that I loved her; and I was happy. We were happy. And who knows what even the next hour would bring, let alone tomorrow. We were runners in the Marathon des Sables – and we had lived only for the moment.

We were a mile from the finish line and we could see the flags and the white blimps and the Commissaires' gleaming white city when we heard a Land Rover rumbling up behind us. It was an open-top Land Rover with two people in the front and one in the back. The car swept past and then stopped.

In the front passenger seat was the jolly doctor who we'd seen at the second checkpoint.

And in the back was Del. His head flicked from side to side, and his face was contorted into this wild grimace. Around his neck were his smashed sunglasses. His eyes were rolling, like a wild beast that's been caught in a trap. White foam was speckled around his mouth. His lips were bleeding.

Very gingerly, we walked over to the side of the Land Rover and we looked at Del. He was clawing at his face with his fingernails, and there were great red weals across his cheeks and his forehead.

'Is he going to be all right?' Kate asked the Commissaire.

Del twitched when he heard her voice, peering out from the car.

'We hope so,' the Commissaire said. He shook his head, chewing on his lower lip. 'I have never seen this before.'

Del was thrashing in his seat, back and forth, his head banging into the back of the seat. He'd been strapped into a six-point harness. He strained to get out.

'Will he stay in the bivouac?' I asked.

It was a mistake.

I should not have spoken.

The moment Del heard my voice, he let out a howl of the most manic rage. His eyes rolled and as he focussed on me, he lunged out of the window, fingers clawing at the air. 'I hate him!' he screamed. 'I hate him, hate him, hate him!' He was frantically trying to release the harness, jerking from side to side, his teeth champing up and down. He stared at me with absolute vitriol.

I goggled. Kate pulled me back. Del screeched his rage, 'Hate him, hate him, hate him!'

The car drew away, flicking up the desert dust, with Del leaning out of the back window, his mouth etched into a scream of the most visceral loathing that I had ever heard. I was looking into the face of a man turned mad by the desert.

CHAPTER 22

A Parisian orchestra had been flown in to Merdani, and as night fell over the bivouac, we clustered around a bonfire and listened to the most extraordinary concert. Never in their dreams could Bach or Puccini have imagined their music being played in such a strange setting, or to such a strange audience.

It was cold, and Kate and I had all our clothes on as we'd hobbled over to the bonfire. By now I had all the symptoms of full-blown flu, and, as for Kate, well, her feet looked horrendous. She'd spent over two hours in Doc Trotters. She'd probably finish the final stage, but it would be weeks before she was running properly again. We did not speak about her feet any more. We did not speak about her pain. Talking about it only seemed to make it worse. She took her drugs and she soldiered on.

The bonfire was huge, at least ten feet tall. A stream of sparks were carried high in the wind. Many of the Tuareg had turned out for the show, sitting in clusters around the periphery of the audience. Kate and I edged to the front. We were close to the fire and could feel its heat on our hands and on our faces.

We sat on my sleeping bag, legs stretched in front of us. I passed Kate my bottle of water and as she took it, we looked at each other and we had this spark that only lovers know of. We leaned in and we kissed. We didn't care who saw us.

We cheered as the orchestra came out. The musicians were fronted by the prima donna, a woman in her mid-forties, gypsy-like with long black curly hair, diamond earrings and a pearl necklace. She wore a turquoise shirt and a black corset; she was not the type of woman who stood for any nonsense. Behind her, the green laser beamed into the sky.

We didn't know what she was going to be like, or what was going to happen, but as she began to sing, she enchanted us. She sang Schubert's 'Ave Maria.' I used to know it quite well; the music is Bach, the first prelude from his 'Well-Tempered Clavier.'

Kate and I lay with our heads back on the sleeping bag. We were holding hands, staring up at the stars and the sparks of the flame that whistled in the wind. There was the scent of the wood smoke and the roar of the flames, and over it all this miraculous singing.

Quite unexpectedly, I found that I was crying. I didn't try to wipe the tears away. They dripped down the sides of my face and onto the dry sand beneath my head.

I don't even really know why I was crying. Do you need a reason to cry? It was partly the music. Once, with another woman, in another life, I had been able to play this piece of Bach, and hearing it now was another reminder that even the greatest love affairs eventually crash and burn. And if they don't, if there is no drama, then love's white heat fades to nothing but embers. And these greying embers can occasionally be kicked over, but they will never be a match for the roar of the heat as you open the furnace door for the first time.

I loved Kate.

At that moment, I would gladly have given it all up for her.

And for a while, it might work. But it couldn't work. Not really. I was twenty years her senior, and she was way too young to be settling down with a middle-aged man. She still had many, many adventures ahead of her. And though we might share some small domestic bliss, all too soon I would have become nothing but a deadweight dragging at her ankles.

And the fire roared and the music washed over us, and we lay flat on our backs, staring to the stars. I looked over at Kate and instantly she turned to look at me, and we realized we'd both been crying.

The diva sang Brahms and Bach and Handel's 'Largo' and that Andrea Bocelli anthem, 'Time to Say Goodbye.' The last song was from *Carmen*. Then, being the diva that she was, the singer wrapped herself in a shawl and refused to give an encore; they'd travelled a long way, she said. They were tired. The end of her little speech was punctuated by a loud wet fart. I hoped it was Kurtz giving the concert its final punctuation mark.

As the others drifted off, Kate and I lay by the bonfire. Kate lifted my hand, wagging it in the air. 'Ever wonder how's it going to turn out?' she asked.

'Only all the time.'

For a while we stared at the laser, as it still beamed its blaze up at the stars, as pointless as our pondering of all these abstruse what-ifs and what-might-bes.

Kate rolled over on top of me. She grinned and she kissed me. 'Hey – we're in the Marathon des Sables!'

It was a cool, refreshing bucket of water. Who the hell cared about how things might turn out? We were living the dream.

'Thank you for reminding me,' I said.

And we rolled and we writhed against each other, first her on top and then me, panting, straining against each other, and for a while we were quite consumed with lust, but then it ebbed, like the husks of wood that lay dying in the fire. We tottered back to our tent.

There was more space in the middle now that Del had gone. We brushed our teeth and then both lay together in my sleeping bag. I zipped us up. We were lying face to face in each other's arms, and I might have thought of making love then.

I remember how she stroked my hair. A moment later I had fallen asleep.

*

The next day, I heard the music for the last time, and though it was still as cheesy as ever, when I heard ACDC, I felt goosebumps prickling up my neck. We'd posed for our last pictures of Tent 71, had pricked our last blisters, and had dumped billycans and hexamine and spare food until our rucksacks were down to the bare last kilos. I was shivering, my nose was streaming, and Kate was still in her own world of pain. But we only had ten miles to go and no time limits.

In previous years, they'd had a staggered start on the last day. The runners would divide into three groups, the slowest starting off first and the others following in 15 minute intervals. As a runner ran past, you would both hold out your hands and touch. It showed that you were all in the MdS together, that even the hobbling, blistered walkers were as much a part of it as the race winner.

I would have liked that.

Patrick sent us all on our way. We were to head due north on a stony plateau parallel to the dunes. When we reached the first checkpoint, we were to head off straight through the heart of *Erg Chebbi*. The last stretch was just six miles, barely more than the route we ran from work in Wapping.

The others had long gone; even Kurtz, with his IT band syndrome had managed to crank out an unwieldy jog.

I gave Kate a hug. 'Let's get this thing over with,' I said. 'How much money are you raising?'

'Me?' she said. 'A fair bit.'

'Over five figures?' I asked casually.

'I hope so,' she said. 'I've been plugging it every day in the paper.'

We held hands as we walked over the line. A few of the Commissaires had turned out to wave us on our way.

'Puts my seven grand into the shade,' I said. 'Better make sure you do it.'

'And I haven't even played the girly card.'

'You don't need to play the girly card. We're going to smash this thing.'

'You won't be too tired for our date tonight?'

'Our date in Room 429? I am counting the minutes!'

She sidled up to me, her hand teasing at the front of my trousers. 'So am I,' she said.

Yes – whatever else happened, there was always going to be that.

I don't remember much about the walk to the first checkpoint. What I remember are the dunes. I remember little shanty huts, wondering how people could possibly live in them.

And I remember my feet, so hot in my shoes, and this nipping pain from the previous day's blisters, and on we would trudge through the sand, with this giant of a dune up ahead of us. Kate had shortened off my poles and was using them to drive herself up the sides of the sandy crescents. And then, to hell with the blisters and to blazes with her delaminated feet –we both ran down the dunes, the wind in our faces, squealing for the sheer joy of it all. Then along the ridge of another dune, and down the other side, and more sand, and more sand, swallowing your feet and sucking at your ankles as we slogged ever onwards.

We were halfway through the dunes, in the very lee of *Erg Chebbi* itself when Kate stopped and took off her rucksack.

'Need a pee?' I asked, turning away.

'No,' she said, sitting down on the sand. 'Take off your rucksack.'

I unclipped my rucksack and tossed it onto the ground and sat next to Kate. She had unhitched her gaiters and was untying her laces. She pulled off her shoes and unpeeled her socks. Her feet were only fresh bandaged that morning.

'What are we doing?' I said.

'For the first time in this race, we are going to dip our feet into the sea of the Sahara,' she said. She wormed her feet into the dune until she was knee deep in sand. Her white bandages were completely covered.

She lay back on the sand, lips glossed, face straight to the sun. 'When you've got your socks off, come over and kiss me.'

It seemed like the most fantastically stupid thing to do, and yet also so utterly brilliant. That morning, we had spent over an hour cleaning our blisters, bandaging our feet, putting on our socks and gaiters, and all of it to keep our feet free from the sand. And yet here we were, taking it all off and actually dipping our feet into the hot Sahara.

I eased my bandaged feet into the sand. I was surprised. The feeling was delicious, like immersing my feet into a warm bath.

I leant over Kate and our wet lips kissed. In the distance, we could see people walking the dunes, so intent on reaching the finish line, not realising, perhaps, that when they were done, they'd wish it had never ended.

'One day,' Kate said, 'When you are old and grey, and sitting by the fire in your care home, you will remember this. You will remember lying in the sun at *Erg Chebbi*. You will remember taking off your shoes and your socks. And you will remember how you bathed your feet in this hot sand.'

'I might remember that,' I said. 'The one thing I'll never forget is you.' I stared up to the top of *Erg Chebbi* and dreamed of the sharks that had swum over these dunes so many million years ago; in a million years, would there ever be a woman who was a match for Kate?

'Yes,' she said, and she sat up. 'You'll be the key to all my happiest memories.'

I did not know what to say. We embraced, clumsily, sitting there on the foothills of *Erg Chebbi*, holding each other tight.

'Come on,' I said. 'This is the Marathon des Sables, you know.'

'Kiss me one more time,' she said.

'I will – because I love you.' I leaned in to kiss her and she cupped my cheek; the spell was broken.

We brushed the sand off our feet and pulled on our socks and shoes and secured our gaiters. Then we set off on the last three miles of the race. Gradually we were leaving our desert dreams behind us and emerging into the real world. Children came out to greet us. Four tourists on camels had trekked out into the dunes, clapping when they saw us. In the distance, a green belt of trees and a giant inflatable man pouring Sultan tea. More children and now men and women, standing out on top of the dunes, holding up handmade posters and cheering us on. And on the very outskirts, there was a strange man in a khaki suit, a Westerner, who was calling out to us. 'Well done!' he shouted. 'It's magnificent! You've got to run now! You're nearly there!'

We were weaving through the last of the dunes and this scorch of adrenalin scalded through us as we moved up to a jog and then a run, and I could hear these cheers, massive cheers, from all the hundreds of people who had gathered to welcome us home. To my amazement, Kate was now sprinting, so fast I could barely keep up with her, pounding through the dunes as the sand spurted from her feet, and as we took the next corner, we had a sight of the finish line. We were giving it everything we'd got.

In a flash, in a blur, it was all gone. We were over the line and we were holding onto each other, and we weren't crying, we were laughing, so elated that it was all over. We had done the unthinkable. We had taken the last step and we need walk no further.

We waited for Patrick Bauer to give us our medals. He was an old pro. With every runner, with every hug, he somehow made it personal.

My magical moment was gone in an instant. '*C'est fantastique!*' I said to Patrick, kissing him on both cheeks, and the old rogue smiled and clapped me on the back. 'Bravo, Mr Kim!'

All around us, everyone was going mad. After the tranquillity of the desert, it seemed like bedlam.

We found ourselves a quiet corner by the finish line, and amidst all the noise and the tumult, I remember we were holding onto each other, and after a while we started to kiss. We were kissing again and for only the hundredth time, I couldn't believe that it was Kate who was pressing her lips onto mine. I looked at her softly, through long lashes. Even after a week in the desert, her face was still so smooth and clean.

From off to the side, right in my peripheral vision, I caught a flutter of movement.

I looked up and saw a man who looked like Grubby – Grubby the *Sun* photographer who had first introduced me to Kate all those months ago in the News International canteen. He was some way off. He wore a crumpled safari suit and a grimy white Tilley hat, a couple of cameras slung around his neck. I goggled at him. It *was* Grubby. I could even see the sweat stains underneath his armpits. He was waving at me, repeatedly slicing a finger across his throat – Cut, Cut, Cut!

His meaning was quite clear. I stopped kissing Kate. With my arm loose about her waist I stared quizzically at the photographer.

My two worlds were in collision and I could not begin to make sense of it all. What was he doing here? What could have happened to have brought Grubby out to the desert?

'There's Grubby,' I said to Kate.

She let out a squeal – and even now, as I look back, I don't know whether it was a squeal of horror or amazement. Perhaps even of delight.

A man, a tall man with floppy blonde hair, was climbing over the railings. He was wearing chinos and a purple polo shirt. He jumped into the runners' pen, and my heart did a complete somersault, hard over the humpback bridge and into thin air.

Edward? Edward here too?

He had this hungry smile on his face. He only had eyes for Kate, lifting her off the ground and sweeping her up into his arms. I am struck dumb. I stand to the side, watching as Edward holds her tight and as he smothers her with his kisses. He's babbling at her, but I cannot hear what he is saying.

I am swept with the most complete resignation.

Oh.

Well.

So that was that then. He'd come for her. My little desert dream had turned out to be nothing but a mirage.

I was hot and my legs felt unimaginably tired. I didn't want to watch Kate's reunion. I just wanted to get into the shade.

I went over to the railings, staring out at my old friend the desert, where everything had seemed so clear and so definite, and where the only task in hand was to take the next step. How I wished I was back out there.

I took off my rucksack. I wondered if I'd ever come back. And Kate had gone, I knew it. For a week now, I had been living my life in the moment; and now, all too quickly, that moment was over.

The crowd had started to whoop. I listened. It all seemed so unbearably banal.

What now?

I turned back to find Edward on his knees. He had a small red Cartier box in his hands.

He was proposing to her.

Kate's hands flew to her face, though whether in shock or happiness, I did not know. She fell to her knees. The crowd was going mad as Kate and Edward held onto each other. Grubby was capturing every moment of it on his camera. She was crying, Edward was crying, the runners were crying and the crowd was crying too.

I did not cry.

Without even noticing it, I had slipped back into my old world. I am just the objective reporter, the man who clinically observes, who watches, but who does not engage.

I watched as he kissed her. Edward was kissing those same lips that I had been kissing an hour ago in the *Erg Chebbi* dunes. He had his arms around her waist and was still holding onto the Cartier box. It was open now and inside it there was a fat diamond solitaire. Kate had taken off her sunglasses. She buried her face into Edward's neck.

A deep breath in. A last look to the desert, and I slung my rucksack over my shoulder. I was leaving now. I had a last glance at Kate. She looked young, kneeling there in the sand.

She must have known I was looking at her because suddenly she opened her eyes. For a while we just stared at each other, but I could not tell what she was thinking – whether it was regret or resignation, or anything much at all. Well – we'll always have Ouarzazate.

I raised my hand and I gave her a wave, but she did not move. As I left the runners' pen, I could feel her beautiful blue eyes on my back.

They were serving Sultan tea. I stood at the bar in the shade and I sipped my tea, and I observed this jumbling car crash of thoughts as they piled through my head, one after the next. I sipped the tea slowly, savouring it, realising I could never drink it again. Then I drained the last drop and I was done. It was over.

I bought a Fanta and went and sat at one of the cafés that had been set up near the finish line. I was waiting for my coach back to the Berbère Palace.

Grubby came over. He clapped me on the back and sat down at the table. He was red in the face and his shirt was soaked through from the sweat.

'Congratulations,' he said. 'We never thought you'd make it.'

'Thanks.'

'What a story!' he said. He mopped at his face with a wet grey handkerchief.

'Has it been big?' I asked. I had no idea how our story of the MdS had been playing out in the UK.

'You don't know?' he said.

'I haven't heard a thing.'

'They're going mental for it!' he said. 'Kate survives terminal brain cancer. She skins her feet. She raises over two million and now her boyfriend only goes and proposes to her on the finish line.'

'Really?' I spoke without thinking, without even really listening. I suddenly realised what Grubby had said to me. 'She's raised two million?'

'Probably go up to three now that we've got the fairytale ending.' Grubby patted my knee. He knew. We both knew. Well, what guy wouldn't have wanted to kiss her?

I looked at him and nodded, digesting all that he had just told me. So she'd written about her brain cancer too; she'd not told me about that either.

'She's a great girl,' I said.

'And now, being the hack that you are, you've got to file the splash.'

I was surprised I hadn't seen it days ago. It made sense. Kate's tale ticked all the tabloid boxes: a pretty woman, a cancer survivor, no less, who runs through the pain to complete the toughest footrace on earth. And who's raising money for her favourite cancer charity. And whose boyfriend has flown out to Merzouga to propose to her on the finish line.

And as for the goat who was running with her?

Who cared?

'Yep,' I said.

I turned the facts around in my head, examining them from all angles. 'What are they giving it? Five pages?'

'And the rest.'

I stared glumly at my Fanta. It was tepid. I didn't want to drink any more. I wanted to plunge into the ice-cold pool in the Berbère Palace and stay swimming at the bottom until my lungs burst.

'At least it's Saturday,' I said. 'No hurry.'

Grubby had got out his laptop. He was syncing it up to his camera. 'You've got all the time world,' he said. 'At least 60 minutes. You forgot we've started publishing on Sundays?'

Another jolt to the system. Over the last week, I'd thought so little of my mad masters that I'd even forgotten about their newly launched Sunday edition.

'How much do they want?' I said to Grubby.

'Everything you've got,' he said. 'Running copy, eh? Doesn't it just remind you of your glory days in New York?'

I bought a couple of beers. Grubby tossed me his notepad, and as he started sending over the pictures, I began to scrawl out my copy. I just had to get the first couple of sentences right, and then I'd be able to dictate the rest of the copy off the top of my head.

I wondered what I was trying to say, what I wanted to say.

I wondered – different matter entirely – what my mad masters wanted me to say.

They'd want me to say that Kate had toughed it out on the most brutal footrace on earth; that her handsome boyfriend Edward had been waiting for her at the finish line with a diamond solitaire engagement ring.

Grubby gave me his phone. I was put through to the copytakers; they can type your copy as fast as you can think.

'Copytakers,' came a calm voice that was slightly familiar. 'Sara speaking.'

'Hi Sara,' I said. 'It's Kim here – Kim from the *Sun*.'

'Oh yes!' she said. 'You're the nice man who once bought me lunch in the canteen.'

'So I did,' I said, remembering that day when Grubby had first introduced me to Kate as we'd been queuing for lunch. Sara had been in front of us, and Kate behind. I wondered what would have happened if they'd been the other way round. It seemed like another age and another world.

'I've been reading about you in the desert every day,' Sara said. 'Is it over yet?'

'It's over.' I took a sip from my beer. It tasted odd. It was the first alcohol I'd had in a week.

'Had your colleague Kate on the phone quite a bit this week.'

Another short sharp jab to the gut. Kate had never mentioned the copytakers. It had never occurred to me that there was any pressing need for such huge amounts of copy. 'Really?' I said.

'Thousands of words. She let it run.'

'Oh,' I said. Oh well.

It looked as if, not for the first time, I had been bested on all counts by a younger, less-experienced colleague.

'Ready when you are, Kim,' Sara said.

And I looked up at Grubby and we clinked our beer bottles, and for a moment more I listened to the wind and I gazed out at what was left of my desert fantasy. 'She's the woman who beat cancer, and who then toughed it out in the Sahara to raise millions for charity,' I said. 'And last night, she was finally reduced to tears – after her boyfriend popped the question.' I remembered that all punctuation had to be spelt out to the copytakers. 'Point-par.'

'So did she say yes?' Sara asked.

'I don't know,' I replied. I felt like I didn't know much about anything any more.

*

Grubby drove me to the Berbère Palace. I nosed through the MdS packed lunch. There was fresh bread and cheese, apricots and peanuts, a crêpe, couscous tabouleh, some small salamis and some juice, and it should have been absolutely delicious after the junk I'd been eating in the desert. But I had no taste for it. I ate a dried apricot and looked out of the window of the hired Mercedes. We were skimming through the desert at 70 mph. And now that I was in a car, the Sahara had been transformed into just this dull, featureless wasteland; the desert only ever reveals her charms to the footsloggers.

I plugged in my headphones and slept sightless dreams; nothing could ever be a match for what I'd seen in the desert. Grubby nudged me awake and passed me his phone. It was my mad masters with more of their interminable questions. It does not matter how much you file, the mad masters will still be sitting in their bottomless pit, for ever asking for more.

It was late afternoon when we got into the Berbère Palace. Most of the other Brits had already arrived. I picked up my suitcase and went to Room 429. I don't know why, but a tiny part of me had still hoped that Kate might be in the room, singing to herself as she soaked in the bath.

The room was empty. It still smelled of paint. I peeled off my clothes, ripped off my bandages and had the fabled shower I had been dreaming about for the previous eight days – and, as with so many things in my life, the reality never even came close to being a match for my soaring expectations. I washed my hair and washed it again and then scoured the grime from my ears and my eyes and the back of my neck. Even after my sleep in the car, I still felt unconscionably weary. It was partly the flu and partly just not being with Kate any more.

I looked at myself in the mirror. With my beard and my sun-etched skin, I looked like a hollow-eyed vagrant. I patted my beard and wondered whether to leave it. I shaved it all off. The basin was thick with my stubble.

I put on jeans and a grubby fleece and limped out of the room.

I squared my shoulders.

I clicked my neck from left to right.

And I swaggered into the bar as if I had been reborn as the party king.

So I'd had a reverse. Not a stupendous reverse, just another reverse in love. You'd have thought that at my age I'd be pretty used to it by now, but it still hurts all the same.

Try again. Fail again. Fail better.

I drank and I drank, and after making a hog of myself over the buffet dinner, I drank some more. We told our favourite tales from the MdS, and, three times over, I had to tell my tentmates about how it had all ended for Del, finally driven mad by the desert.

Kate was not there. I did not even know if she was staying in the same hotel. But I didn't care; or, at least, I was attempting to give every indication that I didn't care. She was already fading fast from view, as beautiful, as ethereal – and, perhaps, as unknowable – as the desert herself.

I was lining up the beers six at a time on top of the bar. Now that we were back in civilisation, and now that we had our medals, all was genteel and courteous and, 'No, my dear chap, after you'.

I don't know how long I carried on drinking. We had moved onto brandy, and I left after I'd fallen off my stool. I wandered out of the bar and into the night, and the air was thick with the scent of jasmine. I plucked some orange blossom and tucked it behind my ear. I staggered to my room, and as I thought of that great Niagara of sex that Kate and I had once planned for each other, I laughed out loud. Only ever in my dreams.

The curtains were drawn and I could see that I'd left the lights on. I went into the vestibule and keyed the lock. I dropped the key as I opened the door. I was still scrabbling on the ground when I heard a voice.

'Hello,' she said.

I jerked up, slackjawed and staring – for on this day of unbelievable days, there was still one last shocker awaiting me: my wife, lying in the double bed.

I picked up the key and sat on the edge of the bed. For a little while there was silence. 'Hello,' I said.

'Surprised to see me?' Elise said.

'A little,' I said. 'It's rather been a day of surprises.'

'Good surprise. Or bad surprise?'

'Good – I think.'

For the first time I looked at Elise properly. She had a bit of a tan and I wondered how long she'd been out in Morocco. She had lipstick on too, quite dark, chocolaty lipstick that went well with her tan. She was wearing something in black silk. I could see the black ribbons on her bare shoulders; it suited her.

'And Edward came out and asked Kate to marry him?' Elise said. She nodded at me, as if to prompt an answer.

'Yes he did,' I said. I had my hand on the bed cover. I was playing with Elise's foot. 'How did you know that?'

'I told him to.'

I raised my eyebrows. I had not seen that one coming; in fact I hadn't seen many of the things that had been coming my way that day. I'd lost my touch, my finely tuned antennae now well and truly clipped by the desert.

I shrugged and popped my cheeks. Try again. Fail again. Fail better.

'New hair?' I asked. Elise's hair was still a glorious Titian red, but it was much shorter, cropped close about her neck.

She touched her hair, stroking it. 'Do you like it?'

'Quite sexy,' I said, and in my mind's eye...

I kick off my shoes and I range over the bed to Elise and I kiss her on the lips. We are looking at each other as we kiss, for there are still so many questions that remain unanswered, but they can wait. They can wait till the morning. Suddenly Elise is closing her eyes and drawing me in, and her kisses are firmer and deeper, and her arm is snaking about my neck, enfolding me, ensnaring me, as she strokes my cheek to kiss me as only a lover can kiss.

And in reality...

The reality was better, even, than the most exotic of all my fantasies.

PREVIEW

The next romance in Kim's love life is The Woman Who Dared to Dare, *due to be published by Thames River Press in May 2014. This is the first chapter.*

CHAPTER 1

There are two types of swimmer: those who live to follow the black lines in the pool, length after mind-numbing length, and the wild swimmers, those who live for the sea and for the rivers, and who thrive on the cold and the scrapes and the bruises. And this, also, is how lovers are divided. Are you a creature of comfort who looks for love in the snug of your bedroom, between satin sheets and behind locked doors? Or are you a lover of all things wild and airy, with the stars high overhead as the wind stings at your skin.

I am a wild swimmer. And as for my lovemaking – well, we will come to that shortly. Though doubtless even now you can hazard what sort of lover I am.

I had learned my swimming stroke in the outdoor pool at Cirencester, but I honed my swimming in the rivers of Gloucestershire, and in one river in particular: the Thames.

In Lechlade, near where the Thames rises, it is nothing but a small country river. But then, as you know, it swells and it grows until, by London, it is this wide, dirty brown streak.

I had swum the Thames many times in and around Gloucestershire – and almost always I had swum it with Sasha.

But this time, on a whim, as a dare, we were swimming the Thames in London, and that is much, much more dangerous. It's not the distance that's the killer; we could swim 400 yards, easy. But there are tides in the London Thames, and there are potholes, and around the bridges there are rippling downsurges, which can suck you to your death before you're even aware they exist.

And there are other ways the Thames in London can kill you...

But the Thames is nevertheless the Thames, the most famous river in the British Isles, and so for all us wild swimmers, it is a challenge that has to be swum.

The gauntlet had only been thrown down that afternoon. It was spring in 1990, a Saturday, and Sasha and I had been swimming in Lechlade. In those days we didn't even bother with wetsuits. I'd been watching her from the bank. In the water, swimming above the reeds, Sasha was like a sea otter, lithe and supple. Like all the best swimmers, she was very slippery in the water. Some swimmers are thrashers, but Sasha was fluid; she hardly made a splash. Her body seemed to meld itself to the river, her long dark hair flowing free behind her.

'When are we going to swim the Thames properly?' I called down to her. I'd already got out because it was cold.

Sasha looked up out of the water, her wet head bobbing black beneath the bridge. She laughed and she smiled, her teeth this quite brilliant white against her black hair.

'Why not today?' she said. 'I dare you.'

'Well if it's a dare.'

'It might be.'

And that is the beauty of being in your 20s, carefree, commitment-free: you can do just about whatever you want.

She got out of the water. There were some tourists walking over Halfpenny Bridge, cameras bumping on their fat stomachs. They watched her. I watched her. Her hair fell long and sleek down the back of her neck. She patted it with a white towel. She was wearing a black swimsuit, a swimmer's swimsuit, one that showed off her legs. They were very long, olive-skinned; she was half-British, half-Argentinean.

I had known her for a year. I found her very beautiful.

But I had yet to lay even a finger on her.

She towelled herself down. I admired those legs and her swimmer's shoulders. She pulled on her white towelling robe, and then, very discreetly and efficiently, pulled on some khaki shorts. She turned her back to me and pulled on a white T-shirt.

Putting her wet things into a bag, she slipped on some thongs – and just like that, we were ready to go.

We decided to catch the train down to London. I drove us straight to Kemble station just outside Cirencester. In those days, I was driving a grey Mercedes. It was an old automatic with peppery white plastic seats.

Sasha sat next to me in the front. She eased her seat back as far as it would go, and then reclined it even further. She kicked off her thongs and rested her bare feet on the glove compartment, so that her toes touched the windscreen.

I looked again at her legs. How could I not look at her legs? They were only a few inches from my face. I have always been the world's most complete sucker for long legs. I would have liked to kiss them. I would have liked to pull over into a layby, snatch a rug from the boot, and lead her by the hand to the adjacent field, where, initially, at least, I would have kissed those legs, my tongue trailing down the inside of her thigh and lingering just behind her knee (a much underrated erogenous zone, but a wonderful one for all that).

But, of course, I did not kiss Sasha's legs, nor did I even touch her.

That was not part of the plan.

For if you aspire to date a very beautiful woman, you are going to have to do things very differently from all the other scores of swains who will be yapping at her bedroom door.

So while all the other young Turks were buying her flowers and Champagne and whatever else it was they thought might take her fancy, I was playing a quite different game.

I was in it for the long-haul.

And that meant that I would never – even once – touch her.

Or compliment her.

Or flirt with her.

The plan – and I had stuck to it rigidly – was to be the absolute antithesis of every other young buck in Cirencester; and there were quite a few of them, too. Rich, young South Americans over for the summer to play polo in the park; rich peers come to join Prince Charles's various royal parties at nearby Highgrove; and, above all else, the rich young landowners come to Cirencester to learn their trade at Britain's pre-eminent seat of all things agricultural, the Royal Agricultural College, or RAC, as it is known.

Over the previous year, I had seen many young men making their plays for Sasha. But I bided my time. I watched and I waited. I did not know what I was waiting for. But I hoped that when the time came, I would recognise it. And that I would seize it.

As we drove to Kemble station then, I was trying, as best I could, to have a perfectly normal conversation with Sasha, as if she were just a good, wholesome mate with whom I could drink and laugh and swim, and whose looks had not even registered on my mind.

'Can you get your dirty bloody feet off my dashboard?' I said.

'My dirty bloody feet off your dashboard? Well I might get my dirty bloody feet off the dashboard,' she said, 'if you ever bothered to clean up your dirty bloody car in the first place.'

She opened a can of Coke. She drank and passed me the can and I drank too. I've never much liked the taste, but if you're a wild swimmer then Coke is good for killing the bugs you've swallowed in the swim.

'Are you saying my car's dirty?' I said. We were on a long stretch of straight road, purring along behind a puttering brown Mini.

'It's not dirty, no,' she said. 'It is absolutely, disgustingly filthy. Look at this!' She leaned towards me and wiped her finger over my dusty headrest. Her finger lightly touched the back of my neck. I did not even flinch.

She waved the dusty black finger under my nose. 'Look at this!' she said. 'And you're complaining about my feet on the dashboard! Have you ever even cleaned this car?'

'It was pretty clean when I bought it,' I said. 'I think it was.'

She laughed triumphantly. 'How long ago was that?'

'A year ago,' I said. 'When I got my job on the paper. I needed a set of wheels. It was really cheap, too.'

'You amaze me.' She chuckled as she spat on her dirty finger. She produced a small packet of tissues from her pocket and wiped her finger on one. She looked at the tissue for a moment and made to put into the ashtray in the side of the door. It was already overflowing with sweet papers.

'Toss it in the back,' I said.

'Are you sure?' she asked. 'It just doesn't seem right.'

'Go for it.' With a flick of her thumb the tissue was tossed onto the back seat, where it joined assorted beer bottles, both empty and full, as well as Coke cans, crisp packets and a huge pile of old newspapers.

For a while we drove on in silence. I crumpled the empty Coke can and that was also tossed into the back. Sasha looked at the Mini ahead of us. I could smell its rich black exhaust.

'Are you going to overtake this car?' she said. Sasha always loved speed – whether it was in cars or the ski-slopes, or on her beloved polo ponies.

'In this heap?' I said. 'Do you know about the acceleration in this thing?'

'I know it can go at 120 miles an hour. You showed me.'

'It can go at 120mph,' I said. 'But it takes about ten minutes to get there.'

'Pathetic.'

'We'll see who's pathetic when we get to London.'

We were in luck at Kemble station. The next London train was in a few minutes, so the thrill of the adventure was not dissipated on the station platform.

We found a table and a couple of window seats on the train and I went to the bar and bought four small bottles of red, four small bottles of white, two cans of Coke and ten miniatures of Brandy.

'That's a lot,' Sasha said as I got back to the table.

'And we're going to need it,' I said. 'It's going to be freezing.'

We drank the wine and we plotted our plan of action. We would be getting into Paddington at around dusk. From there, we'd take the tube to Tower Hill. I liked the thought of swimming the Thames at Tower Bridge. It had history. Perhaps we might even end up at the Traitors' Gate.

We'd hide our bags underneath some bush or bench on the north side of the river, cross over Tower Bridge to the south side of the

Thames, find the nearest ladder down to the river, and then finally we would dive head-first into the hostile element.

That was our plan. It didn't seem like that big of a deal, but for us country bumpkins it would be an adventure; besides, how many other people do you know who have swum the Thames at night in London?

'What about the tides?' Sasha asked.

'I have not got a damn clue,' I said. Hah – isn't it amazing to think of it now, this Stone Age era that we used to live in two decades ago, when there were no mobile phones, no internet, no WiFi and no way on earth of learning about the tides of the Thames?

'Can we find out?'

'We'll just chuck in a stick,' I said. 'Should be a pretty good indicator.'

Sasha was not convinced. She was sat in her chair, staring out at the sunset as she stroked the bridge of her nose. She often stroked the bridge of her nose when she was deep in thought; I had come to know this reflex very well. It was an unusual nose for a woman, with a bump in the middle and a tweak to the side. It was the sort of nose you might have seen on a rugby forward. I loved it. It had character. A vainer woman would have had it straightened out by the plastic surgeons, but not Sasha. It would be some time before I learned how she'd broken it: her mother had hit her in the face when she was a teenager.

She looked at me. 'Anything else we haven't thought of?' she said.

I shrugged. I barely gave it a thought. 'Shouldn't think so,' I said. Blithely. Airily. Cockily. In the manner of a young swaggerer who was riding for the most spectacular fall. 'It'll be fine.'

We were delayed at Oxford. It was quite dark by the time we got into Paddington. The wine had all been finished and I had started on the brandy. I was feeling Tiggerish and bouncy; Sasha was more circumspect. She definitely wanted to do the swim, but she did not want to do anything reckless. While we were on the Tube, it was me doing most of the talking. We were both wearing our towelling robes; we must have looked a strange sight.

I could smell the river. You can't smell the Thames if you live in London. But if you're an outsider, with unclogged nostrils, you can smell it. It is a mix of light sea salt and London grime.

The river was in spate. It was roaring and wild, thrashing beneath us like a living animal. There was a hard wind coming in flat from the west, and we could see the white waves crashing against the north buttress.

If I'd been by myself, I would not have swum it then. But we had just caught the train to London specifically to swim the river. And I was with Sasha. Not that I wanted to impress her or anything.

The tide was going out full and hard. I tossed a white plastic cup off the bridge. In seconds it had been swept far off down the river.

'Do you want to stay while I dump the bags?' I asked.

'I'll come with you.'

Sasha squirmed into her swimming costume. I hid the bags under a bush and, barefoot, we trotted back to Tower Bridge. I was wearing nothing but a pair of baggy swimming trunks. We had our swimming goggles.

I don't really remember being aware of the traffic or the pedestrians – or anything much at all. I just remember being hell-bent on swimming the Thames. That's what we were going to do, that's what we were there for, and this one thought turned all else to darkness.

A few cars honked at us as we went over Tower Bridge. A truck driver rolled down his window and jeered. I can't speak particularly for myself, but Sasha was a very striking sight, long, loose-limbed, hair flying behind as she loped along in her black swimsuit.

We took a right on the south side of the river, and after a while we found a ladder down to the water. The river was high and there was no bank to be seen. We just had to climb down a few rungs and then dive in.

'So here we are,' I said.

Sasha looked at the Thames. Now that we were on the verge of diving in, the river was like a winking black abyss, its white tops flashing and frothing as they were caught by the streetlights. 'It's different from Lechlade,' she said.

'I've never swum anything like it.'

And still we dithered, and the longer we waited, the worse the river looked.

I remembered a story from my last year at school. My housemaster Francis Frederickson had run himself a piping hot bath. The water steamed. Frederickson had dipped his toes into the water and had recoiled, but being ex-army, had given himself a pep talk. 'Come on Frederickson, man or mouse!' he'd said and had jumped into the bath. Shortly afterwards, he was taken to hospital with third degree burns.

I spat into my goggles and rubbed the inside of the lens. The spit stops the goggles from steaming up.

I put them on.

'Man or mouse!' I said. 'See you on the other side!'

I climbed down the ladder and hit the river in a flat racing dive. I stretched my legs down. I did not touch bottom.

I turned to Sasha who was standing on the parapet. I had already been swept far downstream. 'Come on in!' I yelled. 'The water's warm!'

Though in truth, the river was freezing, that sort of electric cold that stings your skin and wicks the heat from your core.

I started to swim. Over the previous year in Cirencester, I had learned a very simple, economical freestyle technique. It was never meant for quick little sprints. It was a long, lazy, rolling, gliding crawl, and I could keep it going for a long time.

Most people in the pool are nothing but thrashing windmills. They do a length, perhaps two, and then, utterly shattered, they cling to the side of the pool to get their breath back. These are not swimmers. These are not even sprinters. Their bodies are angular, like a squat square ship ploughing slowly up the river.

As a swimmer, you want to be long and slippery and splash-free, with your hands and arms slipping into the water so smoothly that they don't even make a ripple; and your torso, rolling easily from side to side, as it tucks into the space that was made by your arm. But you keep that front arm outstretched, keep it there until your other hand has all but touched it, and once you can do that, you have learned the secret of the glide. After each arm pull, you glide on your side, easily and efficiently. And as for your legs, well, these naturally want to sink, but they should be counterbalanced by the heaviest part of your body, your head. Your head must be immersed fully and totally into the water. There is a tendency to thrash with your legs, but if you're swimming long distances, your leg muscles will burn through huge amounts of oxygen. Instead, you should strive for just a little two-beat kick. For each pull of the arm, a single kick with the leg. And that's the essence of efficient, smooth swimming; that is all there is to it. Though it is deceptively simple. Much like a happy marriage.

I struck out across the Thames, head deep down in the black water. I could see nothing when my head was in the water, and I could see very little when I came up for air. As you breathe, you only move your head just a little to the side, still streamlined as you suck down the air.

It was a mistake. It was not something I knew about at the time. Although I was a wild swimmer, of sorts, I'd never swum in anything as remotely treacherous as the London Thames. At night.

But I swam and I kicked, efficient and smooth, and I soon got into my old routine. I was almost underneath Tower Bridge itself when I stopped and looked back for Sasha. She was no longer on the parapet. I spotted her about 50 yards away, her arms smoothly easing into the water.

I continued to swim.

Although my swimming technique was about as smooth and economical as I could make it, it did have a fault. It was not a glaring fault, but it was a weakness – and sometimes, though not often, these weaknesses can find you out.

When I swim, I need a lot of oxygen. I need to breathe much more frequently than most long-distance swimmers. Most swimmers will breathe every three strokes, or perhaps even every five, and this means they're alternating the sides that they breathe on – first to the left, and then to the right.

I was taking a breath every two strokes, which meant I was always breathing on the same side, my right side. My other side, the left-hand side, was blind.

That was nothing much in itself, but combined with one other weakness in my swimming technique – not always being aware of what was around me – well, it could be a disaster. It's quite different from swimming in a pool. When you are following the black lines, you can just get your head down and keep on motoring. But in the wild, particularly a busy waterway like the Thames, you have to keep an eye out for anything that should not be there. In practice, this means that every five or six strokes, you should be lifting your head clear out of the water to have a good look round and to check that everything's clear.

And if you don't keep an eye out...

Well, most of the time, it will make no odds either one way or the other. You will reach the end of your swim and nothing untoward will have happened.

Most of the time.

I must have been about halfway across the river. By now I'd been swept clear under the bridge, and I had a very solid rhythm going. The current was much brisker than I'd thought it would be, but that was neither here nor there. It would just mean a slightly longer walk in the cold before we picked up our clothes.

I have my head deep down in the water, so deep that not even the slightest portion of my head is above the surface. And then, after perhaps ten seconds, I roll slightly to the side and take my quick snatch of air, take in the bright lights of London. And I roll my face back into the water, and the darkness is so complete that I might be staring into a vat of black ink.

I didn't see it.

I felt it.

It was a rippling shockwave that pulsed at me through the water.

I registered it and I knew something was wrong. A moment later I heard it. The noise was coming through the water. It was the low droning pulse of a heavy-duty propeller.

I stopped swimming and looked all about me, my head turning this way and that, trying to see where the danger was coming from. I could hear the screws turning, but I could not see anything. Wherever I looked, there was nothing but the black river and the black night.

I stared towards where I thought the sound was coming from and I suddenly caught sight of two white bow waves funnelling underneath the bridge. A moment later, I saw the dredger itself, this huge wall of blackness bearing down on me.

I didn't know if Sasha had seen the ship. 'Sasha!' I screamed at the top of my voice, and then I was thrashing as hard as I could for the riverbank – no time now for easy gliding, for nonchalant two-stroke kicks. I was swimming for my life. This fizz of adrenalin washed through me, and the cold was forgotten as my arms flailed through the water, as fast as I could, thrashing my way out from underneath the dredger's stern. I was enveloped by this wall of thundering noise. I kicked and I thrashed, and I'm not thinking about Sasha or what a stupid way this would be to die; all I'm thinking of is the next pull and the next pull, and keeping my fingers tight together as I try to drag every possible inch out of the water.

The dredger shoots past. I don't know by how much it misses, but we're talking nothing more than a few feet. The next moment, even as I am still thrashing through the water, I am hit by this monstrous bow wave. It sweeps over me, pitching me upside down, tumbling me over and over in the water. I come up for air. I see the side of the dredger shooting past. It looms above me like a black canyon. The ship sweeps imperiously on its way, and a moment later, I am being hammered by the dredger's wake. It is like this white popping field of thunder. I catch a snatch of air and the water throbs over my head, and then there I am, bobbing in the black Thames, watching the dredger recede into the night.

A short moment of euphoria and then anxiety for Sasha. She'd been a way behind me, and I wondered if she'd been right in the path of the dredger. I looked out into the darkness of the river, but I could see nothing, no bobbing head, no tell-tale arms.

I swam to the north bank. There was no way out of the river. I had to swim some way downstream before I found a ladder. I got out and ran to get our clothes. I put on my towelling robe and, shivering, went over to the embankment to start scouring the river.

I looked upstream and I looked downstream, looking for any glimpse of Sasha's arms or legs – but I could see nothing at all, not a thing, just the black Thames glittering in the streetlights.

I was starting to think the unthinkable. She couldn't be dead.

Could she?

I was imagining all manner of nightmares. Had she been hit by the dredger? Concussed and drowned, or swept to her death, and even now lying dead on the bottom of the river?

I continued to look upriver. I realised she couldn't be upriver. If she'd been in the Thames this long, then she must have been swept way, way downstream.

I must have been out of the water for fifteen, twenty minutes. I was getting cold and my teeth were chattering. My eyes were smarting from staring out over the river so long.

I didn't know what to do.

Should I call the police? There certainly didn't seem any point in just blindly waiting by the river bank.

But she couldn't be gone – she couldn't be! Not my Sasha, the woman who I had loved from afar for so long, and yet who I'd never once touched.

I'd give it five more minutes. Then I'd call the police. And then I'd get the dressing-down that I so richly deserved.

I heard the patter of footsteps slapping on the pavement. They were coming from upriver – from towards Tower Bridge.

I looked up, and there she was, running towards me. Her swimming suit was ripped at the neck and there was blood dribbling down her shoulder.

I stared at Sasha in the most complete astonishment. I had no idea where she'd popped up from.

She threw herself into my arms and I gave her a hug to end all hugs.

Now that she was safe, she started to shiver and then she started to cry. I held her, and she buried her face into my shoulder and she wept.

I pulled out her towel and her robe. She had a bad graze and a cut on her shoulder. I pressed my towel hard against the cut and I helped her put the robe on.

I got out the brandies and offered her one. She took it and drank from it, and let out this monumental sigh of relief. She finished the bottle and tossed it into the river. She put on her thongs and, very slowly now, we started shuffling back to Tower Bridge and to the Tube station.

I gave her another brandy bottle. She drank it in one and, again, hurled the empty into the river.

I was carrying both bags. She had her arms crossed in front of her. She was not crying any more.

At length, I said the thing that was uppermost in my mind. 'Thank God you made it.'

She did not reply. She took another brandy bottle. The brandy poured down her cheeks and throat as she upended the bottle.

'What happened?' I said.

'Bow wave knocked me into the bridge,' she said.

'Jesus.'

'Had to swim back,' she said. 'Ages to find a way out of the river. Ran back over Tower Bridge.'

'Wow.' It sounded rather lame. 'I'm sorry.'

'You should be,' she said. 'Stupid, stupid idea.' And then she stopped and she gave me the most resounding slap across my cheek, a real roundhouse blow that rattled my teeth.

I didn't say anything. I didn't move. I looked at her.

She took a fourth brandy bottle from the bag, opened it and drank it. As she drank the brandy, her eyes never once left mine.

I found another miniature, and I also drank the brandy – so there we were, cold and drinking brandy and realising that we had both come within an inch of killing ourselves.

And that, I think, was the moment when I realised that the tide had turned. After a year of quietly and patiently biding my time with this woman, the moment was upon me. And I had to act fast. For we lovers must take the current when it serves, or we shall lose our ventures.

Lightning Source UK Ltd.
Milton Keynes UK
UKOW04f0820110913

216989UK00001B/3/P